Mary Clayton was born and brought up in Cornwall, and read History at Oxford University. After university she went to America as a Fulbright English-Speaking Union Fellow to Ann Arbor, Michigan, where she taught in the History Department. She has lived in England, Denmark and Italy, and now divides her time between America and Europe. As Mary Lide and Mary Lomer, the author has written historical novels and sagas. Mary Clayton's first two novels to feature ex-Inspector John Reynolds, PEARLS BEFORE SWINE and DEAD MEN'S BONES, are also available from Headline.

The Prodigal's Return

Mary Clayton

HEADLINE

First published in 1997
by HEADLINE BOOK PUBLISHING

First published in paperback in 1997
by HEADLINE BOOK PUBLISHING

10 9 8 7 6 5 4 3 2 1

ISBN 0 7472 4961 X

Printed and bound in Great Britain by
Cox & Wyman Ltd, Reading, Berks

HEADLINE BOOK PUBLISHING
A division of Hodder Headline PLC
338 Euston Road
London NW1 3BH

For my family – with love

Chapter 1

John Reynolds, ex-police inspector, formerly of the Devon and Cornwall Constabulary, stretched his long legs comfortably. Lounging as he now was, feet up on the coffee table, a can of beer, Tinners, in his hand, he could have been mistaken for a man half his age. Trim of build, athletic, having retired early to write books and pursue his hobbies of gardening and hiking, he had settled in this quiet corner of Cornwall, close to what had once been his family home. Although born in Cornwall he'd been brought up in what his present neighbours would call 'foreign parts,' that is, any place east of the Cornish border. Yet he had taken to living back here like a duck to water.

Through the open windows the sounds of a late August evening came pleasantly familiar – a man walking his dog down a cobbled lane, a wren chirping sleepily in a holly hedge; if he strained he could hear the distant chuckle of the little stream that gave St Breddaford its name and the faint splash of indignant coots disturbed among the rushes.

He smiled indulgently. With his garden finally tidied, with his new book, a detective thriller based on his own experiences, already reaching bestseller proportions, with his suitcase and haversack packed and ready in the hallway for an early start tomorrow, he was entitled to feel complacent. On holiday for a change, he was

1

thinking lazily, car set to roll, off where fancy takes me and scrambles into isolated countryside will keep me nicely occupied—

The ring of a telephone startled him from his pleasant musings.

'It's me, Johnny. Thank God you're there. There's been an accident.'

The voice, a woman's, was husky, insistent, a faint ripple of hysteria kept in check. 'I thought of you at once. I'm alone. Everyone else is away. Come quickly, please don't let me down.'

And then, as if it had only just struck her that he might not know who she was, 'How are you? It's been so long since we've been in touch . . .'

He stiffened, holding the receiver at arm's length as if it had bitten him, heard without listening the directions she was giving, Bodinnick Ferry across the River Fowey already closed so he'd have to come inland through Lostwithiel, he'd know the manor house when he got there of course . . .

No other word of explanation, no pleasant preamble. Only one woman ever called him 'Johnny' in that tone of voice; only one would ever ring him out of the blue, as it were, expecting him to recognise her instantly without any idle chitchat. Only one ever talked of his 'letting her down'.

The unhappy marriage, the painful divorce seven years ago, seared him. He hadn't thought about it, or her, had deliberately shut all that out of his mind for so long he was surprised that it still had the power to hurt. When he'd retired he'd put the divorce, along with his professional life, behind him. He hadn't seen or heard from his ex-wife since the day she'd told him she wanted her freedom from what she had then called 'twelve years of hard labour' – along with the exact, cruel, reasons why. She'd made no effort to contact him since and he'd made no effort either, had allowed the solicitors to handle everything. He didn't even know where she was living. And that's the way it should, must stay, he told himself. I can't be caught up in that nightmare again.

Without a word, he put the phone down while she was still talking. 'No,' he told himself, striding about the room where the harmony already seemed invaded. 'No, and no.'

The phone began to ring a second time.

Chapter 2

En route to Lostwithiel, the medieval market town
whose bridge across the Fowey was his closest route to
the opposite side of the estuary, he was still surprised
at his own reactions. 'No,' he'd said, and meant it. Yet
here he was, over the bridge, driving ever deeper into a
maze of twisting country roads that even locals confessed
would be less confusing if left unsignposted. He had no
easy answer to his change of attitude.

Curiosity was part of it. There, he had admitted it. If
curiosity was a fault, he had it in abundance. It was
probably what had led him to take up police work in
the first instance. He hadn't heard from her in so long,
and then out of nowhere, her voice, as if nothing had
changed between them. But still nothing of her personal
life, still no interest in his. She'd shut up like a clam
when, during her second call, he'd at least tried to
question her on details. What was she doing in
Cornwall? he wondered. And where was she actually
living? And what was the 'accident' she'd first mentioned,
and then, later, had ignored with typical inconsistency.

But if she hadn't been explicit about who had been
injured or how, she had certainly been frightened. He
knew her well enough to recognize that. She'd also
emphasized she was alone. So where were the other
members of the household where she was staying? She'd
been vague about that too, hadn't spoken again of them,

5

only told him where the house was, repeating that he would, of course, 'know it'. She meant 'know' in the sense of being on social terms with its owners, as presumably she was, a frequent visitor to be there on her own. But he'd never even heard of the place.

Who are these new friends she's been making? he wondered. And for God's sake why make them here in Cornwall where I've staked out my own piece of turf? For that matter, why ring me at all? Even a child knows how to dial an emergency number. He felt resentment grow that she should have encroached upon his hard-won privacy, and once more was tempted to turn back.

But he didn't. For there was more than curiosity involved, more than the idle interest of seeing her again and finding what had become of her during these seven years. And now as he edged his way round a series of zigzag bends he let himself consider what else it was.

Not love, he told himself. Wipe that idea out, to start with. He'd long ago ceased to love his ex-wife, probably when she'd begun to boast about her love affairs, taunting him with her 'adventures', as she called them, although now he honestly couldn't remember what his early reactions had been. But if not love, then something akin to it – responsibility, sense of duty, guilt . . .

'Why?' he asked himself, savagely twisting the car round another bend. 'She's no concern of mine, I owe her nothing.' But he did feel guilty and he did feel responsible. Living with her had left him with nothing else. Just as living with him had taught her, only too well, how to play upon those feelings, how to gouge raw wounds until they festered. But all these thoughts were ones to put aside, too complex, too revealing, too deeply embedded for present exploration. Later he'd come to them.

Her directions had been explicit, thorough and concise

as if, he now thought as he negotiated a blind corner more slowly, she'd written them down beforehand and had memorized them. Without her instructions at this point he might well have lost his way, for the road had narrowed to a single track from which small side lanes sprouted like stalks. The narrowness was accentuated by the bushes on top of the typical Cornish hedge. They met in an arch, so thick they blocked all views at either side and even the car headlights bounced ineffectively off the interlocking branches. Yet as he emerged from this natural tunnel into more open space, where swathes of cut grass still released a momentary scent of summer, he caught a fleeting glint of water far beneath him, a thin snake coil, and felt the stir of wind with its rich smell of tidal mud and rotting seaweed.

Still cursing his weak will, or his innate inquisitiveness – even now he couldn't be sure which – he followed the track away from the river, passing eventually between vague gateposts and along a rutted drive, until the dark silhouette of a building showed against the grey of the sky.

No light shone from the windows, the house indeed looked empty, but as he drew up he glimpsed two cars, parked inconspicuously off the drive as if deliberately out of sight, one behind the other – ready for a quick get-away, he thought, as he switched off his own lights and eased himself out of the seat. He passed the cars on his way to the front door, out of habit noting their licence plates, then hesitated a moment before mounting the shallow steps. As he did so, the door opened, or rather was thrown open abruptly. His ex-wife stood in a sliver of pale light, looking down at him as she had so often in the past. He braced himself for the full force of her invective: 'You're late. Where have you been? You know I had these plans, these arrangements . . .' all the familiar abuse and criticism that had filled the last years of their marriage, making life in his own house untenable.

'So there you are,' was all she said, as if he had been on a short walk. She gave a fleeting smile, the sort reserved for strangers. 'How are you?' she asked again, then, without bothering to wait for an answer, 'Come in.'

She ushered him into the hall. No real interest then, no 'Thank you for coming'. His own conventional words of greeting died on his lips. What did one say anyway to a woman who had done her best to destroy him? He merely asked her how she was, in formal fashion, before noting how she carefully closed the door behind him and turned off the light.

The hallway was low, he had to duck his head under beams, and in the semi-darkness he caught only fleeting impressions of other rooms and, as he passed, a large carved chair, over which a woman's jacket was draped. Under it was a handbag and what looked like a brown paper parcel.

He could see little of his ex-wife's features. Her hair, he thought, was longer, she might have lost some weight, she was dressed in a fashionably long skirt which swished as she moved with her usual vigorous stride towards a corridor that opened on the right. 'Down there,' she said, and for lack of any reason to linger he followed, aware that on the left another half-opened door led to what looked like a dining room. He had the impression of shrouded objects, of furniture draped with dustsheets. Not much in use then, he thought, puzzled. A holiday home perhaps?

The corridor was also dimly lit but she showed no hesitation, and as he came behind her he was conscious of soft carpeting beneath his feet and what looked like antlers towering above his head, rows of game trophies, something of an anachronism in this modern world of animal rights.

The brightness of the light she switched on at the end of the corridor was blinding. He paused to blink, seeing before him the entrance to what he thought was an office, and taking in again the grotesqueness of the wall decorations to which the more mundane rows of boots and shoes beneath them, the tiers of outdoor gear that hung against the wall made a homely contrast. There were strange marks in the thick carpet, as if something had recently been dragged across it. Then he was in the room and she was closing the door firmly behind him, as if, he thought suddenly, she wants to keep the light from being seen. Or wants to prevent my leaving.

He was wrong about the room being an office. It was a small sitting room, the sort used on informal occasions, filled with family clutter and scattered with books and papers. Heavy curtains had been pulled tight across the windows, making an effective blackout, and a fire smouldered tentatively in the grate. A pair of sagging chairs was pulled in front of the hearth, and in one of them a man's figure sprawled, feet towards the fender.

'Who's that?' he found himself asking, and at her gesture which suggested that he stop asking questions and introduce himself, he moved in front of the man, bending to look at him. 'Good evening,' he started to say when something about the man's appearance stopped him.

The feet were stretched out in normal fashion, and the arms rested naturally on either side of the chair, but the face was twisted against one shoulder as if it was being deliberately hidden. As Reynolds bent lower, a strange, half-remembered smell came overpoweringly

9

up towards him, a mixture of vomit and blood and some other smell he couldn't identify yet knew he ought to. Gently he turned the man's face round, feeling for the pulse in the neck, saw the shock of brown hair fall forward from its natural peak, saw the glimmer of blue beneath the eyelashes. The mouth sagged, the lips pulled back to reveal a row of teeth in parody of one of those snarling animal masks on the wall outside. A young man's face, which once must have been handsome, now grotesquely twisted and distorted.

His ex-wife had stayed by the door, was leaning against it, watching him as if waiting for him to do or say something. 'What happened?' he found himself asking, and heard her give the little sigh that meant she didn't want to answer.

'He choked,' she said at last. 'He was sitting just like anyone does, eating, talking, drinking. Then he collapsed.' She paused.

'And?' he prompted.

'I didn't know what to do,' she said, 'so I rang you. I couldn't think of anyone else. Is he all right?'

He turned to stare at her. He could see her clearly now, the unlined face that made her look younger than she was, the soft hair, the pursed lips – he'd forgotten how beautiful she was. And how self-centredly devious.

'You know very well he's not all right,' he said. 'He's dead. And my guess is he was dead before you ever rang me.'

He ignored her cry.

'So how did he die? And where? And why in God's name did you move him?'

Chapter 3

She continued to stare at him, with the wide-eyed stare she'd developed as camouflage, while he continued to talk, giving himself space to overcome his revulsion.

'He's been poisoned,' he said. 'If he was eating and drinking, as you put it, then he's eaten or drunk something poisonous. And since you say you're the only other person in the house, that makes you the most likely suspect.'

She was indignant. 'The suggestion's ridiculous,' she snapped.

Without any further signs of shock or grief – typical, Reynolds thought – she went on to explain that the victim had taken a homemade pie out of the freezer, had himself heated it in the microwave, brought it to the table and helped himself when she'd insisted she wasn't hungry. The story sounded plausible, and to some extent could be verified. 'Who is he?' he asked. 'And what were you doing in an empty house that's been shut up?'

'It's his house,' she said defensively, ignoring the first question. 'Or rather his mother's. He had a key. He said the family were on holiday and he could come and go as he pleased. He asked me to meet him here on business. And for the record, I don't really know him, we'd only met once before.'

She isn't going to identify him, Reynolds was thinking.

But maybe she doesn't know his name. Wouldn't be the first time she's picked up someone from some bar or pub. A good-looking young man, this one, in his late twenties, not so well-heeled as she was used to and not her usual age group, a little young for her. Here on 'business' indeed. It's perfectly obvious she had something very different in mind.

'You're telling me someone you've only met once brings you to an empty house that he claims is his mother's, then suggests an intimate little meal – which all goes horribly wrong?' Reynolds made no attempt to hide the sarcasm in his voice.

'It's not what you're thinking,' she cried as if she had guessed his thoughts. 'He was a genuine client of mine.' She stared at him defiantly. 'He wanted my advice. He lives somewhere on this side of the estuary, Polperro I think. I drove myself—'

'That's your car outside?' he interrupted her. 'The red Rover?' What does she mean by 'client', he wondered, and where does she get the money for a sporty car like that?

'It was latish when I arrived,' she went on, ignoring his question, 'and when he explained there weren't many places to eat out close by, we decided to have a bite at home instead.'

'But you know he wasn't supposed to be here,' he said. And when she began to argue, 'Forget the key. He could have stolen it, or even found it and kept it to make a break-in. Why did he make a point of coming so late in the evening, when the people who live here are absent, and the staff, or whoever they have to run a place like this, have gone for the night? What about the way the cars are parked, out of sight? What about the drawn curtains, the lack of lights? No one bothers to be so careful unless he doesn't want to be seen. Or unless whoever plans to murder him takes the same precautions – all of which makes explanation more difficult for you.'

He paused to let that sink in. 'To say nothing of dragging the body down a corridor out of sight.'

At last he had broken through to her. Or perhaps the actual use of the word 'murder' had done it. He could feel the fear in her now, hot and sweating (if so elegant a woman could be said to sweat). But she still had some fight left.

'It is his mother's house,' she insisted. 'All right, perhaps he's quarrelled with his father and so chose not to come when his father was at home. But if he's been poisoned, then it's just sheer bad luck. It's nothing to do with me.' At that, her face crumpled. 'And if I'd been hungry I might be dead too,' she cried as if the thought had just occurred to her. 'I made do with fruit and cheese that I'd brought in the car. The only thing we shared was a bottle of wine. Thank God for that.'

She might be telling the truth, he thought, again incensed by her myopic view of events. She wasn't stupid. Why would she deliberately summon him as a witness if she'd committed the crime?

'You didn't eat in here,' he said. 'After he collapsed, you dragged him down the corridor. Why?'

'I thought he'd be more comfortable. I thought maybe he was drunk and would feel better by the fire. He lit one here after we arrived since the furniture in the other rooms is all sheeted over. He was irritated by that, wanted to pull the covers off. And you're wrong that he was dead when I rang you,' she went on. 'He was certainly alive, he was breathing.' She was silent for a moment. 'Since he helped himself from the kitchen, presumably the food wasn't even intended for him given that he doesn't live here. Surely that's proof

I couldn't have been responsible.'

The thought had already occurred to him. At the moment it was the best alibi she had. He stopped himself from pointing out that she could have slipped something in after it was cooked. Some other poor sod, a real police official, would have to pursue that line of questioning. He'd heard enough.

He straightened up. The warmth of the fire was drawing out the smell he'd first noticed; he felt it had permeated his own clothes, he could almost taste it. God, what a mess, he thought. Accident, she'd said. But if she'd said death, would he have come more quickly, or any more willingly? And what was he to do now that he was here?

He said abruptly, 'The police will have to be informed. You should have rung them in the first place. You'd better ring them now.'

For a second time her face crumpled like a wet rag. 'I can't.' Her hysteria was real. 'You know they won't believe me; they'll say I did it. You know how to speak to them, Johnny, you've got to make them see I'm telling the truth.'

He raised his eyebrows at that. 'You must ring them,' he said in a mild voice that didn't conceal the bitterness. 'You've forgotten I'm not an acting officer, thanks in part to you. But even if I were, my advice would be the longer you hesitate, the worse it looks. Your only chance is to tell them what you've just told me. If you're innocent, they'll know it.'

'You just want to turn me in,' she snapped. 'Like a common criminal. See me in jail. Isn't that what you want? To pay me back.'

He stared at her. The tension in the little room seemed to spark and crackle like an electric current, all that pent-up hate. What good does it do us? he thought, forcing himself to calm down. What's the point?

Perhaps she felt the same. She drew in her breath, fighting for control. 'Even if you're off the force,' she said, 'you know how to handle them.'

Handle the whole thing, she meant. And that of course was why she'd rung him. To heap the whole damn burden on his shoulders. To lure him here and then implicate him. Because, better than anyone, she understood these twin aspects of his character, his curiosity and his sense of duty. And because, again better than anyone, she knew how to play upon them to make him vulnerable.

Even in his anger at his stupidity, he couldn't help noting the primitive shrewdness which made self-preservation her main objective. On the other hand, he was pretty sure she wasn't a poisoner.

'Where's the phone?' he asked.

He looked about the room, half listening to her tearful explanations that she'd had to search for it in the dark, it was at the back of the dining room, of all places. This is a case for Derrymore, he was thinking. He's a good friend and neighbour as well as the local police sergeant. We're just on the border of his jurisdiction here but he won't quibble. And he'll be sympathetic. It's the least I can do for her, and she's damn lucky to get that much.

Cutting short her explanations he propelled her in front of him, along the corridor where the animal heads snarled down at them in frozen rows and the scuff marks on the carpet took on a more sinister aspect. At the entrance to the dining room, she dug in her heels, peering round the door as if fearful of what she might find inside.

The room was in darkness and the curtains were drawn. Its air of heaviness, as if something was weighing it down, was intensified by the white dustsheets that shrouded most of the chairs and the long sideboard, the sort of covers, Reynolds thought, that were always used in Victorian times, suggestive of excessive cleanliness and moral primness.

There was no sign of anyone having eaten here recently, no plates, no cutlery or glasses. Damn, he thought. She must have cleared it all away. Another stupid move. The covers had been removed from two chairs, however, and not replaced, and the chairs themselves had been left at either side of the table where a couple of candelabra, large, were arranged in the middle. I bet if I look on the floor I'll find all the evidence I need, he thought, and I bet if I touch the candle wax it'll still be soft. And her fingerprints are probably everywhere! Strangely, this inept attempt to conceal evidence struck him as pitiful rather than sinister. How could she imagine she'd get away with it?

It was this same sense of pity that caused him not to insist when she refused to go through the door. 'I can't,' she said with a shudder. She didn't add, 'Because of what happened in there.' She didn't need to, the look in her eyes told him. He'd seen that look in others, too many to count, mirroring the realization of some tragedy too awful to contemplate.

'Wait here,' he told her peremptorily, then, resisting the temptation to poke at the candles, picked his way along the room towards the far end, careful not to touch anything and blur all those fingerprints he knew must be there.

The telephone had been installed in some sort of cubicle, like a public phone box, and the telephone itself was of strange design, what he called modern Californian. He wondered whose taste had chosen the ceramic Donald Duck figure as he fumbled with a handkerchief before picking up the receiver, housed in the beak. Getting the hang of the dials under the wings, he rang Derrymore's number.

He heard his friend's soft Cornish voice with relief, which he hoped didn't show as he outlined briefly what had occurred, and with even more relief listened to Derrymore's prompt response. It was only after he tried to explain where he was and heard Derrymore's sudden hesitation, then quick reply, 'I remember the place,' that he began to wonder what Derrymore meant. And it was only when he had hung up that he realized the one thing he himself hadn't explained was who the woman was.

'She rang me this evening,' is how he had put it, and Derrymore had accepted that without comment. Reynolds hadn't meant to hide the fact of his ex-wife's presence, it was only that, at that moment, explanation seemed cumbersome. When Derrymore arrived would be the time to make things clear. Then, face to face, introductions and explanations would come more naturally. But when he returned to the hall, he realized that even that save-face was to be denied him. The 'woman' in the case, the ex-wife, had already gone, taking her jacket, handbag and parcel with her.

Chapter 4

Gone, done a flit, scuttled off and left me to cope. Furious, Reynolds checked that the red car was gone as well, then, resisting slamming the house door shut in case he couldn't re-open it, he leaned against it, cursing in several languages, legacy of his army days. Never should have trusted her, should have expected she'd set me up. The woman who used her infidelities to 'punish' me, even with a best friend, ex-friend, he thought, hasn't altered much. And why should I expect her to? A leopard doesn't change its spots. I'm a fool to have imagined otherwise.

Round and round his thoughts ran. Was I to blame, for being the man I was, for having the job I had, for leaving her too long alone, for having married her in the first place? All those familiar accusations came flooding to the surface. Guilt and responsibility – albatross-like, they hung round his neck. And the most damning thing of all was that he himself would never have broken with her, not even when she had told him about that last and most cruel betrayal; it was she, not he, who had asked for the divorce that released them both from misery.

For a moment, the rehashing of this old, depressing tale sickened him. I've no reason to stay on here, he told himself. As a private individual I'm free to go, and be damned to her. Let the law cope.

Except the 'law' was someone he knew well, coming at his explicit request, deserving all the help he could give.

When he heard the sound of a car jolting up the drive, he went to meet Derrymore with a sense of temptation overcome – tempered with regret that once more the sergeant would be saddled with a crime overcharged with personal complications.

By now the moon had risen, and the front of the house was bathed in a silver glow. When Derrymore heaved himself out of his car, he appeared reassuringly solid, his shoulders wide and dependable against the sky. He's put his uniform on, Reynolds thought. Always correct. Here comes the helmet, settled firmly over the nose. Officially on duty then. He half smiled, moved out of the shadows by the door. Together the two men went inside, Derrymore's boots echoing loudly on the flagged hall.

At once Reynolds felt the younger man's unease. Derrymore wasn't the most talkative of people but usually he exuded youthful confidence. Aware that he had no business here at all, that he was a retired officer, what some would call an old has-been, he took a quick glance at Derrymore's face.

His being an outsider had never mattered to the younger man before. In fact, in other cases they had worked on together, it had usually proved an advantage in the end. And we've worked often together now, he thought; I know him as well as he does me, we've few secrets from each other, so what's wrong?

He considered and rejected the possibility that Derrymore was resenting being rooted out so late. Derrymore always claimed that village policemen, like doctors, were always on call. And despite his recent promotion to sergeant, he was too sensible to take umbrage over petty issues. Nevertheless something was certainly bothering the younger man, as if, sudden intuition struck him, Derrymore had also felt obliged to come out of some personal sense of duty.

Concealing these observations, Reynolds concentrated on filling in details. He'd got no further than explaining where the body was when, instinctively, Derrymore turned towards the corridor. Reynolds said no more, not even when, again with unerring instinct, Derrymore felt for the switches which brought the passage blazing to life. He's certainly been here before, Reynolds told himself as they tramped along under the staring animal heads. Only at the door did Derrymore hesitate, as if drawing breath before going inside.

The fire had dwindled, and for a moment even Reynolds could imagine the figure was asleep, so life-like did it look. Or so life-like had it been arranged. While Derrymore bent over the body as Reynolds himself had done, for the first time the ex-inspector let himself dwell on what effect his ex-wife's actions would have. He almost expected the sergeant to ask, 'Was the body moved to divert attention from the scene of the crime?'

Instead when the younger man straightened up, his round face had gone unnaturally pale. 'God,' he said through greyish lips, 'that's young Mr Edmund. I'd no idea.' He felt for a chair and sat down unsteadily. 'God,' he repeated. 'Hadn't heard of him for ages, mind, but then that wasn't surprising. When we were kids we used to play together in this very room. Makes you think.'

Whatever it was he was thinking was brought to a halt by the loud crashing of the front door. A man's voice bellowed in alarm, and a man's footsteps came thudding down the corridor. 'Who's here?' they heard him shout, and then he was upon them, a strongly built, oldish fellow, sunburnt-faced, thin-lipped, with eyes that narrowed like a cat's. He was dressed in faded jeans and shirt, and armed with a shotgun.

'What the hell's going on?' he cried, shouldering his way into the room then stopping mid-stride, obviously taken aback at the sight of the two men.

It was then he saw the body by the hearth. Lowering his gun, he took a step forward, stared, after which, as Derrymore had done, he sagged into a chair, burying his face in his hands.

With Derrymore seemingly still in shock, Reynolds felt called upon to take charge. 'You recognize this man, sir?' he asked in a mild voice which nevertheless suggested steel beneath its sympathy.

And when neither the newcomer nor Derrymore answered, 'He's supposed to be a son of the house.'

It was the newcomer who spoke first. 'Yes,' he said dully, 'I suppose you could call him that. But I don't understand what's happened here.'

'That's what we're trying to establish.' Reynolds was soothing but firm. 'First your name, if you will, then his.'

'I'm Joe. Joseph Fletcher.' The man made an effort. He pointed to the body, said bleakly, 'He's Edmund Gatterly.'

'And you work here?' Observing Fletcher's clothes, his choice of weapon, his weather-beaten face, Reynolds assumed he was a gamekeeper or some such, perhaps reduced in these less affluent days to a general caretaker or handyman.

Joe Fletcher noticed Reynolds' pointed look at the gun, double-barrelled, the sort used by hunters. Rather shamefacedly he uncocked it and took out the shot which he stuffed in his pocket.

'I used to be the steward here,' he explained. 'That's the Cornish name for bailiff. Before the place was sold.

Now we just help out. Saw the lights and heard a car.' He glanced about him with grey eyes, even more narrowed. 'Can't be too careful these days,' he added belligerently. 'And with the house empty, well, it's an obvious attraction.'

'Of course.' Reynolds gently brought him back on line. 'You mentioned "we", Mr Fletcher.' He paused to let the other explain that he and his wife lived in what had once been the steward's cottage, now rented by them from the estate, or what was left of it, set back from the road, nice little place with its own acre or so of land, but too far away to keep a proper eye on things.

'And Edmund Gatterly's mother, Mrs Gatterly, is the owner of the estate?' Again Reynolds broke in upon Joseph Fletcher's lengthy explanations.

The man half turned at the name to take another fearful look at the body. 'Did own,' he said. 'Or rather her family did.' He shifted uneasily. 'Gatterly was her married name. She was a Trewithen.'

It was Reynolds' turn to be confused. 'Was?' he repeated. 'You mean she's dead?'

'No.' The man stirred indignantly. 'Although better for her perhaps if she were. It's just she's not living here as she ought, more's the pity. Her family owned this place for ever. Always been Trewithens on the Fowey River.'

'So the victim is her son by her first husband?'

'Her younger son, there are two.' As if suddenly aware of where he was, Fletcher stood up. If he'd had a hat on he would have pulled it off in respect. 'Twins,' he said, surprise at such ignorance of local history showing. 'Edmund here was the younger. They left with their mother about fifteen years ago, turned out like unwanted lodgers when the place was sold. Then, when it came on the market again, several months ago, seems

Mr Gatterly found the cash to buy it back. But not for her.' He leaned forward intently. 'He's not her first husband.' He emphasised the 'first'. 'She's never remarried. Why should she want to? He did the rummaging for a new wife.' Thought everyone knew that, his voice implied, where've you been living all your life?

Comprehension came. 'You mean Mr Gatterly lives here now with a second wife, after recently buying his first wife's old family home. And his son, Mr Edmund Gatterly, was a frequent visitor?'

'Not likely.' Again the voice was full of contempt. 'Not after what his father did to his mother. He'd more respect for her than that.' His voice rose. 'After his first family's turned out, Mr Gatterly goes to live abroad with some foreign tart. Then, out of the blue, he comes back a rich man and buys the place up, lock, stock and barrel.'

'That's right,' Derrymore's voice was strained but he had got control of himself. 'It was in all the papers. I . . .' He turned to Fletcher. 'You won't remember me,' he said, 'but my mother's Mazie Derrymore.'

Fletcher started, and again his eyes narrowed. 'Well I never,' he said. 'Haven't seen or heard of you, boy, since the break-up. But I stayed on, you know, been here through thick and thin. Miss Trewithen, Mrs Gatterly that was, asked me to when the house was originally sold. Well, the new owners weren't all bad, not Cornish, mind, but then you can't have everything. Didn't keep the game up of course, more's the pity, and bit by bit sold off the land. So me and the wife – yes, I'm married now, one child – took what there was, the cottage I've just told you of. But it's been a struggle.'

'And you stayed on even when Mr Gatterly returned?' Derrymore couldn't keep the surprise from his voice.

'I'd have cleared off fast if I could.' Fletcher's tone

was defensive. 'But things are tough these days for the likes of me. Where'd I find another job like this, for one thing, or a house at such low rent?' He hesitated again. 'And my missus didn't know what it was like before the break-up. She—'

'Where's she now, your wife?' Reynolds had had enough of family chitchat for the moment. And whatever Derrymore's personal interest was in the Trewithen fortunes, no doubt he'd come to it in time.

After being assured that 'the wife and child' were safely at home, one knitting by the fire, the other in bed, Reynolds now suggested that Mr Fletcher show them round the house, especially the kitchen where the food had come from. Out of the corner of his eye he saw Derrymore's face whiten again at the mention of the possible cause of death, but as he said nothing Reynolds let it pass, merely watched how, with tightened lips, the sergeant strode unerringly back along the corridor to the hall, past the dining room and along another short passageway which opened into a modern kitchen.

'She had that done.' Fletcher stood looking gloomily at the white plastic-coated doors and steel appliances which gave the room the macabre appearance of a city morgue. 'The new Mrs Gatterly. Some US fashion.'

By which Reynolds was given to understand that Mr Gatterly's second wife was American, the same, presumably, whose taste in phones he himself had found so hideous.

The steel counters were bare, wiped clean and shining. Not a cup or plate or knife was out of place, everything restored with pristine precision and as the switch to the dishwasher was off, she must have washed everything by hand, then turned on the waste disposal unit in the sink to take care of the remnants. Suddenly angry, he thought, Why, in God's name, if she's innocent, didn't she leave well enough alone? He knew the answer already, she'd given it to him: 'They won't believe me.' Damn right they won't, he thought. You've made it virtually impossible.

There was no trace of any cooking utensils although the microwave was conspicuous. After Fletcher had pointed out that microwaves needed special non-metallic pans, many of which were disposable, under one of the counters Reynolds found a sort of rubbish bin, what was known in America as a trash compactor. Although it, too, had not been switched on, it was possible some clues might be found inside.

Reynolds sighed in exasperation. All these modern gadgets were beyond him. The most undomesticated of bachelors himself, if he was hungry he opened a tin of baked beans, put the beans in a saucepan on a gas ring, then chucked the empty can out and stacked the dirty dishes for 'another day' until he'd run out of clean ones.

When Derrymore suggested that if the pie dish had been non-metallic it could have been got rid of in other ways, burnt, for example, in the fire in the little sitting room, Reynolds nodded grimly. If there were any traces in the ashes of a used cooking dish, then the case against his ex-wife would become really serious.

The freezer, a large chest variety, located in a back scullery (which, fortunately for architectural sanity, had been left in its original state) was stocked to the brim with food of various sorts, among which were several pre-cooked pies, carefully labelled as to contents, each wrapped in its own special container ready for reheating.

'Any idea who made these?' Reynolds asked, as Fletcher closed the freezer lid and prepared to usher them back into the kitchen. His question might be casual but the answer was important. He was disappointed when Fletcher shook his head. 'Since they comed back they went all native, helping the neighbourhood economy, they called it. Used to get various local people to make them things. My wife isn't no cook,' he added, with another of his narrow-eyed glances. 'Tidies up and such, she's good at that. But not her job in the kitchen. Mrs Gatterly oversees that.'

Oversees too much, his disapproving tone suggested. He went on to explain that when he brought his wife here as a bride, the new owners used to have her come in once or twice a week to help with the house, and she'd kept it up after the Gatterlys returned. 'Light housework only,' he insisted. 'They've a cleaning service for the rough stuff. And as I've said, nothing in the kitchen.'

Lengthy explanations for a question that wasn't really asked, Reynolds thought. I'd like to talk with the lady herself. He glanced at Derrymore. But Derrymore had gone off into some world of his own again and wasn't being of much use.

'And where are the Gatterlys now?' Reynolds asked.

He should have inquired earlier and was relieved by the prosaic answer that they were on holiday somewhere abroad, Fletcher wasn't sure where but the wife would know.

Damping down the thought that on holiday was where he ought to be himself, he asked, 'Might we have a word with Mrs Fletcher?' Ignoring Joe's sudden frown, he continued in a voice that suggested nothing more than friendly cooperation, 'We need to reach the family as soon as possible. And your wife might have heard or noticed something useful that we've missed.' Such as what lights you noticed, he said to himself. And why you came running when you heard Derrymore's car. You certainly didn't when I arrived. Did you when Edmund and his 'guest' turned up? Or were you expecting them? And what about the key Edmund's supposed to have

27

used? He hadn't gone through the pockets, perhaps it was there, but where had it come from? He pushed aside the other thought that there wasn't much time left, what with head office needing to be informed. And he still had to fill Derrymore in on the most important detail of all, so far not even mentioned: who the woman was that had summoned him here, and where she'd gone.

Waiting until they'd made a brief but thorough search of what in police parlance would be called 'the premises' – the house was smaller than it seemed and, except for the ill-fated little sitting room, all of the main rooms on the ground floor and the bedrooms above were obviously shut up and deserted – and after Derrymore had put through the necessary call to head office on his mobile phone, he geared himself up for this difficult task. Unexpectedly, Derrymore forestalled him.

As they followed Fletcher through the bushes, Derrymore stopped dead in his tracks. He turned to face Reynolds. 'There's something you've got to know,' he said. 'I used to live here once in the old days, before the house was first sold. My mam was housekeeper. I was just a nipper, mind, and the two boys were not much older. Mr Edmund there and I were friends. Never knew his brother well, but Edmund and I got up to some tricks down by the river. He taught me how to swim and sail, for one thing.' For a moment, like Fletcher, he seemed lost in reminiscence. 'When the house was sold there wasn't a place for us so we moved on.' After a while he continued, 'But Mr Gatterly wasn't a bad sort. At least,' he amended, 'not to my mother. Over the years he kept in touch. When he came back, he rang her up. Said he always remembered what she'd done for them.'

He mused for a moment. 'My mam's getting on in years,' he said, in the same defensive voice Fletcher had used. 'No need now for her to work at all, not with my promotion and all. But she likes cooking. A great cook, my mam. About those pies,' he said. 'Don't go on about who made 'em. My mam did.'

Chapter 5

Here was a bombshell. Reynolds felt almost deflated as Derrymore went on to explain that he had immediately recognized his mother's writing on the food labels in the freezer. Mazie Derrymore of all people, Reynolds was thinking. What rotten luck.

His own problems receded even further as Derrymore continued to protest – quite unnecessarily, Reynolds thought – that his mother wouldn't have put poison in her own baking. Remembering the good-natured elderly lady and her whole-hearted Cornish hospitality, Reynolds couldn't for the life of him imagine anyone even hinting it. Yet more than hints there would be, as soon as head office became involved.

These days, head office hadn't much liking for village policemen or village crimes. With city violence on the increase, they had no time for petty rural vice. And even less time for this particular village and its surrounding countryside.

If St Breddaford and its inhabitants weren't popular, this was mainly because of Reynolds. For various reasons, complex personal ones not of Reynolds' making, over the years since he'd retired he'd become persona non grata with the force he'd once dominated. Let them find out that Mazie Derrymore did the baking, he thought with grim certainty, and learn that I and my ex-wife are involved; they'll tear us to bits. His 'Don't

31

worry' to Derrymore was singularly fatuous. Of course Derrymore was worried, as worried as he himself was. When he was rewarded with one of Derrymore's jokes, 'Well, I'd been warning my mam for years her cooking'd kill someone,' both men's smiles were as strained as the would-be witticism.

Fletcher was beckoning to them impatiently. The house door was open and a woman, presumably Mrs Fletcher, was peering anxiously out. The three men crowded past her into the narrow passage. She was a little woman, skinny, outlandishly dressed in a sequined jogging top and black velvet trousers, a style that Reynolds suspected originated across the Atlantic. Much younger than her husband, with bright red lips and made-up eyes and a mop of fluffed out hair, she seemed as out of place in this country setting as the steel kitchen appliances. Melodramatic, Reynolds thought, recognizing the signs. She'll be wringing her hands in a moment (a fine Victorian phrase), except she was carrying what he took to be a ball of wool and which turned out to be a large orange and white cat.

'What is it, Joe?' she cried in a girlish voice, the sort that immediately grated. The accent was peculiar, one he couldn't pinpoint, certainly not local, showing traces of what he'd call 'affected British' overlaying an unspecified twang. Whatever brought her here to this backwater? he wondered, eyeing her discreetly. And whatever made her settle down as a steward's wife?

The living room, equally narrow, was dominated by a large television set which continued to flicker garishly after Fletcher turned off the sound. His subsequent explanations to his wife, revealing all the grisly particulars, didn't seem to upset her as much as the unexpected presence of what she took to be two police officers.

'Oh my,' she said once or twice in the same high voice, and, 'Oh my goodness,' but without emotion, seeming more occupied with stroking her cat. Only when Joe had finished did she become more animated, batting her false eyelashes.

'We're in such a muddle here at the moment, apologies,' she piped, putting the cat aside and attempting to clear away her knitting, balls of brightly coloured wool that seemed intended for a man's jersey, along with the tea and biscuits that she and her husband must have been enjoying before they were disturbed. As if she would have preferred a week's notice of our arrival, Reynolds thought. Or as if housekeeping's the issue here, rather than murder. Perhaps that's why the owners of the main house 'keep her on'; in their eyes she'd be a treasure.

As was correct, Reynolds left the questioning to Derrymore. He noted with relief that as the sergeant gradually regained his confidence, he warmed to the task. The gleanings, however, were small, mostly by default, just enough to whet interest – which again, Reynolds noted thankfully, Derrymore kept dampened down.

Although Mrs Fletcher, she was called Mary Lou, explained that she had not heard or even seen anything untoward this evening, other than what Joe had told them, she hinted darkly that she 'wasn't surprised', a remark which, after a look from her husband, she amended to, 'Always people lurking about, only a week or so ago we scared a couple off.'

Before they could question her about these strangers, her husband interrupted, muttering that Mary Lou was merely referring to passing hikers. And anyway hadn't he already mentioned that he tried to keep a careful watch, look at the burglaries these days. And the local police not doing a damn thing about them – here he glowered at Derrymore.

Resisting the temptation to argue, Derrymore pressed on. 'Have either of the Gatterly twins been here recently?' he asked Mary Lou, to be answered in no uncertain terms by her husband that how could she know anything about visits to the Gatterlys, only to have her pipe up again, 'I know the older twin, Justin, comes,' a second slip which merited a second glower. And finally that she'd never met Mr Edmund Gatterly and could not explain where he'd got the key ('The locks were all changed years ago, so it couldn't be his mother's') nor why he'd want to 'snoop round late at night', as she put it. 'Heard he didn't get on with his father,' she volunteered, substantiating Joe's claim, and earning a third narrowed look from her husband.

Asked where Mr Gatterly and his family were at present, from a tin box on the television set she instantly produced a piece of paper with an address and telephone number on it. 'Left with me especially, in case of emergency,' she said, a trace of pride showing.

'Emergency' hardly seemed strong enough to cover this occasion, Reynolds thought wryly. And he couldn't help noticing that although Joe Fletcher seemed upset, twice mentioning how dreadful this death would be for Edmund's mother, Mary Lou appeared strangely immune.

'The Gatterlys are Mary Lou's particular friends,' Joe announced. 'Perhaps she ought to speak to them.'

Looking coy, she echoed him by saying, 'I could call them collect if you like.'

It was the use of the American phrase 'call collect' instead of the English 'reverse charge' as much as the declaration of friendship that helped Reynolds finally locate Mary Lou's twang as Mid-American, overlayered by English of dubious origin. The ladies' common background might be the link that united them. And perhaps that was the reason for Mary Lou's being here in Cornwall in the first place, trailing in the second Mrs Gatterly's footsteps. But with one woman married to the lord of the manor, as it were, and the other having to make do with his ex-steward, that might put a relationship under a lot of strain. Reynolds eyed Mary Lou thoughtfully.

Emphasizing that the police would be responsible for the sad task of informing relatives abroad, as well as Edmund's mother, Derrymore passed the address on to Reynolds – a posh-sounding hotel in one of the more exotic Greek islands. And while Mary Lou nattered on about how disappointing to have the holiday end so soon, Reynolds thought about Mr Gatterly. Surely he, too, would be devastated by the news. Children can't be blamed for their parents' break-up. And a firstborn can't be disinherited from being first in his father's affection, even if he is one of twins. Unless there's some reason for hating him of course. Or wishing he were dead. He remembered the hints about some quarrel.

At this point questioning came to a standstill. There were no other leads for Joe Fletcher to block, and there was little time before head office arrived. Let head office sift through all the complexities, he thought, as Derrymore pocketed the paper with the address, and thanked the Fletchers for their cooperation.

Obviously relieved, Joe ushered them into the hall. 'If I'd known,' Mary Lou twittered brightly over his shoulder, the drawled vowels betraying her American origin, 'I'd have had a cake all ready. But I'm no cook, as poor Joe will tell you; never learned.'

Proof, if proof were needed, of her lack of feeling. And substantiation of what her husband had earlier emphasized, about her having nothing to do with the kitchen – unwittingly, or previously rehearsed? And was she as ignorant of the family history as her husband had suggested?

Reynolds glanced at Derrymore and was relieved to see his expression mirrored his own thoughts.

Fletcher caught the look. 'Hush,' he said to his wife, raising a warning finger. And as the other men stared at him, 'The child,' he said in an exaggerated whisper. 'Upstairs asleep. Don't want to wake the child.'

As they left the pair behind in the doorway, Derrymore cocked his thumb backwards. 'There's a rum couple. Never thought old Fletcher'd get married. And his wife . . .' He whistled under his breath. 'Not what I'd expect,' he confessed. 'Not your average home body. But get her on her own without her husband, we might find out something.'

They had returned to the drive now and were standing beside Reynolds' car, both of them, for differing reasons, reluctant to go back into the house. At least Reynolds knew why he was reluctant.

'About the woman who phoned me originally,' he began, and was relieved to hear Derrymore say, 'Ah,' in his old way, as if he'd been waiting for Reynolds to come to that. But when Reynolds had explained who the woman was, and what, when he'd reached the manor, he'd found she'd done, all Derrymore said bluntly was, 'What do we do now?' Then he added, 'You're in a worse hole than I am. At least I know where my mam is!'

His attempt at humour was half-hearted but genuine. It was like him, Reynolds thought affectionately, to show concern for a friend's predicament in the midst of his own difficulties.

'Come clean from the beginning.' Reynolds' display of assurance was far from his true feelings. In fact, ever since Derrymore had confided in him the problem had been gnawing away at him. 'My advice, old son,' he continued, 'for what it's worth, is explain your mother's part straight off. As you and your mam have nothing to hide, that's no skin off your teeth. It's a damn shame, I know, but if you try to hush it up, it'll only make things worse when it does come out.'

Derrymore was listening intently. He suddenly looked so much older, Reynolds wanted to put his arm round his shoulder and tell him to cheer up. All he said, however, was, 'They may make a fuss but the worst they can do is take you off the case. Too close to the whole thing, they'll say. The real problem, however,' and here he did hesitate because what he was about to say now was only a theory, and was one that didn't help the sergeant's mother so much as Reynolds' ex-wife, 'is what about my ex-wife? You see, I don't believe Mr Edmund Gatterly was the intended victim.'

After he had explained his reasonings, and Derrymore had mulled them over, he added, 'It's possible that the stuff could have been put in tonight, but only if the poison was a type that could be added easily.' He began to expand on this idea. 'It's not simple to do the adding on the spot,' he concluded, 'without the intended victim becoming suspicious, and since my ex-wife claimed she never went near the freezer and Edmund Gatterly did all the cooking, there may be clues to substantiate her claims. But I think at the moment the strongest point in her favour is that if she's only met Edmund Gatterly once before she'd have to have a damn good reason to bump him off. That's another thing to check on,' he went on. 'The length of their relationship.'

He paused, letting these ideas sink in. 'On the other hand, whoever put the poison in that pie had to be familiar with the household and its routines.'

Derrymore nodded. 'Or be an actual member of the household, one of the Gatterlys themselves.'

'There's the new Mrs Gatterly.' Reynolds began to name them. 'And Mr Gatterly. And of course there's the former Mrs Gatterly, Miss Trewithen, and the other twin brother, Justin. Then there's Joe Fletcher, who's made no bones about his dislike of the whole family, and Mary Lou Fletcher. Any of them could be suspects.'

Derrymore nodded again. 'To my mind, Mary Lou Fletcher talked about several things Joe felt she shouldn't. And both of them must be in and out of the house all the time, especially now the family's away.'

'Fletcher suggested that Edmund wasn't on good terms with his father,' Reynolds switched thoughts. 'My ex-wife mentioned the same thing. That might be significant. And what about the twin brother? Is he on good terms with his father? Mary Lou suggested he comes to the house. Be interesting to know what access he has when his father is away. What do you know about him?'

Derrymore frowned, trying to remember. 'Always acted as if he were too important to mix with the rest of us; know what I mean? Of course we were children when Mam and I were here, so you can't go by that. He might have changed. I haven't seen him in years either. But if, for example, Edmund had been the intended victim, Justin could have a lot to gain.'

Then he shook his head. 'The twins never were close, like most twins I know. Didn't even look alike and didn't have much in common. But they didn't hate each other either, not that I remember.'

He and Reynolds exchanged looks, their thoughts working in harmony as always, Reynolds providing the main ideas, Derrymore testing their validity. It would be a damned shame, Reynolds thought, to have the partnership broken up, just because of what head office would call 'personal considerations'.

There was one last thing to sort out. After a pause, somewhat reluctantly, Reynolds said, 'If my theories make sense at all, they'll hold in my ex-wife's favour, in spite of her stupidity. Either way, I'd like to be the one to bring her back.'

Derrymore looked at Reynolds, his eyes like his mother's, kind but shrewd. 'Agreed,' he said slowly, 'but you should clear off fast now. Leave me to deal with them.' He meant head office, who by now would be converging on the Fowey estuary, trailing all their paraphernalia of pathological and forensic science, all their modern skills and apparatus geared to solving crimes. 'I'll keep your name out as long as I can,' he added, meaning he would do all he could short of lying. 'And I'll keep her name out as long as possible too. How on earth will you trace her?'

'I've got the car number.'

Thankful that memory hadn't let him down, Reynolds recited the number of the red Rover that by now must be speeding back to wherever she lived. He was about to say, 'Surprised you didn't pass her,' but thought better of it. In that maze of lanes there might be many ways of threading a passage out.

Derrymore had turned to look at the house with its gruesome burden. Seeing his expression, for a moment Reynolds was tempted to change his mind and offer to stay. It's not every day a man has to face the prospect of a dead friend, murdered in full throttle, as it were, the prodigal son returning to a feast where poison is the welcomer.

But, like his mother, Derrymore was practical. Already he was using his mobile phone. As Reynolds returned to his own car, he heard Derrymore asking for a tracer on the licence plate he'd just given him. If he stayed, what use would he be? Once head office heard his name, he'd be barred from the case anyway. His ex-wife would be arrested, and any hope he might have of finding the real murderer would be closed.

These arguments were sensible and logical. Yet it was with the feeling of a rat leaving a sinking ship that Reynolds drove off, leaving the police sergeant to handle the delicate issue of his mother's involvement, and the even more delicate problems of how he had been informed of the murder, who his informant was (even if he didn't mention Reynolds, the Fletchers might) and who the mysterious woman was who had so carefully cleared away all the evidence she could put her hands on.

Upstairs in the bedroom the child straightened up from where she'd been listening through the floorboards. She heard the front door slam and her parents move into the living room where immediately the blare from the television drowned their voices. Blast, she thought. She leaned back against the bed, playing with the cuffs of the outsize man's jumper she was wearing and considered what to do next.

'Child' wasn't the right word for her, although Joe always called her that as if unwilling to acknowledge he'd spawned a daughter of her size. Squarely built like her father, with her father's narrow eyes and her mother's hair (in her case lank and greasy) she was what was commonly called a 'buxom wench' of about fifteen who looked thirty.

Edmund, she was repeating to herself, more in surprise than sorrow. Why I never! And then, with her mother's coolness, it must have been fate, she decided.

She believed in fate, in horoscopes and stars. Without

a sound, she rooted under the bed among the Coke bottles and discarded chip shop papers to find the box where she kept her astrological charts. They occupied more of her time these days than geometry or French verbs. Edmund Gatterly, she was thinking, trying to remember the date of his birthday. Surely she'd asked him once when he'd last seen her fishing, and argued with her that it was wrong. I fish to eat, she'd told him, when I'm hungry. Nothing wrong in that. Besides, you taught me how to fish, don't you remember? How poor Edmund had cringed.

She knew Edmund was often about the place. Her father and mother were lying when they said he never came here. Course her father wouldn't think it unusual as he believed the estate, the remnants of it, that is, should belong to the twins anyway. And after Mr Gatterly came back, the older twin was certainly all over the house, sucking up to his father. Made you sick.

On the other hand, if Edmund had gone into the house tonight, he must have had a reason. He was the sort of serious person who had a reason for everything. It irritated her that she didn't know what it was. Usually she knew about all sorts of things.

If she'd been in the sitting room she'd have made it her prime concern to find out what the police knew, or guessed. And she would have been there if her mother's whinnying hadn't driven her upstairs, nag, nag, nag, all day long. She didn't care twopence about fashion or what she wore, not like some people she could mention (here she gave her father's glower), who spent more than they could afford on clothes. Keeping up with the Joneses, she called it, except the name wasn't Jones!

Sucking on a long lank of hair and settling herself more comfortably into the folds of the sweater (picked up in Truro market, second-hand, none of her mother's

knitted cardies for her), she began to think of the
questions she'd have made sure were answered before
the bobbies left.

First, if Edmund had arrived sneakily, after dark,
what was he after? Not just to pig out on some hideous
pie in his stepmother's hideous kitchen. Equally
important, who was the person who'd come with him,
the person the police hadn't mentioned? She frowned at
the thought. Her parents hadn't mentioned that either,
although they must have known Edmund had invited
her; there were two cars.

Most important of all, why didn't the police ask
outright who could have put the poison in the food? Or
who the poison was intended for? They must have
theories; on the telly, the police always had theories and
when they kept them to themselves that meant the
situation was serious. If she'd been there she'd have
prodded them about what they knew or didn't know,
she was good at that.

As for her parents, they were wet behind the ears,
she thought, babes in the woods, not to have told what
they knew when they had the chance. If nothing else, it
would have turned suspicion away from them. Any fool
could have seen that the police were trying to pry into
her parents' secrets. If they weren't careful, they'd end
up being blamed. They should have attacked first.

Not that she felt much loyalty towards her parents,
her lips curled, but what a wasted opportunity for
herself. Oh, my, what a chance to stir things up! She
thought about that for a moment, her eyes shining.

So what happens next? The police swarming around,
the place humming with reporters – well, she could do
without them. But there would be consolations. Her
parents under surveillance, for one thing. Serve them
right. Get them off her back. The holiday abroad

interrupted, the family summoned home at a moment's notice, that'd be something to look forward to, a bonus of major import. And everywhere confusion and distress. All written in the stars. She wriggled her bare feet in joyous anticipation.

Chapter 6

It was late when Reynolds reached home, where the cases in the hall stood mutely accusing. 'Hell,' he said, kicking his way past them and throwing himself into the same chair where earlier he had been enjoying the prospect of freedom. 'Bloody hell.' Find her, he told himself, haul her back and then clear off, that's the best solution – and the best I can do for her. The names of possible suspects continued to buzz in his head, with reasons and motives tangled together like strands of netting. Despite his common sense telling him to back off he knew he didn't want to be excluded from a case that promised (if that wasn't the wrong word) all the complications that he excelled in solving, and all the difficulties that roused his fighting instincts. He also knew that he, and possibly Derrymore too, would be sent packing as soon as their part was known.

Morning dawned dull and grey with the hint of sun later, the sort of day when fish bite and birds are out along the tidal flats. Derrymore rang with the information he wanted, a weary sounding Derrymore despite his cheerful veneer.

'Can't talk,' he said tersely. 'Holding, but not for long. Just hope my mam's bearing up. If you can, could you . . .' His voice trailed away but his meaning was clear. He was keeping his promise not to implicate Reynolds, and he was hoping that at some time Reynolds would

45

pay his mother a visit. Fair enough, Reynolds thought, that's the least I can do while he holds head office at bay. As soon as I've tracked down my own game I'll do that very thing. Once my ex-wife comes forward, Derrymore's mam will be in the clear.

He had steeled himself for a long search, but Derrymore informed him that the Rover was registered under his ex-wife's maiden name, and when he double-checked in the telephone directory, there it was in black and white: Audrey Linton. She was living in St Ives, not more than an hour's drive on a good day. It made him feel better somehow to think of her as Miss Linton, more impersonal. But for God's sake, why St Ives, the most famous artist colony in Cornwall? What was she doing there? She'd never shown any interest in art as far as he could remember, at most a course at the Women's Institute. Her rendezvous at the house had certainly been out of the way for her if not for Edmund Gatterly who, Derrymore confirmed, had had the key on him, lived where she'd said, but whose rooms, when searched, had revealed no new clues.

This was not the moment to quiz Derrymore since he was in no position to speak freely and every word could be heard. Saving other questions for later, Reynolds headed westward, along the main A30, where unfortunately the promise of a fine morning had tempted tourists out. Forced to creep in traffic queues slowed still further by repair works, he reached St Ives much later than he planned, and in no good humour.

Situated in the north-west corner of Cornwall, St Ives had once been a working fishing village. Its position along a curving bay, enhanced by the quality of its light, had become much admired by painters who had flocked there in the last century. Sometimes, Reynolds thought irritably as he manipulated his car through the narrow, twisting lanes looking for a parking space, I wish all cars were banned from beauty spots. Or, better still, that beauty spots themselves were banned. Or that I was still an official police officer and could leave my car wherever I wanted.

By the time he'd parked, his early reaction of relief that his ex-wife had been traced so easily had given way to something akin to anger. If he'd been annoyed that she'd come to the Fowey estuary for what he'd first taken as a mere weekend stay, how much more infuriating that she'd settled in the same county as himself, and must have chosen to do so, almost in defiance of him.

She knew where I lived, he thought, as he strode along the narrow cobbled streets; in the early days she was in touch with my solicitors often enough, and through my books I was frequently in the news. He found her apparent indifference to his whereabouts, an indifference, it seemed, as great as his, the worst irritant of all. But when he finally reached the address he was looking for, he was surprised out of his bad mood.

The crescent existed, as did the number, 35. Except it wasn't a house, or a block of flats. It was a shop. Or rather, it was an artists' gallery, trading under her own name, according to the sign prominently hung outside, and by the looks of it, a successful one.

He crossed the street to scrutinize the display in the window. It consisted of various paintings in various modern styles; the elegant arrangement was augmented by pots of flowers which set the works off to advantage. None was priced, always a bad sign for prospective buyers and indicative of the sort of expenditure expected. This is no fly-by-night establishment, he thought grudgingly, here's class.

He pushed at the fashionable stable door. It wasn't

locked and inside he found an equally elegant room, lined with more canvases. The lighting was subdued but functional and when, after a moment or two, Audrey herself emerged from the rear of the gallery, her cheerful manner was almost alarming. Only the traditional, 'How may I help you?' suggested that she meant business.

Realizing that silhouetted as he was against the now dazzling sunlight, she didn't recognize him, he shut the door with a bang before moving towards her. This morning she was dressed in a greenish skirt and blouse which accentuated her figure, and her hair was swept back in a chignon. She looked what her gallery suggested, stylish, at ease in an exclusive milieu, familiar with the painters who created the canvases she dealt in. How the devil had she managed to move into these circles? he found himself thinking as he barked tersely, 'Get your coat and shut up shop. There's a posse of policemen waiting to interview you.'

When she stared at him as if nonplussed, he added on impulse, 'And while you're at it, bring whatever Edmund Gatterly gave you and you took when you ran out on me.'

The expression on her face didn't change, as if that bright efficiency was frozen. Then she shrugged, said grudgingly, 'I suppose you'd better come up,' and, gesturing to him to follow, went up some back stairs which led to what apparently were her living quarters. He found himself in a long sun-bathed room running the full length of the building. The entire end wall had been removed to make way for French windows, opening on to a balcony with a spectacular view of the harbour. Seagulls swooped and called over a range of chimneypots; sea and sky merged into an expanse of blue against which a vase of yellow sunflowers was framed. He might have been looking at a living reproduction of a Van Gogh painting. For a moment he was stunned.

She noted his reaction at once; she never missed things like that, and, as if enjoying his astonishment, sat down on the sofa in front of the balcony, moving a pile of art books so that he could join her on the sofa, an invitation which he ignored. Even in the harsh light she looked twenty again.

'I've already phoned the police,' she said bluntly. 'I talked it over with a friend and we agreed I should go back to talk to them.' She emphasized the word 'friend'. And as he continued to stare at her, added, 'I was just sorting through papers before leaving.'

My God, what cheek! As if murder can wait for papers to be sorted. And who's this bloody friend whose advice is so important? He felt anger start up again.

As if anticipating his reaction, she stubbed out her half-finished cigarette defiantly. 'They gave a number to call on the local news this morning,' she told him smugly. 'Just mentioned there'd been a murder, no other details. I didn't give my name or address,' she continued. 'She, my friend that is, pointed out that there's no need to have policemen homing in on the gallery. But I've assured them I'll be there as soon as possible.' She made a gesture. 'And if you don't believe me, phone them yourself and ask. And while you're at it, explain how you're involved.'

Touché, he thought. Before he could protest, she sat up and gave him a triumphant smile. 'It's the least I can do,' she said virtuously, as if letting him in on a secret. 'We thought about that side as well. I decided I owed Edmund Gatterly some return. Helping find his murderer is something I can't turn my back on.'

Twaddle, he thought. What's really made you change

your mind? Not me, for sure. Still, if she'd come to her senses, so much the better. But to announce it in that way, as if nothing he'd said made any difference! He had been so sure she wouldn't come, had so geared himself up for argument, he felt let down.

'If Edmund gave me anything,' she was saying, 'what's it to you? In any case, I promised him not to talk about it.'

You don't know what light it might shed on the whole matter, Reynolds wanted to protest. It might be connected with the murder. And don't talk to me about promises, I've never heard you give, or hold to, promises before.

She glanced at her watch, a dainty diamond-studded contraption he didn't remember. 'I don't want to quarrel,' she told him as if she were a schoolteacher and he an erring school boy. 'Just because I panicked and reverted back to old ways in a crisis doesn't mean the reversal is permanent.' She suddenly smiled. 'And it's taken me years of therapy to admit that much.'

Therapy? he was thinking. I suppose she means psychoanalysis and all that claptrap. He grimaced. He wasn't a believer in psychoanalysis; as far as he was concerned, it too often made self-centred people more self-centred.

She gave another smile. 'We're not all made like you, you know,' she said, her voice deliberately studded with irony, yet having a ring of truth underneath. 'Macho man, coping with every emergency, a modern Captain Marvel. So certain women can't do anything on their own, so patronizing towards us, it makes me sick.'

Her assessment of his character surprised him; he'd never thought of himself as patronizing to women, and hadn't known she did.

'You've made a new life for yourself, I've heard,' she

went on, bitterness just showing. 'Your books are bestsellers. Well, I've made a new life too. I used the settlement money to go to art school in London, then afterwards, with the help of my new friends, started this gallery. I found I had a knack for putting artists and their prospective clients together. But I had to work at it. And I'm not ashamed of turning to professionals for help,' she went on. 'The best thing I ever did. And my friend encouraged me to see the analysis through. But I am ashamed that at the first crisis I leaned on you so hard.'

He was embarrassed. That was another thing he didn't like about psychoanalysis, the mumbo jumbo of soul-searching that went with it.

'Better lean on those you know,' he quipped although he didn't feel like laughing, 'than those you don't.'

She didn't laugh, simply looked through him into space. Then, as if making up her mind, she said, 'Edmund shouldn't have had to die like that.'

Her echo of his own thoughts was also surprising. So was what she said next. 'Now you are involved, I hope you'll stay on. For his sake. Not mine. I don't need you any more.' She fixed him with the wide-eyed look he had once dreaded.

He didn't know what to answer. Abruptly changing the subject, he asked her what she had meant when she said Edmund and his father had quarrelled.

She hesitated. 'If I did,' she said reluctantly, 'I shouldn't have. It had nothing to do with his parents' divorce, no matter what others say.' She blinked. 'I can't reveal any more. Again, that wouldn't be fair to Edmund. You'll have to dig for it.' She gave a little giggle. 'Isn't that what you're good at, digging for clues?'

He ignored the sarcasm. 'It might be important,' he urged her. 'You said you met him on business. Did the quarrel have anything to do with it? And what was that business anyway?'

'Oh, you do so harp on things,' she told him with a return to waspishness. 'You never let go. I'm not talking. Can't you take no for an answer? I know murder's more important than my art or my gallery, or anything connected with my life here. I'm not that dumb. But it's no good your preaching, I can't stand your preaching, never could.'

And with that he had to be content.

He returned to St Breddaford feeling somewhat rejected. He hadn't had to use anything for leverage, not even Derrymore's mother; his powers of persuasion hadn't been needed, he might just as well have stayed at home. For whatever reason she had done the right thing for once, though he suspected that the unknown 'friend' had had more to do with her decision than even she'd let on. He was convinced that she was keeping something hidden. Whatever it was, like the cause of the Gatterly quarrel he'd have to dig for it.

On the other hand his own relief should have been great. So great that, had he been a melodramatic man himself, he should have stopped the car and jumped out to shout aloud. It had nothing to do with the case in hand of course, was purely and simply personal. For the first time since he'd known her, without his prompting, without blaming him for her own inadequacies, she'd done the right thing. And there's the rub he thought, with a rueful grin. Years of wanting her to stand up for herself, when she does, I resent it. As Derrymore would say, makes you think.

Against these revelations, even the dreadful fact of murder had retreated. Which, when he realized, made him ashamed of his own brand of self-centredness. His ex-wife's request, unexpected as it was, that he stay on the case, now came home to him in a new light. Things might still be difficult between them, and between him and the investigating team, but for Edmund Gatterly's sake he felt a special commitment.

As he drove, he tried to piece together what Audrey had told him, as well as what she had not told. For the first time he concentrated on the package she'd taken. He assumed that she still had it in her possession. Small enough to be easily carried, oblong in shape, it could be a book or a bundle of papers. More likely, if the meeting really was a business matter, it was some work of art. A small painting perhaps, left in the house at the time of the original sale. But if he was right, why was it suddenly so important that fifteen years or so later Edmund Gatterly had to come back secretly to take it? Steal it, the law might say. And why give it to Audrey? To sell, to raise money for some purpose? Although, like the Gatterly quarrel, it seemed to have no bearing on the case, yet his intuition told him that, somehow, it was important.

With these questions, as well as others, filling his mind, he reached the village where he made a detour to keep his promise to drop in on Derrymore's mother. Besides, she might have information he could use. If Mr Gatterly kept in touch, she might have insights into the family. If they were the intended victims he needed to find out as much as he could about them.

Mazie Derrymore and her son now lived in a cottage scarcely a stone's throw from Reynolds' own, a typical St Breddaford building of grey granite, brightened by a garden full of flowers. He left his car in the lane outside, confident that no one would try to move it or block it in, or, as had happened recently, scratch an obscenity across its side. This was a quiet place; traffic and tourists had not yet made life unbearable here.

He found Mazie where she usually was at that hour, in the kitchen. It was close to one o'clock, and, when she saw him, like all good cooks she immediately thought of food. She wouldn't let him say a word until she had settled him at her dining table with a bowl of soup and homemade bread, then, with a typical joke, said, 'If you're not frightened of my cooking, that is. Although won't Mrs Aintree laugh. She'd told me for years my pastry was tough.'

Clearly, for the moment fear of implication in murder weighed less on her mind than concern for village gossip – or her genuine grief at Edmund's unexpected death. Reynolds let her talk, by gradual degrees turning the conversation round to her time at Trewithen Manor.

'She was a beauty.' Mazie, who could never have had that said about her, even in her youth, was surprisingly tolerant of the second wife, even if she had destroyed the household, and for that matter destroyed Mazie's own position in it. 'Only saw her once, but clearly Mr Gatterly was besotted.'

The Biblical simplicity of the word struck Reynolds. 'Besotted.' It must have been a lightning flash in what was still a Victorian-minded world.

'Mind you,' Mazie continued, 'Mr G, as we called him, was never suited to country living. He only stayed on in the first place because Miss Trewithen insisted. And the second Mrs Gatterly wasn't suited either. American, you see, all bustle and go. Could have knocked me down with a feather when I heard they was back to stay.'

She poured cups of tea from the large earthenware pot, not happy at being questioned and too good-natured to speak ill of anyone. Yet, as Reynolds knew from past meetings, her own brand of honesty made it impossible for her to prevaricate. Like her son, she told the truth bluntly, as she saw it.

'Don't know all the ins and outs of why the house first had to be sold,' she said in answer to his next question. She pushed the sugar bowl across. 'But there was talk.'

'Talk?' he prompted.

She looked uncomfortable. 'They said he'd put money into local businesses,' she said at last, flustered at his insistence. 'Money that belonged to his first wife. He didn't have anything of his own then, you see. When the business failed, he lost it all, the house included.'

She sipped her tea and sighed. 'In those days money was always tight, sometimes I didn't get paid for weeks. Not that Derry and me wanted much. But I was cook and housekeeper there for eight years, so I knew what went on. Many's the time we'd have gone supperless if the boys hadn't gone fishing.'

She took a satisfying bite of cake, an old countrywoman for whom things had finally fallen into place.

'But for all he did his family wrong, Mr Gatterly was good to us.'

She said this as defiantly as Derrymore had done, expecting to be contradicted, then added, 'Of course, you weren't living here, you don't know the scandal the split-up caused. But in spite of that, Mr G found us this cottage in St Breddaford. He told us Miss Trewithen was too upset and didn't have the time.'

That doesn't sound right, he thought. But he didn't query her statement. 'What happened afterwards?'

'He started to stay away, weeks at a stretch,' she told him. 'Working, they said, in London, but I don't know about that. Course by then the twins were off at school and Miss Trewithen kept more and more to her own rooms. Sometimes me and Derrymore had the run of the whole place to ourselves. Funny,' she mused, 'people down that way always called Miss Trewithen by her maiden name even when she was first married. I don't think Mr G liked that.'

'And you've not heard of the twins since?' Reynolds coaxed.

'They was with their mother first off,' she explained, 'then once they'd grown I suppose they went their own way. Most boys do these days.' Although not my Derry, thank goodness, she seemed to be saying.

'And do you ever see her now, the first Mrs Gatterly, I mean Miss Trewithen?'

She shook her head. 'She was always very proud.'

Again her dislike of speaking ill of anyone made her pause until she was persuaded to go on talking. 'They say she's a real recluse now,' she continued. 'And she was such an active lady. Course she's younger than me, but 'cept for one spat over Derry we got on right enough.'

Questioned about this incident, for the first time she waxed eloquent. 'Miss Trewithen was one of the old aristocracy,' she explained. 'Kept you in your place. Well, one day she came to me in my little sitting room at the end of the passage.'

The one where the body was, he thought with a pang.

'She told me she didn't like our sons playing together. Edmund wasn't to be encouraged to spend time with us, and Derry wasn't to go out in the boat with Edmund as if he was his equal. "If Derry's not welcome to come and go as he pleases, within sensible reason that is," I says, "then I'm not welcome neither." Told her straight, I did, and she backed down. As if my Derry weren't fit to associate with her boys, why, the older twin was always into trouble. But there, boys will be boys and it was a bad time for them.'

Here, clearly reluctant to say anything about her former employers, she launched into a recital of

Derrymore's virtues, how he'd left school as soon as he was old enough to help out and take a job, then when he could, he went into the army and sent her virtually every penny he earned. And now that he had a good job and a promotion he was always after her not to work at all, even when Mr G had asked her, oh, about six months ago, to do some cooking for a reception. After that she had got in the habit of sending over some things every month or so. 'In the old days, Mr G was always partial to my baking,' Mazie said, 'and these days, every penny helps, doesn't it?'

And how many other people knew of that partiality? Reynolds wondered. At least to make use of it. It was an important line of investigation especially if, as he believed, Edmund wasn't the intended victim. But when he asked Mazie outright if she knew of anyone with a grudge against the Gatterly family, as he suspected she was shocked by the idea.

Another thought struck him. 'Why do you think Mr Gatterly's come back?' he asked. 'Did his new wife suggest it?' He was told in no uncertain terms that after their marriage the second Mrs Gatterly had made no secret about not wanting to live in England, let alone Cornwall, had more than once openly said she'd not spend the rest of her life in a damp medieval hovel lumbered with medieval plumbing. In fact it was commonly held that the second Mrs Gatterly's return was something of a miracle. 'I should have thought that when she found he meant to live here permanent,' Mazie leaned forward confidentially, 'she'd have been furious.'

'So the present Mr and Mrs Gatterly aren't on good terms?'

'Oh, I wouldn't say that.' Mazie looked alarmed. 'They have a son too, you know. And it must be fifteen years or more since they got married. Why would they break up after all these years? Mr G only mentioned the new Mrs G's objections for fun like,' she added in explanation. 'When he was paying me for the baking. I can see him, large as life, standing in this very room, pulling out his money and saying, "How can we make her happy, Mrs Mazie," he always called me that, "now I've got the wherewithal to set things right?" And to think it might have been the very pie I'd made him, it's downright upsetting.'

Mazie began to sob while Reynolds reassured her over and over again that no one could blame her, nothing was her fault, the whole thing was a hideous mistake.

When she had dried her tears, remembering what Audrey had claimed, he asked if there was any recent reason why Edmund and his father might have quarrelled.

Mazie shook her head. 'Never mentioned the boys,' she said. 'But I know he didn't see them after the divorce, so I suppose there might be some hard feelings.'

Seeing Reynolds' expression, she added quickly, 'I don't know anything about it really, but for what it's worth, I'll tell you all the same why I think Mr Gatterly's returned.'

She leaned forward, more than ever like her son, her rosy face puckered with concentration. 'He wants to make amends, get the manor in order for the twins. It was his fault it was lost; this is his chance to make things right for them now he has "the wherewithal". Just like he said.'

Reynolds was considering this idea when the door opened and the object of Mazie's pride stood on the doorstep, a worried Derrymore, his face looking if anything more pinched and grey than it had last evening.

He said in his kindest voice, 'Sorry, my mam, I can't

stay now. But everything's come out all right so don't you fret. I'll tell you later.' And then to Reynolds, 'A word, sir, if I may. Was on my way to find you and saw your car. There's something I thought I'd better let you know before you heard it yourself.'

She didn't keep her word, Reynolds thought dully as he stood up. She's tricked me again. The albatross weight about his neck returned, heavier than ever, as he followed Derrymore outside.

Chapter 7

'Miss Linton didn't ring,' Reynolds heard himself say flatly. 'She didn't come.' He turned blindly towards the village green where the little stream trickled slowly in its summer course.

If Derrymore was surprised by the use of that name, this was no moment to show it. Instead, even more agitatedly, he insisted, 'But she did! When she said she would. That's not why I'm here.'

Reynolds felt his heart thump as if it was struggling to catch up. Breathing deeply, he walked beside the stream, passing the wider gravel stretches where children fed the ducks. 'What is it then?' he said, trying to act normally although relief threatened to flood him.

It came out in fits and starts, how Derrymore had managed to stall all discussion of an 'unknown woman' and, better still, delete all references to a 'second officer', so far fortunately not mentioned by the Fletchers. And how, when both father and mother had been informed, and the dead man's twin had made a definite identification first thing this morning, a woman had rung the inquiry team, soon after Derrymore and Reynolds had spoken in fact, just in time to rescue him from his predicament. 'Although if they find out the truth,' he said in a gloomy aside, 'they'll have my stripes for garters.'

He knew it was too quick for Reynolds to have persuaded her, nevertheless the anonymous caller promised a mid-morning arrival. And despite the scepticism of the others in the inquiry team now firmly installed at Trewithen Manor – 'Murder always draws out cranks,' they said – sure enough, about mid-morning she'd shown up in the red car, looking, Derrymore said somewhat apologetically, 'businesslike. Sensible and cool, even when the cross-examination started.'

What his real impression of Reynolds' ex-wife was, he was too shy, or polite, to reveal, although Reynolds knew there wasn't much he would have missed. As for her story, Derrymore went on to say that by the time she appeared at the house, pathology and forensic had completed their nasty business and the inquiry team had torn the place apart in their search for evidence. In short, fortunately for her, the investigation had already progressed far enough to make her version of events sound plausible. More than that, several clues had been discovered to exonerate her completely.

Hearing Reynolds' sigh of relief, Derrymore added he'd get back to all that later. It was what happened at the end of the interview that was important.

'They roasted her, of course,' he continued. 'Mind you, she stood up very well. Didn't mention you, merely said she'd called the police, which fitted in with my version. Went through every move, just as you'd described, but swore the man was still alive when she summoned help. The worst strike against her, apart from leaving, was clearing things away, but in a state of shock, I suppose it might be possible. I've heard of people stopping to tidy out their cupboards when their house is on fire. Anyway, she admitted she'd acted foolishly and so on, and her story held together in light of what we'd found. So they let her go.' Again he glanced at Reynolds.

Reynolds felt the cold touch of impending disaster. 'And then?' he prompted.

Derrymore stammered that the details had just come in over the blower. At the nasty bend where cars queued for the ferry, a car had gone out of control. A red Rover. 'Witnesses said she was driving too fast.' Derrymore was speaking more quickly now that he'd finally brought out the news and given Reynolds time to recover. 'Seems she couldn't make a turn and skidded. There were parked cars waiting; it was lucky she didn't hit them. It could have been much worse.'

Once, when he was in the army, Reynolds had been wounded. He hadn't felt a thing, had actually continued moving forward until, quite unexpectedly, his whole side had frozen as if turned to wood. He felt the same wooden feeling now. All he could see were the flowers in her living room, yellow against the vivid blue, and the triumphant smile as she turned to face him.

After a while, he pulled himself together and began to ask the questions people always ask in such circumstances, the mundane routine questions that hide the true anxieties. Was she conscious? What was her condition? What could he do? What about the car? To be told firmly but kindly, as he himself had so many times done in the past, that she was alive when pulled from the wreckage, serious injuries though, a helicopter had been summoned to take her to the nearest special unit but there was hope. 'Nothing you can do at the moment, sir,' Derrymore concluded. 'I'll let you know.'

'You said she was driving too fast,' Reynolds said, putting his anxieties to one side and turning to Derrymore who was hovering protectively, if such a large man could be said to hover. 'Any reason?'

'They're checking that too, sir.' Derrymore's smile was sympathetic. 'But I'd drive fast myself after the way Old Clemie drummed her.'

'Clemie?' For a second time Reynolds felt the tingle of

premonition. 'Not Chief Inspector Clemow of the Devon and Cornwall Constabulary?'

Derrymore looked as though he wished he'd bitten off his tongue rather than make such a careless slip. He himself had had more run-ins with the same inspector than he liked to recall. He told Reynolds that although Clemow had not actually taken part in the interview, he'd made sure he could listen, setting up the interrogation in such a way that he could sit behind a screen and, well, eavesdrop, was how Derrymore put it. When the official questioning had ended, he'd come forward. 'As if he wanted to confuse her,' Derrymore added. 'After all that secrecy, he suddenly appeared in person to ask more questions, all to do with private matters, such as how long had she been living in St Ives and what was she doing there, as if he had the right to know. Milking the situation, I'd say; getting the most out of it. I can't think why.'

'I can.' Reynolds didn't elucidate. Anyone who had fallen foul of Clemow, as, for various reasons, he and his ex-wife had done, would understand how the inspector would enjoy the opportunity to crow over them.

'And there were several other strange things,' Derrymore went on. 'For one, although Clemow didn't make anything of the name she'd given, as soon as she arrived he recognized her. Until then he'd made it very plain he wanted to conduct the interview himself. And although he kept back and let someone else take over, it was clear he was hoping, well, let's say looking, for something to hold her on. Myself, I don't think the old devil really means to let her go; he's dangling her on a string, just waiting to reel her back in. You should have seen his face after the news about the accident come through.' He was silent for a moment. Then, apologetically, 'Gets her off the hook, of course, for a while at any rate.'

Reynolds was only half listening. Clemow, he was thinking. The main reason why he had retired when he did, and the main cause of his subsequent failures to deal with the force. Clemow had been Reynolds' partner and friend – until his affair with Reynolds' wife had fed him gossip to fuel the smear campaign Clemow himself had started against Reynolds. And he hated Reynolds all the more for finding out.

Of all the people head office would have chosen, Reynolds thought, Clemow spelt disaster. For me, and for my ex-wife. Clemow will never forgive Audrey either, for chucking him afterwards, for making it painfully clear there was no real or lasting attraction between them, for telling him she'd used him merely to hurt me. Clemow will jump at the chance to get his own back.

Reynolds swore under his breath. The last thing he needed was Clemow supervising every move. And if Clemow found out that he was already involved, or that he and the sergeant had cooked up a story between them, it wasn't only Derrymore's stripes that were in danger. They'd both be crucified.

'I'm sorry, sir,' Derrymore said.

'Don't apologize to me.' Reynolds hid his true concern. 'He's my problem. I'll handle him.'

He stopped mid-stride. Here came the crucial moment when he made up his mind, either to tell Derrymore he intended to leave well enough alone, by far the wisest move, or to go on, as every instinct now cried out. He brooded for a moment, considering his options.

His immediate part was finished. He was free to go home, pick up his bags and leave. Or he could wait to ensure Audrey was all right. Once she'd recovered, and there was no reason why she shouldn't recover, he'd find the means somehow to break down her resistance and get her to explain all those hints she'd dropped, make peace with her . . . Come off it, Reynolds, he told himself. Be realistic. She's already made it clear that she doesn't need you; she has new 'friends' and a new life.

Her words echoed in his ears. 'Now you are involved, I hope you'll stay on. For Edmund's sake. Not mine.' But neither of them had known then that she would have to face such a malevolent antagonist, or pay such a heavy price. The clear possibility of her death came to him in spite of all his efforts to keep the thought away.

'Macho man,' she'd called him, always in control. 'I can't stand your preaching,' she'd said. He didn't feel he had the right to preach to anyone, and he didn't feel in control. All he had ever known was his work. If, in the past, his profession had been the greatest antidote to personal stress, now it must be again.

He gave himself a mental shake, moved forward. 'Now, Sergeant,' he said firmly, 'if you will, back to those vital clues you mentioned.' He spoke formally, to show Derrymore that he had put the news behind him and was on course again.

'Right.' Derrymore, obviously thankful that the worst was over, was eager to begin. 'First, in the kitchen. Although her fingerprints were all over it, and everywhere else she said she'd been, none showed up on the microwave or freezer although the dead man's did.'

He went on to explain that there was no evidence of anything being burnt in the fire; the remains of the pie and pie dish, a special microwave one, were where Reynolds had suggested, in the compactor gadget. They had found enough crumbs and bits of food on the dining room floor to confirm that that was where the meal had been eaten. The most significant discovery, however, was in the freezer itself.

'Every item of homemade food was contaminated with the same poisonous substance,' Derrymore said gravely. 'Every single piece had been sprayed or injected, I don't know which, then carefully re-sealed and the labels replaced, to look as if nothing had been touched. Not possible in a hurry,' he pointed out unnecessarily. 'So you see, despite all she'd done to harm herself, there was no reason to hold her.'

Reynolds nodded. 'And that finding surely substantiates the idea that the food can't have been meant for Edmund.'

'Although I don't believe Clemow sees it that way yet,' Derrymore confessed. 'But who on earth would dream up such a way to wipe out an entire family? The whole thing sounds like some Sherlock Holmes scenario, mass poisoning, a real Victorian shocker.' He shook his head. 'Horrible.'

'What about the poison?'

'Don't know for sure what it is but there's a rumour it's the sort that's been out of fashion for years. Not something you'd buy over the counter or carry about with you, like, waiting for a chance to use. And not just my mam's baking tampered with,' he concluded, satisfaction just showing. 'She'll be that relieved.'

'Did Miss Linton say why she and young Gatterly actually picked the manor as a rendezvous?' Reynolds asked. 'Or mention a package that he'd given her?'

'She never spoke of him giving her anything.' Derrymore was sure of that. 'And no one asked specifically why they were there. I think, you know,' he added tactfully, 'it was assumed they just met, being friends and all, and left at that.'

Another of Clemow's bad habits, Reynolds thought,

remembering the times they'd worked together. Always jumping to conclusions, too ready to accept the obvious, never working anything out.

Derrymore had been thinking too. 'Can't have been easy for her,' he said after a while. 'And then to crash like that. Doesn't seem right. Real bad luck.'

'Perhaps.' Reynolds was terse. In his line of work he'd never had much faith in luck. Cause and effect, those were what counted. It was only a question of finding the link. Again he stopped walking. 'Who else was in or about the house this morning when she arrived?' he said. 'I mean besides the police?'

He mentally ticked off names as Derrymore gave them. Joe Fletcher. The other twin, Justin, who'd left immediately after he'd identified his brother. And the rest of the Gatterlys. 'Flew back by private jet early this morning,' Derrymore explained. 'Landed at Plymouth, then came on by car. Fletcher doubles as a chauffeur, it seems, so was detailed off to fetch them.'

Noticing Reynolds' raised eyebrows, 'One of the luxuries of grief I suppose. At least,' he hesitated, 'we assume Mr Gatterly was motivated by grief. When he was first told last night, they say they could hear someone in the background, carrying on about not having the holiday spoiled. But I think Mr G was persuaded that the whole family had better return together and that's what they did.'

'So they were all there when Miss Linton arrived?'

'Yes, but I didn't see much of them. As I've explained, Justin left immediately. Fletcher went off in a temper, partly I think because he'd had to get up so early to drive to the airport. Mr Gatterly was ensconced with the police for a while and when the interview was over, he and his wife and son went straight to bed.' He grimaced. 'Hard work, an all-night flight.' By which

Reynolds understood that Derrymore's common sense was affronted by what he would call the Gatterlys' wimpish approach to tragedy.

Reynolds considered. With the Gatterlys back, the first move would be to talk to them. But if they needed their sleep, and if Clemow was allowing them that indulgence, it wasn't likely he'd get much out of them today. And with Audrey in hospital and also not up to questioning, that line too was closed. Derrymore was right, he'd be no use at her bedside, even if he could get close to it. But there were other leads he could busy himself with, if he chose. And he did choose, although he could foresee all sorts of trouble ahead, including what to do and say to Clemow to explain his presence. But he'd handle that in due course.

'What's your next move, Sergeant?' he asked formally. 'Because, if you've no objections, I'd like to come with you to look at the scene of the crash and, as long as we're not stopped, see what we can find out together.'

Derrymore brightened. 'Well, as even the media's been shut up at Clemow's insistence, "No further news until later", that sort of nonsense, you can imagine everything's on hold back at the house. In the meanwhile I've been detailed off to see Edmund Gatterly's mother. We could take in the car crash on the way.' He took off his helmet and wiped his forehead as if in anticipation of what was to come. 'Miss Trewithen's already been informed,' he reminded Reynolds. 'Last night. All the same, it's not a pleasant prospect. As I remember, she's a fair old tartar. Never liked me,' he confessed. 'And the job's a real put-down. Clemow's idea of fun. All he thinks I'm capable of, I suppose, before dropping me like a ton of bricks. Still, I mustn't be hard on the poor lady. It's her son that's been murdered, in her old home. But I can't think she'll have much to add.'

'Except,' Reynolds spoke half to himself, 'what she thinks about her husband's return with a woman she must hate, and how much Joe Fletcher keeps her informed about the internal workings of the house. And why Edmund disliked his father so much, and why Justin showed up so early this morning. And what was taken from the house last night that was valuable enough to put Edmund's life at risk, and possibly my ex-wife's.'

And with that list of questions buzzing at the back of his head, he strode back to Derrymore's Panda where Derrymore, after a quick stop to tell his mother the latest developments, joined him.

They left St Breddaford in glorious sun which, with typical Cornish inconsistency, had disappeared under clouds of indeterminate grey by the time they reached the car ferry to Bodinnick, just outside the town of Fowey.

As they negotiated the narrow streets leading to the ferry, despite his preoccupations Reynolds was entranced, as always, by the tantalizing glimpses of river and sea, framed through the gaps in the houses, their chimneys nestling together like broody hens. A timeless place, he thought, never changing.

By now the river had also turned grey, suiting their sombre mission, reflecting the sky like a pewter dish, and as they waited for the ferry to return from the other side they heard people talking about the dreadful accident which earlier had blocked the road opposite, only now reopened.

The crossing was short. They followed the other cars off the ferry, turning immediately left and driving as slowly as they could past the scene of the accident, clearly indicated by the flutter of tapes across a gap in the hedge although the car itself was gone. Eventually they pulled into a gateway that served as a lay-by and waited until the last of the cars had passed, then started back down again on foot.

Reynolds, who was not familiar with the ferry crossing, noted that two roads merged at Bodinnick, opposite the landing place. The first, very steep, ran straight up from the jetty and had been used by the diverted traffic, although it was mainly frequented by walkers heading towards the cliffs. The second, the left-hand one they'd taken, was the official motorist route, and cars were already lining up along it to take the ferry back. As he and Derrymore approached, the waiting cars began to move forward slowly, and after a while the throb of the ferry could be heard as it started on its return trip.

Once the cars, filled with their freight of happy holidaymakers, had gone, all sounds died away as if the heaviness of the sky acted like a muffler. Again Reynolds was struck by the timelessness of his surroundings; he could have been transported to any period or place, suspended, waiting. Then, just above where the last car had been parked, the ragged scar in the hedge jolted him back to the present.

The sheered off branches looked like so many bones, surrounded by a tangle of police tape. There were deep tyre marks beside the hedge and mud tracks in the road, showing where a service vehicle must have pulled the Rover away.

As Derrymore had explained, it was pure luck she'd gone into the hedge at this particular spot. A few yards further on, if she hadn't collided first with cars waiting for the ferry she would have smashed through the intersection into the stone wall on the other side, which would probably have killed her.

With doubts beginning to form, Reynolds turned and

tramped further up the hill, Derrymore faithfully tagging along behind him. Here, the road became steeper and narrow, running in a series of curves, the tall grass along its sides bent under a weight of summer dust. When Reynolds turned to look back, he could no longer see the flutter of police tape. Not a road meant for heavy traffic, not a road for driving fast.

Why at that exact place? he thought. Why, if she was driving too fast, didn't she crash further up here where the road first curves?

Derrymore was thinking along the same lines. 'To my mind,' he said, 'if the brakes gave way, normal like, she wouldn't have stood a chance. She'd have gone full tilt into that stone wall at the bottom. Unless she had time to realize what was happening and deliberately drove into the hedge.'

Reynolds nodded. Audrey was a good but not what he would call a particularly skilled driver. Not someone who could manipulate a car like a racing enthusiast. And not someone who would drive at excessive speed, even if upset.

'I thought it strange when I heard,' Derrymore was continuing, his round face showing the sympathy he was too shy to express openly. 'And,' here he hesitated, 'even more strange that a mechanical defect occurred after, not during, her earlier drive along that fast road from St Ives.'

'And after her visit to the manor,' Reynolds concurred.

'As if someone banked on her taking the steep ferry road back,' Derrymore finished.

They looked at each other, in perfect accord. Bad luck, Derrymore had said originally, and Reynolds had expressed doubt; he didn't believe in luck, good or bad. But he believed even less in coincidence. 'In this profession,' he said curtly now, 'there's no room for coincidence. I'm beginning to think,' and as he spoke he became suddenly, cruelly, certain, 'someone meddled with her car while she was with the police. I'd like to know who. And why. And, most of all, what was actually done to it. So let's find out.'

A quick phone call established that the garage where the car had been taken was nearby, on their side of the ferry. Thankful they didn't have to drive past the scene of the crash again, to overhear people on the ferry talking in awed voices about the 'tragedy', they found the garage easily and waited until the owner emerged from his office, straightening his tie.

A youngish man, drifting towards middle age, with the pleasant, red face of a country farmer, he seemed torn between relief that the police had arrived so promptly and nervousness at what he had to reveal. Or rather what his mechanic Terence had to reveal. Shouting for him, he let 'Ter' take over.

Terence, a gnome of a man with a face wrinkled into a myriad of lines, was one of those who delight in bad news. First, in solemn procession, he had them follow him into the workshop where the remains of the car had been hoisted on a lift. When it had been duly lowered, still in solemn fashion he led them round it, pointing out how its bright red sides had been scratched and battered, its windscreen shattered, how one door hung loose and the other was dented, demonstrating in detail the force of the impact.

'Fortunate for she the seat belt were fastened,' he ended. 'And if it'd been a smaller car we'd have had to pry 'un out.'

This drawn-out procedure was too much for Reynolds. He abruptly broke into the recital to ask if anything suspicious had been found, a direct approach that he knew by now seldom worked with country people.

Luckily, Terence's pleasure in disaster outweighed his enjoyment of longwindedness.

'If you'm meaning them brakes,' he said eagerly, 'spotted 'em first off. Look here.'

He tapped his boot against the wheel disc nearest him, then rubbed the mud away with his hand. Dark stains appeared on his gnarled fingers. 'Brake fluid,' he said triumphantly as he dabbed at the stains ineffectually with an even oilier rag. 'And when I opened the bonnet the fluid container showed empty.'

'Could have been accidental,' Reynolds said, half wanting to be contradicted, and wasn't surprised when Terence suddenly leaned forward and jerked up the twisted bonnet with a strength that belied his puny frame.

'Not with them left in this condition,' he said even more smugly, and pointed to the engine, against which two thick cables dangled. A tug, and they came apart. He waved the ends under Reynolds' startled face. 'Cut,' he cried. 'And just to be sure, someone's partly cut the handbrake wires as well. Someone who knows about cars, I'd say, a real enthusiastic bugger. That weren't no accident,' he went on, nodding to himself. 'I'll swear to that on my mother's grave. And she over ninety and chirpy as a cricket.'

'No chance of fingerprints, I suppose?' Reynolds snapped, his emotions getting the better of him. He regretted his outburst immediately when poor Ter's enthusiasm suddenly wilted and he looked about to burst into tears. But there was no denying that the brake fluid cables had been cut, and the handbrake rendered inoperable, with or without the fingerprints of whoever had done the cutting. They had the proof positive they had been looking for.

Chapter 8

'Where next?'

Derrymore was already swinging the car round in the direction of the manor. News of this importance had to be given to the authorities as soon as possible. If someone had attempted to murder Audrey Linton, among other things it would help confirm her innocence. But the man they'd have to see would be the man in charge, Chief Inspector Clemow.

While they drove as fast as the Panda would take them, he asked Derrymore go over all the details he could remember from this morning, searching for discrepancies. Patiently Derrymore repeated his descriptions of how Justin had turned up, and then the Gatterlys. As far as he knew, none of the family was about when Miss Linton had arrived. As for Fletcher, after some fuss about the parking, he'd stumped off home.

'What's that about the parking?' Reynolds pounced. 'You didn't mention that before.'

Derrymore explained that official cars now occupied most of the parking spaces outside the manor. When Fletcher returned from the airport, there had been no place to put the Gatterlys' car, a Rolls. 'Even the garage entrance was blocked. Eventually he had to leave it by the road. There was a right old thrash about it. I suppose,' he continued tentatively, 'you're trying to discover where Miss Linton parked. But the driveway is gravel. Probably stains would sink in.'

When Reynolds didn't reply, Derrymore went on, 'Of course there's the problem how someone could tamper with the car without being seen, what with the police everywhere.'

'Quite.'

At Reynolds' tone, Derrymore slowed down almost to a crawl. 'If you're suspecting Clemow,' he said soberly, 'forget it. Old Clemmie was inside. He'd no time to go creeping under cars.'

'He has cronies,' Reynolds insisted. 'You know who his special pals are. Where were they?'

'They were also inside the house, as far as I remember.'

Given his dislike of Clemow, the sergeant's loyalty to his superior and his professional comrades was commendable, and since he seldom questioned Reynolds, his rebuke struck. Too bad, Reynolds thought. I'd have liked to blame the old buzzard. 'Mind you,' Derrymore added, 'I was inside myself at the time too, so I can't say for sure who might have left the house and returned.' Which was at least honest.

In daylight, the house and its surroundings were more shabby than Reynolds had imagined. Looking at the overgrown garden and the peeling paint on windows and doors, he was surprised at the amount of work needed to restore it to its former glory, to say nothing of bringing it up to American standards. Remembering the modernized kitchen and the infamous telephone booth, he wondered why, if the Gatterlys had been here several months and money was no object, they had abandoned the renovations halfway through, then decided Mazie's information was probably right – the new lady of the manor had blown cold.

The Rolls was parked outside, so some time Fletcher

had found a place for it, among the irregular rows of police Pandas. As they squeezed in beside the Rolls, Derrymore said disapprovingly, 'Far too big for these parts. Although my mam always says if you're going to be run down by a car it'd better be a posh one.'

He didn't laugh and neither did Reynolds.

'Well,' said Derrymore, not looking at Reynolds but staring straight ahead. 'This won't buy the baby a bonnet. Good luck, sir.' And shut his mouth firmly on, 'You'll need it.'

A relatively restrained way of putting things, Reynolds thought. Seeing your reputation's at stake with mine. To say nothing of your future if I blow the interview. But he too kept his thoughts to himself, tipped Derrymore a flick of a salute, and strode off, leaving Derrymore to putter round the car. And if Derrymore was worried, he had the sense to do his worrying in private.

The door to the manor house was wide open this late afternoon, giving the place the air of public property, accessible to anyone on official business. Even from a distance the buzz of activity was like a beehive. Reynolds was thinking that if the Gatterlys could sleep through this they must all be dead, when he was almost bowled over by one of them, a young boy, a tall, gangling lad of some fourteen or fifteen years, who seemed strangely familiar. Muttering a furious, 'Look where you're going,' he deliberately bumped into Reynolds a second time.

Not stopping to apologize, he shouted more loudly over his shoulder, 'Damn coppers,' before stumping off into the thickets, a cricket bat under one arm, his broad, what might have been called 'wholesome' face under its thatch of light brown hair contorted with dislike.

'Cheeky bugger!' Half amused at being identified so readily, Reynolds gazed after him, resisting the temptation to box the kid's ears. It wasn't often he met with downright rudeness; for the most part Cornish children usually retained a smidgen of respect for their elders. For a moment he was puzzled. Then, ignoring the scruffy blue jeans, topped by a torn T-shirt with a faded Californian logo, he focused on the boy's hair and the way it grew from a tufted peak – and made the connection. This bad-tempered young fellow and the dead man of two nights ago bore a vague resemblance to each other.

It was probably his voice in the background, whingeing about missing out on his holidays, Reynolds thought. He continued to stare after the boy who had wandered out again on to the drive and was standing whacking at the nettles which grew along its verge with a certain listlessness that belied his earlier belligerence. Like all boys that age, Reynolds thought, recognizing the droop of the shoulders, doesn't know where to put himself, and bored out of his skull. If he were mine I'd set him to clearing out those thickets properly; do him some good. But a handsome youngster, if he cleaned himself up a bit. Give him a couple of years before the girls find him, or he finds them, and he'll be completely spoilt.

His musings were interrupted by a second near-encounter, this time with a woman. Surely the boy's mother, he thought, as again he was forced to step aside, except she seems too young.

Like her son, she was in a temper, although more in control than Richard, and her drawled, 'Hi, what can we do for you?' hid most of the irritation.

Reynolds didn't answer. 'A beauty,' Mazie Derrymore had called her, and even after fifteen years the word still fitted although the suntanned skin had rather a leathery look, and the hair, once naturally blonde, had

had its colour enhanced. The mouth was beautiful though, even pouting with displeasure, large, sensuous, and the eyes were expressive, grey-blue, fringed with long lashes – no wonder, in younger days, Mr Gatterly had been 'besotted'.

'So just who are you?' she asked, aggressively now. 'Or have you come to stare, for the heck of it?'

Her voice had a distinctive American burr, much more noticeable than Mary Lou Fletcher's, but under the softness there was steel. Somewhere south and west, he thought, straining to locate the source.

She was wearing a dove grey suit, expensive, overloaded with a quantity of diamond jewellery, the stones so big Reynolds' first expression was that they must be fake. Remembering the tasteless gimmickry inside the manor he wasn't surprised. Here was a rich bimbo in all her glory, just as he'd envisaged. The flamboyance disturbed him, evoking memories of his own background when his father, having turned a small company into a big one, began to flaunt his wealth, losing touch with family, and reality, in the process.

Pulling himself together, he gave his own name and former title, and said, 'I was looking for Chief Inspector Clemow. But now you're here . . .'

'Clemow!' Her exclamation spoke volumes. She looked at Reynolds appraisingly. 'You'll find Chief What's-His-Face with my husband. Step right in, make yourself at home like everyone else.' She jangled a gold bracelet in the direction of the house. 'I'm off to get some fresh air.'

While Reynolds considered ways of stopping her, she set off down the driveway, then turned and eyed him speculatively. 'What do you want with him?' she demanded. 'No, don't tell me, let me guess. You're here to order yet another search of my house, as if you haven't turned it upside down already. Or you're here to make an arrest.' She smiled, a rather attractive smile showing a row of pearly teeth, a tribute to American dentistry. 'That I'd like to see,' she said.

When Reynolds tried to assure her he had no such intentions, she ignored him. As if suddenly making up her mind, she retraced her steps, beckoning to him to follow with another jangle of bracelets. 'I'll take you to them,' she insisted. 'You might lose your way in the confusion.'

A not completely unjustified sarcasm. Inside, the volume of noise rose as police officers and forensic experts still scoured every inch of the dining room and presumably the kitchen.

She paused. 'Look at them,' she said, as if speaking of animals in a zoo. 'Upstairs and down and in my lady's chamber. Even in my parlour.'

Nodding pleasantly to several old acquaintances milling about in the hall, tea mugs in hand, aware of the sudden hush as he passed, Reynolds strode out to keep up with her. But when he remarked blandly that he hadn't heard the word 'parlour' in a long while, she told him it was what they used in the part of America she came from, with a twist of her mouth that made him wonder if she were homesick. 'Ollie is always nattering on about doing what the Romans do when you're in Rome,' she added, 'but I say it depends where Rome is. Don't you think so, Mr Reynolds?'

She looked at him with an expression he couldn't quite fathom. 'I mean, America is the modern capital of the world, isn't it? So why would anyone exchange it for a hole in the wall where the natives try to poison you like savages in a jungle?'

Reynolds, suddenly very much aware of her perfume, and her smile, thought, Mazie is right. She's a knockout all right. And if rich, certainly no bimbo. And if I read the signs correctly, she's about to use me to engineer what she'd call a 'showdown' with her husband. Not quite the interview I had in mind!

She had reached the 'parlour' door now, and was waiting for him to open it. He hesitated. Clemow was waiting on the other side, too. Apart from telling Clemow about the brakes in Audrey's car, Reynolds had not thought out clearly what he would say to the Chief Inspector, relying on instinct to get him through. He knew what he wanted of course: the chance to find Edmund Gatterly's murderer, and at the same time catch the person who had tampered with his ex-wife's car. If necessary, he was prepared to carry out investigations on his own, although, given a choice, he'd rather work in harmony with the authorities than against them. What he did not know was how to persuade Clemow to let him stay involved in either capacity.

He didn't expect for a moment that Clemow would accept him happily as an official working partner. They had met from time to time since Reynolds' divorce but neither had ever actually mentioned it, or Clemow's part in causing it. The whole episode had lain between them like an unused weapon. If it would help him now Reynolds was prepared to use it, but he certainly hadn't imagined doing so with the Gatterlys as an audience. The image of the four of them warbling away on different notes to tunes of their own making, like some Mozartian quartet in an opera, appealed to his sense of irony but wasn't exactly helpful.

And there were other causes for Clemow's dislike, over and above this personal issue, all to do with their former professional relationship. To begin with, when they had been in the force together, Reynolds had often had to cover up Clemow's mistakes. It wasn't that Clemow was stupid but his bad habit of jumping to conclusions was too often exacerbated by his stubborn refusal to listen to reason. And if Clemow had come to resent Reynolds' ability to put unlikely clues together and solve cases that he himself claimed were unsolvable, he resented even more what few others knew: that he himself had been offered his present post of chief inspector only because Reynolds had turned it down. Clemow's professional jealousy, therefore, had also changed friendship into enmity, although he had managed to keep the fact hidden for a long while.

All this flashed through Reynolds' mind as he followed Mrs Gatterly into her 'parlour' like the proverbial fly.

The room beyond was long, and in the late afternoon light looked graceful in a dishevelled sort of way. The dust sheets (he presumed another strange American anachronism) had been piled in a corner and Clemow was perched on a new sofa whose style seemed more suited to a Texan ranch than an English country house, the colour of its slippery calf leather blending perfectly with his greying hair and sallow skin.

On seeing Reynolds, his pale eyes bulged and he gave a sort of gurgle, somewhere between a gasp and a snort. All he needs is a Stetson and silver spurs to fit the part of a Texan sheriff, Reynolds thoughts incongruously as he watched with secret pleasure how the inspector struggled to his feet, his short legs flailing for a moment, and gracelessly failing to find purchase on the polished wooden floor.

'Look who I found outside.'

Mrs Gatterly had taken Reynolds' arm and, ignoring Clemow, was leading him towards her husband with a proprietary air as if he were an old friend. 'Inspector Reynolds, to solve our problems,' she said brightly, so brightly that Reynolds cringed. This'll blow my chances with Clemow, he thought. Then he noticed the amused glitter in her eyes. Damn it, if she's playing games, there are some that two can play.

Gatterly was standing by the fireplace with his back to the room, and swung round abruptly at the intrusion. Reynolds would have recognized him anywhere. The likeness to his sons, dead and alive, was unmistakable. Broad shouldered under the dark blue blazer decorated with club brass buttons, about Reynolds' own height and build, with the telltale peak of hair (in his case already streaked grey), he seemed the epitome of the successful businessman, self-assured and forceful. Yet there was something about his mouth that suggested diffidence, something about his eyes and chin that told of weakness.

As Gatterly came forward, hand outstretched in American style, Reynolds thought, assessing him, he's handsome enough, a lady's man, and under the circumstances showing as much confidence as might be expected in a husband about to have his wife come down on him like a ton of bricks. Mazie Derrymore had said he had a 'kinder side'; say 'soft' and that would sum him up. And he was certainly not the sort of man who made enemies, or went looking for them.

'Pleased to meet you,' Reynolds said, his own voice sympathetic. 'This has been a sad homecoming.'

It was the right approach. Oliver Gatterly's face relaxed and he straightened his shoulders. He started to say something but his wife interrupted.

'I said we shouldn't have all gone away on holiday at the same time,' she shrilled. 'One of us should have stayed behind to keep an eye on things.' She made it clear who should have done the staying.

'I told him there'd be trouble if we left the place empty,' she continued. 'And look what's happened, the Cornish all over, the Celtic brooding and scheming in the dark.'

'You think that badly of us?' Reynolds tried to make light of what she'd said, but she didn't smile. And at that point, Clemow intervened.

For the moment he ignored Reynolds and concentrated on the Gatterlys. He was always impressed by the rich or famous. 'Funny people, the Cornish,' he said ingratiatingly. 'Can't understand them myself. Like country folk the world over I suppose. But that's nothing to do with the case in hand.'

'It's everything to do with it,' Mrs Gatterly contradicted. 'One woman's Celtic malice in particular. Miss Trewithen's.' She positively spat the name out. 'I wouldn't put it past her to kill off her own son, or us. I just hope Mr Reynolds here will know how to deal with her. No one else seems to.'

She certainly doesn't mince her words, Reynolds thought, or see any need of hiding her hatred of Miss Trewithen. How will Clemow react to that?

He watched as Clemow's face flushed and the sandy eyelids fluttered, a habit of the chief inspector's when he was caught off guard. Recovering his composure, he let his gaze rest on Reynolds, for the first time. 'Why old chap,' he said jovially, as if only then noticing him. 'Never thought to see you here.' Didn't think you had it in you, his tone implied, didn't think you'd dare.

Sitting down he'd given the impression of being taller then he actually was on his feet, broad and, at first glance, dependable. Or so Reynolds once had thought. As always when he met Clemow, he wondered what Audrey had seen in him – other than the means to make Reynolds himself look foolish. He pushed the thought aside.

With all eyes upon him as he intended, Clemow turned to Mrs Gatterly. 'My dear lady,' he said to her, with a gallantry that Reynolds instinctively knew wouldn't work, 'you can't go around casting suspicion on people like that without any evidence.'

'Then you find the evidence,' she snapped even more fiercely. 'That's what you're paid for, isn't it? Not lolling in my parlour, eating me out of house and home.'

At this her husband roused himself to make shushing noises, looking, Reynolds thought, as if he wished he was miles away. But the flicker of a glance between him and his wife, and then towards Reynolds suggested that it wasn't only fear of her that had kept him quiet.

Clemow broached the silence with his habitual lack of tact. 'As for suspicion,' he said with a smile that could be only called oily, 'I was just telling your husband about the woman . . .'

'Whoever she is,' Gatterly cut in, 'I bear her no ill will coming into my house, if she didn't cause my son's death.'

'She didn't.' Reynolds' interruption was abrupt but authoritative. He knew contradicting Clemow was dangerous but he knew Clemow would make life impossible for Audrey if he didn't intervene. All heads now swivelled towards him as he continued, 'That's why I'm here. I've just come from the garage where Miss Linton's car was taken. The brakes had been tampered with. While she was here.'

He'd caught Clemow off-balance again.

'What the devil are you suggesting?' he cried in outrage. 'Who could have touched her car?'

'What did I tell you?' Mrs Gatterly wailed. 'If he can't protect a woman's car, how's he going to keep us safe? We'll all be murdered first.'

'We'll find the murderer,' Reynolds assured her while a flustered Clemow, again reduced to silence, blinked even more rapidly.

'Do you think there's danger?'

Mr Gatterly's head jerked forward as he spoke, and he stared hard at Reynolds, only to have Mrs Gatterly interrupt once more.

'Sure he does,' she cried. 'And you think so too, only you won't admit it. Someone's gunning for us.'

It was the opportunity that Reynolds had been waiting for. 'Have you any idea who it might be?' he asked, addressing Gatterly specifically. 'Any enemies? Anyone with a grudge?' And when Gatterly didn't answer, 'You do realize,' he said softly, 'that the evidence so far suggests that you and your immediate family were probably the intended victims. Not specifically your son. You didn't expect him to come to the house in your absence, did you?'

His questions seemed to touch some nerve. Gatterly swallowed hard. He opened his mouth as if about to speak, but before he could answer, Mrs Gatterly once more intervened.

'Why should anyone dislike us?' she said indignantly. 'After all we've done to help in the neighbourhood. As for Edmund, we knew he hung about the grounds, but never knocking on your door and saying "Hi there," like any reasonable guy. Ollie always said he'd make peace in his own good time. Well, Ollie was wrong about that, too, wasn't he?'

She turned to her husband, furiously attacking now, her mouth hard. 'If you'd had the nerve to talk to him straight out none of this would have happened. Typical English delicacy. Scared to say boo to a goose. You let him hold a grudge and there's the consequence.'

'Grudge!' Reynolds echoed. 'There was some sort of disagreement?'

'Not what you'd call a real quarrel. Now if it had been Justin,' here Mrs Gatterly glittered meanly, 'I'd not have been surprised. He's after something too, although God knows what it is.'

Gatterly seemed to shrink into the fine white broadcloth of his handmade shirt. 'Nonsense,' he began, then with a forced laugh, 'The police don't want to hear all our little problems, sweetie. If Edmund had been complaining it's because his mother put him up to it.'

He turned to Reynolds. 'My wife's right about her in one way,' he said. 'She is out to make trouble.'

'You see!' Mrs Gatterly was triumphant. 'I knew you'd come to it. And while we're on that subject,' she whirled on her husband, bracelets a-jangle. 'I know we have to live here now, but I'm not having another bite to eat in this house, I swear it, until the murderer's caught. And I'm not sleeping another night under this roof without round the clock protection.'

As if she'd said too much she suddenly stopped and exchanged a quick glance with her husband. Then, with an effort, she went on, 'I'll pay for it, if I have to.'

So that's what she was after all the time, Reynolds thought. A rich woman's solution, buying safety. And if I had a family and was in the same position I suppose I'd feel the same way. But is it all she wants? There's something odd to what she's just said about 'having to live here now'.

He had no time to analyze what made him uneasy. As if a sudden idea had come to her, she added, 'I'd like Mr Reynolds here to take the job.'

She turned to Reynolds. 'Name your price,' she said.

Something in Mrs Gatterly's pretensions irritated him afresh. 'I don't think you need me,' he drawled, a flicker of his annoyance at her suggestion just showing. 'The Devon and Cornwall Constabulary are perfectly capable of looking after you. But you'd be a lot safer if you could give some motive for someone wanting to kill you. Then we can search for a real solution.'

He was rewarded by a second ripple that passed between the couple, of understanding or of fear, he couldn't be sure.

Again taking advantage of the situation he pressed on with other questions: Where had Edmund got the key? Did they know of anything in the house he wanted? Why had Justin shown up this morning? He was rewarded not merely with shakes of their heads, but with those half averted glances that he couldn't quite fathom but that suggested uneasiness. Before he could probe deeper Clemow broke in.

Clemow had been clearly taken aback by this question and answer session in which he had played no part. Now he forced his way back into the conversation, insisting that while he was in charge there was no need to hire anyone, certainly not a private individual.

Here he threw an angry look in Reynolds' direction, and seemed to be on the point of ordering him to leave, when Mr Gatterly took action himself.

With more dignity than Reynolds would have thought possible under the circumstances, Oliver Gatterly gripped his wife's arm tightly, and if not exactly pushing her towards the door certainly turned her to face it.

'You'd better go on about your business, darling,' he said, the endearment barely hiding his nervousness. 'Don't want to be late for the hairdresser. I'll finish with these gentlemen.'

And when, reluctantly to be sure, she had gone, he faced them with that strange straightening of his shoulders which Reynolds found rather pitiful. Suddenly, without preamble, he crashed his fist down on a table. 'I want my son's killer caught,' he said. 'I want him punished. And if Mr Reynolds here can help then I want him on the case. Not as a bodyguard but as a fulltime official part of the team. And that's all I have to say at the moment. I've nothing more to add.'

Turning abruptly, he strode out of the room, followed to the door by Clemow who kept on reassuring him that he and his family were in no danger, and that everything possible to solve the murder was being done. But when Gatterly had gone, presumably to join his wife, Clemow took out his anger and frustration on Reynolds, as Reynolds had anticipated he would.

'What the hell do you think you're doing,' he shouted. 'Thought you'd take over? Thought you'd squeeze something out of them? Well it won't work. Because I'm in charge here. I'll manage this case in my own way.'

And when Reynolds didn't answer. 'Why in hell have you turned up?'

'I told you. I'm here about the car,' Reynolds answered calmly, ignoring the outburst. 'And about Audrey's presence when the murder took place.'

Clemow's eyes flickered. He began to splutter. He has no idea what he's saying, Reynolds thought. He's weaving a jumble of fact and fantasy. Typical. I knew this was the sort of case he wouldn't understand. As always he's jumped to the easiest conclusion and ignored all the difficulties. With head office panting for results he's already classified this murder as a lovers' quarrel. No matter that logic and evidence stand in the way of his conclusion, he won't admit he's wrong.

'Everything that happened that night has been satisfactorily explained,' Reynolds said as evenly as before. 'You can't pretend Audrey's still a suspect when you know she isn't.'

'Officially no one knows she was here last night!' Ignoring the other issues Clemow struck at the weakest point. He could be clever when cornered. 'So where do you get your information from?' He glared at Reynolds.

'You've been talking to some damn blabber mouth,' he said. 'Your side kick, for example, Derrydown. Whose fucking mother baked the fucking pie.' Another thought stopped him in his tracks. 'Or did Audrey tell you herself?'

The implication of that possibility gripped him. He stared at Reynolds, his head jutting forward in a familiar bull-like pose. 'Have you been in contact with her?' he bellowed. 'Has she come whining to you?'

With an obvious effort he stopped himself from adding what he must have been thinking, 'Have you two kept in touch all these years?'

He seemed blinded to the other obvious conclusion: that Reynolds knew because somehow he had been present himself. A fortunate lapse, Reynolds thought, relieved. Although he would probably come to it later. But there was an eagerness to the last questions that Clemow couldn't quite hide. More than eagerness, a sense of bitterness. Poor sod, Reynolds thought suddenly, what must he have felt when Audrey thew him over?

If he'd often wondered what Audrey had seen in Clemow, he'd never given a thought before to what Clemow had seen in Audrey. She was a beautiful woman, persistent. Hard for a man to resist. He'd just assumed Clemow had been flattered and then seduced by her interest. But suppose for Clemow there had been something more to their relationship, something that the Chief Inspector's own life lacked?

Reynolds had no idea what Clemow's marriage was like, knew only that he was married, with children. Was still married. Passed for a happy family man. He should have been content with that, Reynolds thought, hardening his resolve. He was lucky to have that much.

Clemow had passed on to another matter, one equally important. 'In my book she's still a suspect,' he was insisting. 'And I'm keeping her under observation, even in hospital.'

'Good,' Reynolds broke in. 'Because she may still be in danger, and don't you forget it. Don't let her out of your sight again. And don't forget the others may be in danger too. If the Gatterly family were the intended victims, you'd better keep close watch on them.'

Clemow had never liked advice. Power had made him even less receptive. He clenched his fists. 'Sod off,' he bellowed. 'Don't tell me what to do. You're no longer one of us.'

His voice reverberated down the corridor. It seemed to Reynolds that sounds there came ominously to a halt.

'If I find you snooping again, I'll throw you out myself, see if I don't. And even if you had any right, you'd be off this case in two seconds flat and you know it. Suspect or not, your wife's name has been mentioned. That means conflict of interest.'

'Conflict of interest, eh?' Reynolds said loudly. If they were listening outside, then let them hear. There'd always been rumours, a little truth wouldn't hurt.

'Not much of one I'd say, since she's no longer my wife. But if there's conflict of interest where an ex-wife is concerned I suppose the same applies to an ex-mistress.'

At the word 'mistress' Clemow's head shot up. With a leap that seemed remarkably agile for a man of his bulk, he slammed the door shut and turned towards his tormentor, his head jutting forward, more and more like a bull. 'What are you trying to do here, man?' he hissed. 'Ruin me?'

Reynolds shrugged. 'The worst sort of ruin,' he said calmly, 'is the false accusation of an innocent party. Wouldn't do anyone's reputation good. Forget Audrey. Except as a witness she's no use to you. Begin at the beginning as our old mentor used to say. Start fresh.'

Clemow ran a finger round his collar as if his shirt had grown too tight. As, calmly, Reynolds slid the last barb in. 'And remember, Gatterly is a powerful man, rich, used to having his own way. It might be better to humour him.

'There are several other suspects,' he continued. 'And what about Audrey's car? Someone at the manor tampered with it and almost had her killed. To my mind that's also a priority.'

Clemow sat down heavily. For a moment he said nothing, frowning as if in concentration. Reynolds knew him well enough to recognize the signs. Beaten, he'd be thinking up excuses that would make changing his mind more palatable. Sure enough, at last he said slowly, 'I'll see to the car business. And as far as I'm concerned you can have a go at finding out what you can. Just keep out of my way, that's all.' Making the best of a bad job he added, 'The more the merrier, I suppose. And you know the region better than we do. You and your Derrydown.'

Another thought struck him. 'And since he's a nuisance to us at the moment too, what with his mother being involved, take him with you. He'll give you your official backing, for what it's worth, and get him off my hands.' He gave a hollow laugh. 'But don't look to me for support if things go wrong,' he said. He didn't add, 'Remember, I'm only doing this because Gatterly insisted,' but he and Reynolds both accepted it. And accepted how he would resent and work to reverse the situation if he could.

Nor did he have to say, 'I reserve the right to change my mind.' Reynolds remembered the other flaw in Clemow's character. Forced into accepting a course of action, he'd pretend compliance but later, in the company of his pals, would rant and rail, swear he'd been taken in – and wait for a chance to rescind his decision while inflicting as much damage as possible.

But if for the present Reynolds had achieved what he wanted with the minimum fuss, that was what he called a good day's work.

Only as he left did Clemow make one last snide comment. 'Remember, you're answerable to Derrydown. You deserve each other. It's the sort of cosy little family quarrel that you and your village plod revel in.'

Cosy family quarrel, thought Reynolds, yes, I suppose on one level that's what it seems. But I wonder. And whatever Gatterly's forced him into accepting, Clemow won't make it cosy for us long.

Chapter 9

In the outer hall people were rushing about, resolutely turning their backs as if engrossed. No one stopped to wave or chat. Rumours swirled like smoke.

If I were in charge, Reynolds thought, they'd be out rooting for real clues, not wasting time re-inventing them. Such inefficiency irritated him afresh. He swore under his breath.

Away from the overcharged atmosphere inside, he reassessed the chances that he and Clemow would work together again. Clemow's virtues had always been logistical; paperwork was his speciality. They'd made a good team once, Reynolds with the ideas, Clemow with the ability to keep them in order and get them funded. But would Clemow really support him now? He couldn't tell and he wasn't optimistic. The adrenaline which had kept him going flooded out. Suddenly he felt drained.

Looking down the drive he saw Derrymore's stalwart back bent over his car. Blessed with girth of shoulders and waist to do justice to a Cornish wrestling champion, Derrymore gave him fresh confidence. The sergeant would stand by him through thick and thin. Taking a deep breath of fresh air, Reynolds strode down the drive towards him.

The Rolls had gone.

'Mrs was driving, Mr in the back, kid in front,'

Derrymore volunteered, cheerful as ever. 'Mow someone down if they don't look out.'

Damn, Reynolds thought, then changed his mind. He wasn't sure he was up to coping with the Gatterlys again at present. He'd have another go at them later, when he could make sure Mrs Gatterly wouldn't manage the proceedings.

Although Derrymore looked his usual unflappable self, Reynolds was sure he must be anxious to know what had happened at the interview especially as he must have seen Mrs Gatterly lead him into the house. Quickly he outlined the situation with Clemow, without any of the personal details, and without overstressing Gatterly's wish that he stay on the case. He wasn't exactly proud of the way he'd manipulated that request.

'It's still a tricky situation,' he summed up, 'but at least for the moment Clemow's letting me play along. He's agreed that I can continue on the case, in a semi-official way, with you acting as the official presence.' He smiled. 'And as Mrs G wanted to hire me as a body guard I suppose there's always that job to fall back on!'

He laughed at Derrymore's expression. 'You can imagine what Clemow thought of that.'

'And the Gatterlys themselves? How did they react?' Derrymore's voice didn't change although relief was written over him.

Reynolds thought back to the interview. 'Uneasy at being questioned,' he said, 'not giving much away. But Mrs G let slip something strange. She said, "I know we have to live here now."'

'But why shouldn't she say that? After all, Mr Gatterly bought the house so she must have agreed. And unless she left him, she'd have to come and live where he did.'

'Yes,' Reynolds agreed. 'But I don't think she meant it in quite that simple way. I got the impression that she was inadvertently referring to some special reason over and above the obvious personal one. And when you think about it, given that her husband obviously does what she wants, and that her dislike of all things Cornish is so well known, their settling here does seem peculiar. With their sort of money they could live anywhere they liked, in England, or abroad.' He added, 'Your mam suggested Gatterly wanted to make amends to his sons and bought the house back for them. Perhaps he did, but he wouldn't have to live in it. He seemed genuinely shocked by Edmund's death, by the by. But Mrs G certainly didn't express much affection for Edmund or his brother. She even suggested Miss Trewithen had killed Edmund.'

'That doesn't make sense,' Derrymore said stoutly. 'Why would a mother kill her own son? And so far his father hasn't done poor Edmund much good either, has he?'

'So what exactly brings the Gatterlys to live in Cornwall?' Reynolds persisted. 'Something to bear in mind. In the meantime let's see what we can find out from Miss Trewithen. I'll tag alone, if that's agreeable to you.'

This expression, familiar to both men, put Derrymore at ease, confirming his position vis-a-vis the ex-inspector's. He smiled broadly, gave a thumbs up sign, and opened the car door with a flourish, saying enthusiastically, 'Off to Fowey then.'

Reynolds folded himself inside the little car as best he could. 'Where do you get your energy?' he asked. 'You've been on duty most of the night, certainly must have been up before day break this morning.'

'Like my mam, I'm a born work horse,' Derrymore joked, 'never happier than when I'm busy. If they took me off this case, I wouldn't have been satisfied, there's the truth, twiddling my thumbs at home.' He squeezed into the driver's seat, and for the first time Reynolds realized just how committed the sergeant was as well to finding Edmund's killer.

As they left, Reynolds was relieved to see several officers emerging from the house, presumably about to search for the Rover's parking place. A hopeless task, what with the constant coming and going of vehicles ever since, but nevertheless a move in the right direction, suggesting Clemow had taken his advice. A good sign.

Filling in other details about the Gatterlys took them past the site of the accident and on to the ferry. They crossed the river and returned to Fowey where the first Mrs Gatterly, Miss Trewithen, as Reynolds had to keep reminding himself, lived in the main part of the town.

It was coming on for evening now, and everything seemed placidly normal. As he and the sergeant walked down the steep hill towards the river front, people were still strolling through the narrow Fore Street or loitering by the Town Quay where pleasure craft bobbed up and down. Further along the Esplanade, the little passenger ferry from Polruan, loaded with more visitors, chugged into its traditional landing place and then chugged off again, while the car ferry to Bodinnick continued to surge back and forth like a tireless whale.

Miss Trewithen's dwelling (somehow one didn't like to think of it as a common 'house') was up a back street behind the church, in the oldest part of town. Nothing younger here than the sixteenth century, Reynolds noted as Derrymore hammered on a mildewed wooden door, decorated with what looked like a battered coat of arms.

He was not unduly worried when no one immediately answered, although there were sounds from inside. Transition from a past world to the present takes time. Eventually there was a long and intricate undoing of bolts and locks. The door creaked open. 'If you're from the police,' a voice complained, high-pitched and autocratic, 'I've bloody well had enough of you.'

Once more Derrymore had removed his helmet, this time out of respect, but her choice of language made his eyebrows twitch.

'I'm not here to trouble you, ma'am,' he said politely. 'I've come to offer condolences, mine and my mam's.'

The door opened wider. A woman's face peered out, thin, gaunt, with what must have once been soft brown hair screwed untidily into a bun. Face and manner reminded Reynolds of a portrait he'd once seen of a Spanish grandee at the height of Spain's Golden Age.

'I remember you,' the voice said, not changing its imperious tone. 'Mazie's son. You look just like your mother. Not that I've seen hair or hide of her lately but I hear she's running with the Gatterly pack, for what that's worth to her.'

It was not an auspicious beginning. Reynolds glanced at Derrymore. Although he had flushed, he didn't back down. 'Yes, ma'am,' he said, still polite, 'and if you'd let us in, I've a few things I'd like to ask, if you'd be so kind.'

'Who's that with you?' The voice became thin with suspicion. 'Not one of those reporter fellows? I've had them baying round all morning, damn scavengers.'

'This is Inspector Reynolds. Ex-Inspector Reynolds I should say.'

'Don't fuss me with ex's,' the voice snapped. 'I've had it up here with ex's. Still,' the hand on the door tapped, 'if you've got an inspector on a leading rein, why didn't you say so? Always head for high ground, I say.'

With that ambiguous remark she opened the door. Miss Trewithen was revealed in all her glory, tall, imposingly if outlandishly dressed in a black, old-fashioned riding habit looped up at one side to reveal a black stockinged leg.

'Couldn't find anything else suitable in the wardrobe,' she said as if in explanation. She stalked down the hall, even narrower than the one in the Fletchers' house. 'But had to show my respect. Poor Edmund, always a bit of a loser, a back runner, if you know what I mean.'

These callous observations sounded more fitting to a hunting field, or to the pictures in the hall, lined, as if in parody of the old manor house, with various hunting photographs, their sepia tones blurred and fading. Men and women of thirty or more years ago, some top-hatted, dressed in elegant riding gear, stared out solemn-faced, their hounds milling in the background, their horses big-boned and haunched, with extraordinary small heads.

'That was the best mare I ever owned,' Miss Trewithen said as the men paused in front of the largest photograph. 'Heart like a house. Would go through fire and hell water, tore me up to part with her. Had her put down instead. And in any case, all that's over with these days, you know. I'm a reformed character.' She gave a laugh, showing large, yellowing teeth. 'Been talked out of hunting at least,' she said. 'Seen the error of my ways. My son's influence.'

She beckoned them into her sitting room, shabbily if comfortably furnished, sat down in what was clearly her favourite chair with a crowded table beside it, amongst whose objects the opened bottle of whisky and the half full tumbler were conspicuous.

'Know you don't drink on duty,' she said, in the same commanding fashion. 'But nothing to say I can't.' And with what could only be called a practised gesture she tossed off the rest of the tumbler's contents and then refilled it.

Another forceful woman, Reynolds thought. Poor Mr Gatterly seems to have had a weakness for dominating females. He had a moment's sympathy. Oliver Gatterly seemed to have jumped from frying pan to fire in his choice of wives.

He avoided looking at Derrymore. Miss Trewithen's drinking was something else that presumably Derrymore's mam had not mentioned, nor had Mr Gatterly, their expressions like 'keeping to her own room,' or 'being tired,' hiding the truth. Reynolds felt a second twinge of sympathy. There had been a time when he'd relied on alcohol for comfort, and it had almost ruined him.

He heard Derrymore say with genuine regret, 'I'm so sorry about what's happened, and so sorry I was there to find it out.'

'Were you now?' She tilted the glass back to drain the last drop. 'Sorry won't bring him back.' She stared at them with dry, fierce eyes. 'Sorry won't bring back anything.'

She turned to Reynolds. 'Now, Inspector whoever you are, I want some facts. What was poison doing in my kitchen? And why did Edmund feel he had to sneak into the house after dark, like a thief? It is his house.'

Resisting the temptation to point out that neither house nor kitchen were hers any longer, Reynolds explained that her son had apparently used a key, did she know about it? And had he left anything in the house, some childhood memento perhaps?

'A key?' she said, breaking in, looking at him as if he'd asked if she kept a hippo in her bathtub. 'We never locked the doors in the old days. And everything in the house was mine once.'

'Did Edmund mention why he was going to the house?' Derrymore asked.

'I'm talking to *him*,' she said fiercely, pointing at Reynolds. 'Not a whippersnapper whose nose was always running and whose mother was cook and bottle-washer on my staff.'

Her rudeness was shocking. Like a steam roller, with as much sensitivity as a bucket of concrete, Reynolds thought. Again he didn't look at Derrymore but noted how the sergeant, wisely perhaps, kept his gaze firmly fixed on the floor and refused to be drawn. Bitch, Reynolds thought, angry for his friend.

When he explained that the family, meaning the Gatterlys, had been away, she bristled, 'Of course we've been away. We've been away, as you put it, for over fifteen years. Dispossessed. Now if we were squatters,' she added, fixing her bold, direct gaze on him, 'you'd leave us alone if we forced an entrance, wouldn't you? You'd say because we were homeless we had the right to be there. Bloody sentimentalism. It never occurs to you that I'm homeless too. Well, I am. What's this?' She flapped a contemptuous hand. 'Nothing but a holding stall, as far as I'm concerned, a penning area until I get my own property back.

'My boys will get it for me,' she continued in the same fiercely possessive way, but becoming noticeably more and more dramatic, like an actress warming to her lines. 'One or the other. How? The end justifies the means, I say.'

She refilled the glass. 'You think we're finished, don't you? Out of the running. Well, you're wrong. A Trewithen's never done until the last ditch is cleared. I won't deny we've taken a mighty tumble.' Here, her chin began to tremble, and she had to put the glass down so she could support it with her hand.

'The banner passes on. When Basil Grenville led Charles the First's army to rout the Roundheads at

Bocconock, a Trewithen was standard bearer. When Basil and the Cornish died at Bristol, we still held the flag. I've a second son,' she told them, proud as a general, her theatrics at full pitch. 'I've a Justin to render me justice. And now the enemy's back, we're ready to take them on.'

At this mixture of drunken bravado and exaggerated misquotation, Reynolds gave up and let Derrymore take over.

'Quite,' the sergeant said soothingly. 'But there's a question of murder here, you know. You want your son's killer found, don't you, Miss Trewithen? If you know anything that might help us, you ought to let us know. We—'

'Oh, as for who killed him,' she broke in, 'I can tell you that. His father did. And his father's whore. Macbeth and his whore, that's who they are, carving up a kingdom that isn't theirs. Why else did he come back except to crow over us, dead dirt. Why does he stay here? I'll tell you why.' She banged the bottle down. 'So her miserable little bastard, her crookback Richard, can lord it over us. And to make sure he does, they'll kill us off one by one.'

This was the bitter reverse of what Mazie had suggested. And the equally bitter opposite of Mrs Gatterly's accusation. Bitterness was in the next comment too.

'So if you want the murderers, look no further than at home. Because that's where they'll be hid.' She raised her glass. 'We've scotched the snake, not killed it,' she quoted tipsily. 'Let yourselves out, because I'm going to finish this bottle even if it kills me.'

'Mam never said anything about her drinking.' Outside in the street, Derrymore blew out his cheeks. 'Ye gods, I never heard anything like it. What do you make of it, sir?'

'Hell hath no fury like a woman scorned.' Reynolds couldn't resist the quotation. The habit was catching. 'That, and some other Shakespearean tag about the wound isn't as wide as a church door but it still can kill.'

'Meaning?'

'She minds her son's death more than she wants to let on. And she's named her suspects.'

Derrymore stared at him. 'You must be joking. She was in a state when we got here, too far gone to know what she was saying.'

'No, she wasn't,' Reynolds replied. 'I think she's in a state as you call it, for two reasons. One, because she can't bear not to be. And two, because she meant us to notice she was.'

He almost laughed again at Derrymore's bewilderment. 'Being drunk hides what one really feels. And no one expects a drunkard to be coherent.' And if Miss Trewithen gives the impression she takes her fences like a man, he thought, she certainly uses her ability to handle liquor like one.

'In Aden,' he told Derrymore, 'we used to say our commanding colonel downed whisky in such quantities that when he died his body would be already pickled. His only words of wisdom to his young officers, in an Arab war zone mind you, where booze is taboo, was, "Drink your enemy under the table before you tell him anything." Well, Miss Trewithen's followed his advice in a partial sort of way. She may have drunk herself under the table but still she hasn't given anything of herself away – although she's dropped several hints about other people, and made a deliberate accusation.'

'You mean we should take her seriously?'

'Yes,' Reynolds said. 'Partly because of what she's said, but more because of what she hasn't. Next time we talk to her, we'll see if we can pin down exactly what she bases her opinions on. Because if anyone's given a reason for wanting to get rid of the Gatterlys, she has.'

While Derrymore was still trying to work that out, he added, 'Let's leave it at that today. An hour with Miss Trewithen's enough for anyone to crack their brains on. Go home.' He opened the car door and folded himself inside. 'You've been on the go twenty-four hours nonstop, and your mam needs you. Let me put my thoughts in order, and tomorrow we'll have a shot at solving both cases.'

Later, in the little town of Fowey, after the street lights had come on, the narrow house with its clutter of hunting memorabilia remained dark. Miss Trewithen had sunk so deeply into whisky-fumed stupor it is doubtful if she would have heard even if her ancestor's regiment had come banging on her door. But she had not sunk so far that she couldn't remember the last interview and think with pleasure of the clever trail she'd laid, although having to deal with a whippersnapper of a boy whose mother had been her servant made her mouth curl with rage. And not only a servant, a disagreeable one, she thought, with airs above her station, and all too eager to accept help from Oliver Gatterly when it suited her. And, if Fletcher was correct, maker of the food that had killed her son! Her face contorted.

But her encounter with Mazie's son was another insult to be pushed aside. Better to dream of the times she and her mare had gone flying across the ditches beyond Trewithen Manor, in the days when she had been happy, when she was still Miss Trewithen for real, her Papa's heiress. When, after Papa had exchanged his whisky-soaked corner (where his broken back had condemned him to a wheelchair existence) for a heaven where hounds ran every day, she had succeeded to his land

and name and position. She relived the hunting fields she had dominated, the point-to-points she'd won, the horse trials, jumping competitions, the hunt balls. In those days, before she'd 'reformed', as she called it, she'd done it all, reigned as queen over the county. Miss Trewithen, they called her, Cornwall's darling, and so she remained, even after the marriage forced upon her by Papa's condition. 'For the sake of the future when I'm gone,' he'd said.

He was dead before her sons were born, two together, a double offering to the future which Papa at least would have appreciated, even if Oliver Gatterly hadn't.

The man she'd chosen as her husband, and their father, hadn't been Papa's choice, and there had been her first mistake. 'Take someone who knows the county,' he'd wheezed at her from his high four-poster bed in which generations of Trewithens had been spawned, and from which they'd been buried, as he was soon to be. 'And someone the county knows.'

Instead she'd chosen an outsider, a city man, certain she could refashion him into a country gentleman, a man who these days was benefiting from her tuition by aping a country squire. And it had been an even worse mistake to confuse Oliver Gatterly's physical attractions for constructive energy; a mistake to imagine a man who stood six foot in his socks and who liked 'scragging' (his word) would use his energies to rescue Trewithen Manor from its rundown condition and restore it to its proper state. Might as well ask a baboon to give up eating nuts.

'I'm not a farmer,' he'd said, and meant; hadn't even been willing to give farming much of a try, had left the management of the estate to Fletcher who, thank goodness, knew what he was about. Had lounged about in breeches and hacking jacket although he couldn't ride, eyeing the neighbouring ladies, stupid little fillies with about as much sense as fleas. Hadn't lifted a finger, not even in the first days of their marriage when he was still in awe of her, when living in an ancient manor house touched some sense of respect, when 'marrying above his station', as he'd once put it, gave him a feeling of achievement. If he'd married above, she'd married beneath, and that was her third mistake. It had cost her her home, her marriage, her sons' future, all that she and Papa had stood for.

And her sons, they had her husband's weakness in them, a stain in the bloodline, which she knew all about in the breeding of horses and had ignored in her own until it was too late. Edmund, too sensitive for his own good; Justin, cursed with his father's capacity for 'shagging' and his sense of remorse afterwards, unsuccessful inheritor of his father's business aspirations. When had a Trewithen ever cared about the sluts he slept with? Or dirtied his hands with 'business', for God's sake? Justin, then, a loser too. Yet she had to rely on him, there was no one else.

When much later the phone rang, she didn't hear it. But the message was there waiting on the answering machine Justin had insisted that she have. A muffled voice. Menacing. 'We know Edmund's plan. And now we know Justin's. So you'd better stop him. Before it's too late.'

Chapter 10

While Miss Trewithen dreamt the evening away, Justin made a phone call at a seedy hotel he patronized when he was short of cash, although the pub round the corner was a preferred haunt. He'd chosen the hotel now to avoid his drinking pals next door. He'd join them when he was ready.

The dingy lobby was ripe with an early evening smell of disinfectant and gin, over-tinged by hot fat from a take-away fish and chip shop across the street. He dialled, listened to the recorded message, re-dialled. Then realizing there was no one in, slammed the receiver down. Bugger it, he thought.

After a while he tried again. And again.

He'd planned in advance what to say. A little flick to titillate, a little hint, just enough to show what he had in mind. At this stage all he could do was keep things simmering, waiting for the right moment to bring them to the boil. What he really needed was time.

He leaned against his telephone booth door, and felt the tiredness eat into his bones. Never been a day like it, and if he'd known he'd have kept his distance. With Father on his way back from Greece, there'd really been no excuse for turning up at the manor as he had. In fact he'd been a fool to think of it.

His excuse, given on the spur of the moment, 'While

109

my father's away I'm seeing to his affairs,' sounded far too pompous to be true. It hadn't cut much ice with the police, and would have only earned him one of Fletcher's reproachful looks. Fletcher had never liked him; the man's devotion to Mother was all that stopped him from sneaking to Father with what he really thought. Easily tempted, he'd say, lazy . . . stupid too, he thought, angry with himself, so stupid you couldn't keep away. Although that was only the half of it.

He hadn't realized he'd be asked to identify the body. He shivered. But since Ma wouldn't and Father couldn't, the task had fallen to him. But the expression on his brother's face – again he shivered. Think of it as simply a body, he told himself. He could deal with it better if he called it an anonymous body. Not Edmund's. Not his twin brother's.

He stared at the glass partition and his face stared back, hair unbrushed, chin unshaved, mouth tremulous, eyes frightened, the gold earring glinting. Not like his brother's face in any part, but the image of his mother's. Long-headed, like her, narrow-cheeked and chinned, horse-faced. Except, unlike her, he couldn't stand horses, never had.

And not like Edmund in character either, although they were twins. A mirror image, he thought, almost putting out a hand to touch his reflection, everything somehow reversed. The fair, the dark, the idealist, the materialist, the good, the bad. He shook his head, trying to shake off depression.

Edmund had usually accepted the differences between them as a fact of nature. The meeting that was to prove their last was the first time he'd allowed disapproval to show. 'You hang around him all the time. You ought to have more pride. He may be our father but think what he's done!'

The remarks still rankled. Edmund had never badgered like that before.

'I'm not changing sides because I like him. I'm not letting you and Ma down.' Justin's assurances had sounded thin even to him. And whether Edmund believed him, he never knew. Edmund was so Goddamn honest he expected you to be the same. But now Edmund wasn't here to listen while he twisted facts to fit his arguments, would never listen again.

He had guessed most of what Edmund had been after. Edmund had more or less told him. But then his twin had always been too trusting. It wasn't Justin's fault that it had all gone wrong.

Edmund, on the other hand, had had no idea what Justin was up to. Not even Ma knew that. And there was another problem, Ma herself. Ma would never believe he could pull it off. 'Can't run with hare and hound.' He could hear her saying it, her eyes burning. 'All for personal greed and gain.'

And that was the biggest difference between Edmund and me, he thought. Edmund had principles, ones he would have died for, perhaps did die for. I don't. But I do have aspirations. There's nothing wrong with aspirations – look where principles got Edmund. If he weren't my brother I'd say serve him right.

He suddenly felt an unaccustomed stab of pain.

At this point in his musings, the door of the booth rattled. The beerily flushed face of one of his chums appeared on the outside, mouthing through the glass. 'Fuck off,' Justin said. 'Go away, you sodding brute. Leave me alone.'

Deep in self-pity now, he began to think how misunderstood he'd been. Take all the efforts I made to ingratiate myself since Father's return, he thought; the flowers, making me look like a walking greenhouse, for a stepmother who obviously loathed the very idea; the carefully selected child's book for a half-brother whose age I'd forgotten ('Not quite my reading level,' the brat coolly remarked, barely bothering to glance at it); in debt for a suit to impress; my CV, such as it is, carefully re-composed to make the best of a bad job (no pun intended), I certainly spared no time or effort to impress a father who left us to rot. No wonder Edmund was shocked.

It isn't as simple as Edmund imagined, he told himself. And Father's money isn't all that I'm after, although Edmund and Mother may think so. I don't want the house back like Mother does. I've no fancy for country life, that was more Edmund's line. What I want . . .

But how describe what he wanted? More than a quarter of a century old and still crying for the moon. I know my rights, he told himself. A start, a chance to redeem myself, a hand up for an eldest son. Father stole all that from me when the estate was sold. He owes me it. So if I see a chance of beating him at his own game, that's my good luck. At least he'll have to acknowledge me as he should have done years ago.

He felt his face twist then with grief, much as it had when he'd heard the news of Edmund's death. Suddenly he began to sweat. It'll be all right, he told himself, like a drowning man in a rough sea. It can't go wrong. It's the last chance I have.

The realization released the anguish that was bottled up inside. He felt it spew out, hot, clotted thick. Just as it had last night, when without warning his innards had clamped down in a vice – at the very moment when his twin brother had died.

In Naomi's studio the pretty youth with the beaded

waistcoat was mouthing at her above the noise of the music, rap they called it, it made her head throb. He was one of those 'toy boys' who took over St Ives in summer and faded away with autumn, like migrating birds. Because she was an older woman, and rich, he strutted and postured before her, taking for granted she needed him, for sex or patronage, or whatever he'd set his heart on at the moment and so presumed was equally essential to her!

Naomi was Audrey's friend, the one who had persuaded her to talk to the police. For many years she'd been the leading light of the younger artistic set, although she wasn't exactly young. Where Naomi led, others followed. This group here, for example, she curled her lip, drinking her booze and having a good time at her expense, while pretending to be interested in art. Their shadows postured against the white walls, where posters of whales and dolphins and 'Safe Waters for Surfing' served as decoration.

She continued to look through the young man, puffing on her cigarette in an amber holder. A would-be sculptor, he'd said earlier, with a smirk. Would-be, she thought, that's what they all are, would-bes. And she glanced at her guests with one of her famous sidelong looks and blew another smoke ring.

The party was being held in her studio rather than the flat above the gallery which she and Audrey shared, because Audrey's accident had made her feel strange about having people in where they actually lived. The evening was unusually noisy, mainly because news of the car crash gave a special tinge of excitement, like dancing on a grave. But although her so-called friends had persuaded her to go ahead, saying things like 'Audrey expects us to' or 'Audrey wouldn't want us to be miserable', she hadn't the heart to enjoy herself. They

113

didn't care a shit about Audrey. She did.

The young man tugged at her arm again, something about being wanted. 'What?' she said. 'Who?'

When earlier this afternoon the hospital had informed her of the accident, at first she'd still been so angry she'd insisted she didn't know who Audrey Linton was. She was angry with Audrey for making a secret rendezvous with an unknown man, and even more angry with her for turning to an ex-husband when things went wrong. Disloyal, devious, she'd wanted to cry, why should I suffer because of her? Why should I care for her since she so obviously doesn't care for me? It wasn't the sex thing that bothered her so much. She wasn't jealous. It was the secrecy that hurt. That was the blow which had stunned. And she sat here now, the death's head at the feast, with merriment swirling round her, and people coming up and saying things like, 'You must be devastated.' Audrey's accident had shown her how much she had invested in the younger woman— and how badly it had been returned.

And there was another side to the situation. She struggled to formulate it to herself. It had to do with affection, love even. It had to do with childhood memories.

When she'd been a child, wealthy and indulged, she'd had a pet dog she adored. Somehow it escaped from the house and was found broken on the road outside. The servants brought it in, the vet was called. It may live, they said, this dirty, bloodied dog with a leg that now will always be lame. She had wept then too, not because she was afraid it wouldn't recover, but because she was afraid she couldn't love it if it did. Do I want it if it's maimed? she'd kept asking herself. It won't be pretty any more. 'Take it away!' she'd finally screamed.

Ever since that day she had liked only beautiful

things. Perfection, harmony, grace were her gods. Only now had it come to her that love might continue even if the outward appearance was flawed.

The young man tugged her arm again. Damn his impudence, she thought. Everyone here knew of her attachment to Audrey. 'Naomi's new plaything' they'd called her, and when she'd chosen her as a 'soul-mate', everyone had waited for Audrey's fall from grace. But when they saw how Naomi spared no effort and expense to 'launch' her friend into the world she herself controlled, when under her expert guidance Audrey developed her own talents and grew into someone Naomi could be proud of, they laughed on the other side of their faces. How they must be licking their lips now, Naomi thought, in ghoulish anticipation.

The boy mouthed at her again, something about a phone. Then she understood. She froze. It's the hospital, she thought. Bad news. The worst.

For a moment she was tempted to refuse. 'Take a message,' she wanted to say. 'Death has no place here.' Allowing death into this revelry would be grotesque, sacrilegious. And would leave her naked and vulnerable. She had a momentary vision of the silence that would follow the announcement, the sideways looks, the pretended 'ohs' of sympathy. One by one, uncomfortable at this unwanted melancholy, people would slip away, not to grieve but to find some other place to drink and play. She would be left alone to mourn.

But she was proud. And too loyal (although Audrey hadn't been loyal) to hide behind someone else. Pushing aside the boy's hand which he offered to help her to her feet as if she wasn't capable, she resolutely crossed the room with her long stride, the flowing tunic emphasizing rather than concealing her matronly figure, her small head with its close-cropped hair and her wrinkled neck rising out of the tunic folds of gold and brown like a startled tortoise.

The young man insisted on accompanying her and held the phone out with a look that could have been either pitying, or malicious. Impatiently, she waved him out of hearing. Sitting down on a stool, she cupped her hand over one ear. 'Who is it?' she heard her voice say without emotion.

But it wasn't the hospital, telling her Audrey was alive or dead. The message had nothing to do with the hospital at all, but everything to do with Audrey. And the voice was one she'd never heard before.

Back in his own house, Reynolds removed his cases from the hall and slung them in a cupboard, out of temptation's way. Making the bleak, obligatory call to find out how his ex-wife was, he waited in some trepidation, only to be told Miss Linton was still in intensive care, there was nothing he could do. He couldn't come to see her and she was being well taken care of. Slamming down the receiver, he went into his sitting room.

It had been a long day but he was tired only physically. Mentally he was on a high. He kept rehashing the events, the confrontation and disappointment, the revelation. He had reached a turning point, in his relationship with his wife, and in his relationship with a former friend. He had let down his guard with both of them, and in so doing allowed emotions back into his life.

He didn't know whether to regret this; always previously he had felt personal feelings should be hidden, he'd never liked the idea of washing one's dirty linen in public. But it was done, and he must endure the consequences. Know thy enemy, know thyself . . . It was the enemy within that was the hardest to deal with.

Partly to take his mind off these matters he rooted around among the stacks of papers on the low table in front of him. If he'd had a manuscript to work on, he'd have become engrossed, not even aware how much time passed. But there was no manuscript, only an old notebook, used to solve more crimes than he liked to remember. He picked it up with a feeling he couldn't quite analyze – like coming home to a place one wasn't particularly fond of, yet was so familiar one knew it by heart.

Turning to a blank page, he drew a heavy line, wrote the date and time, and under them, the names of all the people so far involved in the case. It was an old-fashioned habit. Forget computers, fax machines, he thought: ink and paper for me. At least then I can see what I write, and know what I'm doing.

Carefully he listed the names, which had suddenly become so familiar. First, Edmund Gatterly, poisoned, by a substance as yet unidentified. Labelled a loser by his mother, 'a back runner' at odds with his father, was he an unintended victim, as seemed most likely?

Second, his father, Oliver Gatterly, another prodigal son, recently returned to his first wife's house with an American wife, an act of gross insensitivity if nothing else. A disturbing mixture of a man, weak, yet pretending to be strong, fond of women, yet dominated by them.

Third, his new wife, manipulative, using charm to get her way, flaunting her looks and wealth. The term 'rich American temptress' might be hackneyed but certainly rang true. And where did the money come from?

Had they had a lucky escape? If so who was 'gunning for them' as the wife put it, and why? As for their return, if they supposedly disliked Cornwall, what lay behind Mrs Gatterly's slip, 'I know we have to live here'? What had really brought them back? Mazie thought it was to make amends; Miss Trewithen thought the opposite.

This brought him to Miss Trewithen herself. An alcoholic hunting enthusiast, despite her claim to have 'reformed' at least from hunting, and an eccentric. But was her eccentricity genuine? And what about her hatred? Was it a motive to kill? An outright snob also, an outmoded autocrat, who claimed that her former husband and his 'whore' were responsible for Edmund's murder and that Gatterly's return was to ensure that Richard, the third son, by the second wife, inherited everything.

Methinks the lady protests too much, he thought, then smiled at himself; he must stop the habit developing! But why, while he was on the subject, had she called Richard 'Richard Crookback'?

Richard Gatterly next. Little known about him. On the surface, bad-tempered, but certainly not physically deformed like Shakespeare's king, quite the opposite in fact. Had Miss Trewithen's adjective just sprung drunkenly to mind? Or was there some ulterior meaning? I must look up the play Richard III, he thought, vaguely aware of school boy readings.

Next, Justin, Edmund's older twin. Except for having identified his brother's body, and having various hints dropped about him, also an unknown. Apparently no one's favourite, accused of worming his way back into his father's graces, a suggestion to which Mazie's more kindly observation, and his step-mother's far from kindly comment, gave weight. But according to Miss Trewithen, a loyal son. What had made him turn up this morning in time to perform a nasty duty? Had he been asked to appear? Or did he know in advance? As Derrymore had pointed out, he was likely to gain a lot from his family's deaths.

Back to the list. Joe and Mary Lou Fletcher. A former estate steward, making no secret of his hatred for his employer, and idolizing his employer's first wife. Married to a woman who was supposedly the Gatterlys' friend. Mary Lou, a chatterbox whom the husband had to shut up. Worth talking to on her own.

Last of all, Audrey Linton. He wrote the name firmly. Despite the evidence that appeared to exonerate her and despite having nearly been killed herself in her car, she was nevertheless still involved. Not because she was present when Edmund had died but because of her hints that she had additional information about him and because she was in possession of a package that she had removed from the house. Was the package the reason for her car being tampered with? Where exactly was it now anyway?

Again he sat thinking. If she herself was unavailable for questioning, perhaps he could trace the friend she seemed to think so highly of.

Adding the words 'Unknown friend' to the list, he sat back and observed it. Not a bad beginning. He'd known worse. Now, he thought, with some satisfaction, all that remains is to fit the pieces together, in my own fashion, without Clemow's interference.

He looked at his clock. Almost eleven o'clock. Not too late to begin right now. He reached for the telephone and dialled Audrey's home number, on the off chance the friend might be there. The phone rang, was finally lifted and the line immediately disconnected. When he rang again, all he got was a busy signal.

Chapter 11

Next morning, a mild Cornish morning with the wind in the west and the smell of rain soft as silk, Reynolds drove once more through the gates into the manor grounds. He'd rung Derrymore, arranging to meet, and he'd rung the hospital, to be told with medical curtness that Miss Linton was out of intensive care but not yet able to receive visitors. She was 'doing as well as could be expected', and was he related?

The question was put with some asperity, and left him without an answer. 'Not connected, legally,' he'd told Clemow, and 'Not connected emotionally,' he'd told himself. So what relationship was left? Now, still puzzling over those niceties, he was surprised to find Derrymore wasn't at the manor before him. The sergeant was always punctual. There was no sign of the Gatterlys or their car either, and no sign, thank goodness, of Clemow. The only person in sight was Richard, disconsolately squatting on his heels, bat and ball in hand, his back to what Reynolds assumed was the garage. This time the boy didn't even bother to look up as Reynolds approached and stopped to peer inside the building.

Like other things about the estate, the garage had had a former purpose. Although there was certainly space now for cars, once it had served as stabling for horses. Reynolds could just make out the mouldering bridles and bits hanging on rusty nails hammered into the stone walls and, beyond the parking area, in the dark recesses, the remains of several stalls. Poor Miss Trewithen, he thought, here's glory run to seed.

The floor was of stone too, with traces in the corners of wisps of hay and straw. It was criss-crossed with tyre marks and mud and oil.

'Looking for evidence?' said a disagreeable voice in his ear. He spun round to find Richard at his shoulder, breathing down his neck as though, he thought afterwards, about to belt him one. In the right hands, a bat makes a good weapon.

Perhaps something in his expression made the boy back off. 'Whoa there,' he said, less belligerently. 'Just wondering what you were doing, Inspector. Didn't mean to intrude.'

He had a grown-up way of speaking, as if he was used to the company of adults, and his voice was neither English nor American, as if perhaps the effect of some English school had brushed off most of the American part. Someone's bothered to tell you who I am, Reynolds thought. Your mother perhaps.

'Who are you waiting for?' he asked, his gaze not quite resting on the bat.

'Justin. He promised to come over for a game of cricket. Well, not a real game, just a batting practice. We've rigged up some nets on the other side of the drive and he's a good fast bowler so I get a few swipes off him. But he isn't here yet so I don't think he'll show.'

'Why's that?'

A lengthy explanation followed about Justin never being reliable. It occurred to Reynolds that Richard might be stretching the truth a bit. What sort of brother plays cricket when his twin has just been murdered? For that matter, shouldn't Richard show more respect too? Remembering the damning comments that Richard's mother had made about Justin, why this sudden about-turn, he wondered, as if they were good friends?

He looked at Richard with new awareness. 'You like cricket then?' he asked, with just a hint of surprise. 'I always imagined Americans never understood it.' But when the youngster protested, somewhat heatedly, that although he was half American and, until recently, had been living in America, he went to an English school now and hoped to get into the first eleven next year, Reynolds grew suddenly tired of all this tortuous toing and froing which was all the Gatterly family seemed capable of. If Richard was lying just for the fun of it, he ought to be made aware that lying wasn't acceptable in normal society and in a murder case was downright dangerous. He glanced at his watch. Still no sign of Derrymore, so he had a few spare moments. 'Lead on, Macduff,' he said determinedly. 'Let's see what you're made of.'

Richard visibly paled. He began to protest, although more politely than ever. He wouldn't dream of imposing, he couldn't waste Reynolds' time.

'Try me,' Reynolds said, cutting short the protests, and shooing him ahead. 'I'll sling a few up for you.'

The nets were certainly there, installed behind the thickets of rhododendrons, new and well-built, a rich man's toy. Ever more reluctantly Richard took his stance at the batting while Reynolds caught up the ball, also new, scarcely used, the gold paint with the maker's name still glinting faintly on its shiny surface. He weighed it in his hand, feeling the familiar stitching with his thumb, and swung his bowling arm several times to test the shoulder he'd injured in a previous case.

He walked back, carefully measuring the number of

steps he took. It was a long while since he had done this but it was strange how readily it all came back. Like riding a bike, one never really forgot. Then, calculating again the distance to the batsman and the stumps behind him, he began his run.

It didn't seem so long after all since he had last bowled like this, spent a whole summer at improvised nets far flimsier than these, practising until he could put a ball on a penny and win his own place in the school team.

Down the pitch the red ball shot. The figure at the other end stepped forward, bat held over his shoulder, like a baseball bat. With a resounding crack the stumps went flying. Not bad for an old man, Reynolds thought. And for a boy who wants to get on the first team, I'd wager he's never even watched a cricket match, let alone hit a cricket ball.

Without saying anything, Reynolds scooped the ball up from the netting. For a good quarter of an hour he bowled with all the returning enthusiasm that a one-time cricketer never quite gets out of his system, at the end coming to the conclusion that although Richard didn't know how to hold a bat until he'd showed him, and had no concept at all of the finesse of the game, the boy at least showed determination when he wanted. As Justin and Derrymore had still not appeared, he thought he might as well take the opportunity to find out what he could about this youngster who seemed not to be able to distinguish fact from fantasy, and was as slippery as an eel.

He asked a string of seemingly harmless questions, all of which the lad fielded well, giving nothing away. Asked about his stepbrother, Edmund, his answers were noncommittal, and except as a partner for cricket he appeared as uninterested in Justin. What was his main hobby then, besides batting? Oh, he didn't know, swimming, boating, that sort of thing, but it was really to cold to enjoy the sea in Cornwall, he was used to warmer water.

'And where does Justin live?' Reynolds asked idly, and after listening to a rather complicated story about Justin's sharing a one-room flat with a mate, asked even more idly, 'What sort of car does he drive?' – to be handed his first fresh piece of information for the day.

When, half an hour later, Derrymore found them still 'practising,' Richard had been clean bowled enough times to show respect and appeared to be enthusiastically listening to Reynolds' tips, while Reynolds, in shirt sleeves, coat and tie discarded, his trousers satisfactorily stained with green, was smiling like a cat that had swallowed the canary.

Hailing Derrymore, he turned to Richard. 'I enjoyed that,' he said, 'thanks. And get your feet moving when the ball falls close.' And to Derrymore, when they were out of earshot, added, 'Just testing out an idea which was partly right, partly wrong. And gathering some useful information.'

He waited until they had come back to the drive before filling Derrymore in. Namely, that whether Richard would ever become a batsman on his school's cricket team he was a better spin bowler than he knew. He'd just tossed Reynolds up two yorkers: first, where Audrey's car had actually been parked yesterday, and second, who might have tampered with it!

Reynolds had concentrated on the car first. How had Richard known where it was parked? Richard had apparently seen Fletcher looking at it. Fletcher actually brought his attention to it. 'Nice little car,' Fletcher had said. 'But Master Justin's no business parking there when the Rolls is stuck outside.'

So Fletcher had made a mistake and thought Miss

Linton's car was Justin's? Had Richard appraised Joe of his error? 'Of course not,' Richard laughed. 'But it's dark inside the building, I suppose anyone could make a mistake like that, even an old fusspot like Fletcher. And Justin always parks his car in the garage when he comes. I suppose he thinks it makes him one of the family!' He gave a shrug of his shoulders as if to say, 'Fat good that'll do him.'

'What then?' Reynolds had asked, hiding his surprise.

'Nothing much.' Richard gave a sideways grin that lit up his face. Like his mother's smile, it was the most attractive thing about him. 'I wasn't going to get involved. I wasn't supposed to be about, you see. But when Justin turned up later, he too saw the car. I caught him peering in the garage like you did.'

'Justin came back?' Derrymore asked, giving his, by now, familiar whistle. 'What do you make of it? Do you think that's true?'

Reynolds shook his head. 'More like false clues,' he said. 'Deliberately dropped. Which makes one wonder what our young lad is up to. But both stories are worth checking out. I mean, he's neatly suggested, cool as a cucumber, that either Fletcher or Justin could have tampered with Audrey's car without being seen. So if it's all right with you,' he said, 'next stop the Fletchers, to see what Joe has to say. And then, since Richard also gave me Justin's address, we'll pay a little call on him.'

'Right.'

Derrymore's voice had none of its usual enthusiasm. Reynolds looked at him more closely. Derrymore was worried, unlike his usual self. He even had what seemed like a speck of blood on his collar which was slightly awry, and a small nick on his chin. A shaving cut presumably, but uncharacteristic. Usually in uniform the sergeant was immaculately shaved and dressed.

'Is anything wrong?' Reynolds asked, expecting a story of Clemow's vindictiveness at the very least. He didn't know whether to be glad or sorry when, reluctantly, Derrymore explained that he was OK. It was his mam. 'She was fine yesterday,' Derrymore hastened to explain. 'You cheered her up no end, and when I'd gone over all about the clues again, she seemed back to normal. Not that she could put it aside completely, just like that. It'd been a shock and all, especially her knowing the family. Well, this morning when I was in the bathroom, I heard her singing away in the kitchen like she always does, and I thought, that's all right. Then the post came, and the singing stopped. And she was in as bad a state as before. And that's why I'm late. Seems there was a letter. I didn't see it, she threw it in the fire before I came down, but it made her all over shaky, crying and carrying on.' He shook his head. 'Never seen her like it.'

'What did the letter say?'

'She wouldn't say at first. Said it was horrible. Said it was what we call a poison-pen letter, labelling her a poisoner herself. You should be punished, it said. Put into prison. Things of that sort. Mind you,' he went on, 'what upset her most wasn't what was said. It was being anonymous. Could be someone I know, she kept saying, someone I thought was my friend. Didn't think anyone in the village would have it in for me like that, and me and my family before me having lived here for so long. Really broke your heart it did.'

'But the details of the case haven't been made public,' Reynolds said gently. 'How could anyone have found out?'

'Oh,' said Derrymore, 'you know how it is. They've said that Edmund Gatterly was poisoned by eating food in the house and plenty of people know my mam did some cooking for them. All they've got to do is put two and two together and bingo, they've made a hit. What am I to do about it, sir?' he burst out. 'What if another letter comes?'

'I expect it will,' Reynolds said. 'Writing anonymous letters is how some people get their kicks. Tell your mother not to open it. She should give any strange letter to you. We need to see one before we can begin to identify the author. Meanwhile, you make a list of people in the village who might hold a grudge against your mother. She mentioned a Mrs Aintree, I think it was . . .'

'Lucy Aintree's our next-door neighbour,' Derrymore protested. 'She's known my mam since childhood.'

Reynolds didn't say what he was thinking, that sometimes it's the oldest friends who turn on you the hardest. And he thought, too, of what Mrs Gatterly had said about Cornish people in general, the people Reynolds himself was so fond of. How she would crow if she found out there was a poison-pen writer in the vicinity! 'Typical,' he could hear her saying, 'just the sort of malice I'd expect.' Yet he knew this wasn't true. The Cornish villagers weren't the way she depicted them, they were honest, hard-working, kind. Like Mazie Derrymore herself. He suddenly felt very angry.

'Come on, old son,' he said. 'We'll crack it. And now let's go and crack the other case.'

After they'd gone Richard collapsed on the grass, out of breath and exhausted, but not completely dissatisfied. Reynolds thought he'd got the better of him; perhaps he'd got the better of Reynolds! Although now he had time to think about it, he'd probably gone too far. But of course that wasn't his fault; he'd been tempted into it. Nothing ever was his fault, he took good care of that.

He wasn't waiting for Justin, but he didn't intend anyone to know who he was waiting for. And they weren't going to play cricket, although that's how they'd met, pretending to toss balls at each other, while his new friend eyed the nets contemptuously. Made him feel a right fool, almost as bad as Reynolds. And that's another reason why he had to set Reynolds up; he hated being made to look a fool.

Most of the time when he was with his new friend he ended up feeling foolish. That was a truth he didn't like. And it was such an effort to keep up that he became more extravagant than he should have been, just to show he was at ease. But every time he tried to impress, he was caught off balance. He couldn't put his finger on it, but it was like walking on a tightrope. And the strangest thing of all, the thing he couldn't understand, was that he'd come to enjoy it; it gave him a high, stronger than any shot of crack.

It's all part of the strangeness of the place, he thought, lying there with the sun glinting through the grass and the gnats dancing in the shade of the old oak trees behind the nets. Strange people, strange habits, strange ways of speaking. It made him feel strange as well. But after that first meeting, when they'd gone down to the river together, he'd suddenly felt happy. Like sometimes after a long rap session with his friends at home, when the pot went round and they'd sniffed a bit and he experienced a kind of peace.

He thought again of home and the young people there he'd run around with, a wild bunch if ever there was. None of them could compare with here.

Once he'd been asked, unexpectedly, what the difference was between his friends here and there. How could he explain? 'Their hair is long and dirty,' he'd said, 'but eventually it gets cut and washed. Although their jeans may be torn and dirty, they wear designer models and their closets are full of lovely gear from all the right shops, like Nieman Marcus. And if they kick up the traces at school, or run foul of the law, their parents are rich enough to gloss trouble over. And the girls never give themselves away to any boy, for love or money. Frigid fricking virgins, cold as fish.'

'Money then is all that counts?' The scorn had made him blush.

It's not just the money, he'd wanted to say, but hadn't. There I was a leader. Here I'm nothing, a bit player who wants to take centre stage. Instead he'd said, 'My friends from home aren't really rebels. Even high on drugs they're always in control. In a year or two the boys expect go into their fathers' law firms or their grandfathers' oil companies, while the girls grow up like those mothers they pretend to despise. They never play for keeps.' Like you, he meant.

'And you?' The question came sharp. 'Can you show you're serious?'

Behind it lay a challenge. No wonder he felt foolish. How was a fellow to prove himself, after all?

Chapter 12

Reynolds and Derrymore walked towards the Fletchers' house, the track clearly visible in daylight. Seeing the thickness of the undergrowth, and the actual distance involved, Reynolds solved one mystery to his satisfaction. 'I'll accept the possibility they heard your car but not the others,' he told Derrymore. 'They still might have been expecting Edmund and his friend. Although of course they can't admit that.'

They'd already devised ways of getting Mary Lou on her own, plans that proved unnecessary because Joe wasn't at home. Mary Lou herself answered their knock and when they asked where her husband was, she told them he was mending a blocked drain down by the river. She was soberly dressed today in dark blue and green, although the skirt was short by Cornish standards and the striped top reminded Reynolds of a rugby jersey. She looked strained, he thought, as she reluctantly invited them inside, her eyes darkened by shadows as if she hadn't slept. Why isn't she up at the manor? he wondered. If she's such a good friend of the family, they might need her.

As if reading his mind, she said resentfully, 'The police told me to keep away. Ordered me off, like I was a suspect. "The two who came before," I told them, "were gentlemen. You're regular New York cops." But they only laughed. Coffee?'

As if, even without her husband to restrain her, she became aware that she must be careful what she said, she skipped off, the too short skirt swinging. Reynolds and Derrymore sat down in a room which all too clearly hadn't been tidied up since their last visit, and probably for some time before that. The dust lay thick on the television set and the wool from her knitting was still strewn behind the sofa where she had stowed it on the night of the murder.

'Now, Mrs Fletcher,' Derrymore began when she came back with coffee, American style, black, strong. 'There are a few questions about the night of the murder we'd like verified, if you don't mind.'

Waiting until she had settled herself, somewhat skittishly pulling the meagre folds of material across her skinny thighs, and then sitting with hands folded, like a child posed for an examination, he and Reynolds both tried her with the familiar questions about how Edmund had got into the house and what his relationship with his father was. But she knew nothing, or more likely Joe had coached her too well, although her lack of interest in Edmund's 'friend' was surprising to say the least. Not even inquiries about the couple she had seen 'lurking about', whom Joe had dismissed as hikers, could tempt her into opening up. 'You'll have to ask my husband,' was her stock answer.

Exasperated, Reynolds changed tack. 'About the manor house, you're the very one to ask,' he said, showing suitable respect. 'When it was first sold, and then recently resold, was it left empty?'

'I don't understand,' she said, staring at him, her arms crossed on her breast, defensively. And listened while Reynolds explained that Joe had mentioned Mr Gatterly buying the place 'lock, stock and barrel'; did that mean complete with furnishings, carpets, books, pictures?

Yes, it did, they were told in no uncertain terms. As far as she was concerned there was too much old junk left, stuffing falling out every time she tried to move the chairs, and curtains in shreds. For her taste, redecoration couldn't be done quickly enough. As for books, there'd been a library but Mr Gatterly used it now so she never went near it. And paintings, family portraits and such, well, the gallery upstairs was virtually empty and Miss Trewithen would have got her claws on anything valuable before the creditors arrived.

'Why do you ask?' she said, stopping herself suddenly and staring at him even more suspiciously.

'Just curious,' he answered, smiling. 'We think Edmund might have wanted something from the house that night. Any idea what it could be?'

At this, her face went white. She glanced imploringly over her shoulder as if searching for her husband.

'It's quite all right,' Reynolds told her soothingly. 'We're only looking for confirmation, everything you say is confidential.'

His smile must have reassured her. 'I suppose,' she said reluctantly, answering a question he hadn't asked, 'Edmund might have blamed his father for lots of things.'

'Meaning he might have felt justified in stealing from him?'

No answer.

'Of course he might not think it was stealing,' he offered. 'He might think it belonged to him.'

'It's nothing to do with me of course,' she said, in an even more frightened voice, 'but he did speak to Joe.' Recovering herself, she added, 'I mean, he and Joe used to meet. Why not? They were friends from way back.' Her eyes were wide again, this time with awareness.

If that's true, Reynolds thought, it seems odd she never met Edmund, or so she claimed before. Another thought struck him. 'The first Mrs Gatterly, Miss Trewithen, does she ever come here?' he asked.

'Joe and she are buddy buddy,' she said scornfully. 'Dances to her tune, I'd say. And when the house was first sold, people said she used to roam the woods, like a lost soul. The new owners pretended not to notice, but I thought it was creepy.'

Another nice little piece of information, Reynolds thought, as Derrymore wrote it down. Now comes the moment to focus on the main questions: who were the real victims and who might have wanted to kill them.

'Joe doesn't like Mr Gatterly, I gather,' he said.

'Joe doesn't like change, a real stick-in-the-mud. Of course,' she glanced under her eyelashes, 'it's different now he's married. Men can be bachelors too long, don't you think?'

'It must have been hard on him when Miss Trewithen left?' Derrymore interposed, following Reynolds' tactics, 'But you wouldn't remember that, would you? Joe wasn't married then. I know Mam and me had to go in, let's see,' he frowned, trying to remember the date, 'spring of nineteen eighty, I can't recall which month but my mam would.'

'I forgot you lived here once,' she said, suddenly cold. 'But you'd only have been a child yourself.' She turned to pick up the coffee cups, her mouth pursed.

Meaning, Reynolds guessed, she doesn't think Derrymore will remember – what? Another lead given away, this time unknowingly.

'But at least Joe's got this little house,' he said sympathetically. He was about to add something fatuous about the place and was glad he hadn't, when she suddenly turned on him.

'Little's the word,' she spat, a kitten showing its claws. 'Not what I was used to, I can tell you. Mind, I'm not saying we aren't glad to have it. But I expected something bigger when Joe first mentioned it.'

'And how did you and Joe meet, exactly?'

He had wondered about that since their last interview, the coupling had seemed so oddly contrived. As if genuinely surprised by his question, she said, 'Mr Gatterly introduced us. I came down here before he married again, you know.'

'Ah.' Reynolds professed amiable enlightenment. Although he wasn't clear why Mr Gatterly would have arranged such an introduction, or why, if she'd visited the place before her marriage, she hadn't known where Joe lived. Again she anticipated part of his question. 'At that time, Joe was staying in an old gamekeeper's hut, I guess that's what you'd call it,' she said. 'A real dump of a place, in the back of beyond. Might have been the Wild West I thought, and said so. I wasn't made to be a pioneer woman. So when the estate was sold, Mr Gatterly arranged for him to rent this house.'

Mr Gatterly not Miss Trewithen, that's odd, he was thinking when again she anticipated where his thoughts were leading.

'Oh, Miss Trewithen wanted Joe to stay on all right,' she said witheringly. 'But she wouldn't lift a finger to help us. And neither would the new Mrs Gatterly.'

He ignored the bitterness, said, 'Of course, you're the Gatterlys' friend, aren't you? So how did you all meet?'

'Mrs Gatterly and I knew each other from childhood,' she said. 'We played together, Barbs and me.'

The use of the childhood name caused her face to soften. 'At the end of the pasture there was a creek,' she told him. 'Makes the Fowey River that they're always on about look like a ditch. We used to catch fish and put them into jars.' The memories had put a glow into her cheeks. 'Mind you, Barbs was always a scaredy cat, couldn't get her to jump across.'

Bet you did, Reynolds thought, suddenly seeing her as a thin kid in faded jeans and plaits, and wasn't surprised when she added, 'It was on the Texas border, so in summer there wasn't much water. There were rattlers though, sunning on the boulders, big as your arm. But they don't bother you if you don't bother them.'

He pictured children leaping across the dried-up river bed from rock to rock, the surface blazing in the sun. He saw the coiled snakes. He thought of their venom. 'And how did you both end up in England?' he asked.

Her face clouded as if the sun had gone in. 'Adventure, I suppose,' she said dully. 'Barbs and I were working in the same firm and were offered jobs in London.'

'Two American girls, taking the old country by storm.' He laughed, but she didn't laugh back. 'And she met Mr Gatterly and brought you down—'

'Wrong,' she snapped. 'I met Oliver first.' Once more, as if she'd said too much, she glanced over her shoulder but no help arrived.

They waited until she went on, 'He'd come to work in the same company, see. In those days they were looking for English recruits; there were plenty of jobs then. He wasn't married when we met,' she added defensively. 'I mean, he was already separated from his wife. He had to be, he was in London, Miss Trewithen and her children were down here. So there was nothing fishy going on when I first dated him. It was all fine, all above board until . . .'

Until he met your friend, Barbs, Reynolds thought, silently finishing the sentence for her. He nodded sympathetically. Everything fine until she cut you out and married him herself. Sometimes beauties have all the luck.

But it wasn't only beauty that Mary Lou resented.

'Anyway, you don't need me to tell you how it ended,' she went on, the Texan accent more pronounced now. 'Barbs and I were friends only up to a point. There was always a difference between us, and it wasn't just looks. My pappy didn't own the company. Hers did.'

And those two simple sentences summed up the whole situation. It must have been a major trauma, Reynolds thought looking at her with something more than sympathy, to move on from Oliver Gatterly to Joe Fletcher. Caught on the rebound with a vengeance, a real 'see if I care' attitude. And then all these years since, well, they mightn't have been so bad. Joe seems a kind enough man and there's a child; she must have come to terms with her life here, he thought, or she wouldn't have stayed. Only to have the Gatterlys come back, lording it over her. No wonder she and Barbs Gatterly don't get on. It certainly gives her a genuine motive for hatred, and explains why her husband wants her to keep her mouth shut. And is that why Joe made so much of her not being a cook, to ensure no one connects her with the kitchen? He looked at her, taking stock.

He caught Derrymore's glance and together the two men rose. 'Thanks,' Reynolds said mildly, without sarcasm this time. 'You've helped a lot.'

'That's a dilly of a story.' Derrymore couldn't repress his astonishment.

Reynolds agreed, but for the moment Mary Lou's revelation preoccupied him less than a mystery that remained unresolved: the parcel that Audrey had taken. 'If it was something valuable, a painting, for example, Edmund might have wanted to try to sell it to get even with his father. But in that case you'd think someone would have mentioned it by now. Why would they keep quiet? Surely not to preserve Edmund's reputation. I can't see Mrs Gatterly the second being that generous.'

He stopped walking. 'I just have a feeling the whole incident isn't so easily explained,' he said, looking at his companion. 'And I also have a premonition it's a real clue. Don't ask me why,' he added somewhat uncomfortably, 'I can't explain it. As for Mary Lou's confession giving her a motive—'

He was interrupted by a rustling in the bushes.

'Who's there?' he said sharply. As Derrymore dived under the laurels, he expected to see Richard hauled forth by his ear. Instead, a large, moon-faced girl dressed in a too big jersey like an over-stuffed cushion came stumbling out. Brushing away the twigs and leaves that bedecked her ample frame, she stared at them with a hard, almost defiant look, before turning on her heel and striding down the path towards the Fletchers' house.

They watched as she went up to the door and stood talking to Mary Lou for a moment. Then she followed Mary Lou inside, with a defiant toss of her long hair, aimed at them.

'Ye Gods,' Reynolds said, taken aback. 'That's surely not Mary Lou's child. From the way Joe spoke, I thought at most she was a toddler.'

Derrymore was still staring after the girl. 'Seen her before,' he said. 'Certain of it. There's a group,' he went on, 'hangs about the local pub. Although they're under age, they try to get people to sneak drinks out to them, and be damned to the law. Been called to chase them off several times recently, the pub owners are in a fair tizz, but what can they do? Trouble if they get drunk, trouble if they don't.'

They continued on their way.

'Fletcher never used to drink,' Derrymore added after a moment. 'A teetotaller of the old school. He'd have a fit if he knew what his daughter was up to.' He turned to Reynolds. 'You were speaking of Mary Lou's confession. Do you think it might be a reason for her to bump off the Gatterlys?'

'I suppose so. Although since she gave it to us gratis, as it were, I doubt it. However Fletcher is another matter. I wonder how much he knows about what his missus told us. Presumably if Gatterly introduced them Joe would be suspicious of their former relationship.'

Derrymore considered for a moment. 'Perhaps not. They say he was an old bachelor, living alone, and by all accounts not having much to do with women until he met her. Mary Lou may have knocked him over like a thunderbolt. And he's the one who stressed she was a good friend of the Gatterlys. Surely he wouldn't do that if he thought she was, well, Gatterly's leavings, like.'

'Perhaps.' Reynolds too was thoughtful. 'On the other hand it may explain part of his dislike for Gatterly. And he's certainly protective of Mary Lou, at least keeps trying to stop her from saying too much. Fat chance of that I'd say.'

'I feel sorry for him,' Derrymore said. 'Joe wasn't a bad chap in the old days. He deserves a good wife.' And I don't think he's got one, his tone suggested. 'And whatever he thinks of his daughter she'll lead him a merry dance.'

'Let's get to him now. Any idea where he is?'

Derrymore's eyes shone with boyish enthusiasm. 'If he's mending a drain, he'll be somewhere at the foot of what we called Big Hill. There used to be a quick way to it, down an old mining track. If we take the car I'm sure I can find it, unless it's overgrown. We'll get there quicker than going on foot from here. And we'll have a car handy for later.'

They had reached the manor now, and leaving Reynolds' car safely parked, to be collected on their return, they bumped off in Derrymore's Panda, turning towards the town of Fowey, seemingly away from the river. As Derrymore drove he peered through the windows.

'The track's been there for centuries.' Unusually talkative, he continued, 'They say it was for taking tin down to the ships moored in the river. I'll tell you something confidentially,' he went on, 'all that boasting about the Trewithens being landowners and such, well, I happen to know they made their money in mining first off, like every Cornish family hereabouts. Scratch any true Cornishman and you'll find a miner somewhere. So there's no call for her to pretend she's any better than the rest of us.'

He slammed on the brakes and manoeuvred the car with difficulty into a small and inconspicuous lane, seldom used by the looks of it. Grass grew along the centre and the sides were overgrown. Fronds swished and tore at the doors as they jolted forward. After a few moments, they came to a gateway, where a sagging wooden gate was easily removed.

'Don't know who the land belongs to now,' Derrymore said, as they drove through, 'but we'll risk it.'

He grinned, a small boy again, and wary of trespassing.

The track they were following ran in a series of steep zigzags through the remains of woodland, cleared and sprouting in a wilderness of tree stumps and brambles. Derrymore clucked under his breath as he negotiated the bends. 'Shame,' he said.

He swung the wheel again, and the river opened abruptly beneath them, the land falling even steeper now, a miniature cliff.

Today the water was a deep blue-grey, with a shimmer to it which the fringe of trees on both banks enhanced.

Lower downstream, on their side, the fringe widened into a thick belt, suggesting what must have existed before the felling took place.

On a sort of plateau, Derrymore stopped the car and got out, looking about him with the air of a man returning to his past. 'There he is,' he said suddenly, pointing. And almost out of sight, close to where the trees widened, a figure looked up.

For a moment, Reynolds could have sworn there was a second figure. But he was looking into brightness against the blue-grey of the river, and when he shielded his eyes there was only the bent back of a man digging. Feeling he must have been imagining things, he slid behind Derrymore, down the precipitous embankment in a rush of old leaves and trampled bracken.

Joe didn't turn as they approached although he must have seen and heard them. In fact he gave no sign of recognition at all. It was only when Derrymore shouted to him that he had the grace to put down his spade and lean on the handle, a long-handled Cornish spade with a thick triangled blade, used to cut as well as dig.

'You,' he said forbiddingly. 'What do you want this time?'

'Nothing much.' Reynolds' reply was matter-of-fact. 'More to the point, what are you up to? Looks like hard work.'

'A bit of proper stuff for a change,' Fletcher said more cheerfully. 'Mind you, in the old days this wouldn't have been my job. Once we'd have had a ditcher to handle drains. But I don't mind.'

'Any fishing still? Or are those rights sold off too?'

The question must have touched a nerve. 'Plenty of fish,' Fletcher said dourly. He dug in the spade between some tree roots, then leaned again on the handle. 'That felling up there,' he gestured, 'shouldn't have been allowed. Just for cash on the spot, nothing replanted for the future, and the erosion plays havoc with the banks.'

He dug out a great root and threw it over his shoulder. 'Bloody upcountry people,' he said. 'But some fishing rights still belong to the estate, so I keep an eye on this from time to time. Better than papering back bedrooms or raking up lawns, I say, which is what they keep me for mostly.'

'Or driving cars around at all hours of the day and night,' Derrymore added cheerfully. 'Speaking of which, did you ever find a place to park the Rolls the morning the family returned?'

No, Fletcher admitted, even more dourly, thanks to police inefficiency, he hadn't. And later, when he'd tried to get it back into the garage where it belonged, some damn car had been shoved there out of the way instead. Mrs Gatterly had finally sorted out the situation. He intimated that he wasn't grateful. In his opinion Mrs Gatterly took too much upon herself.

'And what car was that?' Reynolds asked.

'A Rover. Belonged to some woman who was there giving evidence, although what she had to do with it I have no idea.'

'Not Justin's car then?'

Joe stared. 'I'm not blind,' he snorted. 'I can still tell the difference between an old banger and this year's model. Although after the crash, I doubt if there's much to choose between them.'

'Did you know the woman had been at the house last night?'

Fletcher bent and lifted. 'Everyone at the manor was talking,' he said. 'It weren't on the news.'

'And did you touch the woman's car?'

'I'd have moved it if I could,' Joe said, irritated anew.

'Taking up room that wasn't intended. But I didn't fool with it, if that's what you mean.'

Reasonable enough, Reynolds thought. He moved to another, related issue. 'Did you know Justin came twice yesterday morning?' he asked.

Fletcher gave his narrow-eyed stare. 'He was gone by the time we returned from the airport. I never saw him again.'

'You don't know why he came in the first place, or why he returned?'

'No, to both questions.' Fletcher was sounding testy. 'He doesn't take me into his confidence.'

'Did you tell him about his brother's death?'

'No.' Another spadeful of earth and roots went flying. 'But he was always poking his nose in, well, I thought, you'll poke so hard one day you'll regret it.'

'And Edmund?'

'I told you all I know about Mr Edmund.'

'But you didn't say you met him sometimes.'

Fletcher didn't look ruffled. 'Why should I?' he countered. 'It was our private business. And we never went near the house, only down in the woods. He liked to get the feel of the old place, sit by the river, chat about birds and such. More than the present owners ever think of doing.'

He had a point.

'And you had no prior knowledge that he had a key and meant to go in the house that night with anyone?'

'I'm not a fool.' Fletcher straightened up. 'I suppose you think because I have a set of keys I hand them out to everyone. Wouldn't be worth my job. I keep 'em with me, look.' He reached under his knitted waistcoat and produced a large clump knotted to his belt. 'No one's likely to make copies without me knowing,' he said. 'Don't even think it. And as for who put the poison in the food I certainly didn't, and neither did my wife. We knows each other's ways too well, so there's no good looking for chinks in our armour. Back off.'

An ambiguous warning, but a warning nevertheless. To be followed by one much more explicit. 'But I'll tell you one thing,' Joe said fiercely. 'Them details about the murder, on the telly this morning, shouldn't be allowed. Awful for the family.'

He didn't mean the present Gatterlys.

'You there, boy,' he pointed at Derrymore. 'You should know better. Biting the hand that fed you, I call it. No sense of decency.'

His outburst took Derrymore aback. 'Public information isn't my department,' he protested.

'Then it ought to be,' Joe snorted. 'You were here when it happened. You should be responsible for what's told.' And without another word he went back to his digging.

Downcast, Derrymore scrambled up the embankment. 'What do you think, sir?' he asked after a while. 'I mean about the car and keys and all. Someone must be lying. And if it's not Joe, it's that boy.'

But for once Reynolds wasn't listening. 'Hush,' he said. He put out his hand to stop Derrymore opening the car door. Beneath them, the river ran slow and deep, too far away for them to see the current. The sun glinted off the dark late-summer foliage and, closer to, wasps buzzed around a clump of meadowsweet.

The distant click of Fletcher's spade was the only other sound, except for a low thudding that came in waves, recognizable as the rapid beat of hooves, the horse and its rider hidden among the trees.

'So there was someone else here when we arrived.' Reynolds spoke to himself. 'And who might that be? Only one person I can think of, and she must have a constitution like an ox even to hoist herself into the saddle, to say nothing of staying there. What's she doing in this part of the world, I'd like to know, if not chatting up Joe Fletcher? And what better way to come and go, without leaving a trace?'

'You think that was Miss Trewithen?' Derrymore looked startled. 'I didn't know she still kept a horse.'

They got into the car and drove laboriously up to the track and, via the lane, to the main road. 'And where in the hell does she keep it?' he asked.

'Not behind her Fowey house, that's certain.' Reynolds' answer was thoughtful. 'So here's a task for you. Find out where she stables it, and whether she and her horse ever came up to the house before the first murder. But first we'd better let the inquiry team know what we've found out about the Rover. No matter if Richard's lying, trying to involve Fletcher and Justin. Thanks to Fletcher we can be pretty certain now where the Rover was parked. Should satisfy even Clemow that the stables, excuse me, garage, is the place for clues.' Derrymore's lugubrious expression made him laugh. 'I'd rather keep a low profile for a bit,' he explained. 'Better let Clemow settle down. Your turn to tackle him.'

It was not until he was waiting for Derrymore to finish with the phone, that his own words came back to haunt him.

'First murder' he'd said, as if he was certain there would be another. As if it was not only a question of solving one, but of trying to prevent others. And, although plenty of suspects, still no real clues who the intended victim really was. And certainly no leads to the murderer's identity or motive – although the Fletchers' evidence, at face value, seemed to implicate them and Miss Trewithen more and more – and suggest again, for several reasons, that the family at the manor was the most likely target.

Ending his call with a smile, Derrymore reported that Clemow seemed to take the new information seriously. He'd said he would send men to scour the stables, 'immediately.'

'Good. Off to Truro then,' Reynolds resettled himself in the Panda, adding with a grin, 'And don't spare the horses.'

The address Richard had given for Justin was in what had once been a residential part of the city, now used mainly for offices, down a small side street away from the hustle and bustle of the cathedral and market. They hammered on the door but no one answered. Convinced that Richard had lied about this too, they were about to leave when a downstairs window opened. A sleepy-eyed fellow with a long narrow face and a ring in one ear looked out. He was dressed in trousers which had obviously been hastily pulled on, and not much else, and from his bleary expression he looked as if he'd just got up.

'Justin Gatterly?' Derrymore asked.

'What about him?'

'Police business, sir. We'd like to speak to him regarding his brother's death.'

'All right, all right.' The man's voice rose and his sallow skin darkened. 'I'm coming. Anything to stop that infernal banging.' His head withdrew and a moment later he opened the door. 'I'm Justin Gatterly,' he said crossly. 'So what do you want to ask? Or tell?'

'Plenty,' Derrymore told him cheerfully. 'So unless you want it blurted out on the doorstep we'd better come in.'

The room Justin showed them into apparently doubled as office and sleeping quarters. There was an unmade camp bed in one corner and a rolled-up sleeping bag in the other but the rest of the space was dominated by a drawing board and a large desk littered with papers.

While Justin struggled into a shirt, they took the opportunity to look around. Reynolds inspected the drawing board which was jammed against the wall.

'It's my flatmate's,' Justin told him. 'He's an architect. At least he's as much of an architect as the present building crisis allows.'

'Are you an architect too?' Reynolds' question was bland. He wasn't surprised when Justin answered vaguely that he 'helped his flatmate out' on occasions but that he had no intention of working as an architect fulltime.

'Too many bloody rules,' he exclaimed, and embarked on a lengthy and complicated explanation of various business ventures he was involved in, during the course of which various business partners were criticized.All of this information was rolled out with a glibness that was impressive, and the list of names and companies made Justin's own participating role (according to him, a key one) sound solid enough until, probing deeper, Reynolds realized everything was tentative, nothing specific.

'Actually I'm laid off at the moment,' Justin finally admitted airily. 'Oh, not long, a few months ago. But irons in the fire.'

'What we call an entrepreneur then,' Reynolds said in his same mild, interested manner. 'With your father's blessing, no doubt.'

The observation left Justin looking foolish. Probably on the dole, Reynolds thought, observing him closely. Nothing wrong with that if you're out of work. But you won't find work, my fine fellow, sleeping until noon. You have to be out there hustling for it. And you won't find dependable partners unless you show them you are equally dependable.

Without giving him time to recover, he said, 'I gather when you arrived on the morning after your brother's death, you showed up to see to your father's affairs. What exactly are those affairs, sir, if I may ask?'

A second time Justin opened his mouth and shut it. Then he muttered that he was speaking in a general way.

'You mean keeping an eye on the house and so on? But I thought that was Joe Fletcher's work. Of course, if you had reason to believe something had happened to your brother I can understand your concern. What did you know about your brother's movements that night?'

The question came out like a bullet. To his astonishment, Justin admitted he'd had a good idea Edmund would be at the house. He didn't know whether to be relieved or angry when Justin added that he 'presumed' Edmund was showing off to a 'lady friend'.

Reynolds ignored that remark, came back to his main line of questioning, including what Edmund might have wanted to take from the house and how he had got in.

'I don't know,' Justin answered to both questions.

'Come on,' Reynolds said, bearing down heavily. 'Brothers who share secrets about their women friends aren't usually backward in revealing other little peccadillos. For example, why did he and his father quarrel? And if they'd quarrelled, surely his father wouldn't welcome him. So if you didn't stop him using his father's place as a secret rendezvous, you're not exactly looking after your father's interests, are you?'

Justin slumped forward sulkily. Reynolds regarded him for a moment. Something about the light, a shaft of sun coming through the fly-smeared windows, emphasized the resemblance to his mother. Nothing of the Gatterly side here at all, Reynolds thought. What sort of person is he under that glib exterior? A twin who

148

doesn't look like his brother, who resembles his mother and yet, like his father, crumbles under pressure.

'Let me ask again,' he said. 'What do you know about your brother's quarrel?'

'Nothing.' Justin sounded aggrieved. 'I wasn't his keeper. As for bringing a woman there, that was a first to him. He didn't usually screw around.'

Like I do, he might have added, and did. 'And since I spent that night with a woman friend, don't think I tried to kill him, or anyone else. She'll be glad to give me an alibi.'

'Oh, we know you weren't there that evening,' Reynolds said, in a tone that suggested of course it was possible that on some other occasion Justin could have crept into the kitchen and poisoned a freezer full of food. 'We still aren't satisfied why you showed up next morning. Or why you returned.'

This time Justin was prepared for him. If he'd come, what of it? And if he'd returned he had the right to see what he could do for his grieving family. Besides, he'd heard the police talking about a phone call from a woman. He felt sure she must be the same one his brother had brought to the house, but when nothing about her was mentioned on the news, he had decided to find out what was going on. He wanted to know whether she was in any way responsible for Edmund's death.

Refraining from pointing out that he should have told the police all this much earlier, Reynolds asked if he had seen the woman's car.

Once more the sallow face darkened. 'I looked in the garage for space,' he said. 'I didn't go in, if that's what you're asking. I didn't fix her bloody brakes.'

By now he was sweating heavily, his dark hair (which showed no signs of the Gatterly 'peak') was wet with it.

Not always a sign of guilt, Reynolds thought, although often it is. How does he know her brakes were 'fixed'?

On a last hunch he said, 'What did you think about your father's decision to return to live in Cornwall?'

Justin stiffened. An involuntary spasm, it could have been anger or some other emotion, crossed his face. His answer was the third surprise. 'I think,' he said savagely, 'it was about bloody time he did.'

The bitterness came as a shock. Even he seemed surprised by it. He threw his head back defiantly, so that the earring swung to and fro. Something about his expression made him look more like his mother than ever. 'But don't think I had a reason to kill him,' he said. 'As far as I'm concerned, he's the goose that laid the golden egg. And since Edmund was the one who copped it, you certainly can't blame him. So you'll have to look elsewhere for your suspects. The sons he abandoned don't fit the part.'

While this interview was going on, Derrymore had turned his attention to the side of the room that apparently belonged to Justin. After opening a cupboard filled with clothes, some of them expensive, he'd occupied himself with the crowded desk. Putting aside a photograph of several pretty girls, he now brought Reynolds' attention to the papers he'd found.

As Reynolds moved over to look, Justin was galvanized into action. Pushing past the two officers, he went to stand by the desk, spreading his arms out protectively. 'That's my stuff,' he said unnecessarily. 'I'll thank you to leave it alone.'

Reynolds didn't reply. Among the papers Derrymore had been trying to show him, something had caught his eye. At one side of the desk was a pile of hand printed prospectuses, the sort that small businesses published for local information. Half hidden by them was a pile of what looked like magazines but which turned out to be reports from various bigger, 'up-country' companies. The ones on top were glossy, the work of sophisticated publicity departments. Under them were files and reports, neatly stapled together. Attached to one was a list of names, handwritten in small, cramped letters, with telephone numbers beside them.

'These papers,' Reynolds said, running his finger over them. 'What are they about?'

Justin was sweating more than ever. Fear, Reynolds thought. He let his fingers run through the pages again. He felt the tension in the room, the sort he'd often noticed when about to make some discovery he hadn't anticipated.

'This company for example,' he peered at the heading where a logo was faintly visible. 'TIC. Any idea what it stands for?'

Justin began to hedge, at the same time trying to shuffle the papers out of sight. It wasn't important, just a company he was interested in – an awkward attempt to diffuse interest, almost pathetic, Reynolds thought. For a moment he was tempted to call Justin's bluff and take a handful of the papers away with him. But given his own semi-legal position, and the lack of a search warrant, he didn't want to force the issue, not yet. Although in most cases he'd ever dealt with, the vital piece of information often resulted from such trivial finds.

'Make a note of that name,' he said under his breath to Derrymore. Then, thanking Justin for his time and trouble, said they'd be in touch again.

On the way out he stopped. 'By the by, do you play cricket?'

Justin, whose expression had lightened considerably at the prospect of their leaving, looked positively aghast.

'Cricket?' he stammered, 'Christ, no.' He managed a shaky laugh. 'Hated games as a kid and still do,' he said.

'I'm not sure I'd remember Justin,' Derrymore said as soon as they were outside. 'He looks much older than his brother. And he didn't remember me, just as well. What did you make of him?'

'His outburst against his father certainly was an eye opener,' Reynolds admitted. 'No one's mentioned he disliked him before, quite the opposite. And what he said about the "golden goose" makes sense of Mrs Gatterly's claim that he was "after something" – his father's money I presume. And some of the other things he let slip were interesting.'

Derrymore nodded. 'I reckon, except about the cricket, most of the time he was lying. I think he knew what his brother wanted to take from the house, searched Miss Linton's car, and then, when he didn't find it, fixed the brakes, to use his words. And he practically admitted he's got a motive to kill. Like I thought before, he could inherit millions. With Edmund dead,' he added, 'that leaves only Richard. Kill off Richard, and Justin's the sole heir.'

'You're guessing,' Reynolds' reproof was mild, the sort he was more used to hearing from Derrymore than the other way round. 'You've no proof.' He smiled. 'But my own guess, for what it's worth, is that Justin's no murderer. He's not above a little fiddle on the side, nothing more serious. I admit he seemed to know that the car had been tampered with, but, like Fletcher, he could have heard rumours. More to the point, if he did mess with the car, why, for God's sake, even admit looking at it? The same goes for the murder, why give us a motive that could incriminate himself? And if, as we suspect, the plans for the murder must have been laid long before the actual night it happened, mentioning an alibi for that same night is irrelevant, and could throw suspicion on him. He'd be better off not mentioning it at all. All of which makes me think he's either foolish, or innocent.'

Derrymore looked crestfallen. 'Well,' he said, recovering, 'I suppose he doesn't look the sort to tinker about with cars, or think up a murder. He's too lazy, I'd say.' He opened the car door. 'So we've wasted our time again.'

'No,' Reynolds said. 'On the contrary we've learned a lot. The quarrel, for example, is more serious than I thought, if both brothers are involved. And I'm intrigued by that company, TIC. That's something else to check out.

'And you can add who Richard was really waiting for,' he continued, 'and what his real game is. Because I think I've underestimated him as well.'

He climbed into the car, saying, 'Can you drop me off? I'd like to pay a visit to the hospital on the way back. See Audrey if I can. I'll collect my own car from the manor tomorrow. I presume it'll be safe there overnight.'

His grin hid his conviction that nothing at the manor was safe until victim and killer were identified.

Behind his closed door, Justin leaned his head back and shut his eyes. It wasn't just the effect of last night. God, he was thinking, how much do they know? And who put them on to me so fast? And aren't I the fool again to have admitted what I felt?

Ten to one it's Fletcher who has squealed, he thought, or Fletcher's fox-faced wife. Or baby Richard. Won't I clobber him if I get the chance. Always someone ratting, he thought savagely. Can't trust anyone. And any false

153

move now will blow the whole deal apart.

Watching behind the shabby curtains, he waited until the police car had driven off, then quickly dressed and shaved, even putting on a tie. It was still relatively early when he emerged from the building, unlocked his old car and drove away.

When he reached the place he was heading for, he stopped with a squeal of brakes and hurriedly backed out of sight. The building was a disused warehouse, about to be converted into flats according to his architect mate. He'd be amazed, as would the town authorities, to know what it was being used for today.

Justin only knew because he'd received an invitation, or rather, an invitation had been pushed under his door – by mistake, he was sure, probably a mix-up with names. It was to attend an impromptu meeting being held by Edmund's colleagues, in Edmund's memory.

The meeting was supposed to have started an hour ago. He could just imagine the effect when he made his appearance, the red faces of the committee, the embarrassment, when he strode down towards the speaker's platform without apology, without explanation. This wasn't any old general meeting, after all, this was a real high-class affair, all the bigwigs Edmund used to mention.

The chairman would call the meeting to order. Edmund had often described him. Small, dark, volatile, dressed always in a grey suit that gave the impression of mourning, he was commonly known as the brains behind the operation. The 'beef', as it were, lay with the extremists, the militants whose excesses he claimed he couldn't control.

'We're here,' this small dark man would say, whose articles to the newspapers about conservation of natural beauty spots and wild-life sanctuaries had won so much acclaim, 'to pay our respects to our brother-in-arms who lost his life so tragically.'

He would rattle on about Edmund's dedication, and loyalty, and honesty. But when it came to mentioning Edmund's 'sacrifice' and his 'giving up his life for the cause', it would be time for Justin to make his move.

Such platitudes wouldn't deceive Justin, or the militants. He imagined himself smiling and waving to them, a 'bigwig' himself for once, holding the outcome in the palm of his hand.

'My family and I,' he would begin, tall and good-looking in his own best suit, 'are touched by your dedication to my poor brother, although I understand that you don't have much affection for us.'

With this little joke he'd defuse any open hostility and prevent any interruptions such as scornful shouts and the more ominous drumming of sticks on the old work tops. He knew, again from his brother, how masterly the militants were at heckling.

'I can't speak for my family,' he imagined going on, 'but I speak for myself when I say your cause can be successful if I show you how!'

Sitting in his car in that sultry little square, with the rain clouds now unexpectedly looming, he almost heard the clapping break out among the handful of older members. And when the younger, wilder element shouted 'How?' then he'd tell them. Silence. Growing understanding. Tumult. Worth every penny, they'd say.

But suppose they didn't cheer and clap. That was what had caused him to sit here and have a little rethink. Suppose instead of acceptance and adulation they took the opposite tack.

'Cut the crap,' someone might bellow, while another, coming up close, might yell, 'Why should we believe you? Your family is shit.' Worse, a third might insist, 'Let's see the colour of the goods before you see our money.'

He imagined this last spoken by one of those thin intense people who dominated the movement these days. 'They're monsters,' Edmund had told him, caught between admiration and mistrust.

Faced with such opposition, how could he defend his position, say truthfully he couldn't actually produce at the moment, and even if he could, he was really more keen on negotiating the best price?

He began to sweat again, in his imagination seeing them crowd round him, like a pack of snarling dogs. He found he was gasping for air. And suppose the invitation hadn't reached him by mistake? Suppose they were on to him too, and the meeting was just a trick? Suppose Edmund, before his death, had already revealed what his own intentions were? That was something he hadn't considered before; it was on Edmund's *not* having said anything that he had pinned his hopes.

My God, he thought, suddenly realizing what a narrow escape he'd had, better not deal with them at all.

He put his foot down hard on the accelerator and skidded away from this danger to confront another elsewhere.

Chapter 13

The hospital was large, impersonal, gone the days of country hospitals where patients were cosseted and matrons kept order. Reynolds wandered along several long corridors before finding the right section. There a large nurse with a forbidding manner demanded what he wanted.

When he told her, she disappeared, returning to report that the policeman on duty had said 'Inspector Reynolds' should come ahead.

'Third door on the right,' she told him. 'She's heavily sedated still. Don't know when she'll really come round, so you may be wasting your time.'

The officer, sitting on a bench outside an observation window, jumped to attention. Reynolds' relief that Clemow was still having Audrey watched gave way to pleasure as he recognised a former colleague. 'So you're the reason why they let me come in so easily,' he said, remembering the man as a youngster at the time of his retirement. And when the policeman tactfully offered to take a half hour break in the hospital canteen he accepted gladly. He preferred to have the actual moment of meeting take place without official observers.

Steeling himself to be shocked by his ex-wife's condition, face swathed in bandages, bed surrounded by pulleys and tubes, he opened the door.

The room was darkened, the only light came from

the window opening on to the corridor. The figure on the bed lay still. But there were no disfiguring bandages, just a covering of a small head wound, probably caused by glass, and a series of tubes attached to steel poles, dripping discreetly. Whatever injuries she'd had must be all internal, hidden, like her own life now.

He could find all about her condition if he wanted by asking, or there was a chart at the foot of the bed, if he could understand its medical jargon. It seemed too much like prying. Instead he took a seat at some distance from the bed and watched.

She was pale, her flesh almost transparent, and she appeared strangely thin. For a moment he wondered if she really were alive. Then her steady breathing reassured him, and a green light from some machine to which she was attached glowed comfortingly in the semi-dark. He remembered a day early in their marriage before it had gone sour. He had come home one evening, in the dark, to find her asleep like this, on a sofa in a cold, fireless room. The noise of his key had awakened her; she'd started up, her face as white as the one on the pillow. 'Johnny, is that you?' she'd cried and he could hear the panic in her voice.

She had clung to him. He still remembered how he had had to disentangle himself from her clutch. He had relaid the fire while she crouched on her heels and watched him, rocking herself to and fro. It was the first time she'd made him feel how much she depended on him. And the first time he'd known guilt.

It was peaceful in this room, a kind of cocooned security, no decisions to be made, no effort, the strange and disturbing interviews he had had today seeming of little consequence, even the questions he had so wanted to ask her suddenly unimportant.

The figure on the bed stirred; he half rose, then as

she slept again sank back in his chair. He had spent a lifetime, he was thinking, of watching people who'd been injured or killed by the hatred of others, of assessing the damage done by hate or cruelty or greed, of trying, usually too late, to stop further damage. What made people want to kill and destroy?

He thought, too, of poor Mazie Derrymore – what made someone want to frighten her? Was frightening as bad as trying to kill, or actually killing? The law distinguished between murder and murderous intent, but what about the many fine differences among all the secret neuroses, the twisted malices that turned spite on others? Who legislated against them?

A slight tap at the door broke into his thoughts. He glanced at his watch. The half hour wasn't up but the officer was back then. As he rose to leave, half sorry not to have spoken to his ex-wife, half glad he hadn't had to, a strangely garbed figure came into the room, almost as tall as he was with a hood drawn over its face like a monk's cowl.

'Are you Audrey's ex-husband?' The voice was decisive, harsh. A woman's voice.

'Who are you?' he asked, startled. He found instinctively he had taken up a defensive attitude beside the bed as if he expected the woman to pounce on him, or even attack Audrey.

Her laugh was low and genuine. 'I'm not armed,' she said. 'And I'm certainly not here to do Audrey harm. I'm . . .' she hesitated, then said firmly, 'Audrey's special friend.'

She stressed the word just as Audrey had done. Of course, he thought, the friend whose advice she took, preferring it to mine. He gazed at the woman, wishing he could see her face, and realized she was gazing at him as intently. Here's a weird situation, he thought, the two of us eyeing each other over my ex-wife's inert body, as if, the thought was ironic, we're both about to make a grab for it, two children squabbling over a doll.

'How do you know who I am?' he asked.

'I've been waiting.' Her answer was surprisingly practical. 'If you were as she described you, you'd be bound to turn up sooner or later. I got your name from the duty nurse just now.' For the first time she looked at the patient. 'How is she?'

'Coming along well, I'd say.' Reynolds tried to sound positive, but in truth he wasn't sure how she was. 'Is this your first visit?'

'They wouldn't let me in earlier. And I suppose I didn't think it would be safe.'

She said this so calmly that again he was startled. 'Why?' he asked.

She didn't answer.

'Safe for you or for her?'

'Her, of course.'

She bent over the bed. She didn't say any more but as she straightened up, he caught a glimpse of her face. She was ugly, with small head and wrinkled neck, but it was the expression that struck him, misery nakedly revealed. She looks like I used to feel, he thought. And she wants something from me. God knows what Audrey's told her.

'I need your help,' she said suddenly and abrasively, as if she wasn't used to asking for help from anyone, let alone a man. 'We're in trouble, Audrey and me. I had a phone call last night. Threatening to kill me.'

She said this calmly but he guessed she'd been shocked. And he sensed something more than the threat was troubling her, something else which she was keeping hidden. He couldn't help contrasting her restraint with Mrs Gatterly's hysteria.

At this point there was a masculine cough outside the room and the policeman passed in front of the window. She spun round in alarm.

'It's all right,' Reynolds found himself saying. 'He's on duty here. Hold on a moment, while I talk to him.'

He went outside, to explain the woman's presence, and when he'd given her a few minutes on her own with Audrey, stuck his head back in and without directly looking at her suggested they go somewhere in the hospital to talk.

'No,' she said, 'I don't want to be seen if I can avoid it. Certainly not with you. The last thing I want is to give the impression I've come running to the police.'

'So you haven't informed them about the threat. Was that sensible?'

'Yes. Under the circumstances, I think so.' She rose from the chair she had pulled beside the bed, wrapped the cloak about her. 'But that's why I must speak to you.'

Not as much as I want to speak to you, he thought. 'I'll leave now,' he told her. 'Give me five minutes, then follow. There's a kind of covered terrace that runs the length of the hospital, where cars pull up. I'll be standing by the taxi rank.'

A thought struck him. 'I don't have a car with me, do you?'

'I don't drive,' she said. The firmness had come back into her voice.

Not 'can't drive', he noted, 'don't'. This isn't a woman who relies on public transport, he thought. The image of chauffeurs and limousines suddenly came to him. 'I'll be in a taxi then,' he said. 'As good a place as any. I'll wait until you come.'

And again tactfully he withdrew, explaining to the officer that he'd vouch for her, and leaving her to make her farewells in her own way and time.

Downstairs, in the open, he was surprised at the daylight, although the drizzle that had been threatening had already started. Sitting in that darkened room he'd lost contact with time. As he strolled along the covered walkway where a few patients lingered and visitors came and went, fortunately a taxi drew up, one of the older models with a glass partition between driver and passenger. He got in and sat back, scrutinizing anyone who came near. Everybody looked perfectly harmless and yet something of the woman's caution had communicated itself to him. No one approached until she did. When she had settled herself and her extraordinary flowing garment, he told the driver to pull up a few yards along the road and wait. Then he shut the partition firmly.

'Now then, can you remember exactly what the message said?' he asked.

Folding her arms she recited bleakly, '"If you don't give us what we want you'll end up like Audrey. Dead or in hospital. And your gallery will be destroyed."'

He made no comment on the personal threat, decided he might as well come bluntly to what primarily interested him. 'I presume,' he said, 'that what they want is something Miss Linton is supposed to have been given by Edmund Gatterly.' He felt her tense at the mention of Edmund's name. 'You've no idea what it is?' he pressed her. 'You know of course he's dead.'

'You don't have to remind me,' she cried, he thought angrily. 'His murder's been on the news, non-stop. And of course Audrey told me how he'd been killed the night that they met. But . . .'

She swallowed the end of her sentence. He guessed she was about to say, 'But Audrey didn't tell me he'd given her anything,' except she found it too painful to admit. So Audrey hasn't changed so much after all, he thought. Even a special friend can be cheated on. Once again he wondered what it was about Edmund Gatterly that made her remain loyal to him.

'Suppose Edmund gave her some work of art,' he said, 'say a painting. What would she do with it?'

He watched closely for any sign of reaction, but she said merely that anything intended to be sold on would be listed in a log book. 'There wasn't any such listing the next morning,' she told him. 'Mind you, I left early for my studio.'

Perhaps Audrey meant to keep it secret. 'Did you recognize the voice?' he asked, and when she shook her head, 'Would you at least recognize it another time?'

'I'm not sure. There was a lot of noise. It was . . .' she hesitated, 'muffled,' she said, 'as if it was disguised.'

'Do you remember the time?'

Her reply that she wasn't sure, she hadn't looked at a clock and she never wore a watch, wasn't helpful.

'It's important,' he persisted.

'I had guests that night, one of them answered the phone. He might remember if I ask him.'

'Did you go back to the gallery yourself, between ten and eleven o'clock say?'

She shook her head. 'No, certainly not. I was hostessing a party for a large number of people at that time.'

'Could anyone else have got in, a mutual friend for example?'

'Why these questions?' she asked sharply.

'I rang the gallery just before eleven. Somebody picked up the phone and immediately put it down again. If my call was around the same time as you got yours, we might be able to trace it from the phone in the gallery.'

'Or pinpoint exactly when someone was there who

shouldn't have been,' she said even more sharply.

Their eyes met at last in understanding.

'If you haven't called the police and if you're not going to,' he said, 'you ought to see what's happened at the gallery. There may be clues.' He didn't have to add, 'Or damage.' But he did say, 'I could go for you. There's no need for you to accompany me, you know, if I could just have a key. Save me breaking in, at least.'

He waited to see how she would react and was relieved when she gave a half smile. 'Someone might notice you,' she said.

He felt himself grin back. 'Well, believe it or not, I've had some practice at coming and going so people don't notice.'

He could feel her debating with herself. 'Better I come too,' she said with some asperity, which didn't hide the relief at his offer. 'I might spot things that you wouldn't.'

While Reynolds opened the partition to give the driver directions for St Ives, she settled herself back again, with a firmness which he had to admire.

But as they drove through the wet twilight, she suddenly burst out, 'I don't care for my own safety. And why should I care that Audrey met a man secretly? But I do feel responsible for her accident. I've come to realize that what I said to her put her in the path of a killer. And so did you. If there's blame, we share it.'

Her logic defeated him but it seemed to satisfy her.

'I advised her to go back to the manor,' she added, as if in explanation. 'I don't know what your reasons were, but mine were partly selfish. I didn't want disgrace to touch our gallery. I wanted to minimize the effect. I didn't even think much about the victim, and I was angry with Audrey.'

She said these last things calmly, accepting them.

When he didn't comment, she went on. 'You do realize,'

she persisted, for the first time her voice bitter, 'she might have been killed.'

'There wouldn't be an officer on watch,' he reassured her, more gently than he'd usually sound, 'if the police didn't think the crash was deliberately engineered.'

They had come to the end of their drive now and were turning towards the windswept harbour, moving very slowly while their driver waited for directions. Sending him to amuse himself for an hour or so, they approached the gallery on foot.

They entered through the main doorway, and it was immediately apparent that someone had broken in. The lights had been fused, and glass was scattered on the floor to the rear of the gallery, from a small window leading directly to a cobbled patio, easily accessible over a neighbouring wall. Beside it, wrapped in newspaper, lay the brick that had broken the glass.

In the gallery itself, only the paintings in the main window seemed untouched, possibly because they were easily identifiable from the street, or possibly because the intruder was afraid of being seen. All the rest, the elegant arrangement he had admired, had been torn off the walls. Some had even been ripped out of their frames and tossed in a haphazard heap. Not a normal robbery then, he thought, as he struggled to separate and set them upright without disturbing possible fingerprints. The intruder had been looking for something. But the job was unfinished.

Wondering why, he remembered his own phone call. Could that have been the cause? Had the intruder lifted the receiver to stop the noise, then panicked and left?

Apart from this observation, his immediate reaction, like the woman's (it came to him that he didn't know her name and she certainly hadn't volunteered it) was to find some reason why certain pictures had been discarded and others closely examined. Using a torch (he always carried a flashlight with him) he began to sort through the canvases, difficult to do in the dark.

The woman tried to help him. He asked if she noticed any pattern to the original search, for example had it been made by artist, or style, even subject matter?

'Most of the paintings are abstracts,' she told him somewhat sharply, stopping that line of logic. 'And I've no idea why they've been cut from their frames except to make them easier to carry away. But as far as I can tell nothing has been taken.'

Afraid of doing more damage if they pulled the canvases about any more, they then went upstairs, expecting to find it much as normal. Instead, they found total devastation. Even in the torchlight, the destruction was clear and alarming.

Thank God no one was actually in the flat, was Reynolds' first thought as he moved from living room to bedrooms. There was something dreadfully ruthless about the way furniture and belongings had been thrown about and then systematically smashed, as if in a wild frenzy. He was puzzled why neighbours hadn't heard the noise, then noticed that the crowbar which had done the damage had been covered with cloth. The frenzy, then, had been premeditated, and controlled.

She walked behind him, wrapping her cloak closely round her as if she was cold. If I'm remembering what the place used to look like, he thought suddenly, what must she be thinking? This was her home, she helped create this. But she said nothing. Once more he sensed the struggle within her, and admired the restraint.

When they had picked their way from one end of the flat to the other, she straightened up, her arms on her ample hips, looking round her just like a fisherwoman, he thought, ready to do battle. He guessed she was already planning what could be salvaged and what must be discarded, was steeling herself to start afresh. Her spunk, that was the word, impressed him.

'Those pictures in the front window,' he said suddenly. 'Let's go down and check them over.' He gave a grin. 'Better to be thorough,' he said.

She stood holding the torch while he clambered up and across the wide sill of the window and began the task of removing the paintings from their stands. The pictures themselves were large, heavy; he remembered looking at them from the street the first morning. Carefully he removed each one and lifted it down so she could examine it more closely. Finally there was only one left, another large abstract. He lifted it – to find something underneath, a much smaller canvas, tucked out of sight.

'Here's what we're looking for,' he told her without hesitation. Whoever would put one painting on top of another, except to hide the under one? He ripped off the tape that held it in place and handed it to her.

It was small, not heavy, easily carried under one arm. Climbing back down into the room he held the torch while she studied it.

To his immense disappointment it was an old-fashioned oil, rather nondescript and dark, framed in what looked like a gilt-edged wooden frame.

'I've never seen it before,' his companion proclaimed. 'It's not the sort of thing we usually sell.'

She turned the painting over. Its wooden back was bare, slightly dusty. A label gave what was presumably the title, something Valley or Wood, he thought. The writing was badly faded and he couldn't tell from looking at the front exactly what was depicted.

'Typical early Victorian,' she said coldly, wiping her fingers on her cloak. 'Perhaps a little earlier. Never heard of the artist, probably some home-painted thing by an amateur. Nothing special. Certainly not valuable.'

Damn, he thought. There goes a pet theory. He sensed disappointment, too, in her voice. Perhaps like him she had been hoping for some forgotten masterpiece, a Rembrandt, or Vermeer at least, which would have made some sense of Edmund's actions. But why had Audrey thought it so important that she'd hidden it?

'I'll keep it if I may,' he said. She nodded, he thought dispiritedly. As they restored the window display, he asked her suddenly if any of the gallery's paintings were hers. When she nodded, he looked at her once more in amazement. And not a word, he thought, not a sign that her own work had been ravaged. His admiration for her grew.

After he had found nails and a hammer and at her request boarded up the back window, he let them out and stood on the pavement by the front door, thinking she can't stay here. And she's right, it won't be safe for her anywhere, not even in her own studio, wherever that is. The man who did this means business.

'You can't go home,' he said, anxiety making him stern. 'Do you have a friend you could doss down with?' She didn't answer. 'What about a hotel?'

'I'd prefer a hotel,' she said. 'You could drop me at one I know on your way back. I could stay there for a few days. I often go there to paint. I'm not in the habit of running away,' she added fiercely. 'But I didn't imagine . . .' Her voice trailed off, uncharacteristically.

He guessed she had been about to say that she hadn't imagined the destruction would be so total, so devastating, so absolute. He was wrong.

'I didn't imagine you'd be so helpful,' she finished.

Not a man, he thought, not Audrey's ex-husband, and

an ex-police officer at that. He took what she said for a
compliment.

They weren't attacked or mugged on the way to the
taxi, and they found it waiting where the driver had
said he'd be, the ticking meter running into real money
now and the driver looking very pleased with his night's
work. They took the fast road back towards Truro, and
after a series of diversions to make sure they weren't
being followed, they reached a small hotel, which by its
isolated location deep in the countryside must have been
known to very few people. And no doubt correspondingly
expensive.

'They know me here,' she told Reynolds as he
accompanied her to the front entrance and waited for
the door to be opened. 'And I know them. They lock
everything up at dark, but someone is always on duty
to let latecomers in. I'll be fine here.'

She had uncovered her head completely, and her black
hair, cut mannishly short as if deliberately to emphasize
the smallness of the head, was now covered with
raindrops. In the light from the door lamp, her dark
eyes glistened with intelligence. 'If anything happens,
I'll be in touch.' And then, as if it was the last thing she
was revealing, 'Naomi's the name.'

The door opened and a man, Reynolds presumed the
hotel owner, greeted her effusively. Just as the taxi was
turning round, she called out something. He rolled down
the window to hear her say, 'If we need watching, I mean
privately, I can pay you for your help. From both of us.'
Then she and the owner turned and went indoors and
the door closed. He heard the lock click.

Another wealthy client, he thought, as the taxi
continued its way towards St Breddaford. Suddenly
my path's paved by wealthy women clamouring for
protection, positively eager to pour cash into my lap.

He had to laugh. But it was the difference between the first offer and the second that impressed him. And suddenly he realized that he liked Naomi very much.

Earlier that evening, just as the rain started, Richard had gone aboard an old boat with his new friend. The boat was moored by the river bank, upstream from the former manor grounds, and had been left there to rot. Now, with the tide still low, it rested on a sort of cradle of broken wooden stays which kept it upright when there was little water.

His friend, whose name was Sybil but whose father called her simply 'child', preferred to be known as Syb. She was leaning over the scuppers, dragging at a fishing line. The timber was so rotten that if she pushed against the railing, bits dropped off and rested on the mud, or sank under it with a horrid sort of gurgle. But in the main stream, what was left of it, there might be fish and more would come as the tide turned and brought them up the estuary.

Although Syb passionately loved all animals, and wanted to protect them, she liked fishing. She threw out a line baited with bread pellets, a trick she'd learned long ago from Edmund, although Edmund had given up fishing himself. She didn't tell Richard that, and she didn't tell him that she had liked Edmund better than anyone else she'd ever known, so much so that when she was younger she had trailed behind him like a lovesick puppy. Of course she'd outgrown that phase but still at times the memory lingered.

Fishing was a patient sort of occupation, and when she wanted she could be patient. Waiting for things to happen. Like now.

'I'm a Cornish Aborigine,' she'd told Richard once when he'd complained how dull life was. 'I'm prehistoric. I can let flies walk on my naked eyeballs and never flinch.'

She'd stared him down.

'You've no concept of such things,' she said.

Richard had gone below deck, where the planking was riddled with so many holes she was surprised the boat ever stayed afloat at high water. He told her that if he trod cautiously along the main ribs he could move about in relative safety but she had no intention of going below just so he could show how clever he was.

Richard had claimed he'd made a momentous discovery. He was fond of momentous discoveries; since she'd known him there had been several. This time it was an old rusting engine. She grimaced. All afternoon he had been trying, without success, to see if he could start it, although as she had already pointed out, probably if he did the whole contraption would shudder apart.

'I know all about engines,' he'd told her angrily, 'so leave me alone.'

All very well, my fine fellow, she thought, but even if you could get it to start, where would it take us?

He emerged from the waterlogged bowels of the ship with his hands and face liberally smeared with oil and grease.

'Don't come close to me, you smell like a sewer,' she told him. 'And if you really want an engine, better spend your energy in getting your dad to buy you summat new that works.'

She knew Richard didn't like her references to his dad's money; that's why she spoke of it so often. He thought she was sneering at him, and so he told her now. It made her laugh. 'Not all of us worship money,' she taunted him. 'We're not like you Yanks.'

'Your mother's as American as mine,' he countered, in the superior way he had sometimes. 'And she and my mother are from the south while Yanks are from the north. So you're wrong twice.'

She hauled in her line without speaking. It came up coated with sticky black mud that stuck to her hands and arms and clothes.

'Talk about mess,' he said disagreeably, 'and talk about smell.' He held his nose.

He's disappointed about the engine not working, she thought.

Syb's relationship, she didn't use the word 'friendship', with Richard Gatterly was dicey, to put it mildly. She didn't like him much. But she needed him, so she had to humour him. That was the way most men were handled, most men she'd ever met, that is, even his half-brothers, needing instant gratification. Men have to be indulged, she thought, coaxed. Only when they're thoroughly malleable can you introduce the idea you've been hanging on to and sit back while they snap it up like a fish taking a pellet. It was so easy, so predictable, once you knew the trick.

She'd heard about Richard long before she met him. When the Gatterlys had first come back to Cornwall, he'd been carefully kept apart from the 'natives'; sent off to boarding school (which he claimed he hated – who wouldn't?) and in the holidays carted off abroad. He said it was his mother's way of insulating them from the shock of living in England, but Syb suspected he said that to impress.

'I don't like foreigners,' she'd told him in retaliation when they'd first come upon each other the previous Easter. She'd looked at him coldly, assessing him. 'They don't talk like us. And most of them look alike. I can't tell one from 'tother.' That'd teach him to try and impress.

From that inauspicious beginning their acquaintance

had grown at remarkable speed, thanks mainly to her contrivance. Although he was not to know that. And only of course when he was here. If Richard had not been obliged to return because of his half-brother's death she probably wouldn't have seen him this holiday, and she suspected that he wouldn't have cared one way or the other. She, on the other hand, cared very much, but not for any reason he could possibly imagine. And although they were inseparable these days, she still held him at a distance. She knew what she wanted out of him and how to get it, but it entailed keeping the upper hand somehow. That meant being as waspish as possible when the occasion demanded.

'Your yapping doesn't help my fishing,' she snapped now. 'Make yourself useful. Light the fire before the rain gets everything wet, if you can manage matches, that is.'

She knew he couldn't stand being told what to do. Well, neither could she. But she had come to realize that faced with things that were strange to him, like being on a Cornish river in the rain, he could be led by her, baffled as it were, by her superior knowledge. And if his interest could be roused there was nothing much he wouldn't try, just for the heck of it. Two useful bits of information, typical, she knew, of his Zodiac sign.

Without letting him see, she watched him watching her. He's thinking it out, she thought. Do as I say, collect wood to make a fire (he has a fresh box of matches in his jeans pocket). Or refuse, tell me to go light it myself. And then I'll have to show him who's boss, tell him to clear off, and leave me alone. But he won't want to clear off yet.

Not because of the fish or fire, of course, but for the something else she'd given him, the something she suspected, for all his boasting, was really new to him.

And which she'd made sure once he'd tried he'd never give up wanting again.

He didn't move, but he didn't actually refuse either. After a while he said, 'That inspector chap who was here this morning, Inspector Reynolds or some such, he's not a bad fellow. My mother says he writes detective stories. Set in St Breddaford.'

'The more fool he,' she retorted. 'And you be careful. He's smarter than you think.' She broke off a piece of bread from the stale loaf beside her and dipped it in the water before rolling it into a ball and baiting the hook. She always used bread for bait, she'd told him when he'd asked. 'I like things that work, things you can use and see results.' He hadn't argued with her over that. But he did argue now about the inspector.

'He played cricket with me,' he told her. 'I said I was going to be in the school team, and I was waiting for Justin. And he believed every word.' He looked at her expectantly.

He's waiting for me to say how clever he is, she thought. 'And what else did you tell him?' she asked coldly. Although the idea of Justin playing games with Richard made her want to laugh. She couldn't believe what Richard said next.

Smirking a little, he explained in detail how he'd hinted he'd seen Justin looking at the red Rover, the car the woman had driven into the hedge.

She rounded on him then. 'Blabber mouth,' she told him trembling with real fury. 'Reynolds isn't that dumb. Why did you tell him that?'

Richard answered in a superior voice, 'He's just a village bobby. And I thought it'd be amusing.'

His stupidity was amazing. Thinking he was so smart, never seeing danger. Why, he'd disregarded her whole plan just for a moment's glory.

Dropping her line, she launched herself at him. As he staggered back under her weight, she hit him with both fists, as hard as she could, and he went down with an almighty crash that shook the boat from stern to prow and sent bigger bits of wood into the water. Before she could jump out of the way, he hooked his leg round hers so that she too came falling to the deck. Twisting and turning, she fought to get free of him, at the same time pushing him towards the gap in the railing.

They went over the side together, only breaking free when they hit the surface. The water was shallow, but the mud beneath was thick. She felt him cough and retch as he struggled to his knees, while she caught hold of a dangling rope to pull herself round the stern into the deeper current.

'Bugger off,' she wheezed. 'For heaven's sake, leave me alone.' And then seeing his face as he stood floundering on the bank with the mud all about him and the water running in dark rivulets down his face, she began to laugh.

'You could have drowned us,' he cried. 'What did you do that for?'

'Why not?' she said, pushing back her hair and beginning to peel off her clothes, throwing them with careless abandon towards the shore. 'It'd be a new experience, wouldn't it? Something to look forward to.'

She stood there naked, and again began to laugh, until he had to laugh as well, the summer rain making splashes all about them, which fish might mistake for flies.

As if knowing what he was thinking, she beckoned. He ran towards her, the rain splashing his body making little silver darts, while she showed him how splendidly, wildly naked she was, her pendulous breasts swinging, her massive thighs blue with cold and streaked with mud.

Later, when they'd lit a fire with extra matches she had, she returned to the river edge to gut the fish she'd caught. The tide was already coming in fast now, a line of bubbles out in the main race. Already the boat was clear of the mud and hung in its wooden cradle with its prow turning towards the bank. She stood by the water, lifting her face as if drinking in the rain, wrapping her hair round her throat. Then, still holding the bloody knife, she began to dance, tossing her head and howling out strange words in a strange tongue. And suddenly she was more than just a country girl, daughter of someone who worked for Richard's father.

Chapter 14

It was long past midnight when Reynolds returned from seeing Naomi to her hotel, too late to ring Derrymore or the incident room with his findings. Early tomorrow he'd persuade Naomi to let him tell them, and then allow him and Derrymore into the gallery. Surely the intruder would have left traces somewhere.

Who the intruder was he had no idea, except he must be linked somehow to the murder – and immediately Justin's name sprang to mind. Perhaps that's what he had been doing last night . . . although again somehow the image of Justin as a frenzied attacker didn't really fit.

Expecting to be kept awake half the night with these new preoccupations, he surprised himself by sleeping like a log and waking only when the alarm went off. The rain had gone; instead there was a good Cornish wind but the sun was out. He found he was whistling as he shaved. He'd just poured his first cup of tea when the doorbell rang. Derrymore, looking harassed.

Not another anonymous letter for his mam, Reynolds thought, beckoning him inside and slipping in an extra bag to make the tea strong, hoping Derrymore wouldn't comment on his sloppy housekeeping. Derrymore was too preoccupied to notice.

'You'd better come quick,' he said, putting the mug down untasted. 'I've been up to the manor, and there's hell to pay. First, from St Ives, a neighbour reports seeing two people last night near the Linton gallery. Acting funny. Later, she hears breaking glass and when at her insistence the local police go round, sure enough there's glass on the ground and other signs of break-in. The neighbour's a typical busybody,' he went on. 'Claims she wasn't surprised. Complains there's always wild parties at weekends, and the gallery is a cover for a spy ring! But when questioned hasn't a clue who actually lives there, except she's seen a well-dressed woman and what she calls a "freak" coming and going at all hours. And if that isn't enough,' he added gloomily before Reynolds could set things straight, 'Joe Fletcher turned up with an equally wild story. Pushed his way in to see Clemow, shouting at the top of his lungs. Brought the Gatterlys out in a rush, I'll tell you. They said Mrs G the second gave him a good blasting, but it didn't shut him up.'

Reynolds listened while Derrymore explained how Fletcher claimed he was there at Miss Trewithen's insistence, had actually driven to Truro for her first thing, in the Rolls, to find Justin. Not that he had actually admitted using the Gatterlys' car, but as she didn't drive and neither of them owned a vehicle, he must have done. And how on hearing that, Barbs Gatterly had screamed, 'I didn't buy a Rolls to have that woman use it as a taxi cab,' or words to that effect.

'As for poor Oliver Gatterly, felt right sorry for him,' the sergeant continued. 'Caught in the middle, red-handed like, between his present wife and his ex-wife's mouthpiece, standing there in his pj's, ruby-coloured, satin. Made you want to laugh. When Mrs G turned on him, she didn't mince words, I'd say. Even Clemmie couldn't shut her up, and you know what he's like, pussy-footing round the ladies.'

Recollecting that that wasn't perhaps the wisest

comment for a mere sergeant to make about his superior, he went on to explain that in the end Fletcher won. The Gatterlys withdrew in confusion while Fletcher was left still insisting Clemow take him seriously.

'What on earth did he want?'

'Justin,' Derrymore said simply. 'As if he thought the Gatterlys had had him for breakfast. Miss Trewithen thinks he's gone missing. He's not at his flat, Fletcher checked there.'

Reynolds gave a start. My God, he thought, dismayed. And then, before he could stop the thought, why has his mother drawn attention to his disappearance – unless embarrassing the police, or more likely the Gatterlys is too strong to resist. He kept his thoughts to himself.

'And what do you make of the whole thing?' he asked.

Derrymore shook his head. 'Justin was asleep about noon yesterday. His chum, the architect, swears he'd gone by late afternoon when he himself returned. Seems he's been working in an art shop to earn a little cash, which I'd say is better than old Justin, lolling in bed at all hours!'

Reynolds had never heard Derrymore so critical. Taking Miss Trewithen's insults into consideration, and remembering Derrymore's own hardworking background, he wasn't surprised.

'We may be the last people to have seen Justin,' Derrymore continued. 'And when Clemow heard that, he was furious. I suppose he didn't know for sure that we'd been there, which put him in a fix. Couldn't say we had gone without his knowledge. Couldn't blame us if we had. Anyway, according to Fletcher, Miss Trewithen's got the wind up good and proper. Fletcher himself told Clemmie that if he was supposed to have put a police guard on the Gatterlys, why wasn't Justin included? "It's his brother who was murdered," he said dourly. "So why waste money on the murderers?"' Derrymore whistled. 'Mind you, he's only saying what Miss Trewithen told him to, but that doesn't alter the situation.'

'And Clemow's response?'

Now Derrymore grinned. 'Clemow points out that people go missing every day yet turn up safe and sound. The police can't put a search warrant out for a man who's only disappeared for a few hours, and anyway the most likely explanation is he's sleeping off another drunken binge somewhere. "I'm to tell you this," Fletcher says, standing like a ramrod. And bless me if he didn't spout off something. Let me see if I can remember it.' He frowned with concentration. '"I had an Edmund and a Richard killed him", something like that. Followed by a long list of killings and names of people who were supposed to have killed them. What on earth did he mean by that, sir?'

'More misquotes from Shakespeare, I'd say.'

'Anyway, I think the quotations just about finished Clemow,' Derrymore concluded. 'But if Justin has disappeared, could it be he's done a runner? I had my suspicions about him yesterday.'

'Could be.' Reynolds was noncommittal. 'So what happened in the end?'

Derrymore looked even more harassed. 'After Clemow promised he'd look into it, Fletcher left. Then Clemow himself went ape, baying for our blood, I'm afraid. So I skipped off to fetch you while he cooled down. But,' he hesitated, 'I get the impression he's not so happy with us being on the case.'

'That's the understatement of the year.' Reynolds' retort was rueful. He gulped his tea, pulled on tie and jacket and got himself out of the house. When Clemmie finds out what I was doing last night, he thought as he folded his lanky frame into the Panda, he'll go more than ape. And at the moment, that means unfortunately we've two emergencies: Justin Gatterly's whereabouts and Chief Inspector Clemow's state of mind.

En route to the manor, Reynolds found the opportunity to recount the story of his strange meeting of the previous evening, and the finding of the painting. 'I've stowed it away at home,' he concluded. 'We'll ask the Gatterlys about it. I suppose it might have some family significance. As for the neighbour, if she heard anything, it must have been me, nailing up the broken window.'

Derrymore concentrated on his driving. 'You're sure of that, sir?' he asked diffidently. 'I mean, this Naomi character sounds really weird. And the mysterious phone call sounds fishy. She might have smashed the place herself out of jealousy or something, and then having dragged you in means to let you shoulder the blame like your . . . well, cause more trouble,' he ended lamely.

Reynolds sighed to himself. Like your ex-wife, Derrymore meant. And he had a valid point. But what might be true of Audrey didn't have to be true of her friend. Naomi had more or less admitted she had reason to distrust Audrey yet bore her no ill will, and in her restrained way she had shown how fond she still was of the younger woman. She seemed genuine, both in her explanations and in her acknowledgement of his help at the gallery.

Of course it was possible, as Derrymore suggested, that she was furious with Audrey and wanted to get her own back. She certainly made no bones about what she thought of men. A real hornet's nest you've stirred up for me, old son, he thought, irritated. The irritation was at himself. If Naomi had meant to deceive him, she'd certainly succeeded. But he didn't want to believe it. Although there was no proof, either way.

'I'll get in touch with Naomi,' he said at last. 'Explain the situation, see what's best to do. In any case, we'd better call off the St Ives police for the moment, can't have them blundering about wrecking clues.'

And as Derrymore busied himself with the phone, when Clemow learns we've interfered with the St Ives branch, he told himself, there's another nail in our coffin.

The manor and its surroundings looked unusually peaceful in the morning sun, whatever chaos, professional and domestic, Fletcher had stirred up. Just as Reynolds was about to comment on this to Derrymore, as if to give the lie to his impression the front door burst open. A group of officers came rushing out, followed by Clemow. Some ran to the side of the house, past the batting nets where the path towards the river started; others took to their cars. As Clemow passed, he rolled down his window and shouted. The wind blew most of his words away, but they caught 'Justin' very clearly, and 'I blame you for this'.

'Something's up,' Derrymore said, staring. 'Never seen the old so-and-so move so quick.'

Reynolds felt his skin prick as it always did when things began to happen. He jumped from the car before it had come to a standstill and ran towards the open door where Oliver Gatterly had appeared, still dressed in his satin pyjamas. His face had a stunned look, as if he'd had a body blow and when Reynolds asked what was the matter, he simply shook his head as if he couldn't speak. It was the duty officer left behind who told them, as, joined by Derrymore, the three of them attempted to coax Mr Gatterly back inside.

'A car,' the officer said tersely, 'caught in the mud. Just been spotted. Down towards Bodinnick. Our side of the river. Wasn't there yesterday,' he shouted as

Reynolds raced back to the Panda. 'Must have happened between the tides.'

'Pilltown way, I imagine, the river's deeper there.'

Derrymore spun the wheel, straining to remember the topography of an area he'd once known like the back of his hand. 'Best take the logging track again,' he told Reynolds. 'Hold tight.'

This time he had no hesitation about where to turn. They bounced over the same rough track to the parking place. Fletcher wasn't watching them from the river bank today, and the path through the woods, taken by the rider on horseback, was empty. They ran, not even stopping when Reynolds pointed mutely to the circle of trampled grass and pile of horse droppings, almost washed away by last night's rain, close enough to Fetcher's ditch to suggest the chat between him and rider must have been lengthy.

Through the branches they caught glimpses of the river, brown, fast-flowing after the rain, the sheen of mud just showing where the tide was draining out, like bath water pouring through the hole when the plug has been pulled.

Reynolds could hear his own heart pounding and in front of him Derrymore was already beginning to wheeze. A big man, Derrymore, built for wrestling, not for long-distance sprinting, yet he'd go until he dropped. By now they knew they were ahead of the officers on foot; they could hear them far behind. Derrymore had been right about this, too; this route was quicker. Derrymore might be right about many things. Even Naomi. Even Justin.

Ahead of them the trees began to thin. The path went uphill here, across a stile into pasture, but they kept to the banks. At high water this would have proved difficult as the river reached the tree roots but now with an outgoing tide a series of large rocks provided them with easy stepping stones. They reached the little old jetty almost at the same time as the official cars drew up and Clemow got out to take charge.

Seeing them, his mouth turned down and he lowered his head. Reynolds almost expected him to howl at them to clear off. But he didn't. Like Reynolds himself, his attention seemed riveted on the flat mud bar appearing before them, each lap of the river uncovering more grey expanse, along with the mud-encased outline of a car, as if it had dived head first into deep water and was stuck on the bottom.

A group of people had gathered: the fisherman who had originally spotted the set of tyre marks, still plainly visible in the wet ground on the bank; the cottage owner from the village, whose phone had been used to dial 999 when the shape of a car first appeared; the neighbours who had heard the commotion, all of whom swore they hadn't heard a car go by last night or any sound when it hit the water.

'Must have been last night,' everyone insisted, as they waited for a breakdown truck to drag the vehicle out. 'High tide was after seven. Must have missed his way in the dark, poor sod.'

Missed his way perhaps, Reynolds thought. But surely Justin would know all these roads along the river, unless he was drunk. And if a car freewheeled down the hill it would have gone over the bank with an almighty splash. His attempts to examine the marks left on the mud were interrupted by the recovery efforts, as the heavy ropes attached to the car groaned and the truck took the strain, its wheels skidding slightly in the soft ground.

Up the car came slowly, with a sucking sound like being pulled out of treacle. Water swirled off it. The flotsam and debris of the river poured out in a dirty flood from the open driver's door. When one of the towing crew peered inside there was a collective sigh of anticipation which turned to disappointment. 'No one,' they shouted, as they crowded round to satisfy themselves. 'Must have gone downstream with the current.'

'Let's have a look.' Knowing he should keep in the background, Reynolds' impatience got the better of him. Pushing his way past Clemow he leaned inside the car. Ignoring the dirt and mud, he struggled with the glove compartment under the dashboard, while Derrymore wrestled to force the back door open.

Clemow hadn't moved from his vantage point but already one of his inquiry team was checking the licence plate. Before he could even try to make a positive identification Reynolds had retrieved what he was after – the car papers with the name of the owner. And from under the seat at the back Derrymore came up with a set of keys and a wallet.

'Justin Gatterly,' Reynolds said.

At that, Clemow positively glowed. 'Just as I thought,' he said, 'drowned with his car.'

'Hold on a moment—' Exasperated, knowing under the circumstances that anything he said was risky, nevertheless Reynolds couldn't prevent himself speaking, even if he cut Clemow short. 'Why drowned? The car door was open. He could have got out and swum to shore.'

'Not bloody likely,' Clemow snapped. 'And if he did why didn't he shout for help? Of course,' his eyes narrowed, 'I suppose it could have been an accident. *You* write the scenario then, you're good at that.' He glared at Reynolds. 'He's drunk and falls asleep at the wheel. Or he parks and forgets to put on the brakes. Next thing he knows, plop, he's in the water. But what was his reason for coming here in the first place?' Again he glared at Reynolds. 'Not to commune with nature, or sob over his dead brother. If he had a reason, I'd say it was because he was frightened. And in my experience, people who're connected with murder cases are most often frightened when they've something to hide. And if they've something to hide, then they must be guilty. And suicide's a perfect answer to guilt.'

Suddenly Reynolds could see where Clemow's mind was taking him. A Justin, dead by his own hand, would provide the perfect answer to finding a suspect for Edmund's killing. Better by far than Audrey, having a real motive. It doesn't add up, Reynolds thought. Knowing he should keep quiet he interrupted Clemow again, as, in full swing, the Chief Inspector began to shout instructions about contacting the harbour authorities, who'd know about tides and currents.

'I admit he might have been drunk. But have you looked at the marks left on the bank? They might tell us something?'

Reluctantly Clemow had one of his men give a casual glance, then, without waiting for his opinion, gave his own. 'Those prints don't prove a thing. All the world's been along this bank before we arrived.' He whirled back on Reynolds. 'Plain as a pikestaff to me what's happened. But you never could see the wood for the trees. If Justin was frightened off, you're to blame.'

He jabbed a stubby finger. 'You mucked things up. You blundered in on him and blew his cover. Thanks to you, a major lead in this case is lost.'

Even although he agreed in part with Clemow's assessment, Reynolds couldn't let things go. Ignoring Derrymore's anxious shake of the head, he said, 'I might as well claim that Justin's still alive and suggest looking for him inland. Why so sure this was deliberate? If

someone wants to drown himself there're easier ways
than sitting in a car and heading it into the river. Besides
even his mother never mentioned suicide as a possibility.'

'His mother is crazy,' Clemow said, with some
justification. 'As for looking inland . . .' His voice rose
several notches. He made a scornful gesture. 'Impossible.
He could be anywhere.'

'No.' Again unwisely, Reynolds contradicted him.
Paying no attention to Derrymore's warning tug on his
sleeve he said, 'If he is alive he couldn't have gone far.
How's he to move about? His own car's in the river, his
mother doesn't drive, and the only car at his disposal is
the Gatterlys' Rolls, with Fletcher to drive it. The Rolls
would have been missed last night if it had gone
anywhere, and in any case it was there early this
morning, to go to Truro.' He looked round him, willing
the team to listen. 'And how'd they get it down these
narrow lanes?' he went on persuasively. 'In my opinion,
if Justin's alive, he left here on foot and is holed up
somewhere out of the limelight.'

'But if he's gone to all that trouble, what on earth
for?'

It was a logical question. Unfortunately Reynolds had
no firm answer.

'He may know something about the original murder
that he hasn't told,' he admitted. 'If so, probably his
mother knows too. Ditto Fletcher. They certainly must
suspect something. If I were you I'd get the pair of them
in fast for questioning. They might shed some light on
what's really happened.'

It was too late to sound ingratiating. And whereas
Clemow might once have accepted Reynolds'
suggestions, even paid tribute to his intuition, that
wasn't so now.

'You're crazy too,' Clemow allowed himself a smile.

'I'm organizing a search for Justin Gatterly. Presumed drowned. By his own hand.'

He turned back to his team. 'Let's get this river thing sussed. And those who think they know better can scour the whole damn countryside on hands and knees if they want to, looking for non-existent evidence. Or better still, save their breath to defend themselves when we serve them with a summons for breaking and entering.'

He let this last out in a gigantic roar, which made his fellow officers jump. 'I've had it up to here,' he added with a vulgar gesture, 'with theories that don't have a leg to stand on.'

A triumph of mixed metaphor. But a triumph for Clemow too. Derrymore gave Reynolds a despairing look. 'He'll have my stripes for garters,' he'd said in the beginning, and it looked as if Clemow would.

'Just one thing,' Reynolds, still calm, calculated a last throw. Clemow wouldn't want to explain, but he might be tricked into boasting. 'What, if anything,' he asked, 'put the idea of breaking and entering into your head?'

The taste of victory was too much for Clemow. 'It's come to our attention,' he said, his voice unusually thick, 'that we've not heard all the truth about the night of the murder. A bird, or rather two birds, have let it out of the bag that someone was there who shouldn't have been.'

He rounded on Reynolds. 'Mary Lou Fletcher and her husband are willing to testify that you were poking • around,' he said. 'So we've got some serious questions to ask you. And if I catch either you or your shadow near the manor again I'll have you arrested. Derrymore's suspended until further notice.'

With a final grin that emphasized his success, he turned his back.

'Damn the Fletchers,' Reynolds muttered to himself,

while Derrymore said, 'Of course. Remember how she fluttered on about the first two officers being "gentlemen"? I could wring her scrawny neck.'

He didn't add 'And I could wring yours, for getting me in this predicament,' but his aside, 'What shall I tell my mam?' implied it. Reynolds felt a sudden rush of justified guilt. While he was merely left stranded, barred from a case in which, by now, he was fully engrossed, Derrymore had much more to lose. Here was real blame! His own muttered apology was turned aside with Derrymore's quiet insistence that, 'had I been in your place, sir, I'd have done the same.' A gentlemanly return, but one that for the moment got them nowhere. They were left with little to do, except fume in private whilst watching a search they didn't believe in, and from which they'd been forbidden to take part.

At Clemow's insistence, the inquiry team began its hunt along the river for Justin's body. As a safety measure, road blocks were set up on all the major roads out of the county and enquiries made at the nearest rail and bus stations. And becoming more certain by the minute that the case was cracked, the chief inspector seemed on the brink of naming Justin as a prime suspect in his brother's death.

Chapter 15

Reynolds was the first to rouse himself. 'Come on, old son,' he told a downcast Derrymore. 'Either we let Clemow stomp all over us, or we continue as before. What have we got to lose? Trust me, I'll make sure your job's safe if it's the last thing I do. And in the meanwhile your mam can have a go at cleaning off that mud. Wish I had a mam to clean me off,' he added, which at last made Derrymore smile. He looked at the younger man. 'But before we leave, there are a few things I want to check on first.'

They waited until the villagers had dispersed and Clemow had moved on down-stream. Then, avoiding the remaining officer, they made their way towards the cottages to find the fisherman who had sounded the alarm.

Not loath to be identified, he was happy to tell his story again, especially to sympathetic listeners. He insisted he had been careful to keep people off the bank, he knew better than let them walk all over the place. And since his house was halfway down the hill he would have heard any car pass last night.

He was indignant that his word had been doubted. 'But there 'tis,' he said, biting on the stem of his pipe, 'them city fellows always do know best.'

He eyed them for a moment, then, leaning forward confidentially, said, 'And I'll tell you summat else. About last night. The old woman at the foot of the hill was in some state about it. Her cottage is closest to the river, see, and when I went down to fish this morning she was leaning over her gate. She's sort of peculiar like, and I was surprised at her speaking to me. She went on about being in her garden late last night, and seeing two men walk up the hill.'

Reynolds and Derrymore looked at each other. 'What was she doing there herself?' Reynolds asked, to have the man admit that most of the cottages still had outdoor closets, no fancy plumbing jobs here for them. 'But the thing is,' he continued, 'she insisted she knew one of the men. Joe Fletcher.'

Again Reynolds and Derrymore exchanged glances. 'Is she sure? Can we speak with her? Who was the other man?'

'She didn't say nothing about him. But she was certain one was Fletcher. As for getting her to say anything to the police,' he shrugged, 'you can try. Like I said she's peculiar. Keeps to herself. That's why I didn't mention her to that chief inspector fellow. If he wouldn't accept what I said he certainly wouldn't get much out of her.'

After his assurance that he would be 'happy and proud' to give evidence at a later date, they left to talk to the woman. Since Derrymore was still in uniform, the task fell on Reynolds. But although he struggled through the brambles and nettles in the back garden, and although he heard movements behind the locked door, she never opened it or responded to his voice. And as there was no official way of persuading her, they were forced to leave it at that.

'It's hearsay evidence only,' Reynolds pointed out. 'But what were the men doing here? And if one of them was Fletcher, who was the other? Fool that I was, I shouldn't have mentioned to Clemow about having him questioned. He and Miss Trewithen will really be off-limits to us now.' Unnecessarily, he added, 'So getting a closer look at those marks on the bank is even more imperative.' Derrymore had already worked out a way of achieving this.

As they had to go back along the river bank towards their starting spot where they'd left the car, they had an excuse to pass the spot, now carefully taped off. While Derrymore distracted the officer left in charge by chatting to him, and, as consolation, receiving his commiserations on 'a piece of bad luck', Reynolds waited until the two men were deep in conversation, their backs turned, before he ducked under the tape.

The mud had already begun to dry out so the tyre marks were plainly visible. Normally Clemow would have made sure that these were carefully examined and matched with the wheels of the car. But in his eagerness to find a suspect and to prove Reynolds wrong, it was possible that he had skimped on the work. In any case it was the footprints that Reynolds was after.

The dry condition made the job easier, and revealed several. The fisherman's claim that no one had walked there was not completely accurate. But most were at a distance from the actual marks of the wheels. Only two, close to them and slightly to the rear, proved specially significant.

Both sets were clearly male, one booted, one shoed. They appeared twice, in a rough parallel line, the pattern of the soles distinct and the toes dug in deep. Quickly making a rough sketch of their shape and position Reynolds strolled away along the path, where Derrymore joined him later.

When he showed what he had drawn, Derrymore immediately came to the same conclusion as himself. 'Two individuals,' he said, 'facing the water. And pushing something heavy. Look at where the pressure marks are. I wish we could take a look at Fletcher's and Justin's footwear, but old Clemie will never allow it.

'That old car of Justin's would be some weight to move,' he added. 'But if one of the men was Fletcher, what's he doing there? And where's Justin?'

'Quite.' Reynolds' voice was dry. 'Think about it. Two men push a car into the river. If Justin was in the car he wasn't committing suicide. Either he was dead or about to become so. And we may be talking murder.'

Derrymore looked shocked. 'But surely Fletcher's devoted to Miss Trewithen? Why would he kill her son? He raised the alarm at her request and . . .'

'Let's write another scenario, as Clemow put it. Suppose he's there to help Justin. Together they push the car in the river, together walk up the hill and are spotted. Which leaves us with another puzzle. Again, as Clemow pointed out, why go to all that trouble? And when you think of it, if you want to hide something, the Fowey river is not a good place. Out goes the tide, leaving the evidence behind.'

He was staring in front of him, intent on working something out. 'If Fletcher is involved you can be sure Miss Trewithen is too. Could even be what they were planning when we spotted them down by the river. Now if anyone knows about the tides and such on the Fowey River, Miss Trewithen does. So one could put a case forward that she intended the car to be found. Which • she doubly ensures will happen by drawing attention to it beforehand.'

Derrymore looked dubious. 'Where would Justin have gone afterwards?'

'That's what I'd like to find out,' Reynolds said grimly. 'My guess that he would still be close by isn't so far-fetched after all. This is all former Trewithen country;

one of his mother's old tenants might be cajoled into hiding him. Anyway, that's where I'd start looking, except with Clemow prowling the region it's out of bounds for the time being. So I suggest we do some home sleuthing on our own. Let's find out what we can about Justin's movements yesterday. There's his architect flatmate to question for starters. And the girlfriend he was supposed to have spent the night with when Edmund was murdered. They may even know something about that company we haven't yet investigated.'

They drove back to the manor to hand over Derrymore's official Panda, a bitter blow to the sergeant who had been proud of it. Then while Reynolds retrieved his own car, Derrymore turned in his badge, a second humiliation which Reynolds would have given a lot not to have had happen. Returning to St Breddaford to allow Derrymore to change out of uniform, and he himself to put on clean clothes, they set out for Truro, starting with Justin's flat, where they found his mate.

He knew about Justin's disappearance from Fletcher's visit, but they didn't elaborate on it or mention the car in the river. Instead they said they were looking for general information. He was happy to oblige, taking them at face value as plain clothes officers, which was what they'd hoped. He agreed that when Justin went out drinking he tended to over-indulge but pointed out that he never went anywhere else to sleep off his excesses and seldom more than once a week. So drinking wasn't the cause of his present disappearance, as he'd already told Fletcher. 'Can't afford it,' was his cheerful explanation. 'Although recently Justin's been brag – talking about his rich relatives. He might have a bit put by that I don't know about. If he does, he owes me two weeks rent I paid for him.'

As for the papers that they'd seen the day before, they were gone. Justin's desk had been hurriedly swept bare and his flatmate had no recollection what the various folders referred to.

'Old Justin always was a dabbler,' was his only comment, not meant unkindly. 'And his desk was always a mess as far as I remember,' he added, staring at the blank surface.

Asked about the girls in a photograph, retrieved from where it had been carelessly shoved in one corner, he identified them vaguely as 'mutual friends' from a previous summer, long forgotten. But he did know Justin's current girl friend and supplied a name and address.

Sally Heyward worked as a secretary in a large law firm. They approached her as she was leaving work for the day and fortunately she didn't ask either of them for their identification.

She was remarkably pretty, so pretty Derrymore couldn't keep his eyes off her as she sat opposite them in a small bar on the main street. 'Lucky bastard,' Reynolds heard him mutter, and agreed. Like his father, Justin seemed to attract good-looking women.

Again, they did not reveal all the reasons for their visit, but she seemed to take them on trust and did not push for more information. She admitted freely that she and Justin were seeing each other and that they had been together the night his brother died. She hadn't known he had a twin brother and when the news had broken she had rung Justin to ask if they were related.

When pressed she admitted Justin often boasted of his father. Like his flatmate, she seemed reluctant to fault this tendency, suggesting if nothing else that Justin's old friends were nicer to him than perhaps he was to them.

It was as if he was driven, she went on, always planning ways he could convince his father to let him join the family firm. She'd actually rewritten Justin's credentials several times for Justin to give to him, although she wasn't sure he ever had. This obsession had begun about eight months ago, before she'd met him but other people had mentioned it to her since. The general opinion was that it had ruined Justin. He wasn't very successful before, was always in and out of jobs, but at least he hadn't put on airs.

'Did he seem different the night he spent with you, the night of his brother's death?' Reynolds asked.

Here for the first time she hedged. 'What do you mean by different?' she asked. 'He stayed in my flat all night, if that's what you're asking. I don't suppose he acted differently except he was quieter than usual, and he fidgeted. Especially after he'd had a queasy spell. And he did get up early next morning. Usually he leaves after I've gone to work, but he was off before me that day. I thought it was because he'd felt rotten earlier on.'

What did she mean by 'feeling rotten'?

Again she tried to hedge, then said simply, 'It was weird. We were watching telly, or at least I was. I'd had a hard day at work and we planned to eat late. Suddenly Justin rolled off the sofa. I thought he was joking but he fell to the floor and lay on his side. He was, well, sort of groaning,' she said. He wasn't actually sick, and this had happened sometime between nine and ten o'clock, before they'd eaten, so it couldn't have been the food.

Reynolds and Derrymore exchanged glances.

'Have you spoken to him since?'

'I rang him as I told you,' she said, 'when the news about his brother came out. I've only left messages since. I've not heard from him direct.'

'So you've no idea where he is now?'

'No,' she said. And when they explained, in a deliberately low-key fashion, that his mother was worried about him, mentioning in the same breath their interest in his current business concerns, she said cheerfully, 'Oh, he'll turn up. He's a survivor. But what his future plans are, he never really told me. So I can't help with anything specific. Of course,' her blue eyes sparkled, 'my guess is he's not really cut out to be a big tycoon like his father. I told him he'd be better off in a small place with a steady job and income. Mind you,' here she became more protective as if she didn't want to seem disloyal, 'he's had a lot of problems, you know, what with ventures failing or partners flaking off, and not having sufficient capital to shore things up by himself. I think it's really mean of his father not to help him. And his mother's not much better, she's always on his back.'

'Something to be said,' Derrymore commented, 'for small family units.' To which to his surprise she gave a hearty hurrah.

The last questions were the most sensitive. If Justin had been with her the night of his brother's murder, did she know where he was the following night? Had he been with her? Had he been out drinking?

'I don't drink much myself,' she admitted, and seemed about to add, 'And I wish he didn't.' Instead she said, 'His drinking pals could tell you. They're usually in the Bull and Garter.' She gave directions. 'But I'm not sure he was in the mood to drink that night. He was queer,' she finally brought out, for the first time looking worried. 'He seemed, I don't know, nervous, stand-offish almost. Preoccupied. As if he didn't want to talk. I offered to come over but he said not to bother.'

Something about the way she said that suggested that her offer, made no doubt out of affection and kindness, had been dismissed in a peremptory fashion.

They separated soon after, giving her Derrymore's number in case she heard from Justin or had anything to report.

'Well, there's his alibi,' Derrymore muttered, while they stood watching Sally hurry away. 'And with a girl like that, who'd want to be anywhere else? Sticks up for him, doesn't she? I like that.'

'And there's one explanation of how he might have learnt about his brother's death,' Reynolds added, to have Derrymore stare at him. 'He *felt* it. No one told him, he didn't foresee it, but he seems to have experienced it. So he went to see what had actually happened. Poor devil.'

'Maybe,' Derrymore said doubtfully. 'He may still have tampered with Miss Linton's car though. Or broken into the Linton gallery. But as I don't for a moment believe our visit frightened him, we still don't know what he's running from.'

It was coming on for evening now, the searchers along the river would be giving up. Now was the opportunity to find where Miss Trewithen kept her horse, and possibly her son. They had time along the way to stop in at the Bull and Garter. Here they separated, Derrymore of an age to mix more freely with Justin's former drinking companions.

The news of his disappearance hadn't reached them either. Thank goodness, Reynolds thought, suddenly feeling sorry for the cheerful young woman they'd just left. They could have broken it to her more kindly than letting her hear it coldly on TV.

Justin's pals were a mixed lot, but no one had seen him yesterday. 'Came in and went the night after his brother's death,' they added. 'Understandably.' Although one insisted he'd tried to root him out from a telephone box in the neighbouring hotel. The time was about nine, he thought, give or take half an hour or more. Justin had been there for a long time. Perhaps he couldn't get an answer. (Derrymore thought of the phone call to Naomi.) At any rate, if Justin had gone drinking later that same night, the general opinion was that it wasn't with them.

'Phone call or not,' Derrymore concluded when he and Reynolds rejoined forces, 'there was time for him to go wandering. To St Ives, for example.'

With these new facts in hand, Derrymore and Reynolds resumed the last part of their programme. But although they drove up and down the river, stopping at as many out-of-the-way farms and isolated smallholdings as they could, no one had news of Justin, and no one had stabled Miss Trewithen's horse.

That next morning, before Reynolds and Derrymore could continue their own search, and before an unsuspecting dog owner had even thought about his day's walk, prior to Clemow restarting his own investigations along the river, several events took place. Seemingly disconnected, each was linked to the next, although not even the participants themselves could have admitted how.

Imagine a revolving stage. Each of the actors, for a moment, holds the centre, then steps aside. The first in the limelight are Oliver Gatterly and his second wife. The setting, again the manor house, where since Fletcher's appearance yesterday, armed with Miss Trewithen's accusation, followed by the subsequent finding of his son's car in the river, Oliver has been struggling to recover his composure.

If he knows that his first wife has been questioned about Justin's disappearance, he hasn't made much of it, although his second wife has. And if he knows Miss Trewithen has once more accused him, he has chosen not to speak of it. As for what has happened to Justin, he hasn't said a word. From his general behaviour one might assume that for him the whole exercise is a waste of time. Any moment now, Justin will appear, affable and smiling, like Oliver's younger self when at that age he first wooed and won Cornwall's 'darling'.

Although it is early by his and his second wife's standards, Oliver is already dressed in what, these days, he considers 'correct' clothes for a business tycoon living in the country. Today this consists of tweed suit, silk shirt, bow tie. It is very important to him that he always appears well dressed, as if nothing should seem to disturb his composure, the man in control. But his face is drained of colour so that the soft green of the shirt seems to reflect his own unease. In reality, Oliver Gatterly is under so much pressure, only attention to detail keeps him from falling apart!

He is standing in the 'parlour' which Barbs Gatterly has tried so hard to turn into a facsimile of her American home, recreating both the 'old-fashioned' atmosphere so beloved by southerners, as well as the 'up and get 'em' style of the modern Texan. Has tried and failed so dismally.

She herself hasn't bothered yet to dress. Lying on the leather sofa, as if exhausted by yesterday's encounter with Fletcher, she is still wearing a sweeping negligee, cream, collared with mock feathers, too flimsy for cool English summers. Yet the feathers fluffed around her face enhance her air of bewilderment, as if she expects any moment now Miss Trewithen will pounce upon her, taking her by surprise.

She and Miss Trewithen have never actually met. They have never talked, nor acknowledged each other's presence, not even when the second marriage was looking probable and Ollie had to fight for his divorce.

'After all these years,' Barbs now says indignantly. 'I don't understand how her hatred can, can . . .' she searches for a word, comes out with, 'fester so long in secret. If you want the truth, I'm shocked that after fifteen years or more she feels the break-up of her marriage happened last week. You know it was over long before we met. Where I come from, people divorce and remarry and divorce again without all this fuss.'

This fluffy indignation is not all an act. When Barb speaks, her voice is still strident. She, too, has something on her mind, and being who she is she can't let go of it. Unfortunately, she can't permit Oliver to let go either.

'He'll worm the truth out of you,' she tells her husband, not for the first time. 'Reynolds is persistent, not like that other guy. Don't you dare give way.'

The command in her voice is flint-like and when her husband doesn't answer, 'Don't even think of it, Ollie,' she warns him. 'Be sensible. It'll ruin you.'

Poor Oliver always tries to be sensible. That is the role he has played since their marriage and more than ever since his return to England, the role his 'Englishness' has prepared him for, the role her 'pappy' pays him to assume. He's not sure now that what he thinks is 'sensible' is in line with her and her pappy's concept of the word.

'Face up to facts,' Barb now says. 'If Justin's gone as well as Edmund, there's only Richard left. But you don't care about him. You don't worry what Richard does all day, hanging about this dump, knowing no one, doing nothing. You don't even think to ask where he is now. Well, I'll tell you.'

She strikes a pose, her arms outstretched, 'I've told him to make himself scarce for a few hours, out of the way. He needs something to keep him occupied. He's bored. You know what happens when he's bored,' she warns.

When Ollie doesn't make any comment, 'There, you see, it's nothing to you. But he's your lifeline, Ollie. He's important. Pappy dotes on him so.' Even if you don't, she means. 'He's Pappy's only grandson and my heir. Don't ever forget that.'

It isn't Justin's disappearance that has made Barbs so frantic. It's what the effect will be on her husband.

'What if he's not dead?' she now cries. She tries to explain what she means by saying Edmund's murder at least was clear cut and obvious. Sure, it caused her terror, for her own and Richard's safety. 'Yours, too, Ollie,' she adds as an afterthought. Justin's disappearance seems worse, she says, simply because it raises so many unanswerable mysteries. 'I don't like mysteries. They're too Celtic. Imponderable. Besides,' she adds, arranging her long sleeves, 'we all knew Justin; he was one of us.'

When Oliver reminds her, as he's justified in doing, that she's never shown much affection for her stepson before, 'That wasn't my fault,' she snaps back, not liking to be contradicted. 'But now he's gone, you still have the future to think of. It's not just your future, you know. It's Richard's. And mine.' She draws herself up to deliver her final salvo. 'Pappy will be furious if he thinks we've let him down.' If you let him down, she means.

But Oliver Gatterly doesn't pay attention. He isn't really listening. He has gone to stand by the window and is staring out down the driveway. If Barbs should ask what he's thinking, he will not tell her.

He has returned to the time when he first lived here, when the twins were born. As soon as they can sit upright their mother puts them on a horse. Actually, as she explains later, it isn't a 'real' horse; it's a pony. An old, lovable family pet she's had since a child, and so fat with being out at grass it can hardly waddle. She herself holds the infants in the saddle, while the groom – there is still a groom in those days – leads the pony by the bridle.

He comes storming out to drag the babies off.

'Trewithens have always learnt to ride before they can walk,' she insists. 'My father taught me, and I'm teaching them.'

'Damn the Trewithens,' he shouts, so loudly one of the twins, Edmund he thinks, began to cry. 'And damn your father, with his twisted body and his twisted brain. Riding crippled him. It shan't cripple my boys.'

Something worse than being crippled has destroyed them. And something as distorted as that old man in Oliver's first marriage looms over his second. If after all these years the memory of Squire Trewithen, imprisoned in his wheelchair, still has power, how much more powerful is the shadow cast upon this quiet corner of England by Barbs's living 'pappy' from his mighty empire, half a world away.

I married daughters who hoped to escape from dominant men, he thinks. Instead they brought their fathers with them, into my marriage bed. The reflection is sobering, not to be shaken off lightly. Just as the responsibility for his eldest sons can't be shaken off.

The expression on his face changes, his teeth grind with strain. 'Stop, stop,' on one side. 'Go, go,' on the other. Like a man being torn, how is he to endure such seesawing back and forth? And what will Pappy say, the living Texan, if he breaks apart?

The stage turns, a new set appears, peopled with another group of actors, this time the son whom his mother accuses his father of not thinking enough of. This third son is on an early morning train. With Syb

Fletcher, whom he isn't supposed to know.

Nor is he supposed to be on a train. His mother believes he is on a harmless expedition to some country market, which, with myopic vision, she has envisaged as an Italian-like festival, complete with lowing oxen and carts of fruit and vegetables, picked by smiling peasants from sun-drenched fields. Instead of what it really is, a line of dreary stalls of shoddy clothes and second-hand videos, confined to galvanized sheds like cattle pens.

It's because he's been pestering her that she's given way. 'What's there to do otherwise?' he's been whining. He knows she can't stand his whining. But she can't stand boredom either. In their world, boredom is next to death.

'It'll get you out of the way,' at last she says brightly, meaning she doesn't want him underfoot while the search continues for the missing Justin (whom no one has asked his opinion of, not even Inspector Reynolds, and whom he hates as a matter of course, seeing him as a potential rival for the family loot. Just as he's sure, under the smarm, Justin views, or viewed, him).

He doesn't know if he should think of his half-brother in the present or past tense, hoping against hope for life (ha, ha) or anticipating death!

His mother doesn't know that on the way he has the taxi stop to pick up Syb. That's why he insisted on going by taxi rather than the Rolls. 'Fletcher's still helping with the search,' he argued cunningly (meaning, as they both recognise, that the old bastard's under suspicion – perhaps his little hints to Reynolds have come home to roost! As is the horsefaced biddy who is Justin's mother, about whom there are now as many whispered stories).

'This way, I can get a taxi back whenever I want. And

you can have Fletcher drive you, without having to bother about me.'

'Thoughtful darling,' his mother coos. Strangely, she likes the affected English 'darling' rather than the more familiar 'honey' or 'sweetie'. He grins. Whatever happens, she mustn't find out about his relationship with Fletcher's daughter. Her American belief in the so-called 'classless society' would flip to admit he's 'dating' a servant's daughter! She can be as snobby as apparently Miss Trewithen is.

Equally he mustn't let Fletcher know that he and Syb are going together. Fletcher doesn't like him: another reason why he couldn't resist implicating Fletcher in fixing the Rover's brakes. He prefers to avoid any dealings with Fletcher for the present. And anyway if Syb is in one of her moods, she'll never ride in the Rolls. 'Great flash thing,' she says.

Richard and she have not met since their river encounter. At first he pretends it is his choice. But he senses she has only come today, or rather, let him come with her, because he has the cash for the tickets. Great of her, he thinks sardonically, as they settle in the hard seats smelling of ancient dust and cigarette smoke. Forgiving me for paying her way. Her apparent dislike of his family's wealth doesn't prevent her using it. Not for the first time he tells himself that she must be envious.

He has obtained the money on the way to the station, using his mother's bank card. He has more than ten times the amount Syb said they'd need, tucked in his pocket. And if he has to, he can get more, using the same method. There's plenty where it came from!

The joke is, his mother will never miss it. He's used this method often enough. When Syb twits him as, sooner or later, she's bound to do, he can always say truthfully it isn't his father's money that's paying for this little jaunt.

Although completely businesslike when it comes to high finance, her father's daughter in company matters, his mother is obligingly offhand about what she thinks of as 'petty expense'. Her refusal to take her English bank seriously, Monopoly money she calls it, as, no doubt, to her it is, provides a veritable goldmine for her son, and a fortune for Syb Fletcher. But if he gives it to Syb, will she accept it? He never knows beforehand which way Syb'll jump.

A quick stop at the market site to maintain a vestige of truth – he's learned early that the best lies keep as close to fact as possible. Then another taxi to St Austell station and they are on their way. Arranged and organized by him. Feeling in control at last, he begins to relax. Until suddenly she turns all serious, explaining the reasons for this excursion, and what it means to her.

He is resentful when she turns serious. It makes him uncomfortable as if he is in church. He doesn't come with her to be preached at. He tries not to listen but she has a way of looking at him that makes switching off difficult. He plays with a discarded Coke tin under the seat, and attempts to appear nonchalant.

Syb is looking more extraordinary than ever today, he thinks, her hair matted, as if she's deliberately combed it with mud. Dressed in a purple jersey with a great hole in the front (which someone, presumably not her mother, has cobbled together with yellow wool) with the knapsack she insists on carrying, stuffed with their gear, she looks so conspicuous he's uncomfortable. I thought you said we were expected to keep a low profile, he wants to complain, but doesn't. It's too early to start a row. That will come later, in due course.

Instead he listens while she lectures him about the ecological projects that interest her, the badger sets she's protected ('What the hell's a set?' he thinks) and the otter cubs her group has saved. Dolphins, whales, foxes, there isn't an animal that she doesn't love. He isn't exactly excited by this list.

As if she guesses now what he's thinking, she suddenly stops her recital of all these good deeds, as if she's a real missionary, he thinks, remembering how they gather at home: Fifth Day Adventists, Holy Rollers, Reborn Christians, all have that same virtuous look.

'You come from another country,' she says, with a telling stare. 'From a foreign city. If you're going to live here, in a rural environment, you have to act responsible.' She scowls. 'And if you're the only one of your family left, learn to care for the land you'll inherit,' she says.

It is the first mention she's made of Justin today. He hasn't mentioned him either, or the row in the manor yesterday. That's the sort of story that needs expansive telling. He looks round him, but the other occupants of the carriage are too engrossed in their morning papers to eavesdrop, and fortunately, at least for now, the news is still under wraps.

Wondering if it's still too soon to speak of his half-brother in the past tense, 'Do you know what's happened to him?' he asks and is dismayed at the flicker of doubt he can't suppress. She catches it and smiles maliciously.

'How much will you bet he's dead?' he asks, matching coolness with coolness.

To have her answer pat, 'All your mother's money, hidden in your pocket.'

Instinctively he clasps the wad of banknotes.

'Who do you think done him in?' she probes. She grins

maliciously again. 'My dad says Miss Trewithen blames your parents, and they blame her, so that makes things equal. In the normal way of things I'd back Trewithen. She's a Celtic witch if ever there was one. She'll put a hex on you that'll make you pine away.' She lets out this extraordinary statement calmly, no trace of blame or surprise. Then adds even more calmly, 'But I think it's someone else.'

She doesn't know what she's saying, he thinks, she's only guessing. The trouble is he can't be sure.

She leans forward and he sees the reflection of her face with its startling eyes outlined against the carriage window as the train enters a cutting and the outside light dims.

'You be careful, little boy,' she says with a look that isn't funny, is determinedly serious. 'The stars never lie. You may be next.'

She settles back. 'I heard them talking,' she now says in a more normal voice, ignoring the effect of her last remark, instead answering his previous unexpressed doubts. 'Those police. I told you that Reynolds fellow was smart. So now we'll give them a good run for their money. If you're game, that is.'

As suddenly she pulls him towards her, whispering in his ear, telling him what she really has in mind. Boredom is forgotten. This is for real. But even as excitement flows, once more his own inadequacies are plainly revealed. Never in his life has he envisaged running riot for a just cause.

Not to be outdone, he whispers back, improvising, enlarging, making his own mark. And for once she listens.

The train chugs out of the cutting into the clear again. The Cornish countryside unfolds as it passes Truro where Justin lives, or used to live. The landscape is so different from anything he's ever known, the yellow-stalked fields after the August harvest, running down to a valley so deep it looks like a mine; the copse of beech trees outlined against the hillside opposite, like a circle of standing stones. Stay here for ever, he thinks, with a sudden sense of revulsion. Not on your life I shan't. But if she shows me excitement, why shouldn't I add to it?

The stage turns again. The train has already left. Joe Fletcher is just returning home. He has been deep in consultation with Miss Trewithen and is beside himself with rage that both she and he have been questioned by the police. For himself, he can stand it. He feels having been detained is a sign of his devotion. But it's not right that a lady of her station should be treated like a common thief. She blames Derrymore for her present predicament but that is only because she remembers the name, dragging it up from her past, he thinks. He reminds her that he has already given the sergeant a good ticking off. In his mind the fault is Oliver Gatterly's. He and his hell-bitch wife.

When he and Miss Trewithen meet they often discuss the way their lives have changed. But he has never before imagined hatred will sink so low. Money buys all things, he thinks, the Gatterly millions. He feels helpless, an old guard dog without its teeth.

Now he is on his way back to his own home, oblivious of danger to himself, to receive an even greater blow. A neighbour, spotting his daughter at the station half an hour ago, has come straight back with the intention of telling, his large mouth grinning, and is lurking by Joe's house to catch Joe when he, in due course, returns.

'Saw your little maid,' he emphasises the 'little', 'with that Gatterly boy. Off on some early jaunt together then?' The grin shows he knows Joe's feelings. Joe has never been discreet where the Gatterlys are concerned.

Joe's anger rises to boiling point. Within inches of knocking his tormentor down, he restrains himself, instead storms into his house to catch his wife by the arm.

Mary Lou is washing up the breakfast dishes. There is a lingering smell of frying bacon. 'Just what are you playing at?' he shouts, making her drop a plate. And when she screeches and pulls her arm away, 'You know what I mean. Where's the child gone?'

'She's fifteen and more.' Mary Lou has spunk too. She doesn't prevaricate, say Syb's in bed or, worse, pretend surprise and say she doesn't know. She nurses her arm, eyeing him with a look more becoming to a snake than a loving wife. 'She's too old for me to babysit,' she says.

'Which you never did.' In Joe's anguish, old wounds are opening fast. 'Never time for her. Only for yourself. How did she get to know that boy? I've told her to have nothing to do with them.'

Mary Lou shrugs. 'They're here,' she says. 'We're here. Young people get together. It's natural.'

'I'll not have my daughter led astray by them,' he shouts, but he knows it is too late. 'Not have them say it's my daughter's fault. And with this murdering lark you can't be too careful. You should have kept them apart.'

She shrugs again.

'Bitch,' he says, and hits her hard.

He has never hit a woman in his life, never anything female, not even his hunting dogs. He is appalled. His hand drops. He looks at it as if it belongs to someone else.

'I didn't mean that, Mary Lou.'

His use of her name is unusual these days. He never calls her by it any more, as if he doesn't want to hear it cross his lips. Using it is his way of making amends. And after a moment or two he tries to explain all that he has heard, coming up to her with a hangdog look to add, 'It's just I'm that bothered. About the case and all. With them here, it's all gone wrong. And, I'm, I'm so jealous . . .'

His admission of wrong doesn't mollify her.

'Jealous?' she cries, her eyes gleaming. 'When it's me that should be jealous. When everyone's talking about what you and Miss Trewithen are up to, hours together in the woods. And why are you to blame when it's her son that's missing? Is it something to do with what she said to you, down by the river bank? Oh, don't deny it.' He is backing away, as if she has struck him a blow in turn. 'I saw you. And so I'm sure did those policemen fellows. I told them where you were.'

Out come her own accusations, tumbling over each other. 'Why do you take so much upon yourself? What's she to you? She's mad enough as it is.'

Venom, pent up, pours out. It blinds her to reason. And again he tries to plead, explaining all the extenuating circumstances, asking forgiveness, repeating that it is only his concern for Syb, his love for his daughter, that counts.

Chapter 16

Morning then. Dull, with the promise of sun later on. More than twenty-four hours since the car was discovered and Justin went missing. Since dawn the searchers have been out, joined by Clemow earlier than usual. Now Clemow ordered the hunt to concentrate upstream, and when his puzzled helpers questioned this decision, 'Could be something to it,' he grumbled, meaning even he was beginning to doubt that Justin had drowned.

Above the trees, Reynolds and Derrymore, having arrived again in Reynolds' car, had parked and were trudging towards yet another farm. It was warm up here, the sun beginning to break through the mist that covered the river bottom, another lazy, late summer day, perhaps the last of the season. Horseflies were biting and bees buzzed in the late gorse flowers and from time to time a sheep trotted out of their path.

They could hear but not see the policemen, moving slowly up from the river banks through the trees. They could also hear a little brown terrier yapping in the undergrowth, an incessant barking.

'Rabbits,' Derrymore said cheerfully. 'And there's its owner whistling for it to come.' But the dog didn't obey the command, instead it broke out into even more frenzied barking. 'Something wrong,' Derrymore said, stopping. 'Dogs don't keep on like that for nothing.'

Together he and Reynolds turned and slid back down
through the bracken towards the sound. Even before
they reached where the dog had been scrabbling under
a bush they glimpsed the pale colour of disturbed soil –
and, beneath the faint scattering of leaves over it, the
outline of a body.

The inquiry team came scrabbling up at Reynolds'
shouts, a puffing Clemow in tow. The pathologist was
summoned, and soon joined them. He'd been on call since
the day before and seemed glad finally to have
something to look at.

'Recent,' he pronounced. 'Late last night or, more
likely, early this morning. Blood's still fresh. But I'll know
for sure later on.'

Always cautious, caution was his profession, he got
up from where he'd been kneeling, fastidiously wiping
his hands on a towel he kept in his bag.

'Bound and shot at close range,' he added. 'Ritual
killing, I'd say. Mafiosi.'

'Long after his car went into the river!' Clemow, still
out of breath what with the climb and the discovery
afterwards, stared as if hypnotized at the ground where
the raw edges of a shallow grave had been hacked out.
He wiped his face with his handkerchief as if wiping off
his disappointment.

In the grave the terrier had discovered, Justin lay on
his side, his profile just showing, the shattered side of
his head hidden. His mouth had been taped. His bound
arms, tied in front, suggested some mute appeal never
listened to. In death, a family resemblance was
unexpectedly revealed. The hair, stiffened with blood,
had hardened into the Gatterly peak.

Reynolds stood unusually still, looking down at him.
He hadn't expected this either. Yet a 'first murder', he'd
said, and from the start he'd anticipated a second. What

he hadn't foreseen was Justin as the next victim. A wave of pity swept over him. Poor Justin, with his gold earring just glinting under the smother of earth. All his plans and hopes, his 'irons in the fire' gone cold. And poor Miss Trewithen, so free with talk of her 'missing' son, how would she react to the news of his death?

Once more the team was faced with the wheres and whys of another killing. And with who was responsible.

Reynolds was shocked. He'd never expected such an ending. Yet he himself had mooted the possibility of murder after they had heard about the 'two men walking up the hill', and Fletcher's possible involvement. But according to some of the officers present, Fletcher had undergone questioning since, and hadn't been released until this morning, so he couldn't have shot Justin. And since Miss Trewithen, also under questioning, had denied any knowledge of what had happened to her son, no fresh leads were expected from her. Where Justin had been since his car went in the river was still unknown, and why it had been put there.

Reynolds expected another explosion from Clemow, but misjudged the Chief Inspector. Clemow was genuinely shaken by the discovery. As the stretcher went past, carried by policemen and some farm workers who'd heard the commotion and come running to help, he waited beside Reynolds and Derrymore in respectful silence, together with the rest of the inquiry team. But after the bearers had disappeared along the track, he turned to Reynolds. 'For God's sake, John,' he said, almost as he used to do, 'what's going on? I don't understand,' in a tone of voice that almost made Reynolds pity him.

Derrymore had been shocked into speechlessness too. He turned at the same time, saying through clenched lips, 'This is worse than his brother. And what does Mafiosi mean?'

'Mafiosi!' Clemow pounced on the word. 'Nothing a country policeman would know about,' he sniffed, recovering some of his composure, 'Thank God, I'd say. I've met it only once or twice myself in the inner city, never in secluded areas like this. But come to that, why should country areas be immune these days? They're becoming hotbeds of every other sort of crime.' He glared at Derrymore angrily as if it was his fault, his head thrust forward, expecting opposition, looking for it. 'And nothing to do with this case,' he bellowed. 'God knows what this case is about.'

Reynolds, who had been about to say something suddenly stopped. Beckoning to Derrymore, the two of them stepped out of Clemow's way as he bustled off.

'He'll be here all day,' Reynolds said quietly, as Clemow, taking hold of himself, began giving orders, redirecting his crew to hunt for clues in the vicinity of the grave site. 'This is the sort of minutiae he usually thrives on. While he's occupied, what do you say to a foray into enemy territory? Back to the ranch, for example.'

He didn't exactly explain what he wanted at the manor house, and he didn't actually say, 'At last Clemow's turned to us for help.' He didn't even claim that help was what the Chief Inspector had asked for, but the sudden cry was genuine, at least at that particular moment, typical of Clemow's about-turns. Encounter any real difficulty, and Clemow always backed away. If now Reynolds took advantage of the situation, used it as a way to do what he knew was essential, that is, try to solve this new murder before Clemow could ruin the opportunity, that was only natural. And Derrymore, who was still half in shock himself, had no hesitation in following Reynolds' lead.

As they stealthily made their way back to the car, taking a round-about route to avoid being seen, and hoping Clemow would be too preoccupied to notice their absence, the sergeant couldn't stop his thoughts returning to the dead man.

'So that's what the Mafia do to their victims,' he exclaimed. 'Shoot them deliberately, execute them? I've seen executions like that in Northern Ireland,' he continued, 'but a civil war's going on there. And why Justin? What had he done for someone to treat him like that? What sort of people are we dealing with?'

Before Reynolds could answer, Derrymore's phone rang. When he heard Sally Heyward's voice, his face lit up, then, as she continued speaking, his smile faded. He held the receiver out so Reynolds could listen.

'A man,' she said breathlessly, 'tailed me when I came to work this morning. And now a phone call.'

Not another, Reynolds thought. He gestured to Derrymore to keep her talking before the threatening panic took over. 'He said I'd end up like Justin,' she cried. 'If . . .'

'If what, miss?' Derrymore probed gently.

'If I called the police, or told anyone. You're not actual policemen, are you?' she went on. 'I mean, you're some sort of special detectives, right? And I don't know who else to talk to.'

Glossing over their status, Derrymore questioned her. 'What did the man want? How do you know it's the same one as this morning? How do you know he was following you?' The routine of answering gradually forced her to overcome her fright.

Bit by bit the story unfolded. A man in a suit waiting at the end of her street, taking the same bus and then coming up beside her. Watching her furtively.

'Men sometimes do that,' she said, suggesting without false modesty or vanity that her good looks often had that effect but that it never bothered her one way or the other. 'When I got off in a hurry, he tried to catch me up, actually grabbed my arm. I ducked down a side lane and lost him. But he must have followed me somehow.' Again panic threatened as she added, 'Now he knows where I work.'

He knew all that already, Reynolds thought, where you work, where you live. Why else would he have been waiting so close to your home? Where did he get that information, and why? He listened while the girl continued to explain that on the phone the man asked why she'd run away, and then, without warning, 'What did Justin give you?'

The same familiar story.

'Can you describe him?' was Derrymore's next question.

She hesitated, trying to remember. 'Tall,' she said, 'fattish. Eyes small, piggy. His voice sounded sort of muffled, perhaps foreign. The suit was certainly not English. It made him look, well, like an inverted pear.'

A vivid description, if not the 'eyes and hair colour' they were more used to.

Before they could ask any more questions, 'And what did "end up like him" mean?' she asked anxiously. 'Justin's all right, isn't he? Nothing's happened?'

Derrymore looked at Reynolds who took over.

'Listen, Miss Heyward,' he said in a tone that gave people confidence. 'Everything's under control. We'll tell you all about Justin presently. Here's what you must do now.'

An elaborate list of precautions followed. She was to stay where she was, in no circumstances to leave her place of work. Did she share an office with someone?

Good, tell that girl not to leave either. An officer would be on his way within moments, together with a woman colleague, and they would be there themselves as soon as they could. They would give her the full story then.

'He's dead, isn't he?' she broke in. 'You've found him and he's dead.' They heard her give a deep breath like a sob.

'I've expected it,' she said, 'ever since we talked. I was so sure he'd be OK and then suddenly I wasn't. It must be that group he was going on about.'

They heard the rustle of her reaching for something, tissues probably, dabbing at her face, presumably trying to control tears.

'The one he said would make his fortune,' she continued after a while. 'I always thought he was joking, like you say "When I find a silver lining", or "When my ship comes in".'

'What was the name of this group? Do you know its location?'

'No,' she said, 'I never asked. I thought it didn't exist.'

After emphasizing again the need for care, they rang off. Using his own authority, Derrymore immediately set things in motion with the Truro branch, to have an officer detailed to her until he arrived, and be hanged to the consequence.

When he'd finished he blurted out, 'Doesn't it remind you of something?' He turned to Reynolds, his face furrowed with new anxiety. 'Naomi, Audrey's friend,' he almost shouted. 'Down to the same sort of threat. So it's got to be the same man. Looking for the same thing. And incidentally means that Naomi can't have been lying.'

Reynolds nodded. He'd already come to that conclusion.

'I'd decided in Naomi's case it had to be Justin,' Derrymore now confessed. 'Prejudice, I suppose. Of

219

course that's impossible here. But this time we do have a description of sorts. And I suppose that blasted picture is behind it. Where is it, by the way?'

'In the back of the car,' Reynolds answered absent-mindedly. 'Forget it for the moment,' he went on. 'Go back to what you said earlier, about what sort of people. Ruthless. Threatening. Would-be killers. Mafia-like. In this case, nothing to do with Italy, but nothing to do with the sort of local business ventures we can imagine Justin being caught up in either. If we're talking of organized crime, death threats, ritual punishment, then Clemie's right; they aren't common in rural areas. In my experience they're always connected with bigger issues, involving bigger companies. International concerns even. The sort of business world we understand Mr Gatterly deals in.'

As if to underline the significance of his observation he repeated it.

'And the only person connected with the case who has that sort of clout is Oliver Gatterly. So let's get on to him while he's still reeling from this last shock.'

Ignoring the callousness of his remark, for he knew it was callous even if essential, with a swift turn of the wheel he reversed and began the drive back to the manor. And although Derrymore was concerned at the delay in reaching Truro, and probably disappointed, he made no comment about this change of plan.

As they drove along, Reynolds enlarged on his theory. How it made sense that, rather than fear of being found guilty of some crime himself, fear of this sort of reprisal might have forced Justin into hiding in the first place, assuming Justin was trying to hide. It could be behind the elaborate car hoax, making Justin seem dead to his would-be murderers. Although how they discovered him was still unexplained.

'And take the way he was killed,' he finally said, 'and the way the body was buried – typical ritual killing, as the pathologist said.'

'You mean,' Derrymore had been listening intently, 'if his killers had wanted to hide the murder they'd have dropped the body over a cliff miles away, no one the wiser, not buried him where they knew the police would already be searching. Buried him deliberately to be found.' He nodded to himself. 'But why?' he went on. 'And how can Mr G be personally involved?'

His points, as ever, were practical. Gatterly had a round-the-clock police watch now on his house, he couldn't shoot Justin himself without being seen. And even if he had quarrelled with Edmund (never substantiated) only Justin had ever hinted that he, too, might hate his father; his father had never suggested it.

'Besides,' Derrymore finished, hesitating before saying firmly, 'We've been assuming all the time that he was the victim, not the murderer.' Before Reynolds could reply, he added gloomily, 'Anyway, what are we going to charge him with? We've no evidence. And talking to Miss Trewithen will be like squeezing blood from stone.' As if suddenly aware of how inappropriate that sounded, he stopped.

Derrymore's objections made sense. Yet somewhere between them and what Reynolds was feeling his way towards there had to be a logical explanation. 'Evidence or not,' Reynolds finally answered, 'we've got the chance at last to question him properly. As long as we keep Barbs Gatterly out of the limelight. She has the same unhelpful influence on her husband as Joe Fletcher has on his wife.'

And there's more ways than one to skin a cat, he told himself. If Gatterly won't give way, and Miss Trewithen won't either, then by God I'll contrive a means for them to confront each other and see what that brings forth.

How to arrange this was something to which he hadn't yet applied himself, and had no immediate way of achieving. But for once luck (which he didn't believe in) was on his side. When they reached the manor, part of their difficulty was solved.

'It's a stalemate if ever I saw one.' The duty officer in charge looked haggard. He and the second duty officer, the only two left in the house, both Cornish, both, as it turned out, less than happy with Clemow's tactics, admitted being shaken by the news of Justin's murder. But this wasn't the reason for their dilemma.

'She pushed her way in,' the first explained. 'Shrieking we was all murderers. Never heard such a to-do. And now she's in, she won't leave.'

He shook his head, looking over his shoulder fearfully, as if the noise might break out again.

'I suppose she heard the news about her son somehow,' the second added, 'because we'd barely got it ourselves. And when we suggested we'd escort her home, all proper like, well, you'd have thought we was trying to kill her too. We're all that's left here at the moment,' he explained unnecessarily. 'The others have been detailed on the search. We've no orders how to handle a situation like this.'

Not one we'd expected, his tone suggested. It's not fair. We'd be more than glad to have someone take over, good luck to them.

'Where is Miss Trewithen now?'

Even by that simple question Reynolds absolved them of responsibility.

'She stuck herself in the small room off the hall. And there she stays.'

'And what about the Gatterlys? What do they know?'

'Everything!' The first officer looked even more glum. 'The missus was down in a flash, giving us what for. But she wouldn't go in and confront her. Backed off from that. As for Mr Gatterly, he looks terrible. Can't even mourn in private, poor fellow. But he won't deal with her either. "Let her be," he said. Which didn't please Mrs Gatterly.'

He looked at Reynolds and Derrymore appraisingly. 'Why don't you try your hand, sir?' he said cunningly. 'It's beyond us.'

I've heard that expression before, Reynolds thought. An idea was forming. All he needed was a little time, and a little help. And although he himself had expressed his distrust of coincidence or fate, luck sometimes does lend a hand.

Suggesting Derrymore stay with the others in the hallway, keeping watch to prevent the Gatterlys from disappearing, at the same time seizing the chance to sort out some of the 'dangling strings', he knocked on the door.

Miss Trewithen was seated in what must have been a small anteroom, mercifully not the one where her younger son had been found. On seeing Reynolds she drew herself upright, her eyes very fierce, no tears, no weakness, the last Trewithen taking up the banner on the battlefield. As if all her caterwauling had drained her she said nothing, only looked, a look of such hauteur that Reynolds felt like the executioner facing Mary Queen of Scots. 'Go away,' it said, 'I've nothing to add. Except I told you I'd come back one day. And I have.'

Regarding her defiant face, her thin body, so thin he thought suddenly even its bones seem compressed, he became aware of her desperation. And was as suddenly reminded of Naomi. About the same age, the same generation, one never having beauty, one presumably having lost it, both had had position and wealth. Yet Naomi had made a success of her life. What had Miss Trewithen done, except feed off past glories soon to be forgotten by everyone. Yet, he told himself, she's more brains than the whole lot put together. What scheme did she hatch with Joe Fletcher? What went wrong?

He said, with real feeling, 'I'm so sorry. But you shouldn't be here. Let me take you home.'

Only to have her turn her back on him.

He gazed at her. What did you persuade your sons to do to get this house? he wondered. Is that why the Gatterlys think you're to blame?

And, the other side of the same question, what has their father done to make you so sure he's his sons' murderer?

He said persuasively, 'I'm not here to question your choice of residence. You're free to come or go as you choose. I'm still interested in only one thing. I want to solve these murders. Help me.'

He might have been speaking to a wall.

Suddenly he was angry. Last time you hid yourself under drunken misquotations, used whisky as a buffer, he thought. Now it's silence. Well, silence can be broken. And by God I'll break it if I have to.

Returning to the hall he spoke to the duty officers who, having had a nice little 'bitch' about Clemie's tactics with Derrymore (whom they knew well and thought had been badly treated) had settled down to do some serious telephoning. Thank God for that, Reynolds thought. The more we can do before Clemie shows up the better.

'Just keep an eye on her, there's a good chap,' he said to the first officer, slipping easily into his old role and taking control as if it came naturally. 'Get her tea, black, but don't let her lace it with anything stronger even if she asks. And whatever happens, don't let her go yet, even if she changes her mind, which I think's unlikely. Stand by, I may need you later. In the meanwhile, can your mate help Derrymore here with this phone call to the hospital. If Naomi isn't there, here's her hotel number. Make sure she and Miss Linton have still got police surveillance; make sure the police know the seriousness of the case. Broadcast the description of the man who hounded Miss Heyward.'

He winked at Derrymore, on a roll himself now, the earlier confrontation with Clemow, with all its distressing implications, put aside if not forgotten. And if the duty officers had qualms, dislike of the Chief-Inspector's bullying, allied to their preference for one of their own, overcame all twinges of resistance. In short both co-operated willingly, and Derrymore, who knew perfectly well what Reynolds was doing, equally ignored the effect these possibly 'illegal' actions might have on him.

'Be hanged for sheep or lamb,' he said, turning back to the most urgent matter: giving priority himself to Miss Heyward in Truro – to learn that all continued well, a woman officer was with her and she'd calmed down.

Finally, leaving the officers with the task of tracking down any other farms or cottages belonging to the estate, including the one they had been heading for this morning, Reynolds added the major puzzler: what could anyone find out about Gatterly's business concerns, what type of business was it and where was its headquarters? And what was the connection between it and a company whose initials were TIC?

And having set all this in motion in a few moments, he and Derrymore went into what Mrs Fletcher had called the library, to plan their attack on Mr Gatterly, (minus his wife) armed with an official-looking tape recorder, never switched on – and a brown paper parcel.

As Oliver Gatterly was slow in joining them (not surprising under the circumstances) they prowled the room, looking for clues, from the start the name 'library' clearly a misnomer. With only a few volumes remaining from what must once have been a considerable collection of books, the room was furnished like a modern office.

The mystery of where Oliver actually did his 'work' was now solved. Here, thanks to a vast array of electronic equipment such as computers, printers, Fax machines, E. mail modems, and a large clock, dominating the remaining wall space, giving the precise time simultaneously in different parts of the world, anyone could conduct his business, whatever it was, in perfect seclusion. All that was needed was an efficient secretary – Barbs Gatterly herself, the obvious answer. Who'd worked for 'Pappy's company' before her marriage! Reynolds was vexed by his own obtuseness in not spotting the link before. But her behaviour, although meant to intimidate, had seemed so much like that of a 'society' woman without a serious thought in her head, except fixing her hair (as indeed Mr Gatterly had intimated) he'd overlooked the possibility that she too might play her part in 'Pappy's affairs'.

The only regular piece of furniture, left over from other days, was a desk, large, ornate, looking more suited to a Victorian solicitor's office. Its drawers were conspicuously empty, any papers innocuously stamped with the manor's private address. Odd, Reynolds thought, that amid all this array of office gadgetry there isn't anything tangible in the way of records and such, locked up I suppose in those steel boxes of computers. Well, computers can be riffled and their secrets read.

He made a note to have that done as soon as they were through here.

Balked at one line of sleuthing, he whiled away the time searching through the remaining books. Surely there must be an obligatory Shakespeare among them. And found a complete set, in one volume.

'Look at this,' he said, flipping through the pages, straining to read the small print. 'That last quotation which Fletcher spouted, not so much misplaced after all, except it's an Edward not an Edmund.'

About to read aloud he was stopped by a voice in the doorway. 'What can I do for you, Mr Reynolds?'

Oliver Gatterly had come in unobserved. For a big man he could move quietly when he wanted. Strike one to him, Reynolds thought. But he came alone, without Barbs dancing attendance. That was to their advantage. Even terms then.

Gathering his thoughts together, Reynolds slipped the book into his pocket, and put the paper parcel on a small side table. 'This is a sad day for you, sir. Our sympathy.'

Gatterly's face twitched but he didn't comment. Without offering the others a chair he seated himself, almost automatically, behind the desk. Crossing his hands upon the polished surface he waited, as if any moment now, Reynolds thought, he'll glance at his clock and tell me we've wasted so many minutes of his time the whole world over. But behind the facade there was pain. He could see it in the eyes and the tic of a nerve beside the mouth, in the nervous adjusting of tie and shirt cuffs.

Another one who keeps his real thoughts bottled up, he thought. He and Miss Trewithen certainly deserve each other. Well, if we can't break through his facade either we'll try shock tactics here too.

'I regret I have to ask you some questions, sir,' he

began softly, but immediately Gatterly interrupted.

'What about my son?' he asked. 'That's my main concern.'

Here his eyes closed, but he kept his voice even. 'I need to know how anyone could kill him,' he went on coldly, 'with half the county police force swarming up and down the river banks. If you can't help with that I've nothing more to say.'

Gone was his friendlier manner of the previous meeting. Something's made him change his mind towards us, Reynolds thought. He beckoned to Derrymore and the two of them sat down, without being asked.

'We've reason to presume Justin's death may be linked with other unfortunate events,' Reynolds said, brusquely for him. 'Namely the murder of your other son and Miss Linton's car crash. Any thoughts on that?'

Gatterly shook his head impatiently. 'First I've heard of any link,' he said. 'No idea.'

Round two, Reynolds thought, again stalemate. If anything, slight advantage to Gatterly. He could feel frustration mounting as he let Derrymore take over the questioning.

'And I think you said there was no reason why Edmund should hold a grudge against you,' Derrymore continued the attack smoothly. 'And we were under the impression you and Justin got on.'

Again Gatterly struggled for composure. 'Why is that so important?' he finally got out, in a strangled voice.

'We need a motive for their deaths,' Reynolds answered.

The effect on Oliver Gatterly was startling. Reynolds had guessed he had a violent nature, the sort that weaker men display when they're under tension. He suddenly squared his shoulders as he had the first time they'd met, as if forcing himself to take action, and with the same over-emphasis struck the desk with his fist.

'Is that all you're capable of, trying to pin blame on me?' he shouted. He pushed his chair back as if to indicate the interview was over. 'You've no right to suggest anything. I don't have to listen to you.'

He leaned across the desk. 'Not when I've reason to believe Miss Linton's your ex-wife,' he continued, no less angrily. 'And you were in my house with her the night Edmund died. You didn't even have an official reason to be there. You're retired.'

He turned to Derrymore. 'You've been suspended. And your mother made the pie that killed my son! Under the circumstances it's an insult to have either of you question me. I should be questioning you.'

Someone's been having a try at discrediting us again, Reynolds thought. Damn Clemow's impertinence. He kept his expression bland but underneath he was seething.

Gatterly continued to look from him to Derrymore, as if he'd settled the matter. 'If you want to talk to me,' he concluded, 'you can talk to my lawyers first.'

'I hope that won't be necessary.' Reynolds returned Gatterly's gaze thoughtfully. Clemow certainly hadn't wasted time in telling the Gatterlys all the unfortunate details of that night; he'd probably told everyone connected with the case, the best stroke of luck he'd ever had, the perfect opportunity to cast doubts on Reynolds and discredit Derrymore, and render them both ineffectual. Derrymore's right again, he thought. This isn't going to be easy. And the possibility of Clemow turning up before we're through and blowing his stack again adds to our difficulties. But I've still got one card up my sleeve, and by God I'll play it. I've had enough of being fooled around with.

'I've been asked to solve a murder case,' Reynolds' voice was mild as milk. Out-doing Clemow, smugly smooth, he knew he'd hate himself afterwards. 'But if that's your last word on the subject, and you won't change your mind, I wonder if you'd do us a favour, sir? Just for a moment. I want to show you something.'

Picking up the parcel, he stood by the door, willing the other man to follow him. Lay on the gush, he was telling himself, remembering his training in the early days. Lard them with 'sirs' and lick their boots. Catches them every time. And if that doesn't work, play the heavy afterwards, when they least expect it.

Derrymore, clued in advance, was closing behind Gatterly, ushering him on, not exactly towering over the older man but at least in breadth and girth overshadowing him. They were in the hall now. Reynolds nodded to the duty policeman who opened the other door. Before Gatterly could realize what was happening, or make good his escape even if he'd wanted to, he was in the same room with his ex-wife.

Chapter 17

Miss Trewithen didn't turn, was still seated in the same curled position, the cup of tea beside her untasted. But Gatterly recoiled. 'What's this?' he cried, and Reynolds sensed the fear now. 'Let me out of here.'

She heard him, looked up. Leaving it at that for the moment, Reynolds let Derrymore start. Pretending to turn on the recorder, giving date and time and place, making it clear this was a formal interview, Derrymore began.

'As you know, sir,' he said, also punctiliously polite, 'Miss Trewithen has made some serious accusations concerning you and her sons' deaths. Perhaps you'd like to comment.'

'She's mad,' Gatterly broke in, but his anger had gone and his voice was shaking. 'I'm surprised anyone would take her seriously. And tricking me here like this, it's outrageous.'

'As, in turn, you, and especially Mrs Gatterly, have made similar accusations against her,' Derrymore continued, his manner admirably unperturbed. 'Have either of you anything to substantiate your suspicions?'

Gatterly began to bluster, but Miss Trewithen said nothing.

'Because if not,' Reynolds now took over, 'it would be helpful if we got down to business.'

He turned to Miss Trewithen. 'Let's start with the

first murder,' he said, 'caused by poison in food which Edmund ate by accident. The most likely victims were the present occupants of Trewithen Manor.' He made these statements flatly, no point in emphasizing that there was still no proof when he hoped to force it out of them.

'We're looking for motives,' he continued. 'And you've made no secret of your hatred for your ex-husband and his new family. You accused him of gloating over you, showing you and your sons were nothing, "dead dirt" I think your expression was.'

No answer.

'We know you can come and go through the manor grounds as you please,' Reynolds continued, trying to goad her into speech. 'We've seen you and your horse.' (A partial truth, but he couldn't stop to quibble). 'Probably you could get into the house easily, with Fletcher's help. Fletcher would do anything for you, wouldn't he?' He paused, then added, 'And how did you pay him back when the manor was first sold? Didn't raise a finger to help him, according to his wife.'

That finally touched her. 'You don't know what you're talking about.' Her mouth quivering, she turned round and stared at him. 'There was no money left. He took it all.' She pointed at her ex-husband. 'Used it to set himself up in business, threw it around like water. You can't imagine what it's like to have everything stolen from you. To be left virtually penniless, with so many • people dependent on you. Only Fletcher understood. He'd go through hell and high water for me.'

She'd used the same expression about her favourite mare. Keep the pressure on, Reynolds told himself.

'So Fletcher helped you in lots of ways, didn't he? He could have helped put poison in the food.'

'He isn't a murderer,' she said, calming down. 'And

neither am I. But he is.' And again she pointed at Gatterly.

Leaving her for a moment, Reynolds whirled on Gatterly. 'Why exactly did you decide to live in your wife's old home? Wasn't it to get even in some way with her, pay her back, incite her into enmity? It certainly wasn't to take your former family into the bosom of your new one. You didn't even offer your sons real friendship.' His voice hardened. 'The dispute between Edmund and you was so strong he never even spoke to you after you returned. Suppose you explain what you quarrelled about.'

'What enmity?' Gatterly was still floundering. Strange, Reynolds thought. A man so large, so seemingly forceful, so free with his anger, yet he reacts to his first wife's presence like a frightened schoolgirl.

Reynolds continued his line of attack. The poison had been put in food intended for the whole family. Gatterly must have some idea who was the most likely suspect. And why that person, or persons, would want to come 'gunning for them' as Mrs Gatterly had once suggested. On the spur of the moment, he added, 'If someone knew of your partiality to those particular homemade foods, was it possible the murderer's aim was to kill you specifically?'

Gatterly reacted to that suggestion angrily. 'I told you before,' he shouted. 'My wife and I have done our best to make friends in the neighbourhood. I've no enemies. Except Miss Trewithen. All she wants is to drive me out of this house. She doesn't care about her sons. She uses them.'

This sort of slanging match would lead nowhere. The anger must be directed. Again, for psychological reasons, Reynolds ignored Gatterly's outburst and focused on Miss Trewithen.

'You must have known your son very well,' he flattered

her. 'Why did he visit the house secretly? And what was he doing there on the night of his death?'

He was still sure these were crucial questions, having bearing on the whole case. He might finally learn what Audrey Linton had hinted at but wouldn't tell, what he had sensed before but never managed to clarify. But he felt nervous. As a witness, Miss Trewithen was unpredictable.

Continuing to ignore Gatterly, he picked up the brown paper parcel, pulling off the wrappings with a flourish, like a magician retrieving a white rabbit from a top hat.

'Has this anything to do with it?' he asked.

He laid the painting on the table between the two of them, watched them looking at it, and finally at each other.

In the light of day its appearance was even more lacklustre than before, its varnish dull. What could it symbolize that made it of such importance?

Miss Trewithen's mouth twitched again. 'It used to hang at the end of the Long Room, upstairs,' she said. 'Edmund went to find it that evening. I didn't know at the time, Justin told me later. How did you get hold of it?'

'He gave it to Miss Linton,' Reynolds said. 'We think that's why her car crashed, and her gallery was ransacked. Edmund died getting it,' he told her and her ex-husband. 'And I believe it's why Justin was killed.'

During this last exchange Oliver had remained standing close to the door, as if mesmerized. Now he reached for a chair and sat down heavily. 'I've never seen the damn thing before,' he said. 'And if it's what Edmund wanted why didn't he ask for it? I'd have given it to him willingly.' Sweat was pouring down his face but he ignored it.

'It's a painting of an old mining valley,' Miss Trewithen was saying, with a sort of repressed glee. 'Down west. Called Wheal Cosmuir Valley, after the mine itself. In the Cornish language the name means "The mine in the great wood". Funny thing, a great grandfather owned it a hundred or so years ago. I imagine the painting was done soon after the mine closed. And you're lying, as usual, when you say you don't know what it is.' She glared at her ex-husband. 'That's what you and Edmund quarrelled about. Wheal Cosmuir is to be re-opened. And your company is doing the re-opening.' She spat out the words.

Before Gatterly could reply, if he had any reply ready, she added scornfully, 'And not even his own company. Although he puts his name to it and pretends it is. It really belongs to his whore's father. All sham. Like the rest of him.'

She turned back to the painting. 'The mine hasn't been worked in years,' she said, 'so the valley that surrounds it is a beauty spot. But more than that, it's become a wildlife sanctuary. Trees, animals, birds, Edmund's abiding passion. I don't know all the details, and again what I know Justin told me afterwards, but I suppose Edmund thought this painting would be useful to show what the place looked like once.'

She didn't sound convinced. Whether Gatterly knew about the picture or not, Reynolds thought, she's as puzzled as we are why Edmund wanted it.

'And after Edmund's death,' he prompted. 'Justin went looking for this same painting?'

'Of course,' she said. 'Edmund told him about it. Only him, mind you, no one else. His father tried to create a barrier between them, but they were too strong for him. And the picture belonged to us; Justin had the right to look.'

235

'And when Justin didn't find it in Miss Linton's car,' Reynolds finished for her, 'nor in her gallery, and when we came asking questions, he turned to you for help. You decided it was time to keep him out of trouble. You and Fletcher had already made a plan. Where did you put him by the by?' he asked conversationally.

'Where I stable my horse,' she answered simply. 'The Grangers are former tenants. They were sending some colts upcountry next week and he was to go with them. When things had quietened down.'

It was the farm they were supposed to have visited this morning! Reynolds and Derrymore exchanged wry glances. Always be thorough. But if they had gone to the Grangers' farm first, would Justin's death have been prevented? That was one of the awful facts of murder, afterwards one saw choices that before one never knew were there.

'I believe, Miss Trewithen, when Justin first disappeared, you raised the alarm.' Now it fell to Derrymore to take up the attack. 'Or rather your former steward, Joe Fletcher, did.'

Miss Trewithen frowned. 'You don't know what loyalty is,' she exploded. 'You're not fit to mention his name. You're a traitor, you and your mother both.'

'Loyal is as loyal does,' Reynolds said, smoothly interposing. 'I think Miss Trewithen means she persuaded Joe to lead us a merry dance.' His voice suddenly hardened. 'What was the real reason you and Fletcher hid Justin?'

He noticed how her hands which looked so frail gripped the arm of her chair, rider's hands, used to controlling and encouraging horses, strong. But all she said was, 'When I first saw you, I thought, here's a man who won't baulk at his fences.' She might have smiled. 'I had a phone call,' she said. And when she'd explained,

God, thought Reynolds despairingly, why the hell didn't she tell anyone?

'I had to act then,' she said. 'I was frightened for him. And finally he saw the sense of it. And agreed. He realized he'd stirred up trouble, although he didn't tell me what it was. He was always easily swayed, you know, weak,' she went on, appraisingly. 'Like his father. But he hadn't done anything wrong. He never touched that car,' she insisted. 'He never wrecked the gallery. But someone came upon him in the dark. Ask his father who it was. He must know.'

Ignoring these accusations, Oliver began to talk about the advantages of opening Wheal Cosmuir, emphasizing the new jobs it would create. 'I told you I want to do good to the local community,' he ended. 'It's stupid to pretend I meant harm. And Justin agreed with me. Justin wanted to be part of the plan. He saw it as a fresh outgrowth of Cornish industry, a chance to bring tin mining back again.'

'So Justin and his brother didn't see eye to eye on the matter?' Reynolds broke in.

'Here's another dreadful thing,' Gatterly said bitterly. 'Two grown-up sons I hardly knew, one set hard against me, one urging me on.'

'Then why didn't you take Justin on as he wanted?' Derrymore, recovering well from Miss Trewithen's outburst, was equally puzzled.

When Gatterly started to say, 'He'd no experience,' Miss Trewithen broke in.

'Neither did you once,' she pointed out. 'You needed a hand up to begin with; your whore's money, to be precise. You could have done as much for your son.' (A repetition of Sally Heyward's sentiments.)

Gatterly continued to speak over her. 'And we were dealing on a higher level than he could handle.'

'Ah,' Reynolds broke in, bringing the interview back on course. 'We haven't discussed that yet. What Miss Trewithen has also mentioned. By higher level I assume, like her, you are speaking of your father-in-law.' He tightened the screw. 'What exactly are your father-in-law's interests? And what has the reopening of this mine to do with a company whose initials are TIC?'

It was a shrewd thrust. Gatterly reacted like a man struck to the quick. Sweat started again around his hairline, he gripped his chair. Again, he began to babble. He wouldn't deny that his father-in-law was interested. And he himself had been asked to manage a deal on his father-in-law's behalf, communicate with the authorities, the local council, in effect, things of that sort, as a man who knew the region well . . .

'So that's why Mrs Gatterly talked of "having to live here"?' Reynolds interrupted. 'Staying at the manor as you do, you are still personally essential to these negotiations?' He made himself sound incredulous.

Vehemently now, as if his importance had been challenged, Gatterly insisted that these days men of business didn't have to go to work like office clerks. They didn't keep ordinary office hours, not with contacts round the globe. But his father-in-law was a hands-on man. He wanted and expected management on the spot. Nothing wrong in that. Tough breed, those old Texans. Why, he knew his father-in-law had once—

'Remind him that Edmund was poisoned here in this very house,' Miss Trewithen cried. 'If he didn't kill Edmund, Edmund died instead of him.' She took a breath. 'Tell him exactly what happened to Justin.'

Before Reynolds could stop her, she went up to her ex-husband. 'Gagged,' she said, spitting the words into his face. 'Bound. Shot at close range. By your father-in-law's men.'

She couldn't have known all these details, but she sounded so positive, it could have been easy to take her accusation seriously. Except her actions told against her. In a way people were correct, her words were those of a crazy woman. And yet . . .

Miss Trewithen's last accusations at least had this effect – they found the weak spot that Reynolds had suspected lay beneath all Oliver Gatterly's bluster.

They all listened now while he broke into a long, impassioned recital of how he loved his sons. After the divorce it was their mother who had kept them away as if he was a leper. And how he'd worked hard to achieve success in spite of all the obstacles in his path. And how he had returned to Cornwall to make a go of things, not have everyone band against him because of envy.

A maudlin litany, self-pity mixed with excuses, in which the claim was even made that he never wanted his marriage to end, had always been faithful – a lie that perhaps he had persuaded himself was a truth.

'She encouraged Edmund to act against me,' he concluded. 'Edmund, who never hated anyone. As for Justin, I thought he genuinely wanted to become part of my world, and admired what I was doing. But he was also bound to her. If she put Justin into hiding,' he went on, 'it was to protect him from the consequences of his own ambitions. Don't they say, Inspector,' he turned round so that the light catching his hair made the resemblance to his younger sons even more marked, 'the sins of the father are visited on the children? Well, can I help it if Justin had ambitions like I once had? That's not my crime. You can't arrest me for that.'

But when they asked him again what he knew about his sons' deaths, he cried, 'I didn't kill them. And I'm not privy to all of my father-in-law's schemes.' Turning on them like a trapped animal himself, he added, 'You'll

have to ask Barbs all that. She's his real right-hand
man.'

Guilt oozing out of him, he collapsed back into his
chair. We'll get no more out of him today, Reynolds
thought. And in her half-mad way, Miss Trewithen has
also told all she knows. But we've been given some new
leads, particularly about Gatterly's business concerns
– which it seems aren't his, and which his wife appears
to run. I've misjudged her too, he conceded. The last
thing I imagined was that she was capable of managing
a business.

But although they'd established plenty of reasons why
the sons had reason to dislike their father, there were
no new clues that they, or anyone else, had actually tried
to kill him. And the identity of their own killers still
remained a mystery. He nodded to Derrymore and
stepped back to let the sergeant take over.

'I think you could have revealed these facts earlier,
without all the waffle.' Derrymore had kept quiet since
Miss Trewithen's outburst, and his sensible observation
made both her and Gatterly jump. Leaning forward he
pretended to switch off the tape recorder to indicate the
interview was over, then went on to sum up some of the
unanswered questions.

'You, Mr Gatterly, still haven't explained the real
nature of your father-in-law's interests. Or for that
matter what brings a big international company into
our little world. And you, Miss Trewithen, haven't •
explained why your son, Edmund, needed to steal a
painting from his father's house, nor why your other
son, Justin, needed protection, so that you had to disrupt
a whole police force with a hare-brained attempt to hide
him, which didn't succeed. As for your accusations
against each other,' he added, 'I think you're one as bad
as the 'tother.' A solid Cornish judgement that rendered

both speechless. 'And I'm warning you that you could be held for various offences,' he continued, his voice level, as if he was used to handling cases of this importance, and as if his suspension from the force wasn't in operation and he really had the power to make formal charges. 'Obstruction of the law, pending the revelation of business affairs, for one. And, for another, the deliberate deception of the police about the whereabouts of Justin Gatterly. So hold yourselves prepared to answer to these counts. I also suggest to you, Miss Trewithen, that Justin is still a prime suspect in the attempted murder of Audrey Linton, and the destruction of her art gallery.'

'I've told you Justin didn't touch the car,' his mother interposed angrily, while Oliver contemplated the floor. 'I can vouch for that. And if he went to the gallery, which I don't deny, he didn't do the damage. So you're wrong on both points.'

She shook her finger. 'And having to defend him against these lies comes hard when I think you were once a boy who used to black our boots! I never thought to see the day that you'd threaten us.' She glared at Derrymore as if he were a child again and she could cow him with her look.

This time Derrymore didn't back down. 'And so you don't make that mistake about threats again,' he said stoutly, 'I'm reading you your rights.'

This he proceeded to do with some relish. 'I accept what comes,' she cried loudly. 'It was worth it. If nothing else it'll drive Oliver Gatterly from my house.' But Oliver was a broken man; he made no reply.

In the doorway, Reynolds stopped. Partly in fun when they'd first met, he'd said, 'Hell hath no fury like a woman scorned,' but he hadn't really known how deep that fury went. Oliver Gatterly had said, 'The sins of

the father visited on the children,' as if it was a law of
nature he was only now beginning to understand, as if
he didn't realize that no action can take place in a
vacuum. Somewhere, sometime, its effects come back
to haunt us, like stones thrown into a pool.

'God help you both, he said. 'Because we'll find the
truth in the end.'

Outside in the hallway he turned to find Barbs
arguing with the officer they'd left on guard, her face
flushed with determination.

Seeing Reynolds, she launched herself at him instead.
'What've you done to him?' she cried. 'This is
intimidation. I've called my father's law team, they'll
be here as soon as possible on the company jet.'

'Mrs Gatterly,' Reynolds said pleasantly, a ripple of
steel beneath the charm, 'we'll talk when we know the
full facts of your father's plans. Which I think we'll find
in the office there and which I give you warning we're
about to have searched. Business ventures which
include,' again he hazarded a guess, 'your father's own
company and another whose initials are TIC. And which
your husband had just intimated you know more about
than he does.'

He noted how Barbs, too, paled, although she didn't
back down. 'I'll have *you* arrested,' she shouted, 'if you've
forced him to confess. Or implicate me.'

'Madam,' said Derrymore, stepping from behind. He
spoke with a simple dignity Reynolds had never seen in •
him before. It silenced even Barbs Gatterly. 'In this
country we're not a gun-toting, rascally sort of people
like the ones I imagine you're used to. So I think you'll
find your husband has volunteered all that's needed to
incriminate himself, and possibly you, without help from
anyone.'

Barbs, unable to break through their calm, left them

and they heard her berating her husband through the doors of the library that he'd been a fool to let them trick him into talking, the least of her accusations, and they'd no right to question him at all. Miss Trewithen remained in her former waiting place meanwhile, as if she intended never to move.

'My God,' Reynolds said, shaken more than he liked to admit, 'my ex-wife told me I never gave a woman credit for anything! Well, she's right. Secretary! Barbs Gatterly runs the whole show all right. Miss Trewithen's met her match there.'

Derrymore, equally disturbed, added, 'I knew Miss Trewithen resented our accepting help from Mr Gatterly. I think she expected my mam to stay on in her employ even without any wages. But I didn't know she hated us for going our own way. And making good.'

Now once more the house buzzed with police activity, as Derrymore enlisted the help of the other two officers, more than glad to co-operate. Their efforts were directed to one end: to find out what was known about Wheal Cosmuir, its history and its future, and how it tied in with Gatterly and his father-in-law's concerns.

'There must be plenty of computer experts,' Reynolds said, for once furious at his own lack of knowledge. 'Set them ferreting. And,' an afterthought, 'when the reports come back about the poison used on Edmund, see if there are any links.'

While this was all going on, the first euphoria over, he wrestled with a problem. It had been haunting him since the interview with Oliver Gatterly and Miss Trewithen had finished, a flaw in his reasoning that he couldn't get straight. Like not seeing the wood for the trees.

'I know it's only a beginning,' he said speaking to himself, but getting Derrymore to listen. 'I know it doesn't mean the hunt's over, only tells us in what direction to run. The snag is, and it's a big one, if their father's right, the brothers were on different sides.'

He fixed Derrymore with his customary look, as if he expected to find the answer written on the sergeant's puzzled face. 'I think I've made a big mistake,' he went on. 'I've let myself be side-tracked by various other clues. I should have concentrated more on the first murder. I've presumed all along that Edmund's death was an error,'he continued. 'Logically, I just assumed the poison was meant to finish off the Gatterly family. I should have focused on that more from the start.'

He paused again. 'But if the Gatterlys were meant to be the victims, and I admit I have no proof of this, we have some new suspects, the nature conservationists, who hated Gatterly for trying to destroy a natural beauty spot and wild life sanctuary.'

'My God,' Derrymore stared at him. 'That's Edmund's group. What a tragedy. And Miss Trewithen would be right. In a way, Oliver Gatterly would have killed his son.'

'But I've never met conservationists who were killers,' Reynolds went on, as if Derrymore hadn't spoken. 'Normally they want to conserve, not destroy. And here's another thing. Whoever meddled with Audrey's car, or attacked her gallery, or as we now know, threatened all these other women, including Naomi and Miss Trewithen as well as Miss Heyward, they're not necessarily attached to the naturalists. They could just as easily be their opponents: what I'll call the pro-Gatterly, pro-mine side for lack of a better name. And that'd be Justin's side.'

Again he brooded. 'So another contradiction. Justin, too, could have been killed by people he supported. His father's men. Just as his mother claims.'

'But if Justin was in favour of his father opening up the mine,' Derrymore interposed, 'why would his father's men want to kill him?'

'I don't know. But there has to be a reason.' Here Reynolds sprang up and began to pace the room. 'Could be something his father said about being too ambitious, whatever that means. On the other hand,' he added, again acting the role of devil's advocate, 'it's also possible we've been barking up the wrong tree all along. Instead of thinking what all the events have in common, we should be concentrating on their differences.'

'Meaning?'

'We may be talking of two separate murders; and possibly two or more separate murderers. As if one wasn't enough. At the moment the only thing they have to hold them together is Oliver Gatterly's father-in-law's determination to reopen Wheal Cosmuir,' he went on. 'And the acquiring of a painting of a valley where the mine is located. Neither of which, despite Miss Trewithen's rhetoric, seems enough to do murder for.'

The phone rang. Reynolds reached for the receiver, heard a voice he recognized, asking for him by name. It was Naomi. 'I've news for you,' she said.

Reynolds felt a shiver of expectation. He'd often noticed that just as a case seemed impenetrable, suddenly clues appeared one after another, like a stack of falling cards. Beckoning to Derrymore, he listened as Naomi related her story, adding several missing pieces that so far had eluded them.

Earlier that morning, Audrey had stirred into full consciousness. For the first time since her accident, she had become aware of where she was and what had happened to bring her there.

'She confirms that she felt the brakes give way,' Naomi said in her deep, mannish voice. 'She doesn't remember more. Instinct must have taken over to force her into the hedge. She can't move yet,' she added. 'She's still in pain, but I have her permission to tell you what she wants to say.'

Reynolds had a sudden image of how the sick woman's eyes might flicker, and how a hand might grasp for another's. He forced the image aside. It wasn't meant for him.

'It's all right,' Naomi was continuing, as if in her strange way she guessed what Reynolds was thinking. 'I've told her about the break-in, and although upset, she sees how wrong it is to keep quiet. I know now what Edmund gave her. And nothing was as we thought.'

Her voice rose a little in triumph. 'First he didn't give it to her,' she said. 'She took it. After he died. She thought she shouldn't leave it when he'd explained why it was so important. And dangerous. That's why she didn't mention it; that's why she kept it hidden. Because she was told of the danger.'

He could hear the excitement beneath her usual calmness. Audrey vindicated as a heroine, he thought. She can live with this. And 'dig for it,' Audrey had said. Had she meant that as a joke – he remembered her little laugh. But that still didn't explain why she was at the manor in the first place.

Again Naomi must have guessed where his thoughts were taking him. 'She admits,' she said more soberly, 'that she was tempted to meet him. She only met him once before, you know, she honestly didn't know his name or anything about his background. But he spoke so convincingly about what he was doing, she wanted to take part. And he,' they heard her sharp intake of breath, 'asked her to help because she was a dealer in paintings, and could give him advice. But he also liked her,' she finished lamely, as if the words were acid to her tongue. He heard her swallow hoarsely, all triumph gone.

So both Audrey and Justin had told the truth, or guessed it, about some details of that evening, he thought. But whether Edmund took Audrey there 'to show off' and whether she liked him back, better draw a veil over those.

'And it wasn't just a painting,' Naomi had recovered herself. 'It was there under our noses all the time. Taped to the back, Audrey's handiwork, between canvas and frame. An old map. He found the painting in a back bedroom, but the map was under a floorboard, kept there, he said, from the time he was a child. He loved things like that, he told her. He had several of the maps once, all cut out of a book in the library. And that's why the other pictures were ripped about in the gallery. Someone else must have known. Although she swears Edmund told her it was a secret. Only he and his brother knew. No one else.'

Reynolds and Derrymore exchanged glances. That corroborated what Miss Trewithen had said. But if Edmund had told only two people, who had Justin told? Or, for that matter, Audrey herself, although of course her accident happening so soon afterwards must have prevented her speaking.

'She isn't sure what the map is about,' Naomi concluded. 'Edmund was rather vague, deliberately so, she thinks. I suspect now it must be of the mine workings under the valley, the one in the painting. I can't think who would want it, though, can you?'

At least two opposing groups, Reynolds thought. Those who want the plan to go ahead; those who want it stopped.

When Naomi had hung up, saying she planned to go to the gallery to help the police with a search there, and promising again to be careful, he and Derrymore took the picture they had all decided was without taste or charm and pried it from its frame.

Taped to the backing was a folded piece of paper, yellowed with age and frayed about the edges. Together they unfolded it and spread it out, the drawing surprisingly clear in spite of its fragile condition. And as Naomi had surmised, it was a map of the mine works, showing all the mine's underground galleries and shafts.

'This was what Edmund died for after all.' For once Reynolds was excited. 'And it certainly is dynamite. It's what any company would give their right hands for, a surveyors' dream. A map like this will save them months of work, if nothing else. Look at the detail; look at the extent of the workings, all the unexplored veins labelled, where tin or copper might still be found but were too difficult in those days to get at. It's like handing the owners all the information they could ever want or need, where to begin and where to stop. But equally,' he drew breath, 'what a find for the opposition, needing evidence of the extent of the mine working and the possible destruction to a beauty spot.'

He closed it up reverently. 'Those old mining surveyors knew their stuff,' he said. 'Poor Edmund. I'd come to believe he just wanted an old painting for some impractical reason, propaganda perhaps. Instead he'd found what both sides would kill for.'

And for a moment he was silent.

'I was wrong about Edmund,' he went on. 'And I was wrong about Barbs Gatterly. But most of all I was wrong about Audrey.

'Perhaps Edmund did ask Audrey's help with the taping; that's something an art dealer would know about. And it was searching for these two items and fixing them together that might have delayed Edmund and my ex-wife so they had to stay 'to eat'. If they hadn't – we wouldn't be here now.'

He tapped the paper. 'I can see why Edmund wanted it, to hinder his father's plans to reopen the mine. And I suppose if Justin was in favour of the plan he'd want it even more. But I'm beginning to think there's an ulterior purpose.'

He considered for a moment. 'Remember Mr Gatterly's remark about Justin's ambition? Remember what Miss Heyward said, about him always talking about a "group" that would make his fortune? If his father kept him at arm's length and wouldn't take him into the family company, perhaps we're right that Justin tried to use this map for his own benefit. Perhaps he was trying to sell it on the open market, as it were. Or more like offer it to one side against another. In which case blackmail was his game. And either side could be wanting it. But my guess is the one that would have the money to pay him most wouldn't be the naturalists.'

He tapped the map again. 'I vote for blackmail,' he said soberly. 'Blackmail of his father's firm. And that's how they knew the map existed. And probably, if he was stupid enough to keep up his dealings with them even after his mother tried to hide him, how they knew where he was.'

'Not a pretty picture,' Derrymore agreed.

'So,' said Reynolds, 'all that remains is for us to find out if it's true. But,' he hesitated, 'most of all the map would be lethal if the mine was used for a purpose other than actual mining.'

It must have been intuition, that sixth sense he so often relied upon. Derrymore had just asked in his sensible fashion, 'What purpose?' but before he could explain, there was a commotion in the library (which the Gatterlys had been obliged to leave, Barbs not above grumbling why should Miss Trewithen stay where she chose while she and Ollie, actual owners of the mansion, were shifted from place to place like pieces of furniture.)

As Reynolds had foretold, the cracking of the computer's secrets was child's game for experts. And the second of the duty guards was that. 'Piece of cake,' he said, positively gloating at the thought of getting his fingers on all this expensive imported machinery. And whatever his father-in-law's orders, Gatterly, or rather his wife, had become complacent, seeing nothing threatening in this, presumably gentle, Cornish setting. There were no checks or secret codes on the information; the intermeshing of pappy's many companies was soon spread out in all their many details. Of these Texas Industrials Consolidates, TIC for short, emerged as important as they had hoped.

TIC was itself an offshoot of his international empire, whose main source of revenue was oil. It was a large and powerful company in its own right, whose actual ownership would be hard to track down, even for someone interested in the stock market. And it dealt in chemicals.

'Texan Oil!' Derrymore sounded more impressed by the name of the parent company. 'No wonder Mary Lou gave way to Barbs. Barbs could buy St Breddaford ten times over and never notice.'

But Reynolds took note of that word chemicals.

Just as interesting however, was what Gatterly's own business was up to. And it wasn't Wheal Cosmuir's tin! The acquiring of the mine seemed to be a separate venture. Gatterly Concerns as it was called, seemed to have another mission, presumably at pappy's original direction: the purchasing of several Cornish firms, gone under during the recession. The one to make the offers, to trot from door to door as it were, buying rather than

selling, was probably Gatterly himself; he looked and
dressed and acted the part. But the actual
administration involved in uniting them into one new
company afterwards was undoubtedly Barbs'
contribution. Memo after memo, message and
instruction, all bore her name – so much for Reynolds'
having dismissed her as a rich bimbo. Or for his ex-
wife's accusation that he didn't take women's ventures
seriously!

The name of the new company sounded harmless
enough. It even kept a Cornish touch, Trewiddle
Haulage. Its main place of business was, however,
impressive.

Again Derrymore raised his eyebrows as he repeated
it. 'Pryor and Pontings, an old family firm,' he said. 'My
dad used to talk of them, the pride of Penzance, he called
them. What have they to do with haulage?'

What indeed? And a real tangle, pappy's holdings.
One which presumably Edmund and Justin had
managed to unravel in part if not completely, even if
their mother hadn't. Once more Reynolds had the feeling
he was on the verge of greater discovery.

He now made a swift decision. 'We'll leave the original
map here, safely,' he said. 'Take a copy with us. Then
hie off west as fast as we can to see what lies behind all
this, with a stop at Truro on the way to make sure all is
well.'

At this point two other things happened in quick
succession again to make them change their minds, at
least as far as Truro was concerned.

One was a call back from a local newspaper,
explaining what was known about Wheal Cosmuir
officially.

'Been all sorts of conservation rallies up there in the
past,' a reporter told them in a cheerful Cornish voice.

'Not surprising really, a wild life sanctuary is always vulnerable when it comes to councils looking for land to develop. But nothing ever definite. And the rallies are always peaceful,' he went on. 'If it wasn't in favour of badgers it was beetles.'

'Anything recent?'

'There've been rumours.' The reporter sounded uncertain. 'They say any attempt to open up the mine would lead to ructions.'

Asked if he knew what the mine might be opened up for, he said he presumed it would be for tin, what else? And about time too, he reckoned. He was Cornish through and through and too many old tin mines had been left to become derelict, when a little spit and polish would bring them back to life.

Resisting the urge to point out that the spit and polish wouldn't be Cornish, and perhaps tin wasn't the only thing a mine could be used for, Reynolds thanked him for his help and asked him 'to keep in touch' when he had more news.

The second surprise was the appearance of Mary Lou Fletcher, her face red with weeping and a black eye just breaking through the tears. 'Joe's gone raving mad. I don't know what he'll do to himself. He's taken his gun.'

When questioned about what had put Joe (and presumably herself) in such a state she hesitated before saying it was all her fault. Joe was furious that she'd let Syb go off all the way to Penzance. With Richard Gatterly.

Unlike the other women in the house she didn't blame her husband. In fact her despair that Joe might do himself harm was so real that even Derrymore felt sorry for her.

Realizing an exhaustive search for Justin Gatterly had just ended, Reynolds thought it unlikely that anyone would be motivated to begin a new hunt for Joe Fletcher, angry after a family row. But he promised they'd keep an open mind, and if Joe didn't turn up soon they'd make enquiries.

It was only when he asked what Syb was doing in Penzance, that everything came together. She and Richard Gatterly had gone to a secret protest meeting – 'At some valley or other.'

When Clemow and his team finally returned, they found Mrs Gatterly in genuine hysterics that her husband was in trouble with the law (without benefit of pappy's legal team), that her son had gone off with a girl who everyone knew was trouble, and God forgive her if she led Richard astray, it wasn't Richard's fault. And if Miss Trewithen had besieged her house and wouldn't leave then she gave up all responsibility.

She said nothing about herself and her own troubles, presumably too devoted a wife and mother to worry about them – or too shrewd.

Meanwhile, Miss Trewithen, drink in hand (from a whisky bottle she'd found somewhere and from which she kept steadily pouring), was steadfast in her determination that she'd come home, and loud in her condemnation of 'that common little sneak', Derrymore of all people. Oliver Gatterly sat in the parlour without speaking, with only Mary Lou's tears for company, his final 'secrets' discovered, and pappy's anger now directed at him full strength.

On a more practical side, charges against two of the family were being seriously considered, despite Barbs Gatterly's protests, and she wasn't innocent herself.

Information of various sorts continued to pour in, again vindicating Reynolds' and Derrymore's theories. And they, themselves – authors of this mayhem – were already heading west, to find what was happening at

Wheal Cosmuir and what Trewiddle Haulage meant.

In the hospital Naomi drew up a chair beside the bed
relying on the duty policeman to protect her and her
friend inside the hospital.

But she was no longer afraid.

She and Audrey had talked together for a long while,
in between times of rest or fitful sleep in which the
patient tried to keep the pain at bay. Naomi, although
quite unused to nursing and generally impatient with
sickness, did her best to help.

It was a healing process. They spoke of the accident
in whispers, as if it were an old acquaintance, expressing
regret and contrition. Finally they came to the main
question, the answer to which was as dangerous as
anything they'd encountered.

On one hand the question was a simple, 'When I get
out of hospital where will I go?' On the other hand, the
question had deeper meaning.

Naomi's reply was spoken first. 'Things will be as
before.' And when she heard Audrey's similar reply, a
smile suddenly broke out on her face that made it almost
beautiful.

One last thing. In St Breddaford, in her little cottage,
Mazie Derrymore was planning the rest of her day. There
was a cake to bake for the Chapel festival, and some
weeding to be done in the back garden, and Derry's
uniform to sponge and clean; covered with mud it was,
and him plastered from head to foot yesterday just like
he used to be when he and Edmund were boys.

When Derrymore had come in, changed, and taken
off again, without even a cup of tea to keep him going,
she'd wondered what he was up to. He looked tired, she
thought. And although he hadn't said why, she had her

suspicions. Especially since, when he'd returned later, long after dark, and found her still before the fire, he'd scolded her for staying out of bed on his account, and then told her he'd be off before dawn this morning, again out of uniform, so not to think about breakfast.

Derry without breakfast was like . . . She searched for a likeness and gave up. Derry never went off his food unless something was on the go. Or Mr Reynolds had him wound up.

Not that she had anything against Mr Reynolds: grand sort, Derry always said and she agreed, only sorry that he had no family life. Sometimes she thought his being a bachelor had encouraged Derry to be one too, and here she was longing for him to get married and give her a grandson – little Derry the second – although she'd cut her tongue out rather then tell him so. But if something was amiss at the manor it either meant news about Mr Edmund's murder, or the car out of control on the hill, or, her heart began to thump, something else unknown and therefore unimaginable.

So I won't imagine it, she told herself firmly, after putting the cake in the oven and having pulled more chickweed than she ever remembered from between the stones in the path. Instead she got out a basin of warm water and spread her son's splattered trousers on the kitchen table. I'll think how nice it'll be when the whole case is solved. I may not even have to give evidence. I'd not like to stand up in court and explain how I make this and that, and here's my recipe, thanks very much. There're plenty I could name who'd like to get hold of my recipes, and other than them I've no secrets from anyone.

It had been the rattle of the letter box this morning, that had made her so edgy. Derry had told her not to worry after the first letter came and so she hadn't.

Suddenly she'd wished that he were here. 'Post, Mam,' he'd say and collect it for her. Then he could sort out the things she didn't need to see; the bills for a start. And circulars, too many to count.

For the umpteenth time today she peeked in the hall where the white envelope lay on the mat. Could be a regular old letter, she thought, from a friend, say. Or from my cousin in Plymouth asking if she can stop. But it didn't have that look.

As she drew close to it she eyed it much the way she would a mouse that had somehow found its way into her kitchen. Taking up an umbrella, hanging from the coat rack, she poked it until she could see the handwriting, all too familiar and frightening now.

'Keep the next one,' Derry had said. 'If there is a next one, I'll look after it.'

But Derry 'looked after' so many things. A man at eight, after his father died, he always had done. Why should she burden him with a little bitty piece of paper? She opened it gingerly, and stared at the drawing that fell out. A crude suggestive drawing of a woman and a man, with a caption underneath.

'You too,' it said. 'Another of his fancy bits.' And just to make the meaning clear, the figures were labelled. Oliver Gatterly's name. And hers.

Chapter 18

They took Reynolds' car, again on 'unofficial business', and as they drove west, Derrymore busied himself on his phone, the line crackling as information continued to pour in.

First more minor details that were essential to clearing up the case. The telephone calls for example had been traced and yes, someone had made a call from the gallery to Naomi's studio, so the time of break-in could therefore be fixed. Next, the St Ives police reported that they had already discovered several fingerprints in the gallery, at least two sets differing from the owners', one of which belonged to Justin Gatterly. But those on the bar and brick, and in certain other vital places, weren't Justin's – possibly validating his mother's claim that he hadn't actually destroyed anything. And emphasizing that another person was involved.

Equally important, though almost overlooked in the sequence of events, the tracing of brake fluid, now confirmed to have been spilled on the stable floor, although there was still no proof who had done the spilling.

Among these other items came frequent reports that Miss Heyward was being well looked after for the moment, would be willing to identify her pursuer when they had someone to identify, and was only concerned about where to go at the end of the day. Her real home was near Manchester and it was felt she shouldn't return to her digs in Truro. Here, Reynolds, stirring himself from his own preoccupations, suggested loudly that they ought to find her a 'safe house', offering his own if need be – or what about Derrymore's? A touch of audacity which left Derrymore speechless, but not for long.

'If you'll be willing, miss,' Reynolds heard him saying diffidently, 'my Mam'd be delighted. I can always doss down on the sofa.

'And it'll do my Mam good,' he added to Reynolds later. 'Take her mind off things,' which didn't clarify whether he meant her preoccupation with anonymous letters, or with his own regrettable bachelorhood!

Details of the interview with the horse-loving former tenants, the Grangers, followed.

Apparently the Grangers – by all accounts a pleasant family, husband, wife, two children (usually off at school and now during the holidays away at riding camp) – had been surprised that something was wrong. They didn't see other people much or listen to the news, being busy at this season. And they hadn't thought anything of putting Justin up for a night or so, at his mother's request (they were too pleasant to use the word 'command'). All she'd said was that his own flat was being painted and he'd like a lift when they went to Gloucestershire. In fact he'd only stayed one night, in their spare bedroom. The next, after saying he'd made a prior arrangement to meet some friends, he'd gone out late, and hadn't returned. And no, they hadn't thought that odd, Mrs Granger admitted. She supposed it typical of young men these days.

'Idiot,' muttered Derrymore as the interviewer went on to relate the Grangers' horror on being informed of Justin's death. 'He must have played into his murderer's hands. After he presumably persuaded his mother he needed help, why act so stupid?'

Reynolds answered, 'Perhaps he was tempted – he could have been offered a small fortune if he could actually produce the map. But since he didn't have it on him – and didn't know where it was, end of credibility – and the end of him! And so blackmail would be his game. If so, that's what his father meant by "being too ambitious". And his father must have known.'

Finally, there was a subdued Clemow. Beleaguered by the second Mrs Gatterly (who in spite of the evidence mounting against her still refused to admit she was in any way implicated, and who, after another ferocious row with her husband, had apparently banished him to a spare bedroom) and besieged by Miss Trewithen (still ensconced in the house), the Chief Inspector had reportedly latched on to Mary Lou Fletcher. Her fluttering femininity must have been a relief after the other ladies' forcefulness. He had therefore put no obstacles in the way of sending out a small search party for the rampaging Joe, so far without results.

'And serves Joe right,' Derrymore said grudgingly. 'Joe didn't do us a favour.' Suggesting he still held a grudge against Joe for telling Clemow about the 'other officers.'

As for their own search down west, good luck to them, Clemow intimated. He'd had it up to here with Gatterlys and their quarrels. Things had spiralled out of control and he washed his hands of the outcome.

'Meaning,' warned Reynolds, 'he'll disown us again if we fail, and claim the credit if we succeed. But since he's back to acknowledging us that's a step in the right direction. And as I would guess your job's secure, there's one less worry.'

While all this was going on, Reynolds had been wrestling with his own problems. Namely, he and Derrymore might be on the track of Justin's killer, but

they still were a long way from solving the first murder.
He was becoming increasingly convinced it had little, if
anything, to do with the second, except perhaps
'sparking' it off. And it must, in any case, be connected
with the actual family, rather than the family business!

'And all stemming from Texan Oil.'

Having finished for the moment with the phone,
Derrymore harped back to this fact. 'And that's where
the money came from originally. I still wonder what
makes Mrs G's father want an old mine. It doesn't make
sense. What's in it for him?'

Reynolds had been asking himself the same questions,
and coming up with answers he didn't like. 'Could be a
host of things,' he finally answered abstractedly. 'But
with humans the motivation's usually greed. Money
breeds money,' he went on, sounding uncharacteristically bitter as the car swayed and rocked westward. 'I
tell you, Derry,' he used Mazie's nickname inadvertently,
'greed'll take us all over if we don't look out.'

'Not me,' Derrymore said stoutly. 'I was born poor and
I'll die poor. I don't envy anyone their riches. But it may
have been different for someone like Justin. You know
why I really never liked him? He always had a chip on
his shoulder, as if the world owed him a fortune. Edmund
wasn't like that.'

They were approaching the end of the peninsula now,
and as the road dipped and rose they caught glimpses
of the sea on both sides. Today its colour was a deep
blue, almost purple, and although on the south coast it
was calm, the water on the north was flecked with white
far out into the Atlantic Ocean.

The landscape they were driving through was mainly
moorland – treeless, heather-covered, rutted with old
spoil heaps, used these days for rough grazing. Dotted
in between were chimney stacks and abandoned engine

houses, and underneath was a honeycomb of shafts and corridors, some stretching miles under the ocean bed.

In its own way, this mining region had a wild and unusual attraction, like coming into a lunar landscape which had been forgotten. Yet in places, where hills dipped and streams cut through to the coast, there were ordinary farms of green fields, bordered by hedges, the bushes all leaning away from the prevailing western winds. Small groups of cottages formed hamlets, and an occasional church spire poked up its finger. Anything less like Texas Reynolds couldn't imagine. Derrymore's question about 'pappy's' intentions had real validity.

The road dipped one final time, the paved part ending by a large field where a gate with a stile beside it, both new and wooden, brought them to a standstill.

The stile and an arrowed path sign marked the start of a public right of way. The path itself, leading across the stubble field towards the woods, was clearly well used and someone had tacked a home-made sign beside the official one.

'Keep death out of Cosmuir' was its ironic message.

After a lengthy discussion the two men had decided to separate here. Reynolds was to turn back and head for Penzance, making his target Trewiddle Haulage, newly established at the old firm's address. Derrymore, representing the constabulary, was to continue on foot along the valley to see what he could find out at the actual mine site – and incidentally to meet up with the protesters if they were still there.

For a moment they both leant on the stile, gazing towards the upper end of the valley, where the entrance to the mine workings was situated. All seemed quiet in the mid-afternoon sun. The only sounds were of a little stream, and the rustle of wind in the tree branches. If the protesters were somewhere in the wood they were being remarkably quiet. And if work had begun on opening up the mine it wasn't visible from here.

'Pretty, isn't it?' Derrymore said thoughtfully. 'As if the valley's never been touched. I can see how Edmund wanted to preserve it.'

He pointed to the trees. 'And I suppose that's how it got its name. And didn't I tell you the Trewithens once were miners? Seems to her, it isn't so bad as long as her ancestor was the boss, and it all happened in the past.'

Unrolling the copy of the old map, he looked at it again. 'But the mine must be older than she thinks,' he went on. 'They say the Phoenicians came here for tin, which'd be well before the Romans. Fancy! Miners working here two thousand years ago.'

The real map had been so yellowed it hadn't copied very clearly, but they could just decipher its maze of lines. For the first time, with the actual valley and the surrounding countryside spread before them, the extent of the mine workings was revealed.

'The mine's vaster than I thought,' Reynolds said, once more startled. 'Most of the unworked or partially worked areas for example, must stretch far beyond the actual valley.'

He pointed to various natural features away on the horizon. 'If the map's accurate and I don't see why it shouldn't be, there'll be farms, even whole villages, built on top of it.'

He folded the map up and thrust it in his pocket. 'Gatterly's surveyors may have done their job,' he continued, 'but there's no way they can have researched all of this. They'd have had to trace every single passage, test every tunnel and addit, made sure where they all went. And even then they couldn't swear the mine was safe. Suppose they started digging and there's a cave-in, miles away. They'd spend a fortune just in insurance alone. It would never be worth their while to open it all up. I told you this map was dynamite,' he added, 'and now I'd say it's more than that. It'll be the death blow to all of 'pappy's' plans for this area. And I have a feeling that, like his daughter, he doesn't like being thwarted.'

It was a sobering moment, bringing them back to their main purpose. For a fleeting second, Reynolds even debated whether it was wise to separate. He'd felt the hardest job, if not the most dangerous, was dealing with the actual company, while, as an official policeman, even out of uniform, the sergeant was the obvious choice to explore the valley and mine, especially if there was some protest rally going on, however remote that now seemed.

Yet some twinge of anxiety made him hesitate. 'If there is trouble of some sort,' he told Derrymore, 'keep your head down. Don't get involved.'

He wanted to add, 'Be careful,' and then stopped himself. I'm beginning to sound more and more like his mam, he thought. He may not actually have official backing or status, but he can call up reinforcements if he needs them. And he's sensible, not likely to run his head into a noose.

Comforted by these reflections he muttered 'Good luck,' checked again the time and place of meeting, and saw Derrymore leap over the stile and begin his descent towards the woods. Taking the car, he headed on towards Penzance.

- A modern advertisement for Trewiddle Haulage Works dominated the approach road on the outskirts of the town and following its directions he found the site easily. The original building, tall, ramshackle, had always been a landmark, and the old family sign was still faintly discernible, the gold leaf flaking and the 'And Sons' long disappeared.

Driving round the building to the rear, where large

scale renovations were apparently under way, he contemplated his next move. Danger was certainly in the forefront of his thoughts. If this company were responsible for Justin's death, he knew how ruthless they could be.

And even if there was no display of physical violence today, his own days on the force had taught him the strength of what he called 'corporate personality'. Wrongdoers could retreat behind a company name, could plead innocence, could submerge their identity in a composite image and deny all responsibility. Companies had many advantages over individuals: they kept tame lawyers to defend and twist charges and as a last resort, had the money to buy investigators off.

As for excuses, he'd heard them all: the defensive ones like, 'Unacceptable policies don't mean automatic guilt, Inspector'; or 'A man or woman may be the nominal head, but he or she isn't necessarily in charge'. Or the aggressive ones like, 'What is the actual offence here?' Followed by the familiar, 'What is the proof?' While once, in a never-to-be-forgotten case, which might have some bearing on this one, he'd been told that 'Altering the name of the company isn't illegal.'

He'd handled cases dealing with mismanagement of funds, evasion of taxes, even breaking of monopoly laws. Never one in which the scope of the company might have been deliberately hidden. Or the description of its actual dealings falsified.

He didn't even know if this was true here, that's partly what he'd come to find out. And he didn't know what the Trewiddle Haulage company 'hauled', although his instincts were already telling him it was very different from what he might have imagined. And since he himself had never experienced what he supposed should be called 'corporate murder', if such existed, he'd no idea how to go about compiling 'corporate evidence'.

In short he'd set himself an impossible task, but that didn't mean he shouldn't investigate further.

After surveying the layout of streets and buildings, he parked the car beside a pile of lumber at the back of the building, where the movement of work vehicles would help conceal it. And from long experience he'd found the rear of a building was always an easier, if not safer, entrance.

He took the trouble to ask a passing workman if it was OK to leave the car there, and was immediately surrounded by half a dozen men all giving advice in their friendly Cornish fashion; the gist being the car was fine where it was and they'd keep an eye on it, but why was a nice chap like him dealing with a bunch of foreigners.

'All hoighty toighty,' one said, tapping his nose, to be sent about his business by a passing foreman. Trust a workman to know what's what, Reynolds thought, waving his thanks. And always secure your escape route.

Picking his way through the piles of materials to the front of the building and the main entrance, he saw how inside the old stone facade, a new building was going up, gleaming in chrome and glass. His first impression was immediately of 'overkill'. What's a mere haulage company doing with such posh quarters? he thought.

As he gave his name to a receptionist, equally resplendent, with a bunch of flowers on her desk, he realised that if he hadn't been suspicious before, he would be now. One look should have tipped anyone off: this was no local Cornish concern, dealing with other local Cornish companies.

We're looking at a 'big time' company, he told himself, almost certainly funded from abroad, geared to overseas markets, luxuriating in its prospects of large-scale wealth. The sort of world that 'Mafiosi' comes from. But what on earth do they deal in?

The young lady, with a flick of her hair, asked in a bored voice, if he had an appointment. If not, then he must make one for another time. She waved a list at him. 'No one comes in without his name written here,' she said. Pryor and Pontings would turn in their collective graves, he thought, at the idea of a woman on the premises, let alone one this smart and efficient.

Conscious that his trousers must still be grass- and mud-stained, and that his shoes were equally dirty (although out of habit he usually kept them polished to military brightness) he tried charm, giving a bogus name and stating that he was a local writer, true enough, interested in an article on the firm for 'local publication', not true at all.

He'd banked on the possibility that companies, backed by mega-empires, might welcome favourable publicity, especially if they had secrets to hide. In any case Trewiddle Haulage might relish the idea of a tame local reporter, organized in advance on their side. He guessed right.

Relenting, she said she'd check if the director was free, and returned smiling affirmatively. But not before he'd managed to catch a glimpse of the appointment book.

Trying to recall names seen among Justin's papers, he found none that sounded familiar. Yet again, for a so-called local firm, the range of visitors, and the overseas bases of their home companies were impressive. Not your average small town customers.

The inner sanctum revealed even more chrome and glass, spread over an office the size of a cricket pitch. The director, seated at the far end, looked as English as Oliver Gatterly, with traditional tweeds and pipe, except for the large round spectacles more at home in stables than an office. And so out of place in a haulage yard Reynolds wanted to laugh. Remembering the rag and bone merchants of his childhood and the more modern dustmen with their yellow helmets and jackets, he wondered who was fooling who. And wondered even more at the folly of this disguise, when the man told him to 'fire away', in an accent more Texan that Barbs Gatterly's.

Reynolds settled himself in an easy chair, which together with a sofa and several other chairs made a little grouping around an imitation fireplace and gave a false impression of friendliness, while the director observed him from a safe distance, back to the windows. Not quite certain, then, Reynolds thought. On guard. What's he got to hide?

Asking the relevant questions, appropriate to his role of reporter, he listened to a gush of platitudes. Not lies, he thought, writing rapidly. Not quite lies, but certainly not truths. The 'director' continued to expand, in the most friendly fashion now, 'his' decision to set up a 'smallish' company suitable to a 'small community', part of a chain in other parts of England, all calculated to bring work and jobs to a depressed area – the same propaganda that Gatterly had spouted. Although, Reynolds thought, if the workmen out there were anything to go by, there was already bad feeling between 'locals' and 'newcomers'.

'You've got a fine office here,' he broke in, gesturing to the many windows. 'Restoration of this building must be costing a pretty penny?' To be told again most affably, that it was company policy to provide the best conditions for its staff, and 'Let the outer reflect the inner, wouldn't you agree?'

'No, I don't say I would.'

Before the director could think of a rejoinder, a phone rang. He picked it up, barked his name, Jack Bennet, then fell silent, listening intently. Only the sudden stiffening of his body gave away that what he was listening to wasn't welcome news. When he put the receiver down and swung his chair round, it was as if he were forcing himself to face his visitor. As if, Reynolds thought enlightened, he's just heard something that he doesn't like. About me perhaps?

'What did you say your name was?'

Bennet was making an effort to resume his earlier friendly manner but his question was revealing.

And when, making a rapid decision, Reynolds gave his real name, 'That wasn't what you said just now. So you aren't from the local press?' The man's face had paled but he was still trying to smile. 'What do you want?' he asked.

'Nothing much.' Reynolds' reply was calm. 'Actually I *am* a writer. Base my stuff on true experience. Let's say I've become interested in how an overseas firm, American I take it, can burrow into a local community, swallow up an old iron works and change it into a haulage company with a bogus Cornish name. Isn't it a fact,' he asked, 'that Trewiddle Haulage is actually connected with a company run by Mrs Gatterly on her father's behalf? And isn't it involved in plans to reopen an old mine near by. Wheal Cosmuir?'

The last two queries caught Jack Bennet on the raw. •
'What's your interest in all this, Mr Reynolds?' he asked sharply. He bent forward, his glasses sparkling. 'And where have you picked up all this info? It hasn't been made public yet.'

'Straight from the horse's mouth,' Reynolds told him cheerfully. 'Mrs Gatterly herself, to be precise.'

At that, pipe forgotten, Jack Bennet jumped to his

feet, as if Mrs Gatterly herself had just entered the room. 'You know her!' he cried. 'That calls for a celebration. Drink?'

He hurried to a sort of cabinet set in the wall, with a false front which opened to reveal bottles and glasses lined up against a mirror. There was a clink of ice.

'What's your tipple?' Jack asked with a return of benevolence. 'Mine's good old Scotch.'

'Nothing at the moment.'

Another example of trying to drink an enemy under the table. A good piece of advice it seems, the world over. He was more on the alert than ever. That air of friendliness is overdone. And what about the mirror at the rear of the cabinet, possibly a two-way contraption? Or have I been seeing too many American movies? He chided himself but these thoughts made him go more carefully than ever.

'I may not have made myself clear,' he said. 'I'm also here on business. I'd like your help.'

'Sure,' said Bennet amiably, too amiably.

'What does your company actually handle? Oh, come now,' he went on as Bennet began to quibble, 'Trewiddle Haulage of what? Why are you dealing with all those foreign companies I've just seen listed in your appointment book? It's not only what you're going to haul, is it? It's what you're going to dump. In the mine.' Now he was spelling it out clearly it made sense. 'Stuff that wouldn't be allowed in other countries,' he went on, warming to the task. 'Stuff that's too lethal to store just anywhere. Chemicals from TIC, the least of it. What about nuclear waste?' And if that's so, he thought, Edmund certainly uncovered a monster.

'I'm not responsible for company policy,' Jack Bennet was saying through pursed-up lips. The usual excuse. 'My work is with employees, keeping the staff happy.

Meeting prospective customers. PR, that sort of thing. You'll have to ask someone else those questions.'

Reynolds ignored his patter. 'I'm also investigating the murder of Mr Gatterly's sons,' he said. 'Justin Gatterly, and his twin brother Edmund.' Again Bennet mumbled something, 'You must have heard. One a ritualized killing. Either for having learnt too many secrets, or threatening perhaps to reveal them. The other, poisoned by mistake. By some of the chemicals Texas Industrials plans to bury in Wheal Cosmuir.'

Again it was a long shot and it paid off. The whisky splashed. 'How the hell do you know that?' Jack Bennet began, then again steadied himself.

'With a few little extras thrown in,' Reynolds added, 'such as gallery trashing and women intimidating. Where we have reliable witnesses.'

He mentioned this to stir things up further. With good effect.

'These are big assumptions, Mr Reynolds. And pose even bigger problems.' Jack Bennet managed a shaky laugh. 'We're a large company,' he went on, still trying to be the soul of good humour. 'I've no idea what our people do after hours. Or what vendettas any of our employees might have against the natives. In any case, as I've just intimated, I'm only nominally in charge.

'But,' he added quickly, himself changing tack, 'let's keep it that I'm interested in any proposal you might have.'

Reynolds stiffened, all his nerves on edge, adrenalin running. Could 'proposal' mean blackmail? Was Bennet referring to Justin? And was blackmail so much on Bennet's mind that he automatically assumed Reynolds was on to it too? In which case it was Reynolds' good luck that Bennet had somehow given himself away, without having to.

On full alert now, wary, he shifted his own position so that he wasn't hedged in by the coffee table and chairs, feeling in his pocket for the copy of the map.

Making a decision, one he felt he possibly might regret, he pulled the map out and held it in front of him. 'Is this what you mean?' he asked quietly, his own gaze never shifting from the other man's face. 'What's it worth to you?'

Bennet's breath came in quick gasps. His eyes behind his spectacles suddenly darkened, as if in this room of glass a shadow had passed over them. But all he said was, 'Where did you find that, Mr Reynolds?'

'I'm from the Devon and Cornwall Constabulary, actually,' Reynolds lied. 'And if you're interested in it, we are too. So suppose you start by first telling me what you know.'

But Bennet had nothing more to add. He must have begun to take stock of the situation, and realized he'd made a mistake. Or perhaps he'd just remembered he was in England. Policemen here aren't as powerful as they are in the States; for one thing they aren't usually armed. Or perhaps just seeing the map so whetted his appetite he was forgetting common sense.

Reynolds assumed the last when Bennet said abruptly, 'Suppose we make a deal, Mr Inspector. I get the map. You're free to go. And if you come back with full credentials, I'll be glad to help in any way I can.'

Meaning, Reynolds guessed, he'll try his own hand at blackmail first. But why 'free to go'? Who's to stop me if he doesn't? And more to the point, why 'full credentials'. By God, he thought, remembering his original expectations of danger, that telephone call did tip him off. So who was on the other end?

It had to be Barbs Gatterly, if she were as much in charge as he suspected, and Bennet had intimated.

Having heard where he and Derrymore were headed she would have sent a warning. And even if Bennet had become suspicious on his own, he wouldn't dare try something without her permission. And, like her husband, she knew his lack of actual official status.

Angry that he hadn't thought of this earlier, even more angry that he hadn't listened to his own instincts and kept Derrymore with him, he made a quick survey of his position.

He could just up and leave, but even if Bennet didn't stop him he'd probably call up reinforcements, if they weren't already waiting for him outside – he remembered Miss Heyward's description of the man in the suit. And with his cover blown as it were, he didn't have much room for manoeuvre. So he needed something for a lever, to take the pressure off.

'Right,' he said, again coming to a decision. 'You get the map, when I'm outside. First we'll take a walk together.'

Bennet understood what he meant. And such was his desire for the map he readily agreed. Only when they went through into the reception room did Reynolds see why – two men were waiting beside the outer door, just as he'd feared.

It was too late to back-track. Damn, he thought. He was in a bigger fix than before. How had they been alerted? Perhaps the mirror had been a two-way one after all.

The men were large, thugs, he told himself, eyeing them even more warily. They were lounging as if they were prospective clients, with nose and fists like boxers, business suits cut, he told himself, so that the underarm gun holsters didn't show. Making them look like inverted pears!

Remembering Sally Heyward's description he wanted

to laugh. But it wasn't funny. Sally could make an identification, if he could round them up. But they were armed. And he suspected already they could and would shoot.

He couldn't tell if they would dare risk tackling him here, in the lobby, with a bored receptionist looking on. They certainly could do a lot of damage outside. And if they'd been listening in they must know he was not a real police officer, so they'd make sure the damage 'outside' was thorough, and wasn't traceable to them.

All it would take was a strangle hold, and snap. Followed by a smooth cover-up, and, as Derrymore would put it, no one the wiser. Clemow would get a bonus he'd not been looking for and wouldn't do a thing to resolve an unexpected disappearance. And all the information Reynolds had gathered would vanish along with his own dead body . . . No way, he told himself. I've been in as tight a place before. His mind began to twist and turn, hunting for escape.

'Call off your toughies, Jack,' he said. 'They don't look friendly. And,' he improvised, 'I've Sergeant Derrymore waiting outside.'

He knew from the flicker behind the glasses that Bennet recognized the name. More proof, he thought. Bennet must have been told there were two of us. And he doesn't know where Derrymore is. He can't be sure I'm not telling the truth this time.

For a moment he thought his ruse had worked; Bennet was swayed by indecision. Then, making up his mind, he said in his affable way, 'We're going out, boys.' He and Reynolds now continued forward. 'Come with us if you like. Escort our friend, Mr Reynolds, off the premises.' He grinned at Reynolds. 'Then we can all meet Mr Derrymore,' he said, 'friendly like.'

The men who fell in step on either side of them were

as big and tall as Reynolds himself. Overweight perhaps, not in top condition, but together not easy to handle. Already he was assessing them and the situation with a practised eye, rejecting this idea, rejecting that, walking as slowly as he could to give himself time.

He let himself be 'escorted' past the supercilious receptionist. Suppose I shout to her for help, he thought. If I yell 'police' what will Miss Efficiency do? Probably grab her flowers. When I'm in the actual doorway, I'll make my move.

It was a split second decision based on the way the doors opened. They were made of glass, large, imposing double hung. One side was fixed shut. They would have to go in single file, probably letting Bennet go first.

As they came to the door, one man stepped forward to open it for the director. As he did so, Reynolds twisted under the other man's arm, tossed the map so that it slithered across the floor beneath the receptionist's desk. While she screamed and Bennet, with a howl, himself lunged out of line to grab it, Reynolds swung all his weight against the door, pinning the man against the glass. At the same time, with a back-handed jab he caught the second with his fist, then kneed him so he too collapsed. He was through the door and down the steps before they had disentangled themselves from each other.

Remembering the lay-out of the land he had studied previously, he turned towards where he'd left the car • and where he'd seen the workmen. He'd banked on workmen still being about, and for a moment when he saw they weren't, felt the same cold shiver go through him. Ducking by instinct behind a pile of bricks he heard the smack of the first bullet but no other sound. Silencers then. More thorough than he liked.

Both men were behind him now; he could hear them

shouting to each other. He'd miscalculated. On the straight he'd have no difficulty in getting away. But among these piles of building materials there was no straight path. And in any case, a man can't outrun a gun. Again he dived as a second shot whistled past.

They were gaining with each step. And he could only run in short bursts from cover to cover, each time being forced further from the car. He was bruised and shaken; grazed from splintered wood and brick. Another shot shattered behind him. Next time they wouldn't miss.

Now they were right behind him. Just as he thought he'd be done for, he heard, like a sound from heaven, Cornish voices shouting.

The builders had been seated round an open fire enjoying a break, but the sight of running men brought them out in force. Now they came swarming between Reynolds and his pursuers, asking what was wrong. Unable to fire, certainly not anxious to be found with guns, the two men halted, rapidly stuffing their weapons out of sight.

Noting this as he leapt from his last hiding place Reynolds kept on running. 'Thanks,' he shouted over his shoulder, 'nothing serious. Just a little disagreement with some "emmets". If you can, hold 'em off.'

He knew from the laughter and the way the workmen made a defensive ring, that the two gunmen would be kept arguing for a long time – 'emmet' being the contemptuous Cornish word for foreigners of any description.

Flicking a salute, he rounded the pile of lumber, got in the car and was away, too fast now for anyone to follow.

But he had learned all he needed. And even if the men he'd just encountered weren't the actual murderers of Justin, they'd showed him they were capable of murder.

Again it would be difficult to prove. Except for the word of the workmen who had come to his rescue, and the copy of the map which he'd used as bait, he had nothing substantial, although if the map was found in Bennet's possession that might count for something. Any other proof must come at a later time. Fingerprints in the gallery, voice and personal identification, these were details Clemow's team must take on.

Thoughtfully now, as he drove back to the meeting place in the valley, he began to reassess the position.

Much would depend on Clemow's skill and staying power – if Clemow was man enough to sustain the weight. But even if Clemow faltered, surely revealing what the mine was to be used for would lead to public outcry. Followed, if he were lucky, by an official inquiry. Which, as far as he was concerned, would mean he'd achieved part of what he wanted for Edmund Gatterly.

As for Barbs Gatterly, arresting her and her husband would cause an even greater scandal – if they ever were arrested. But whether she had engineered the break-in at the gallery or Justin's murder, she seemed less likely to be responsible for Audrey's accident, or Edmund's death given all the other evidence. Here were two issues that still needed investigation. Besides, he thought, suddenly weary of the greater ones and content to think of the smaller, where has Joe Fletcher got to? And, even smaller, what about Mazie Derrymore's poison-pen letter?

He was late when he arrived by the stile. No one was in sight. After the high rush of excitement comes cold sense. He might have, probably had, blown the whole thing. When Clemow bestirred himself there might be nothing left to find. Penzance is a sea-going port, always has been. A fast ship out with the tide is the best way for someone to hide. Or, remembering Barbs' 'company jet', there were planes too now-a-days.

On the other hand, he had done the best he could under the circumstances. And if Jack Bennet's marksmen had been better shots, or if the builders hadn't appeared in the nick of time, it wouldn't matter a damn if he'd done right or wrong, he'd never have lived to hear about it.

A depressing concept. Where's Derrymore? he thought.

After a good quarter of an hour had passed he got out of the car and leaned against the stile as before. The same scene, nothing changed. Still unworried he climbed the stile and started down the field, noticing for the first time the bruises and cuts, the stiffness in his joints. Show off, he told himself severely. Serves you right.

He came to the trees. It was cooler under them, still no sound except the rustle of dry leaves and the constant trickle of running water, not much of a stream at the end of summer. Despite his preoccupations the whole place interested him, even the oaks were an ancient kind, twisted and small. Wild life would flourish here, animals, birds. A real refuge, he thought. Why is it places like this are always so vulnerable?

There was a path but he kept away from it, skirting through small clearings edged with clumps of hazel and holly. For a moment he had the strangest feeling, as if he were walking beside a very old trail, and these open spaces, surrounded by trees, were all signs of its antiquity, as though all of England had once looked like this. In other parts of England people fought to keep their country heritage; he could understand Edmund's desire to keep this safe.

He stopped to listen. The sound of the stream came louder here as if splashing over rocks. He stepped aside to look, and saw, beneath some boulders, the figure lying on its side, as if asleep.

In her bedroom Mrs Gatterly was trying to do two things at once. She was speaking on the telephone – well, shouting was more like it – while trying to pack, jamming jewellery and clothes into an airline bag. 'Fools, fools,' she kept screaming,' I know I said two, but if he was alone, don't use that as an excuse. You've made a mistake, that's all there is to it. Pappy won't like it. Get him, before he gets you. And find my son.' She shouted even louder. 'I don't know for sure. Try Wheal Cosmuir,' before slamming the receiver down.

She didn't mention she'd had the company plane alerted. When it landed with its pack of lawyers, it would make ready for instant departure. For her and Richard. She didn't tell anyone she was going, or where she planned to go, although it wouldn't take long to find out after she'd left. But once she was out of England they could whistle in the wind before she'd come back. And if Richard didn't show, she'd go without him. She could always send for him later on.

And even when, having waited long enough, she crept down with her suitcase to the garage and found it empty, the Rolls gone presumably with Fletcher, she still didn't let that stop her. Because, as always, she had 'pappy' to look after her. And he had the money to buy a hundred cars and hire as many jets.

Chapter 19

When Reynolds reached Derrymore the sergeant was barely conscious. His clothes were torn and great weals were scored across his body as if someone had thrashed him. One arm at least was broken, perhaps other bones as well, and blood had clotted over two head wounds. Feeling him for other hurts Reynolds came across the mobile phone, smashed, as if someone had hit it with a hammer.

From his war-time experience (in war he'd had too many dealings with serious wounds) he knew that Derrymore should be taken care of as soon as possible. He couldn't tell if there were internal injuries, or if the head injuries were dangerous. He also wasn't sure where Derrymore's assailants, he presumed several of them, had gone. He did therefore what he would have done in wartime conditions: hid the victim as quickly as possible, until he was sure how and where to move him.

Using his coat as a makeshift stretcher he dragged Derrymore still further under the boulders, away from the water and out of sight, difficult because the ground was so rough. There, in a sort of shallow cave, he made the sergeant as comfortable as he could with pieces of torn shirt for a sling, and his own jacket for covering, using bracken (which fortunately grew thickly along the banks) for a pillow, and then piling more bracken over him for warmth. That done, he left for the car and help, but not before he'd whispered in the sergeant's ear what he was doing, pretty certain Derrymore couldn't hear him but, again from his own experience, knowing that if there were a glimmer of consciousness, being told what was going on was a comfort.

He guessed that Derrymore's attackers were members of the protest group Mary Lou Fletcher had talked about. Whether they were the same as the nature militants, and whether Mary Lou's daughter and Richard Gatterly were with them, was, at this point, immaterial. Having revealed how violent and ruthless they were, like Justin's attackers, he had to keep clear of them. Again he was struck by how different they were from any conservationists he'd ever dealt with.

Wishing he could have at least asked Derrymore how many there were and how close, wondering if they'd left Derrymore lying there, or if he'd somehow managed to get away from them, he reconnoitred carefully before starting out.

There were still no sounds, except the usual harmless ones; he heard no startled bird calls, no sudden rustlings in the bushes. Nevertheless, instead of taking the shortest route back to the car he decided to circle round to make sure no one was lying in wait.

Instinctively covering up his immediate tracks, especially the place where Derrymore had been lying – he'd lost a lot of blood – he moved quietly away from the stream taking advantage of the thick cover. He didn't know why he did this, it was just a feeling he had, until he saw, under a bush, a scrap of yellow paper. It was a chocolate wrapper which hadn't been there when he'd passed the spot on the way in. From then on he crawled on hands and knees.

It was a long time since he'd moved like this through underbrush, expecting any moment to run into trouble.

Even now on his wild bird expeditions he didn't resort to such elaborate measures. And the last time he'd been armed himself. He found again, like bike riding, it was a skill one didn't forget, although his shoulders ached as if they'd been racked and his legs felt like rubber.

Like a shadow he crept from one tree to another until he came to the edge of the woods, a long way above the original path. From here, he peered carefully down across the stubble field towards the car. Only then did he see how right his instincts had been.

His car was still there, parked in the late afternoon sun. Beside it was another. Large. Black. Four-wheel drive. When its driver moved out to train his binoculars along the trees, he recognised him, the man he'd pinned against the glass door. Not looking happy. He caught the glint of a gun, and sank back under cover.

His first thought was where's the second man? The answer – somewhere in the wood, leaving his partner on guard – wasn't pleasant. Nor was the answer to his second question: what the devil are they doing here?

He reminded himself they couldn't be looking for Derrymore as they'd no idea he was here and, presumably having arrived after Reynolds himself, they couldn't have been the attackers. It was equally possible they hadn't originally been hunting for Reynolds either; for one thing, as far as he knew, they hadn't seen his car, and wouldn't know he'd come in this direction. Then it occurred to him that they might not have seen him drive off, but Bennet perhaps had. If so, they certainly must be searching for him now.

For the moment, Derrymore was well hidden, although in need of medical attention. As for going for help, even if he abandoned the idea of reaching his car there was no way to cross that expanse of open field to the road without been seen. And as he remembered from the map, there were no farms nearby in any other direction, just wild countryside. His only choice, apart from just sitting and waiting (impossible, given Derrymore's condition and his own temperament) was to track down the gunman in the wood and disarm him, with the intention of then disarming his companion, while avoiding Derrymore's assailants if they were still here, which he'd begun to doubt.

More complicated than he liked, but stalking through an English woodland valley was easy compared with stalking through the desert. And, as he'd told Naomi, it was something he once was good at, unlike the gunman. If he had dropped the chocolate wrapper, that was unbelievably careless.

Returning in the same unobtrusive fashion to where he'd left Derrymore he was relieved to find the sergeant looking better. His colour had returned, his breathing was regular. After moistening Derrymore's lips with river water, Reynolds saw his eyes flicker open. 'Sorry guv,' he heard Derrymore say, 'but they came at me at once. By the mine.'

That was all he said, lapsing back into what seemed more like sleep than unconsciousness. Good work, Derrymore, he thought. Once more replacing the bracken so that the sergeant was completely hidden, he set off in pursuit of his quarry.

Starting from where he'd found the wrapper he began to search for other clues. There were no special marks to show which way the gunman had gone. In fact, as Reynolds studied the terrain more carefully, he could tell several people had already taken the same route today so any distinguishing traces were already lost.

From his earlier study of the map, he knew the valley ran roughly south to north, following the course of the stream and narrowing considerably as it reached the mine entrance, in a high escarpment at the northern end. An old train track began there, running east, presumably used to carry out ore, now petering away in rough moorland after a few hundred yards or so. To the west, nothing but overgrown wilderness. It would be natural therefore for someone starting at the southern end of the valley to work his way north, and on that assumption, Reynolds decided to follow. In any event, as Derrymore had intimated, he'd had his encounter at the mine entrance, presumably managing somehow to give his attackers the slip afterwards. If they were still there, rounding them up, if that were possible, would be a secondary objective.

The going was easy at first. Keeping out of sight he followed the stream until it was crossed by a paved path, the rounded granite stones suggesting this was the original trail to the mine. Here he cut away from both stream and path, continuing parallel, uphill now, under cover, moving cautiously, with many stops to listen.

The going was rougher here, trees giving way to scattered rocks, interspersed with thick scrub and brambles. In one or two places strange mounds appeared, like giant ant hills, covered in gorse and bracken, the soil still glittering with the mica of old spoil heaps. Between them were deep pits, old mine shafts probably, now full of water, some of them almost filled with rotting leaves and sludge.

He edged round them, again reduced to crawling, for the first time sure someone was ahead of him. Not that there was any noise, but he could feel a presence, as if body heat left traces in the air. Several people, not one. Certainly not one man on his own. So where had the gunman gone?

The ground fell away abruptly. He edged towards the drop-off, where he could peer through a gap in the thickets. He had come out on a spur of rock, and was looking down into what seemed like a natural hollow or plateau, surrounded on two sides by cliffs.

He could hear the sound of water clearly, and from the rock face opposite, saw the race of white foam as the stream burst out of what looked like a gap, before curling away and dropping down into the valley.

This must be the mine entrance, he thought, and sure enough, on the crude plateau in front of it, brilliantly lit by the sun like a stage setting, were abandoned wheels, great steel cables, red with rust, and bits of crumbling machinery. To his right, running east, scattered pieces of track marked what looked like the old railway. But all these things were dominated by what was on the left, something that had definitely not been on the map.

Here rocks and earth had been moved recently, shoved out of the way by bulldozers, trees and bushes buried in huge ungainly heaps. A wide flat track of fresh orange soil had been cut out of the steep rock face itself to make a new road. This road veered round to continue in a sweeping curve towards the west, a new road Trewiddle Haulage would use to bring in their waste. Of course, he thought, they've started it here first, hoping it won't be noticed. Later they'll loop it round to join up with the old valley approach road we were on.

There were no workers, but plenty of evidence of their work, together with coils of rope and wire and piles of wooden posts. Several large trucks and a bulldozer lay idle, the name on their sides, Trewiddle Haulage, clearly marked. Something's put a stop to them, he thought, and then realized what it was.

Some of the trucks had been smashed to bits; bright metal pieces were scattered round them like confetti, their wheels wrenched off, and in the case of the bulldozer, its engine ripped out. How's that possible? he thought staring. For a moment the scene resembled a hideous disembowelling.

On the far side of the trucks, close to the cliff opposite, he now picked out movement and a group of people came out of the shadow. He saw how difficult it was to spot them, they were all dressed in camouflage fatigues, and wore black face masks. Never seen a protest group decked out in that fashion, he thought. My God, they look like terrorists. He thought of Derrymore, and his anger, so far held in check began to rise.

He was surprised how many there were: over twenty at least. They were armed too, although not with guns, thank the Lord. Still, heavy wooden clubs, steel hammers, crowbars, could be as dangerous judging by the condition of the vehicles. Again he thought of Derrymore.

Some disagreement seemed to be in progress. Although Reynolds was too far away to hear what was being said, he could tell the argument was becoming heated. Then someone he took to be the leader, began to speak earnestly.

Although age and sex were impossible to judge beneath the uniform and mask, as far as Reynolds could understand, efforts were being made to exhort the 'troops' back to work, which a second-in-command pantomimed by flailing with his crowbar towards the trucks.

Reynolds was just debating whether he should come out of cover himself to stop this further destruction, when there was a rattle of stones further to the left. Someone was approaching along the new road. As he watched, a man came round the corner with a gun in his hand. But it wasn't one of the gang, or even the second of the 'thugs' from this morning. By God, he thought, startled. What's Joe Fletcher doing here? He found himself looking instinctively for the Rolls but if Joe had used it, presumably he'd not been able to bring it along this stretch of new road.

His second thought was, here's help. Then Fletcher shouted.

'Here, you,' he cried, addressing the group. 'Cut that out. I've seen enough of wanton waste. Vandalism, I calls it. And where's my girl?'

There was a murmur, almost a laugh. But when Fletcher raised the gun they backed off hastily. Only two held their ground, the leader, and his second. As they approached together, Reynolds could see them clearly now.

There were still masked, and the way they walked suggested they'd no fear of guns. And they weren't going to have any nonsense from an old game keeper.

'You put that gun away,' the leader told him, as if he were a child. 'And you clear off. This isn't Trewithen Manor. You don't have any say here.'

While the other shouted, 'And forget you've even seen us. Or you won't keep that nice little house of yours long.'

Before Reynolds could digest what all this meant, several things happened. Fletcher had stopped still, several paces away from the last of the vehicles. Dressed in his usual corduroys, with his ammunition bag slung over his shoulder, he was standing in the sunlight, with his gun ready, looking as he might have done in the past, determined to flush out vermin.

The sunlight was made all the brighter by the shadow cast by the cliff, the same shadow from which the group had emerged and back into which most of them were now beginning to sidle. It lit up Fletcher's face, and by contrast the masked faces of the two young people beside him. Young people? Reynolds thought, suddenly appalled. They're *twice* as old as he is, or at least twice as shrewd. He's a child in comparison with them, almost an innocent.

At this same moment, another shout froze them all in place. Along the old railway track another man was approaching slowly, stopping now and then to wipe his face. A tall large man, in a suit, his piggy eyes hidden behind dark glasses.

As he approached, Reynolds recognized him as the man he'd been stalking. Somehow he'd gone astray, and found his way back to the mine along the old railway track, certainly a round-about approach but one which explained why Reynolds had not come upon him earlier.

He also had a definite purpose. Halting some hundred yards off, he too began to yell. 'Richard! Hey Rich!' Reynolds could hear him distinctly. 'Where are you, fellah? I've news for you.' And when no one paid attention, 'Hey there, Richie, your mammy's after you. So you'd better come quick.'

It was only when the second-in-command drew off his mask (against his companion's wishes, but he pushed the other figure aside) that Reynolds recognised the handsome Gatterly face, again transformed by rage into a snarl. Whether Richard recognised his mother's messenger, or would have gone with him eventually, his immediate response was to yell back. 'Fuck off. Leave me alone. Can't you see I'm busy?' His second response was to tell Fletcher the same thing, before shouting at the leader, 'This has nothing to do with us.'

It was when the man repeated that Richard's mother had sent for him – 'Wants you back fast, boy; she told me to get you. The plane's set to leave this evening and you're to be on it.' – that Richard hesitated. And the masked leader really turned on him.

'You're running away.'

The words came screaming out from behind the mask. Surely that's Fletcher's daughter, Reynolds thought, enlightened. Syb Fletcher. So that's who Richard Gatterly was waiting for, and it isn't cricket that they've been playing.

'You think you can leave, just like that! Ditch us without a word, leave us to shoulder the blame. Play act. Just as you've always done.' The voice had become distorted with rage. A purple jersey escaping between the front opening of the fatigues gave a vivid resemblance to a grotesque Sesame Street character with the stuffing falling out. 'You don't have to obey them. Remember how you said you liked that we did things for real.'

At that Richard replied, 'You don't know my mother. Or my grandfather. I've got to go.'

'Got to? Got to?' The voice was razor sharp now. 'No one's got to do anything. The stars say you stay. It's all written in the stars. Set yourself against the stars, you set yourself against nature. The world awry.'

Fletcher, at first overwhelmed by all this confusion, could make no sense of what was being said either. Losing patience, he grabbed what Reynolds took to be his daughter's arm and attempted to pull her away.

'Leave him be,' he was shouting, 'he's no good for you, he'll do you wrong.'

'Wrong!' The hiss behind the mask seemed all the more venomous. 'The wrong's already been done. It's too late to set it right. I had plans for him.'

Instead of trying to wrestle free, as Reynolds supposed, she actually fell back against Fletcher, pushing him off-balance. He remembered the girl as large and heavy. And before Fletcher could prevent it, there was a tussle, more shouts, the rattle of cartridges as the ammunition bag came unfastened and they fell out. Then, the sound of a gun going off.

The noise reverberated off the cliff face and echoed back down the valley. At its noise, the rest of the group, who had been milling uneasily like scared sheep, took off down the railway track, running past the other fellow as if he didn't exist. And he still stood there as if expecting Richard to join him.

But Richard wouldn't join him. Richard was lying on the ground. Forgetting the danger he was in, Reynolds himself began to run towards Richard, while Fletcher took his still masked daughter by the hand and yanked her out of sight into the underbrush. And this time she went with him readily, leaving gun and ammunition bag.

Before he reached the body, Reynolds knew Richard was dead. A gun fired at that close range leaves a hole big enough to put your fist in. He knew it too by the silence that had followed the shot and the way the boy lay. He bent over him, sickened at the sight of the disfigured face and the puddling blood. God, he thought, what's the point of it all? What's the use? This is the consequence of summer's boredom, he thought, remembering his original assessment. Unwillingly, the words he'd read came into his mind: 'I had an Edward (read Edmund) and a Richard killed him'. My God, what else have the pair of them done? he asked.

It was then the gunman on the railway track made his presence known again. He was still too far off to take effective aim, but he could fire his own gun. Which he now did. A splatter of dust rose from where the bullet hit.

Reynolds too had a gun at hand. As he snatched it from the ground and lifted it to aim, he suddenly realised something else. The man on the track was clearly visible, but was looking into the sun. He probably couldn't even distinguish who was actually there in front of him; despite the glasses all he could have seen were dark hazy figures, haloed with a blaze of light.

'Stop there, don't move.'

It was Reynolds' turn to shout. 'If you want Richard, drop your gun.'

The man wavered for a moment. Then, 'You!' he howled, recognizing the voice at least. 'I've been looking for you too.'

Before Reynolds could say anything else he fired again, and at the same time began to run, leaping across the tracks and moving forward at great speed. He must have been so determined to get hold of Reynolds that he put that before the welfare of his employer's son; and he must have gambled on Reynolds still not being armed.

He'd have Reynolds within range in a second. Reynolds lifted the shotgun, steadied it, fired. The unaccustomed recoil hammered into his shoulder, but he'd snatched up a handful of cartridges and rammed two new ones in before the dust of his own shot had cleared.

He'd not mistaken his aim. The man had stopped short, the scatter of shot almost cutting the ground in front of him.

'You want Richard Gatterly?' Reynolds shouted again. 'Throw away your gun, and he's yours.'

But the other man didn't seem to hear him. After that slight pause he still came leaping forward blindly, bull like, Reynolds thought, shooting wildly. All Reynolds had time to do was catch the gun by its barrel so he could use the stock like a cricket bat. As the man charged down upon him he swung with all his weight.

There was a crack; the man's gun dropped. He stood

for a second nursing his shattered arm, an infuriated look of pain mixed with surprise on his face; then with a howl he fell to his knees.

Leaping forward himself, Reynolds grabbed the other gun and stuffed it in his pocket, before the man could make another move.

'Richard's dead,' he told him brutally, more brutal because he knew now the type he was dealing with. And because he was sure this man hadn't shown any emotion or pity when he and his mate bound and shot Justin. 'So there's nothing we can do for him. And you'd better wait here, while I get the police.'

It was the work of a moment to bind the man with all the rope and wire that was scattered among the rubble, while he writhed and groaned, begged for pity, offered money, anything, rather than leave him here beside Richard's body. 'They'll say I did it,' he cried. 'She'll blame me.'

'Shut up,' Reynolds told him finally, breaking his own disgusted silence. 'Or I'll tape your mouth, like you did Justin's.' He tested the knots. 'And you won't be forgotten. I promise you.'

Leaving that reminder for company Reynolds was gone, leaping down the path, not worrying what noise he made. Derrymore's attackers would never catch up with him, lost probably amid the wilderness beyond the old railway. Fletcher and his daughter would be miles away by now. And with shotgun and handgun he had the other 'thug' at his mercy.

But as he ran he knew he, himself, had achieved nothing. He had failed to prevent a killing; and had again failed to see what should have been obvious.

'Crookback Richard'.

Miss Trewithen had got that right at least.

When he came to the crossing with the stream, he

resisted the temptation to see how Derrymore was, went forward more cautiously until he again came to the edge of the wood. Both cars were still there, the second gunman still on guard, pacing nervously up and down. He must have heard the shots and was even more on alert.

It was easily done: a warning shot, then when the gunman dropped to the ground, another shot to make him surrender his own weapon.

He'd brought more rope and wire, and the stile posts made as good a tying post as a tree. Securing his own car by removing the distributor, he took the four-wheel-drive. Unbarring the gate he drove it across the field to the edge of the woods closest to where he'd left his friend. He'd decided that he would drive Derrymore to the nearest hospital, rather than risk the delay of going for ambulance and police and then waiting for them to arrive, and it occurred to him that this would cut the distance to carry Derrymore.

Even so, this part wasn't easy, the sergeant being as tall as Reynolds, and much wider, his mam's cooking, if nothing else, giving him weight. The only way Reynolds could get him on his shoulders, was to make him co-operate. Dabbing his face again with cold water, speaking to him constantly, he finally saw the sergeant's eyes open. 'Sorry,' Derrymore's voice sounded thick as if his mouth were swollen. 'All this trouble.'

'It's no trouble,' Reynolds said. 'Save your strength.' He pressed his shoulder in encouragement.

With some trepidation he had Derrymore try each limb, decided that, although the younger man winced at every movement, except for the arm his injuries were not as serious as he'd first thought. Bit by bit he managed to coax Derrymore to his feet, propped against a boulder, then with a mighty effort stooped and transferred the weight upon his own shoulders in the traditional fireman's lift.

Aware of how painful this must be for Derrymore, he tried to walk without staggering, not easy among the rough boulders and rocks bordering the stream. Gradually, half bent over, he managed a kind of shuffle, which took him longer than he planned, forced as he was to stop for breath after only a few steps.

Derrymore's legs, catching every so often on a tree trunk, with a jar that almost made Reynolds stumble, must have sent waves through the other's body. He heard Derrymore give a short gasp and then sag, even heavier than before. But he couldn't stop, just kept on plodding forward.

When, after what seemed like hours, he reached the Land Rover, he was dripping with sweat. Derrymore was still unconscious, just as well perhaps. Placing him on the passenger side as best he could, he drove up the field and through the gate, leaving his second 'prisoner' still fuming. It was only after he had seen the stretcher carrying Derrymore rush into the Emergency Room that he turned wearily to the policeman now standing next to him.

'There're several more things need seeing to,' he said.

And heard without satisfaction the order go out to search Wheal Cosmuir for the body of a boy, and for two tied-up men, one of them wounded.

Then there were the protesters to deal with. Several stragglers were picked up as they emerged from the rough land beyond the railway track, miles to the east. Those who had got away would be traced eventually. For example, young people boarding buses or trains were stopped and questioned, and if their answers were unsatisfactory, were searched for masks and uniforms. Others, incriminated by evidence given by their companions, were later arrested in their homes. To Reynolds' disappointment many proved to be members of the conservationist group to which Edmund had belonged, part of the random, destructive element which crept so often these days into opposition groups, deplored by the traditionalists but beyond their control.

All those taken into custody admitted that their leader was a young woman but no one knew anything about her, neither her name nor where she came from (although many confessed they had joined in with her suggestions because they were frightened not to). And neither questioning those involved in the destruction at Wheal Cosmuir, nor threatening them with the more serious charge of a violent attack upon a police officer, could budge them from their stand: that they didn't know who the woman was and couldn't identify her as she had always worn a mask in their company.

Enquiries were also immediately focused on Trewiddle Haulage, where Mr Bennet was questioned: an easier nut to crack. Following the arrest of his henchmen, he was more than ready to co-operate, admitting straight away that he knew of Justin's attempt at blackmail and the importance of the map, just as Reynolds had surmised, but had attempted to take the map 'to prevent more trouble': an unlikely excuse. His confessions confirmed Reynolds' suspicions about the company, including the reasons why it wanted to re-open the mine and what it wanted to dump there. And again, as Reynolds had surmised, these had nothing to do with tin!

All Bennet's admissions were substantiated by the findings in Gatterly's computers, even to the list of overseas concerns that Reynolds had spotted while waiting to be admitted to Bennet's presence. Most of them were also subsidiaries of Texan Oil, or had some connection. And the waste that they wanted to have Trewiddle Haulage take care of, by dumping and storing it in the mine, was both nuclear and chemical – stuff that other countries wouldn't allow and were afraid of, and Cornish authorities wouldn't have allowed either had they known the truth.

As for the news of Richard's shooting and the part played by Fletcher and his daughter, this had galvanized Clemow and his team into action – not quickly enough, however, to prevent Mrs Gatterly's leaving.

How she got away had been a masterpiece of deception. Without a car, she'd simply 'demanded' that one of the younger policemen drive her to Lostwithiel, 'for some shopping'; a command which the young fellow nervously obeyed.

Carrying only one large handbag from there she'd taken a taxi to Plymouth airport, and, having abandoned all the rest of her belongings, including her son, was on her way before anyone realized she'd gone. Whether they'd ever get her back was another matter. But the selfish disregard she showed towards her son was startling. His death the punishment to fit the crime.

Fletcher too had arrived back, with Syb in tow. He parked the Rolls carefully in its allotted place in the garage, (he had indeed taken the Rolls, and no one had thought to look for it until Mrs Gatterly did) before coming into the manor to give himself up. Over Miss Trewithen's protests he'd then confessed to a whole slew of crimes: the putting of poison in the food, the giving of keys to Edmund, the shooting of Richard. The only thing he stoutly swore he hadn't done was meddle with Miss Linton's car.

As for his daughter being with the protesters, she wasn't to blame. Richard Gatterly had forced her to come. He was older, more mature, sophisticated, she didn't know what was happening – all a pack of lies. Yet Reynolds felt sorry for the man. What else could a loving father do but protect his child?

Since Reynolds knew what had happened at the mine, he was equally suspicious about Fletcher's other confessions, but another long argument with Clemow, from a distance, was not to his taste. Tomorrow he'd come to it.

His first priority now was Derrymore.

Derrymore was looking somewhat the worse for wear, his hair cut short like a scruffy bear and both eyes rapidly blackening. But, thanks in part to the ex-Inspector, he was not as bad as he could have been.

'He's a dislocated collar bone, a broken rib or two, as well as his arm,' the nurse was proud to relate. 'But we'll have him out of here in next to no time. What've you been doing to him, and yourself?' she wondered, looking more carefully at Reynolds' battered appearance.

'That's what my mam'll say,' Derrymore managed a weak grin.

He'd been filling Reynolds in with details of how he, too, had realized the protesters were ahead of him, and had come upon them just as they were about to start smashing the parked vehicles. Stupidly, he admitted, he'd tried to stop them, been recognized by their leaders (whom he hadn't had chance to identify). Urged on by these leaders then, the second-in-command now identified for certain as Richard Gatterly, the rest of the group had attacked.

He'd not had much of a chance against their metal bars and clubs, but in the end had managed to evade them by hiding in one of those old pits, under the leaves and mud. Then when they'd gone he'd staggered back to where Reynolds had found him. He didn't say 'If they had found me instead . . .' But Reynolds and he both knew what that would have meant.

'Funny though,' he did say, when Reynolds had explained in turn what had happened to him. 'I thought the pair of them were urging each other on, trying to outdo each other, as if there was a struggle between them over who could do most.'

He didn't ask what had become of the two youngsters who had led the attack on him. Reynolds didn't tell him and perhaps he didn't want to know, but he did suddenly try and sit up to say with a real groan, 'Oh, my sainted goodness, what about Miss Heyward? She's supposed to be staying with my mam. And what will my mam say when she hears what I've done?'

Promising to visit Mazie to make things right with her, Reynolds left, suddenly recognizing where he was. He had come in by the emergency entrance; it was the taxi rank by the main one that set him right, the same hospital in which his ex-wife was a patient.

Allowing himself a momentary thought of where she was at this moment, and where Naomi was, he hesitated, drawn back to visit Audrey. At first he wanted to resist, but some thought about unfinished business urged him on.

He found them side by side, Audrey sitting in a chair with a rug over her lap, studying what looked like swatches of material.

'Don't mind me,' he said, as they looked up, startled, obviously engrossed in each other and not expecting anyone. 'I just thought I'd see how you were doing.'

Audrey was looking better, he thought, still pale, but her eyes alive. And when he had told them all that had happened and been found out so far, and when, after a few moments, Naomi left tactfully on some pretext, he was able to explain to Audrey. 'I wanted you especially to know. I thought you would be pleased that Edmund's death has been vindicated.'

'Then that's thanks to you,' she said.

It was a generous answer, one he hadn't expected. She raised herself up, looking at him intently. 'Whatever happened that night,' she went on, 'let's forget it. And let's forget that once we tore each other to pieces. Never again. I know that your not being a police officer any more is mainly my fault,' she added, as if it had been gnawing at her for a long time. 'And when you were, do you know, I hated it. And you yourself, I suppose, for being so good at your job, and letting it come between us. But I always understood that you loved your work. So there's something I'd like to say. I was so jealous,' she paused, 'of you, of all you did, and all you achieved. I had nothing. But now I count for something in my own right. I like what I do. I've grown up at last,' she said. 'Forgive me.'

For being what I was, she meant, for becoming what I am. It was more than a peace offering, it was a benediction.

He left thinking that Audrey had been drawn into this case, and came to grief, because she was fascinated by someone else's desire to set things right. And I was drawn in, and Derrymore after me, because of guilt, and my own desire to set things right, too, when she asked me. But I can't carry the whole world on my shoulders like an Atlas. And behind it all – one man's desire to please a grasping wife and father-in-law – opposed by a son who couldn't have realized what a dangerous force he unleashed. As Derrymore would say, it makes you think.

And feeling better than he had any right to, he paid his final call, on Mazie Derrymore.

It was getting on for dark now, and Mrs Derrymore

was beginning to be anxious, although out of respect for her visitors she hadn't said anything. She and Sally Heyward and the female duty officer had just finished a nice little supper and were about to watch the news on telly, when Reynolds knocked at the door.

Expecting her son, she trotted to answer it. He could hear her scolding as she came down the hallway. Then seeing him, as he stood in the hall light, in a shirt that he'd borrowed, too small for him, minus his jacket, his face and hands a mass of scratches, she couldn't prevent herself from exclaiming, 'Whatever have you done to yourself?' Just as Derrymore said she would. To be followed with, 'And what've you done with my Derry?'

It took a long while to convince her that Derry was fine, he'd be out of hospital in a day or so; Reynolds would take her to visit him tomorrow.

'Such a day,' Mazie said at last, 'I knew it would go wrong. Ever since that new letter comed . . .' She put her hand over her mouth to stop herself.

And so reminded Reynolds of the last piece in the puzzle. Finally retrieving the letter from the dustbin where she'd tossed it, he promised her he'd 'take care of it.'

He also reassured Miss Heyward she was safe to go home. The police had arrested two men, he told her, one of whom he was sure was the one who had harassed her. He didn't explain how or where. He'd come to that later.

Miss Heyward in the meantime was watching Mazie, who was still not quite her cheerful self. 'I'll stay the night here anyway,' she said firmly. 'If Mrs Derrymore will have me.'

She smiled at Reynolds, as if to say that she was not ungrateful, but really much better at looking after people than being looked after.

Nor did she say, and I'll come and see Derrymore with you and her tomorrow. It was too soon after one loss, too soon for either Derrymore or her to look ahead. But Reynolds sensed in time they would.

And with all that personal and professional business so far tidied away satisfactorily, he went into his own home, where sleep never felt so good.

Chapter 20

The next morning, in the light of day, Reynolds was at last free to sift through all the remaining pieces of evidence and make sense of them.

Starting with the beginning, the murder of Edmund.

According to Fletcher's statement, riddled with flaws, Fletcher himself had allowed two unknown hikers (presumably the original ones he and Mary Lou had mentioned) to come into the house. He hadn't asked what their intention was, had let them in to do whatever mischief they could, 'out of hatred for my employer' (his words).

Out of the same dislike and in his effort to help Edmund against his father, he'd later given Edmund a key. He hadn't asked what Edmund wanted it for, it wasn't his place to do so, although he had in fact been on watch in the bushes, 'on guard' he called it, all evening, to make sure nothing went wrong. He wouldn't have dreamed of interfering if he hadn't seen the police car coming up the drive. The original difficulty of what he and Mary Lou could have heard or not heard from their house was thus finally solved, this part of his testimony at least accepted as probably true.

As for Justin, if Miss Trewithen hadn't claimed that responsibility for herself, he would have tried to take the blame for the whole scheme. Under the circumstances the best he could do was admit she had often discussed Justin's 'difficulties' with him, such as the day by the river when Reynolds and Derrymore had come upon them. And she'd told him of the phone call. He couldn't identify what Justin's problems were because like her, he didn't know their full extent, but when, in a panic, she'd suddenly rung him up for help, he'd pushed the car in the river, and arranged for Justin to stay at the Grangers' farm. Again probably true. Reynolds had been right about the reason for the plan, but got the timing wrong when it was arranged – that is, it had to be after the visit to Justin's flat, not before. But all in all as Reynolds had surmised, nothing new there.

That left only the killing of Richard. Joe's claim, that he'd come to the valley with the express intention of shooting Richard, rescuing the 'child' and coming back to face the music, was dubious. Intention perhaps, Reynolds granted. But that wasn't the way it had happened.

'So Joe was the main culprit all the time.' A satisfied Clemow let out a long sigh of relief. 'I gather the two fellows you caught,' he added reluctantly, 'have confessed to Justin's murder, in that each has blamed the other. And they've given the reason, Justin was blackmailing their company. Over some map, which I think you and Derrymore found, behind a picture!'

He tried to keep the chagrin out of his voice. It would never do to let on so much had happened that he hadn't known about.

When Reynolds merely said, 'I'd put my money on the one who tried to shoot me,' Clemow looked blank, going on to say, 'One or the other presumably made the phone call to Miss Trewithen. As well as attacking the gallery, and harassing a Miss, Miss . . .' He consulted his notes. 'Miss Naomi. And a Miss Heyward. Who the devil are they?'

When Reynolds explained, he grunted noncommittally. 'Well,' he said with a heavy sigh, 'just fill it all in when you write your report. And give a mention to old Derrywhat's it, injured in the line of duty. He did well to track those protesters down.'

A grudging compliment.

He turned to Reynolds. 'As for Mrs Gatterly,' he said, 'fancy, a nice woman like that. Rich as Hades too. I pity the husband. I knew all along he wasn't involved. And such a tragedy about their son, Richard. Must have been led astray don't you think, by local hooligans?'

Reynolds felt like saying, 'No, he wasn't. And no, I don't call it a tragedy. It was inevitable.'

Instead he said, 'I think you should make a check on Richard Gatterly. Get his school records, here and in America. Find out all you can about him. Even grill his father. Because, if what I suspect is true, Richard isn't as innocent as you'd like to believe.' And, as Clemow gave a groan, he added, 'When Derrymore sends in his report, he'll give a very different version about the attack at the mine. I think you'll find that Richard was as much to blame as anyone. As for Mr Gatterly,' here he did hesitate because he too had some residue of sympathy for the man. He went on firmly, 'you know ignorance is no defence in law. Oliver Gatterly was well aware of what his wife was doing. And what his sons were like. If he didn't foresee the effects, he should have done.' And when Clemow once more began to argue, 'I think you'll agree that Justin isn't an innocent victim. Nor really is Edmund – if he were at all aware of the militants in his group and their probable violence. As for Sybil Fletcher, whom no one has mentioned so far, she's even less innocent. In fact I think she's responsible for all the events at the manor, including Edmund's death.' And before Clemow could regain breath to answer, 'So, with or without permission, I'm going to question Sybil and her mother now. And while I'm at it, try reading this!' And he produced the Shakespeare book from his pocket, opening it to Richard III.

According to her daughter, Mary Lou was upstairs, too ill to come down. But the daughter was in the sitting room, devouring toast and honey, looking remarkably pleased with herself after what might have been taken as a traumatic experience.

She actually smiled at Reynolds, licking the knife. 'I thought it might be you,' she said. 'So everything that happened yesterday has been cleared up?'

If she were innocent, like her mother she seemed strangely immune to the effects of death: in this instance, the shooting of someone whom she must have known well. Reynolds stared at her. Her face was round and bland, her heavy body encased in one of her sagging jumpers. How old is she really? he wondered. And what's ticking behind that vacuous expression, as if she's some cow out at pasture?

'A few details left,' Reynolds said smoothly. 'But let's start with some minor questions. Who's been writing poison pen letters to Mrs Derrymore?'

He already had his suspicions but he thought this was as good a way as any to begin. Start with lesser crimes, move on to greater, was a procedure that had often worked.

'Letters?' she repeated. 'I've always used wax dolls myself. With pins stuck in 'em.' She grinned companionably at Reynolds. 'Just joking,' she added, 'I didn't write any letters. But I'll tell you who does.' She leaned forward confidentially, her too long sleeves dipping into the honey. 'There's only one other witch in these parts,' she said. 'And her name's Miss Trewithen.'

He ignored that for the moment. 'And does she wreck cars? Miss Linton's for example?'

'What do I know about cars?' she said. 'That's Richard's department.'

She gave another sticky grin. 'Richard liked fooling about with engines,' she said. 'If you don't believe me look at the old boat we found. He thought he could make it work. Pathetic.'

Her chatty, almost childlike, disclosures were as calculated as her mother's. He'd expected her to give nothing away at all. Why so co-operative? he wondered. There must be a reason. It suddenly dawned on him that by implicating Richard she was cleverly manoeuvring the inquiries away from herself. And she must be right. He felt angry with himself that he'd missed a vital clue. If Richard had given the false leads about Justin and Joe Fletcher, then he himself had been present, to spy on them. Which meant equally he could have been the one to do the tampering.

'Did you know Richard tried to implicate your father?' he asked, to be rewarded with the first real sign of emotion, a narrowing of her eyes like Joe Fletcher's. But her answer, 'He'd implicate anyone if it pleased him; he liked doing things to shock,' gave nothing else away.

'Why would Richard want to hurt Miss Linton?' he asked, his puzzlement genuine.

To have her shrug and say, 'To cause trouble. Make himself out to be smarter than he was. Show off.'

Reynolds remembered Derrymore's description, 'trying to outdo each other.' I bet you encouraged him, he thought, put it into his mind, as if accidently. Or actively suggested it. He eyed her again, gleaning nothing from her expression.

'About Richard's death,' he pressed. 'Was it written in the stars?' He tried to quote her. 'Can the stars themselves be changed? If so, wouldn't that really make the world go "awry"?'

That got through to her. She put down the toast and licked her fingers, staring now in front of her. As if she's a great bovine lump, he thought, without feelings or intelligence. But underneath, aware, cunning. And dangerous.

'I can testify you were at the mine yesterday,' he told her quietly. 'I saw you myself. I heard what you said and I saw you struggle with your father before the gun went off. You meant it to go off, didn't you?'

'Everyone wore masks yesterday,' she told him. 'It's been on the news. No one could recognize anyone for sure.'

'Then you also know they've all been rounded up now,' he broke in. 'And they'll confess under questioning.'

'Perhaps,' she said, dismissing the idea with a lofty wave of her hand. 'But they may not know.' She had him there.

He reverted to the first murder, the one that had caused him so much trouble. 'The poison has been identified,' he told her. 'Old fashioned stuff, once used to kill rats. It could have been found in your father's sheds.' He didn't add that one of its main ingredients was a chemical that was produced by Texas Industrial Consolidates, but she told him. 'So it's fitting it was intended to kill the man who wanted to dump it in Wheal Cosmuir,' she concluded, virtuously. 'A pity that the • wrong person ate it, is all I say.'

How did you know all that, he thought, to have her add, before he could ask, that Edmund himself had explained what his father's intentions were.

'He told Miss Linton too,' she went on. 'He could have told lots of other people.' She paused, looking at him with an expression that said, 'Got you again.' He had always accepted it as a possibility.

'But I won't deny I saw the hikers,' she admitted. 'Except they weren't hikers. That's when I first got interested in the conservationists.'

She's lying, he thought. If there were any hikers they must have been genuine. They certainly weren't regular members of Edmund's group, masquerading, as Fletcher would have us believe. I was right that genuine conservationists wouldn't use poison. That's the work of militants. And we know now the militants, that is, the protesters at Cosmuir Mine, had a woman as their leader.

'Those hikers you mention,' he hid his sarcasm, 'did they tell you what they meant to do?'

She shrugged. 'I didn't ask,' she said, 'but I was sure they meant to do something bad. An eye for an eye. That's what the Bible says.'

'And how did they get in?' he asked, playing along with her, to have her reply, 'But my father said he helped them. He gave Edmund the house key, you know. Perhaps Edmund had it copied.' She added with a childlike stare that belied her mature reasoning, 'He could have passed it to anyone.'

Clever answers. Nothing childlike here.

'More like you gave it him.' Reynolds' voice was still calm. 'If anyone had the means to get the key, you did. And if anyone had the means and time to go into the kitchen, you did too. When your mother became nervous that we asked questions about the kitchen,' he went on, the logic behind his arguments at last satisfying even himself, 'I presumed she was afraid she'd be implicated, a possibility that Joe's protective attitude suggested. Whatever Joe thought, your mother wasn't afraid for herself. It was all for you.'

'Of course no one expected Edmund to eat the poison.'

Ignoring these points, Syb reverted to her own story line.

'How was anyone to know he'd bring a woman with him and sit down for a meal? Or that he'd come looking for a map? Or for that matter, that Justin would start looking for it too. Think of the trouble their interfering caused – nothing to do with me.'

'You know your father's confessed to all of this,' again he broke in. 'He's taken the blame.'

'The more fool him,' she shrugged. 'He didn't have to. And if you're using him to make me confess instead, you're wasting your time.'

'Is that the best you can do?' he asked. 'Call your father a fool, because he's covered for you? Well, his so-called confession won't hold water either.'

She stared at him.

'I think,' he said, 'you planted the poison. If Edmund hadn't spoiled your plan, you'd have killed off three Gatterlys at once. As it turned out, you managed only one death, by accident, perhaps not the one you meant. Then you got an unexpected bonus. Justin's death evened things a bit. That left only Richard who had a lucky escape the first time round. So you pulled the trigger on him yourself.' He paused, looked at her as if admiringly. 'But I still don't see your motive, if you had one.'

'I could say why should I be overlooked because I'm a female?' Syb's reply was as virtuous as before. 'I was as good as they were. Better. They were all talk. But what you are suggesting is invention, it doesn't mean a thing.' She had recovered herself well. 'And even if I did, you couldn't make use of it. I'm too young.'

'Be careful what you claim,' he told her. 'Too young you say, meaning Richard was older, so therefore he must have led you astray. But suppose I can prove you're the older of the two, older than you want me to think?'

He hazarded his last guess, the most difficult to put into words, and the most difficult to sustain.

'If your father isn't your father, and Oliver Gatterly is, you must be the older,' he said, 'conceived before he married Richard's mother.'

It was a long shot that found the target. She screamed at him then, obscenities pouring out, 'How do you know?' the only thing repeatable. And after it, 'No one does.'

'Except me. And Joe.' Mary Lou, dressed in black today with her eyes grey shadowed, spoke from the hallway door. 'I finally told him yesterday. That's where I went wrong. He would never have gone after you if I hadn't told.'

Too late, her daughter turned on her, again screaming for her to shut up, to look at what she'd done.

'I guessed earlier,' Reynolds addressed Mary Lou. 'From your story. And the way you put Derrymore off when he talked about dates. And then something was said yesterday about a wrong that could never be put right. That's the wrong, isn't it? That your daughter's as much Gatterly's child as the boys were; and deserves as much of his inheritance.'

'Why not?' Mary Lou Fletcher suddenly cried. Her eyes flared. 'Think of Miss Trewithen with her precious twins; Barbs Gatterly with her one son. And little me, cut off without a cent. It isn't fair, is it?'

'Did you know what your daughter's been doing, Mrs. Fletcher?' Reynolds' voice was grim. While the daughter shouted again at her mother to be quiet, Reynolds could feel the frantic searching for a way out of this second ill-timed confession.

'Yes.' At last Mary Lou Fletcher spoke deliberately. 'I guessed some of it. But not about the poison.' She glared at her daughter. 'Could have killed me or Joe instead,' she said.

'But if you knew she was aware of her illegitimacy,' Reynolds could barely repress his distaste, 'why didn't you warn Gatterly himself? I presume he too was ignorant. And what about the half brothers?'

To have Syb laugh at him instead.

'Spoil the fun?' she mocked him. 'Mother doesn't know I've slept with all three of them.'

She grimaced. 'Only Edmund was worth it. And he died through stupidity. I get things done,' she added, her eyes gleaming. 'It's best to get things done, isn't it, Mr Ex-inspector. Take risks. Act on your own. As you yourself do, and your Sergeant Derrymore. Illegal acts.'

She went on with a smile and a toss of her hair, that for a moment transformed her into a woman twice her age, with all the latent attraction beneath the gross overweight. 'I know all about you, Mr Ex-inspector. Doomed to write books but not live yourself. Doomed to solve other people's mysteries but not the mysteries of your own failed life.'

It seemed a long while afterwards when she added, 'And you still don't have proof.'

'I have all the proof I need,' he started to tell her, to have her repeat, 'I wore a mask yesterday, Mr Ex-inspector. You can't swear to hearing me speak, because you didn't know who I was. You can't say I struggled with my father, or pulled the trigger, as I meant. Oh yes, I meant to do it, eventually when I'd finished with Richard. He couldn't escape me twice. And yes, I meant to kill my father with his stupid little wife who thought I wasn't good enough for her son. And yes, I would have killed Justin and Edmund in my own good time. And perhaps Miss Trewithen too, if she got in my way. I had the right to kill, to punish them.'

Her voice had risen into a sort of chant that was mesmerizing. Reynolds had the impression she had gone somewhere far away and may not even have recognized what she was saying. 'Why can I know that? The stars never lie.'

Again a long pause before she went on in an ordinary tone, 'You can't use as evidence what my mother's just said. Or what I've said myself. We'll deny it. You can't swear to anything; you aren't a policeman anymore. And I'm still underage.'

It was the second time that she'd claimed that her age would protect her. 'Underage by law, perhaps,' he told her, harsher than he meant. 'But the law can be changed. In fact it has been changed recently to deal with young offenders. It'll catch you one way or the other. Recognition by voice or recognition by your fellow protesters; the result will be the same.'

He was torn between thinking she was a real monster and accepting that her cleverness must be the sign of madness. Finally steeling himself to the fact that he might never be able to decide, he said, 'The law has a hundred ways to track you down and deal with you as you deserve.'

And as she again screamed at him, 'I only feel sorry for your mother,' he said above the noise. 'Who always says too much at the wrong time. And sorry most of all for Joe Fletcher. Who having found out that you weren't his daughter, presumably had to make his sacrifice to prove to himself that you still were.'

And that was how the case was finally solved and Mary Lou and Syb Fletcher were taken into custody. But not until both had attacked Reynolds with teeth and nails until he was forced to restrain them physically. Another unpleasant task which left as bitter a taste as

Syb's verbal abuse. It was long before he could forget her, or her summing up of his character.

All that remained then, was the problem of the letters.

Several days later, after Derrymore had come home (looking somewhat abashed at his mother's scoldings, and sheepishly admitting that he didn't feel 'too bad'), when he and Miss Heyward, who also 'happened' to drop in, were munching on Mazie's cake and biscuits, Reynolds also stopped to see them.

'I'm off on holiday tomorrow,' he told them, feeling more like a benevolent uncle than usual. 'Better late than never. And don't you worry, Mrs Derrymore, about those letters. There won't be any more.'

He didn't explain that he'd paid a last visit to Trewithen Manor, where the police and all their gadgets had long gone, and where Miss Trewithen was installed, while final arrangements about her future were settled.

She had just heard she was to get the house, at least have the right to use it while she lived, the last thing Oliver Gatterly had put in motion before his arrest. Although everything else about his business was found to be in his wife's name, or through her, in her father's name, the manor house had been bought in his, and he was therefore legally entitled to do with it as he pleased.

Whether he had planned to make amends to his twin sons as Mazie thought, was never proved, although seemingly probable. Or whether he felt constrained by guilt to satisfy his first wife, he himself never said. Still looking every inch the English gentleman he wasn't, he departed from the scene.

Miss Trewithen had been out riding; despite the smell of straw and horse she looked almost attractive, with colour in her cheeks and her hair blown loose from its tight fastenings. Most of her belongings were strewn around her in the hall where the horse photographs were stacked, waiting to be hung again in place. If, as she had once put it, she had been living in a holding pen, now she was rightfully where she belonged.

'I shan't ask you in,' she said, standing on the doorstep. 'When I'm settled, come back for a chat.'

He understood this to mean she might 'grant him an interview' at some other time, but wouldn't invite him for a meal or a drink as she would a social equal; and she made the request sound like a command. She didn't even acknowledge what he had done for her, and she didn't ask how Derrymore was.

She smiled. Reynolds didn't smile in return. 'Only,' he said, 'if you stop writing letters to Mrs Derrymore.'

Then she did look taken aback.

'How dare you,' she started to say, but he wasn't going to put up with any of her nonsense.

'I suppose you couldn't get over Mazie's betrayal, as you'd see it,' he said. 'And when she and her son came back into your world as it were, you couldn't resist the temptation to get even. You must have done it,' he told her. 'You're the only one I know whose shown the least dislike of them.'

'She made the food that killed my son,' she cried. 'And her son found him. Her Derry that she was always on about is still alive, while my sons are dead.'

The excuse was as weak and self-serving as any Syb Fletcher or her mother could make.

'And all out of false pride,' Reynolds told her, wondering. 'Snobbish self-conceit. Mrs Derrymore's twice the woman you are.

'Derrymore's the salt of the earth,' he added. 'I'm proud to be his friend. If you'd trusted him in the beginning perhaps none of the rest would have happened. And I'm as proud to be a friend of Mrs Derrymore. I've learnt more from her and her son what being true Cornish means, than anyone else I've met.'

And with that hoisting of his own banner, he left her standing there, lady of her manor, but of nothing else.